UNDERSTANDING

VESELIN PENEF

PAGE PUBLISHING, INC.
Conneaut Lake, PA

First originally published by Page Publishing 2021

ISBN 978-1-6624-4589-7 (pbk)
ISBN 978-1-6624-4590-3 (digital)

Printed in the United States of America

Flow, flow, flow,
Rush forth, Mighty Life,
Come to us yet again,
Come to us stronger yet,
Oh Mighty Life, cure all that ails us.

CONTENTS

PREFACE

The truth must be revealed. The false must be exposed. The truth must be established. The false must be destroyed. Philosophy is the answer. Philosophy is supreme. The Good is supreme. The way forward is the way of the Good. The way forward is the way of the One Philosophy. All must join the ranks of the One Philosophy.

ACKNOWLEDGMENT

The writings of this book originate mostly from within the world of philosophy. To that extent, and to a great extent, a great debt is owed to the world of philosophy. The world of philosophy preceded the writings of this book. The power and supremacy of the world of philosophy is clearly acknowledged. Philosophy has been dealt with by many great philosophers prior to the writings of this book. The specific and detailed study of those great philosophers was never to that specific and detailed extent carried out. Philosophical schooling was never engaged in. A school of philosophy was not attended. Philosophers love philosophy. One philosophical book is in my possession, that's Plato's *Republic*. Another source of studying philosophy, and to that extent, was the *Encyclopaedia Britannica*. Hegel is one of the superior philosophers. Aristotle also. The basis of philosophical origin is Socrates and Plato. Some ideas were turned to which were deeply influenced by the book of Plato's *Republic*. The term *guardians* originates from the book. The terms *world of ideas*, the *good* also. The call for the philosopher to be king is worked out in fine fashion in the *Republic*. The idea of the choice for the self in the *Republic* is, as far as known, put forth in mystical terms. In the one philosophy philosophical proof for the personal choice for the self is presented. The term *fare well* was first observed in the *Republic*; the term "government sees the one in the many, and the many in the one" was first observed in the Republic. A great debt is owed to the world of philosophy. To a great extent, the one philosophy works out the philosophical issues independent of outside sources; to that extent, the one philosophy is dependent on the one philosophy. All the ideas of the one philosophy have their origin in the one philosophy. All the ideas are presented in the manner of the one philosophy.

The one philosophy is original. The term "he who falls in battle does not die" was first observed in the writings of Botev. The idea of the future, past and present, occurring simultaneously is original. That such a similar idea was heard about as having been advocated by Einstein long after the writings in the one philosophy, at least five years later. Nothing is known of the Einstein idea, what Einstein had in mind nothing is known about. The writings of the one philosophy are there to be studied and examined. All originate from the one philosophy. The proof for all in the one philosophy is presented by the one philosophy.

UNDERSTANDING

When the human personality is described, it is best summed up by one characteristic: the need to live the perfect life, the need to live in the perfect world. The human wish for perfect existence consists of three major fields: humanity's need to know and understand the laws which govern life, the human need to live within the perfectly lawful political system, and the need to lead a peaceful existence. The human effort at living accordingly involves these same fields of development. The human wish for perfect existence is acted upon in the offering of solutions and answers to such involved problems and questions. The answers given are equivalent to humanity. The human effort is complete, and the answers are genuine. The answers are equal to humanity's, or any one individual's, understanding of the issue of consideration. This is so in the instance of all three fields of human development. When human achievement is examined, however, it is the human failure to arrive at the answer and solution to the three areas of human development that stand out. The human effort at the perfect life has been genuine. At times, that effort has been genuinely fraudulent. The need to know life's laws, the need to create the good society, and the need to live in peace are philosophical issues. Only philosophy has the answers to which. Philosophy is the supreme human intellectual development. Philosophy gives answer to the perfect life. Philosophy gives answer to the genuine effort at the perfect life. In so doing, philosophy fulfills the human being; philosophy fulfills the human task at living.

The achievement of a peaceful existence, together with the creation of the perfectly lawful society, and the understanding of life's laws are the most important areas of development. The importance for the establishing peaceful relations being for its own sake, to live in

11

peace as opposed to war, the self, and all that is good being free from malicious harm. The importance for the creation of the perfect society being to establish a setting and atmosphere under which peaceful interaction will have the best chance to be achieved, and humanity may live and develop properly, realizing the full living potential. The importance for the understanding of life's laws is to both know how to behave, as regard to being guided by truth, and for the attainment of a high and the highest human consciousness possible. All governing laws are divided in two categories, those whose instance is capable of being confirmed by the experience of test, those whose instance is capable of being confirmed by the experience of provable affirmation, and those laws which are solely founded upon reason, laws which are confirmed based on thought alone. Understanding of life's laws is humanity's single and only step in intellectual growth. The worth of any one law is determined according to its level of significance.

From the earliest times, people have engaged in evaluating the nature of the living process, from the earliest times people have engaged in the effort to understand life. Through the years, two ideas have been central to human thought; two ideas have been central to the human mentality, the idea of God, and the idea of judgment. Being issues of importance, it is the correct view of both that is desired. The correct view of these issues has a telling effect on any one individual's assessment of life. In attaining the highest consciousness possible and in behaving according to truth, the correct outlook must be possessed regarding these two most basic human concerns.

Certainly humanity has played a decisive role in defining God. Upon examining the definition of God, it becomes evident that there is one characteristic that best defines the definition of God, the characteristic of unlimited power. Though the characteristic of unlimited power does not define unlimited God completely. God is self-creator. God is creator of all. God is everlasting. God is without change. God is in complete control of all. God does all without any effort. It is not just great power that makes these qualities possible but unlimited power. Great power suggests all the characteristics with which the defined God cannot be associated, imperfection, flaw, lack of justice, lack of the good. Great power is not possessed by God, but only by a being other than God. It is in fact the quality of unlimited power that makes the rest of God's qualities possible.

The definition of judgment is that every individual is judged according to the possession, or lack of possession, of goodness by God. The definition is that judgment is the most natural course of action, that it occurs as result of irreversible and most just law. Those who are good, those who have engaged in good behavior are rewarded. Those who have not engaged in good behavior are punished. The idea of judgment does not include judgment of humanity by any other power other than God or the natural implementation of life's laws. The idea of judgment being of great importance to human thought is of great importance to philosophy. The understanding of the idea of judgment is of great importance to the understanding of life's laws.

The theory of judgment is flawed and cannot be correct. Judgment of humanity cannot occur. In attempting to attain the correct view of the issue, the fundamental topic to consider is humanity. The human status is exactly the same as the human status: Humanity is humanity. Humanity cannot be greater than being human. Humanity cannot be lesser than being human. Humanity is not other than human. Humanity is not something humanity is not. Humanity can not be other than human. Humanity cannot become something humanity is not. Humanity cannot do the impossible for humanity to do. Humanity cannot change the human nature. Humanity is limited to being human. Humanity can only do that which exists within the human personality. Humanity cannot do something that is not present within the human character. Everything that humanity does originates from, and is based on, the human character. Humanity behaves only in the manner of the human quality The living quality within humanity is humanity. Humanity cannot behave in a contrary way to the human character. Humanity cannot create the human quality. Humanity cannot make itself different from what humanity is. It is the human quality that creates humanity. It is not the human quality that is the product of humanity, but rather, humanity is the product of the human quality. Humanity is the product of creation, over which humanity has no greater control than the possible limit present within creation. Human control over creation is exhibited only to the possible and existing extent and limit. It is clear that humanity is product of creation. If humanity weren't, that would mean that humanity created itself, that humanity determines and creates the human personality beyond the limit of creation. If that were so, then humanity would be able to become something that humanity is not. As humanity is product of creation, the individual is also product of creation. The individual cannot become something the individual is not. The individual is limited to being the self. The individual cannot determine and create the self beyond the limit of creation. If this were possible, the individual would be able to become something the individual is not. Both humanity and the single human member are products of creation, over which neither one has control beyond the human and possible extent.

Humanity behaves according to the existence of naturally guiding human law, according to the natural manifestation of life's being. Judgment of humanity will not occur as result of the fact that humanity is a member of life and not an outsider.

In order for judgment to occur, judgment would have to be based on a true reason, due to which judgment would take place. There are two possible reasons that, if true and just, would bring about judgment. Judgment would take place based on the idea that humanity has without limit choice of behavior. Judgment would take place based on the idea that humanity has without limit free will. It is then up to humanity to choose between good and evil, and as a result of humanity's without-limit free will, humanity does so. And as it is that some have chosen to engage in good behavior and others in evil, each individual must be judged for the made choice. The second reason for judgment is that humanity engages in good and evil behavior, for which act humanity must be judged. The human free will is then not unlimited. The human free will is with limitation. Humanity is limited and is a product of life, behaving only in the human, life, manner. The human character being due to life law, humanity being product of creation.

If the reasoning for the theory of judgment is that humanity, being product of life, must and will be judged for the taken acts, then under this circumstance humanity always behaves in the way that humanity possibly can, according to life law, according to life's being. Humanity at no time acts in a contrary way to life. Humanity at no time acts in a contrary way to the human nature. Thus human nature has been determined by creation. Regardless of what anyone chooses to do, or does, that has been made possible by the particular personal characteristic. Being product of life, humanity does not create itself beyond the inherent limit, and consequently creating itself in a different way from that of life's creation. Rather, it is life that creates. Humanity fulfills the human character. Humanity, and the individual, creates, does, and improves, always to the present extent and limit. Never exceeding that limit, never achieving less than that limit. This is so in all respects. The individual engages in wrong behavior, or good behavior, not because the taken path was chosen over another and equally alternate path, but each individual chooses the only present path due to that path being the most desired way to behave. No other possible path could have been taken. If it could have been, then the taken path would not have been taken. Proving that there is one path to take, the human path, each individual's single path at life. All choice is made within the human limit. The final choice is the only possible one. Human behavior can improve, or become worse, according to the human quality. Which life determines and creates. Humanity cannot behave in a nonhuman way. Humanity can only be human. Consequently humanity would not be rewarded or punished for fulfilling the human character. Under this alternative, there is no reason for judgment to occur, no justified reason. Under this alternative, judgment could only occur as an act of injustice. There is only one purpose for judgment to exist, and that is to serve the cause of justice. For judgment to be unjust is for judgment not to be judgment but an act of wrongdoing. Under this alternative, judgment would be an act of wrongdoing. It would be for judgment to be an act of injustice. It would be for such judgment not to be judgment.

If the theory of judgment is based on the idea that humanity possesses free will without limit, that humanity has without limit choice in behavior, that humanity according to the limitless free will, according to the limitless choice in behavior, chooses the path at life and must be judged for the made choice, then under circumstance humanity is self-determining beyond the human limit. Having limitless choice, all choice then becomes equal. There is no reason for humanity to behave in any one particular way, especially the human way. One path would be as appealing as another since it is that humanity would have no human reason as its guide. Limitless choice makes humanity lose its human status. Humanity would have no reason to behave in the human way. Humanity becomes nonhuman. Humanity becomes false and unreal. Having limitless choice means that humanity self-creates yet for no particular reason in the human way. Having no reason to behave in the human way, humanity would not be drawn to behave as humanity; humanity would not be drawn to be human. The alternative of the limitless human is mistaken from the start in its understanding of human nature. Judgment would not be based on mistaken and false to life assessment. Judgment therefore would not occur. If Judgment is based on mistaken thought, then judgment would not be an act of justice but injustice. Judgment would not be judgment.

Humanity is the product of creation. The human identity is the result of creation. Humanity behaves according to the human nature and never behaves in a contrary, nonhuman way, to the human nature. Humanity cannot become something humanity is not. If humanity, or any individual, engages in good or evil behavior that behavior takes place only after the impossibility of doing otherwise. If there is improvement in human behavior, that improvement cannot be exceeded but takes place only after the impossibility of doing otherwise. Humanity is at all times faced with choice. All choice is from within the human character, from within the human limit. The human character is in accordance with creation. The human character is in accordance with life's being. Judgment of humanity cannot take place. Humanity is a member of life, not an outsider. Humanity will not be rewarded. Humanity will not be punished.

Part of the problem that humanity has faced in the attempt at the accurate assessment of the idea of judgment has often been that such accurate assessment attributes humanity with greater than human quality. The human state has not been properly understood. Further, the human daily evaluation of good and evil is used for the sacred act of judgment. Such reasoning is insufficient. The nonphilosopher has been involved in the world of philosophy. Giving then nonphilosophical answers. The human personality plays a part in the misunderstanding of judgment. Bloodthirst is often considered to be reasoning. Bloodthirst is substituted for reason. Bloodthirst is substituted for justice. Bloodthirst is substituted for compassion. Inadequate reasoning is used for lawful and justified judgment. Judgment would be of supreme importance. That importance forces equally such reasoning. It is this reasoning that leads to the starting point, the human status, in turn, to life's being. And consequently prevents judgment from taking place.

The theoretical disproving of judgment successfully carries over into reality. The disproving of judgment is based on the issue of right and wrong. The reason humanity will not be judged is due to the fact that judgment cannot be based on a true and lawful purpose. And due to that, judgment would be an act of wrongdoing. Judgment would be an act of injustice. God would never commit a wrong. God would never be unjust.

Being a member of life and product of creation, humanity behaves according to the human boundary. The definition of God is that God is the creator of all, including humanity. Humanity therefore exists and behaves in the way that God has created humanity. It is God who has created humanity. It is God who has determined the human character. And all choice is based on the human status, which was determined and created by God. God would not judge humanity for behaving in the way that humanity was created by God to behave.

If God is defined differently, if God is defined as being the highest natural law but not being the creator of all, including humanity, then humanity exists and behaves according to creation. God would not judge humanity when humanity exists and lives according to natural law. There would be no justified reason for judgment. Such judgment then would not be judgment; such judgment would be an act of injustice, not justice.

Judgment does not exist due to inaccuracy in thought. The disproving of judgment is the proving of life law. Life, Life's Being should be accurately understood. Life contains all. Life contains all justice.

The theoretical effort at arriving at the true view of judgment is an attempt at philosophy. The made conclusion can only be based on reason. The disproving of the idea of judgment is achieved solely through reason. There is no other evidence to confirm this other than reason. But reason is sufficient proof. Accurate reason is by its definition accurate. It must achieve an understanding of life's laws for accurate reason to be accurate. To claim that reason is insufficient proof is to have sided with the false, and hence, no drawn conclusion is then valid. Since it is that the disproving of judgment has been achieved, it then is an act of philosophy. Philosophy becomes credible and must be accepted as a genuine and proper human development and endeavor whose purpose is the achievement of truth. Philosophy is valid human knowledge. The truth of any philosophical view is to be found in its outlook. Any particular philosophical assessment is provable strictly through itself. Any particular philosophical assessment is provable strictly based on its accuracy of thought, based on its accuracy of reason. Accurate reason leads to truth. Philosophy is human thought that has arrived at undeniable truth. As reason is the most powerful human thought, so is philosophy the most powerful human development. As reason is most powerful, as philosophy is most powerful, it is only philosophy that can answer life's ultimate reality. As reason is most powerful, as philosophy is most powerful, it is only reason, it is only philosophy that has access to life's ultimate being. It is philosophy that seeks the greatest knowledge. It is philosophy that seeks the greatest knowledge of life's being. Philosophy thus attains its highest branch, the branch of metaphysics.

The judgment of humanity, and all life, that God would not engage in on the ground that judgment would be an act of wrongdoing becomes, and is, an act by God. God would not judge any life member because it is wrong to do so. Being wrong, being an injustice, God would not judge humanity. Being wrong, being an injustice, God could not judge humanity. In the definition of God, it is understood that God is in possession of the greatest good, and therefore, God is subject to the good's strictest observance. It follows that God would not and could not judge any life member. It is impossible for judgment to occur. God cannot act against God's own good personality. Granting, however, that God, by having unlimited power, would make it possible for God to act against any law, as result making it possible for God to judge humanity, despite the fact that judgment is an injustice. In this case, the definition of God is changed. The definition of judgment is changed. This is no longer God. This is no longer judgment. This would then be a being who lacks the good. Such judgment is equally lacking in good. The judgment would be meaningless. In order for God to be God, God must be thoroughly good. Judgment is an act of evil. God is good. God will do no wrong. God can do no wrong. God observes irreversible laws. The concept of unlimited power is therefore brought into question. If God cannot act in a certain way, then in this field God has limited power. The only reason due to which God may be thought to be unlimited is the reason that God is thoroughly good and will only, and can only, engage in acts of good. The only other alternative for possessing unlimited power would be for God to lack goodness. Lacking goodness, God most certainly will lack unlimited power. If God can reject the good, if God can reject the law of the good and act contrary to the good, God then becomes evil, and once evil, God cannot have unlimited power on the ground that being evil, God is then evil and cannot become good. In which case an evil God is not truly God. To possess the highest law, as God would have to possess the highest law, is to do so out of equal to the law goodness; God must be equally as good as the law, and the law can only be good. An evil God cannot achieve the law; therefore an evil God is not God. The highest law can only be achieved through goodness, God can only be good. It is only God that may be thought to be unlimited. In the understanding of the idea of unlimited power, it becomes evident that God is not truly unlimited, as God cannot be unlawful. God cannot be unjust. The idea of unlimited power can only be maintained on the ground that it is God who creates the laws, laws which God would not and could not oppose. That God chooses not to oppose the good, that God chooses that which is good and just. Thus maintaining unlimited power on the basis that God can only be good, that it is only by engaging in acts of good that unlimited power may be possessed and that nothing has changed in the understanding of unlimited power even if God in this respect is limited, for it is only natural that God would never do something that is wrong. As it is then, God is thoroughly good, and all of God's acts are and can only be of the same thoroughly good nature. God is the greatest good and cannot be less than the greatest good. God cannot oppose God's own personality. To do so is to lack the greatest good. God is defined by God's personality, which God acts in accordance with. God's personality is God. If it is thought that God's personality is a product of God, then it is also equally as true that God is the product of God's personality. For it is that God's personality is in accordance with God. God chooses the good as much as God having to observe the good. If it were concluded solely that God's personality is a product of God, then that conclusion would be made at the expense of the reverse, that God is the product of God's personality. If It were concluded on the other hand that God is solely the product of God's own personality, then that conclusion would be made at the expense of the reverse, that God's personality is a product of God. As result, there must be a middle ground, one on which both views would be correct, where the Nature of God's being is to be found. To that certain extent, God's personality is a product of God. God is to that certain extent the creator of God's own personality.

That certain extent includes the reverse. God is to that certain extent product of God's own personality. God being the product of God's personality, God is the result of creation. If God weren't the result of creation, then God would not be the product of God's personality. Being the result of creation, God's power is to that certain extent limited. Based on the reasoning of the middle ground, God, to that certain extent being the creator of God's own personality, God to that certain extent possesses unlimited power. The middle ground is the answer, where the opposites are to that certain extent correct.

If God's power were not limited, God would be able to self-create beyond a certain extent. God would be able to self-create beyond the limit of the middle ground. If God's power weren't limited, God would in no way be affected by the middle ground. Yet the Middle Ground is the answer. God's power is limited not in one respect but all. The aspect of unlimited power, unrestrained unlimited power, unlimited power independent of the middle ground does not exist. What exists is unlimited limited power. What exists is limited unlimited power. What exists is the middle ground. The middle ground contains all. The middle ground contains all opposites which to that certain extent are correct. Unlimited power contains limit. Limited power contains lack of limit.

The downfall of the idea of unrestrained unlimited power is the equal legitimacy of the opposite, limited power. The opposite being equally as legitimate, the middle ground then takes shape. The middle ground is the creator of all. The middle ground is the creator of all personality. To have unrestrained unlimited power is to deny the middle ground. To have unrestrained unlimited power is to deny personality; it is to behave against personality.

The continuation of the thought of lack of unlimited power is to be found at this point precisely in the idea that there is no self causing life beyond the middle ground. All life is the product of creation. All life is the result of creation. All life the result of the middle ground. The outcome of all is to the extent of creation. The outcome of all is to the extent of the middle ground. No object being self-causing beyond the middle ground. No object, no life unit is self-sustaining beyond the middle ground. Within life's boundaries all of reality exists, including self-cause, self-creation, and self-sustaining. Lack of unlimited power means that every life member's power is limited in all respects. No life member possesses control exceeding the existing limit over the self, where the life member can create and will the self beyond the existing limit, beyond the middle ground. All control and behavior occur within life's living potential. No life member can become what that life member is not. The sustaining power of all is limited, and all lasts as long as the limited sustaining power allows. No life member is everlasting as unlimited power would be required to be everlasting. All life exists within the middle ground. Within the middle ground, all opposites are included, including everlasting life.

The finding of the middle ground is the finding of life's being. Where to that specific extent life self-creates and life is to that specific extent created. Philosophical inquiry has at its center the issue, the question, of life's being; philosophy wishes to understand life's being. In attempting to understand life, the false assessment must be excluded. Doing so, life becomes knowable. It is the false that interferes with knowledge of life. Seeking the truth, all the possible knowledge will be attained. Knowledge of life is attainable. If it weren't, all association with life would cease. By rejecting the idea of unlimited power, the false is excluded. By accepting the idea of life's middle ground, the truth is included. The grasping of the truth is possible for philosophy to do. The grasping of the all-important truths regarding life's being is possible for philosophy to achieve.

Life self-creates, and life is the result of creation. These acts are not excluding of the other; they are not contradictory. This is due to life's nature, life's specific nature. Both aspects of life are true to the accurate extent of which. All that is real, all that exists is from within life's being. Life includes all. As such, all observes life's laws. All exists due to the middle ground. There is no entity that does not. There can be no entity that does not exist due to the middle ground. For if any entity did exist not due to the middle ground, the medium balance would not be struck, such entity would exist at the expense of the reverse alternative. Making itself incomplete and imbalanced. Every entity being the result of the medium makes every entity a member of life. No entity is totally self-creative, disregarding and behaving beyond the medium. No entity has unrestrained unlimited power. Every entity is to that extent the product of creation. Though no entity is the total product of creation, self-creation occurring to that certain extent. The two alternatives presented, self-creator and product of creation, from which the medium was reached are the only two alternatives; there are no other. For in all life there is either the internal or external, the self and all possible outside life. Under all possibilities, the self would be included. The considered issue, that all life has two guiding possibilities for existence, concerns the self as well as all possible other alternatives. Making the self separate from all other alternatives, all other external alternatives. Making the possibility for self-creation separate from the possibility of external creation. Making all that is external separate from the self. Just as the self is separate from all that is external, so is all that is external separate from the self. Making all life the result of the medium between the two opposites, the opposites of total self-creator, and total product of creation. The two such opposites are life's boundaries. All opposites are life's boundaries. The middle ground is life's origin.

The original, unlimited, creator of all is not a fact in life's being. The original, unlimited, creator of all is not needed in life's being. Life exists according to life's limited power life will end. Life will end not only as result of life's limited power but also and equally as much as result of possessing the ingredient which leads to life's end within. If life did not have this ingredient, life would never take part in something life is not. By being foreign to life's end, life could not enter into a state that is not present. Life can only end by possessing the quality which is of the same nature as life's end, life's opposite. If life did not possess life's opposite, life would never end. Life by ending means that life leads into life's opposite. The opposite is possessed after unrestrained unlimited power is lacked. Through limited power, life possesses the opposite. The opposite has a specific part in life's being. Life does not alone set life's path; the path must be set by the opposite, as well as life. If life alone set life's path, life would never end. Life would be unlimited. The opposite exists within Life. Non Life exists within Life.

This being the instance at the most basic level of existence, of life including nonlife within life's being, of life being self-creator and being created, is also the instance with all life manifestations. The opposite exists within each opposite. The opposite to each opposite is included within each opposite. When the power of any one opposite ceases, that opposite leads into the opposite. Each opposite exists due to the strength to do so. Through the needed power, every opposite attains identity. Life attains identity. When that power ceases, the opposite takes over, the opposite which then contains the opposite.

The power of each opposite is limited, thereby ending, thereby leading into the opposite. The process is continuous.

Life exists, and life's origin is life's own. Life exists, and life must have come into existence. Life's power is limited. Life cannot have always existed. Being limited, life must end. Being unable to exist without end, life must have a beginning. Having limited power, life cannot have always existed. Life's origin is found with life's predecessor, leading to the creation of life. In order for life to come into existence, life must do so from a quality which is stable and constant. Life, due to life's limited power, cannot have originated from life. In order to achieve stability, life has come into existence from life's opposite, nonlife. Nonlife has led to the creation of life. Just as Non Life is a part of Life, so is Life a part of Non Life. Nonlife cannot enter into a state that is not present and known. Nonlife, due to the limited power of nonlife, cannot eternally exist. Upon ending, nonlife leads into nonlife's opposite, life. Nonlife that leads to life and nonlife that life leads to are equitable, on the ground that both are opposites to life, therefore the same opposite. The factor which determines each state as such is power, the power to exist in such state. Due to the fact that limited power is possessed by each state, the counterpart inevitably assumes the state of dominance. Life achieves identity by struggling to do so, by overcoming nonlife. It is the quality of limited power that results in both opposites inevitably leading into the opposite.

In this process, life and nonlife are bound together. Life leads into nonlife, and nonlife leads into life. Further, neither opposite is the representation where that opposite exists solely, where the opposite is excluded from within. Nonlife is not unlimited nonlife, unlimited nonlife which excludes life from within. Nonlife is not separate from life. If nonlife were separate from life, nonlife would not have ever led to life. The same is true for life. Life is not separate from nonlife. Neither opposite is exceeding of life's boundaries. Neither opposite is exceeding of life's middle ground, of self-creator and being created to the accurate extent of which. Both opposites are real and true to their nature, existing within life's middle ground of including all opposites to the real and specific extent; for if any opposite were excluded that would be done at the expense of the other, if any opposite were excluded, the existing opposite would become unrestrained in unlimited power. And so it is with all, including life and nonlife. Making life and nonlife real. Making life's middle ground real. Making life's being real.

Nonlife cannot not exist. Unreal nonlife cannot exist. The unreal nonlife, where nonlife is separate from life, cannot exist. If the unreal nonlife did exist, nonlife would possess unlimited power. Unlimited power in nonlife's ability to self-determine beyond the limit of life and exclude the opposite, the unreal life. Such nonlife would have to eternally nonexist, making nonlife unlimited. Such nonlife would have to eternally nonexist at the expense of the opposite, eternal life. Eternal unlimited nonlife cannot exist. Unlimited eternal life cannot exist. To do so is for eternal life to exist at the expense of eternal nonlife. Unlimited nonlife cannot exist. Unlimited life cannot exist. The middle ground between the two opposites is found. Life originates.

Nonlife must necessarily exist. Nonlife possesses life within. Nonlife leads into life. Being unable to exist without end, through nonlife's end, nonlife gives rise to life. Life always leads to nonlife. Life can never not lead into nonlife. Life is Everlasting, Life can never be destroyed. Life receives life from the same source which appears to end life.

When nonlife leads to life, nonlife was not the false nonlife, where nonlife is separate from life, where nonlife does not include life. But is the real and true nonlife, nonlife that includes life. It is the real and true nonlife that leads into life. If life were excluded from nonlife, then nonlife would not have led to life. The stable and constant quality that was needed for life's predecessor is nonlife, not unlimited eternal nonlife. Possessing life within, nonlife is a representation of life. Nonlife is a stage of life's being. Life cannot not exist. If life did not exist, neither would nonlife not exist. The middle ground gives rise to limited life, not unlimited eternal nonlife. Life in ending, life determines the quality handed down, the quality of nonlife. Nonlife originates from life. Nonlife cannot be a quality unrelated to life. As such, and to that extent, the quality handed down is determined by life. Nonlife in ending, nonlife determines the quality handed down, the quality of life. Life originates from nonlife. Life cannot be a quality unrelated to nonlife. As such, and to that extent, the quality handed down by nonlife is determined by nonlife. The quality handed down always has the living ingredient within. Consequently life is never extinguished. Life is everlasting.

The relationship between life and nonlife is one that is forever binding. Life and nonlife are inseparable. They are part of the same. In the process, they present the living existence. It is life's being that is presented. Nonlife has life within. Nonlife is not unlimited nonlife. As result, nonlife is living. Nonlife is life. Nonlife takes place within life's being. Containing life, nonlife is life. It is life that lives life's path. Life containing nonlife, life does not contain unlimited nonlife. Life contains limited nonlife. Life contains life. Having risen from a stable and constant quality, due to life's limited power, life originates from nonlife. Which is not unlimited nonlife, for unlimited nonlife cannot exist. The stability achieved from nonlife is the stability needed. Nonlife cannot not exist. Life cannot not exist. Neither extreme of unlimited eternal life and unlimited eternal nonlife can occur. The medium is found, limited life. Being limited, life leads into nonlife. Life leads into life. Being limited, life originates from nonlife. Life originates from life.

Life is a fact. Life cannot not exist. Life is limited and yet unlimited. Life lives within life's own laws. Life's laws cannot be broken. Life cannot become something life is not. Life's laws are not contrary to life but are very much in accordance with life's living effort. Life's laws belong to life. Within life all the possible good and justice will be found.

Being limited, life contains the opposite. Being limited, no one stage of life is everlasting. No one stage of life is without end. In ending, life leads into the opposite. Life leads into the following stage of life. Which stage in turn contains the opposite. The occurrence is continuous. By continuously leading into the next stage, life achieves life's destination. Life has an objective which life strives for. If life did not have an objective, life would lead a pointless existence, denying the existence altogether. The objective is whatever the objective happens to be, not lesser, not greater. Making the objective achievable. Life cannot be without an objective. The objective is to attain life. The objective is to attain the possible life. It is the objective of life of possible life and greater life that is life's guiding purpose. Upon achieving the objective, and by possessing the opposite, life then leads into the opposite to the stage of destination. In being limited, the stage of destination is not everlasting. Upon achieving the objective, life will have no further to progress. Life will then lead into the opposite, the most basic stage. And life will then once again seek the guiding purpose. Life will once again seek the stage of destination. Which is totally achievable and in the same manner as it was previously achieved. The stage of destination will be achieved in the same manner as it was previously achieved. Life will repeat in the same manner. For it is that life's being is such as life's being is. Life's being will not change. Life undergoes change from stage to stage, but it is life's being that undergoes the change from stage to stage. Life's being will not and cannot be altered. During each stage, life is as life should be. Life will not take on any ingredient during any stage that is not of life's being. Life will not take on any characteristic that is not present within life's being. Making life unalterable. There is only one middle ground, one life, one unalterable life. Upon the achieving of life's objective, life will then lead into the opposite with the one and same life quality. Leading once again to the exact duplication of life's living effort. Life forever repeats in the same manner, achieving all in the same manner. The power required to forever fulfill each stage is in each instance possessed by life. If it were not, life would cease.

Life's objective, life's guiding purpose, cannot be anything other than life's greatest existence. Life's objective cannot be other than the achievement of the height of life. For life to have a different objective from the height of life is for life to have a lesser objective. It is not to seek that which is best; it is to act against the self. During the point of destination, life exists at the height of achievement. Life exists at the height of life. Life is limited, and the stage is not without end. By the stage of destination ending, life then leads into the opposite. Which in fact is a stage of life, the most basic stage. Life then again repeats the same living path.

This world is a part of life and is in one of life's stages of development. Being a part of the living path, the present possesses life's laws and lives by the laws of life. This world can in no way develop in a manner that is not consistent with life's laws, with the fulfilling of life's purpose. This world can only seek to attain greater life. Not to do so is to act against the self. This world has an objective. If there were no objective, then the denial of this world's existence would ensue. In seeking greater life, this world seeks to achieve life's destination.

The idea that life is everlasting is not contradictory to the original idea of limited power and no object being everlasting. No stage of life is everlasting, without end. Due to limited power, all stages will end. The idea that life cannot have always existed is realized in the nature of life's being. Life did not always exist. What existed was nonlife. What always existed was the middle ground. Life's middle ground. Each life stage has an ending. Each life stage has a beginning. Life has a beginning. There is a beginning to each life stage. The stable opposite to life is nonlife, limited nonlife. The stable opposite to life is not unlimited nonlife. It is life that is attempted to be understood. Life's laws are such as life's laws are in order to ensure life's existence. Life is limited. Unlimited nonlife and unlimited life do not exist. Life does not originate, life cannot originate from unlimited nonlife. The stable opposite as result cannot be, and is not, unlimited nonlife. The stable opposite is limited nonlife. Nonlife having life within. Nonlife is life. Life is everlasting.

Life cannot arise from a quality that is not living. Life can only arise from life. Life is eternal. Life cannot have a beginning, Life must necessarily exist. The middle ground must necessarily exist. Life is separate from unlimited nonlife. Making life the primary source of concern regarding the issue of eternity, making life eternal. Life by arising from life arises from the living quality. The actual fact of living life is of concern, for life not to be eternal is for life to have beginning from a source not of life. Life cannot arise from a nonliving quality. Life captures life within life's quality. Life is distinct from nonlife; life is eternal.

With the excluding of unlimited power, life is not unlimited but is limited, limited and unlimited simultaneously. Life is limited and unlimited to that specific extent. With the excluding of unlimited power, it follows that life consists of those qualities which are of the limited nature. Life cannot forever exist without change. Life cannot self-create beyond the limit of the middle ground. Life cannot exist in a different manner from life's own manner. Life abides by life's laws. The laws originate with creation, creation of life. Creation is a natural fact. Creation cannot not be a fact. Creation cannot be lesser or greater. Creation is not different from life's being. In such fact of creation, life lacks nothing. Life is true to the self. Life's laws do not impair or restrict life but free life to live to the fullest. Life is not lesser. Life is not greater. Life is complete. Life is complete within the self. Life's Laws arise from the Middle Ground, from the Reality of Life.

Such life as unlimited life and such unlimited nonlife are life's boundaries. Neither quality can exist. Creation occurs. The middle ground is found. Eternal life originates. Creating, as result of the boundaries, limited life. Creating, as result of the boundaries, life's being. Creating, as result of the boundaries, laws. Laws that belong to life, laws that are life's own. Life's laws are life's own.

Creation leads to one life. One life that is the identity of the result in finding the medium ground between unlimited life and unlimited nonlife. Through the mixture of the two opposites, the result is one life. The qualities of unlimited life and unlimited nonlife are constant. They cannot be not constant. For if they were not constant, neither quality would have any meaning; neither quality would have any substance. Unlimited life and unlimited nonlife are exactly as they are. They cannot vary. If they did vary, neither quality would be such as the quality is. Making the quality different from itself. As result, presenting no quality. Being constant, the result is one life. Present life is a part of the one life. Present life is central to the one life. Present life is the basis of the one life. Life encompasses the universe, the earth, and all laws of the middle ground, all laws belonging to the reality of life. Life is one: There is no other life that is not related to this life. All life is in a stage of existence directly dependent on and related to this present life. Present life is life's basis. There is one middle ground between the constant qualities of unlimited life and unlimited nonlife. Through the mixture of unlimited nonlife and unlimited life, the result is one life.

By living, life enters into the different life stages. Life always struggles to achieve that which is best. Life always struggles to attain greater life. From the struggle for greater life, the earth has been created. The earth bears the mark of creation. The laws guiding the earth originate with creation. The earth has come into existence, and the earth will go out of existence. When the earth was being created, all life concentrated to bring the earth to life. It is only the earth that lives. If life created more than the single living quality, that would mean that in creation more than the required, more than the possible, life needed to create the one representation of life is possessed by life. If life created more than the one living quality, that would mean that life is denying life's one single nature. The earth being the only living planet is the center of all life. All the other planets are undeveloped and cannot develop in the sense of producing the one life. The earth is the dominant planet and is the sole manifestation of life.

The same is true for the universe. The universe is the sole universe. It is the only universe where life in such stage may exist. The current stage of life's existence can only transpire in this and only universe. The universe captures the one life. Any and all life stages are directly related to this one and only universe. As life is one, life captures all life. Life consists of all life. The one universe is at the center of life's being. In creation, in achieving that which is best, life achieved the universe, the one and only universe.

Life has the objective of being true to the self, of being represented only by the self. Life has the objective of attaining the highest aspect of the self, the most representative aspect of the self. An inferior and not representative level to which, to the level of the one life, is pointless after the existence of the one life has been assured. A level not representative of the one life is pointless for life to create after the ensured existence of the one life has been achieved. And life's true existence has been assured, as it is that life cannot not exist, as it is that the one life cannot not exist. With the proven existence of the earth and the universe, life has been achieved and assured. This Life cannot be not representative and inferior to Life's Being because only true life may exist, and the inferior, not representative, may not. Making this the one life. Making the earth and the universe the one life.

The earth and the universe capture life's being. Life cannot not exist. The earth cannot not exist. The universe cannot not exist. There is no need for other life to exist. There is no need for life to take further measures to secure life. And life's existence is secured due to life seeking the greatest life. Life's existence is secured due to life seeking that which is best. Life cannot not exist. Within that fact, life seeks that which is best. Life cannot not exist. The earth cannot not exist. The universe cannot not exist. There is no need for any other creation. There is no purpose for any further creation. In creation, the earth cannot be duplicated. The universe cannot be duplicated. Any other life would vary from the one life. That life would be either a development that is more closely representative of life's being than the earth is, or that life would be a development that is less closely representative of life's being than the earth is. Such life would be either superior or inferior to earth's life. Life by having the objective of achieving the greatest representation of the self, such measures are taken. Those measures cannot fail. The greatest representation of the self will be achieved. If life did not seek that which is best, if life did not have as life's objective the achievement of the greatest representation of life, then life would be acting against the self. Life would be acting against that which is best for the self. Achieving that which is best, there is one that is best. There cannot be greater life to earth's, as there is one greatest and best representation of life, as there is one greatest and best existing representation of life, and that is the earth. The earth's existence is a fact. Only that which is best exists. That is the earth. There is no greater life to earth's life. There is no inferior life to earth's. Only the best representation of life exists. The earth exists. The earth is best. There is no inferior life. Further, life is one. Life can only be captured by one. From the mixture of the constant qualities of unlimited nonlife and unlimited life, one life is the result, the earth, and the universe. There is no greater or inferior life to earth's. For life to exist elsewhere, life would have to be identical to the one life. The identical duplication of life cannot be undertaken under any one occasion. Life cannot be duplicated. The self cannot be duplicated. There is only one self. Proof for this is to be found in the singleness of the self. Any such existence would vary from the self. Making the self the single and one self. Making life the single and one life. As result, excluding all that is outside the one life from existence. Life is sacred. Life's sacred nature is captured by the single and one life.

Originating with Creation, the earth has limited power. The earth cannot eternally exist, nor can the earth have eternally existed. The earth has a beginning, and the earth has an end. By the earth having a beginning, life on earth has a beginning. Life on earth cannot have preceded the earth's beginning. Life on earth exists due to the earth's existence. The one life cannot not exist. The earth cannot not exist. Life on earth cannot not exist. Based on the origin of the earth, the earth's primal stages were such, primal. The primal stages can only have been developed in a primal way. The earth's early stages are not the stages of later earth. Earth's beginning was basic. At the beginning, the objective was to establish the primal existence. Doing so, the earth, life, seeks greater life. The need to establish primal existence was such, and the result was such. Life's, the earth's achievement was equal to the need. Life has the purpose of achieving greater life. Life has the purpose of achieving the possible life present within life's being. Seeking to attain greater life, life has taken such measures. Primal earth produces primal life. No aspect of life is ever identical and same as another. There is only one self. There can be no duplication. Primal life all varied. Each life quality being different, each life quality has searched for greater life in such different ways. The differing life qualities searching for life differently. The differing life qualities, searching for life, life has in each instance to the inherent and differing extent been achieved. In so doing, life becomes different from the most basic life in the differing ways. Life therefore changes. The most basic is built upon. The most basic is further developed. As result life producing change. The primal was primal during the primal stages. Subsequent to that, the equal to the following stages life was produced.

Life has a purpose. Life's purpose is to establish life. Life's purpose is to attain greater life. Life's purpose is to attain that which is best, that which is best within life's being, to the extent of life's being. Life's being cannot be altered. That which is best for life is from within life's being for life to achieve. Life's being cannot be altered. Life's achievement cannot be altered. The achievement cannot be greater. The achievement cannot be lesser. The achievement cannot be different from life's being. Life's path at life is set by life. Life is one. Life's path is one, the best one.

With the establishing of life, life has produced varying life qualities. All life qualities vary, and all contribute to make up the content of the one life. The life qualities all contribute to earth's life. Building on the having been taken steps at life by basic life, the subsequent life qualities never repeat the already taken such measures at life. The original steps at life are never repeated by subsequent life but are built upon to whatever extent that may be. The searched for life is the life attained. The life attained is the possible life to be attained. A lesser or greater level, a different level of attained life to the possible life can at no time occur. That which is not possible for life to attain is not possible for life to attain. That which is not within life's being is not possible for life to attain. Achieving the possible, each varying life quality has sought to create conditions which are most favorable. Each life quality seeks the most optimum conditions. The life qualities seek the best personal condition. To that extent, it is each life quality that decides what is personally best. In the process, the justice rendered is the justice as so decided by the life quality. The justice is life's justice; there is none greater. If that justice is thought to be somehow inadequate, then life's complete being must be understood.

Coming into being at the most basic level, most basic life is life. Most basic life represents life. Guided by life's laws, basic life's survival is assured. Life's laws ensure basic life's survival. As life cannot not exist, so basic life cannot not exist. Basic life cannot perish before the objective has been achieved, the objective of greater life. The fact that greater life exists proves that basic life sought greater life. The fact that greater life exists proves that basic life cannot perish before the objective of greater life is achieved. No event can ever bring life's existence to a premature and not within life's being intended end. Life's fully intended existence is always secured. Basic life cannot be brought to a premature end. Greater life cannot be brought to a premature end. All life phases are within life's being. Life is in control of every life phase. Life cannot not exist. Life's being cannot not exist. Every life phase is to the nature of life's being controlled. Life cannot not exist. Life's living path cannot not occur to the manner of life's being. Making life's living path always controlled by life. No event is by chance. No event ever occurs from outside of life's living path. No event occurs from outside of life's being.

Coming into being at the most basic level, early life's existence is secured. Searching for greater life, it is greater life that is achieved. Seeking life, it is the possible life that is achieved. It is the present life that is achieved. It is the present life that is realized. Basic life's realization of greater life does not consist of a single phase but many. Having realized any one objective, life then seeks the realization of the next objective. The process is continuous. Based on life's being, each phase of existence is shaped into the possible and desired form. Based on each life quality, basic and greater, each phase of existence is shaped into the possible and desired form. As life realizes objectives, so does each life quality realize objectives. During the living path, life manifests all that is present within. Life's being is then revealed. Life's living path occurs in perfect sequence. Each phase of existence occurs in perfect sequence. No phase of life is out of sequence. Each occurs when it is most appropriate. When life is most ready to embark upon that new development. No phase of life achieves more. No phase of Life achieves less, that is Life's Being. No phase of life is different from life's being. Life's being is the reality of life, the middle ground between life being created and life self-creating. Life lives in life's manner and no other. Life reveals life's being and no other. Life does not blindly lead into life's being, into life's living path. All that life does originates from life's being. All that life does is in accordance with life's eternal being. Life cannot become what life is not. No life quality can become what that life quality is not. No life qual-

34

ity is different from such single nature of that same life quality and is from within life's unchangeable being. Every life quality does the possible. No life quality achieves the impossible. Every life quality achieves that which is present within. Every life quality reveals that which is present within. All life qualities always vary from other life qualities. All life qualities are such as each life quality is due to the possession of such and equivalent life from the beginning. The life obtained by each life quality is the possible life to be obtained, which is in accordance with the single being of each and varying from all other life quality. The life obtained by each life quality is under all circumstances different from the life obtained by any other and all other life qualities. No life quality can obtain something that is not present within originally. No life quality can become something that life quality is not. Life's living path occurs in one way, the best way. All that is from within life is always revealed. Life always occurs in the single and best way. Life cannot not exist. All that exists cannot not Exist. All that is life was always present within life. Life is one. Life's path is one.

The one life contains the opposite. The one life contains all. The one life contains the many. As life undergoes life's living path. Life reveals all of life's being. As basic life leads into greater life, and as greater life leads into more life, all that is of life is revealed. With all the life qualities varying and being different from one another, some qualities are to an extent similar. They are similar to the extent where a branch of life is established. A branch of life of similar qualities but different from all other branches and different from the closest other branch. Each branch exists with the aim to establish life, to secure life, to reveal life. The well-being of any one life branch is dependent on the life qualities within the branch. The life qualities seek life and establish life. The vast majority of life qualities within any one successful life branch seek and establish life in a medium measure. There are also the extremes of the life branch; The few which seek and establish life to a lesser extent and the few which seek life to a greater extent, lesser and greater extent as when compared to the vast majority of medium measure. For any one life branch to be success-ful, such successful steps are taken. It serves no purpose for any one branch to be unsuccessful. The well-being of any one life quality is dependent on the well-being of the life branch. With the life branch being stable and successful, it is the medium element, those seeking life in the medium measure, that represents the vast majority of life qualities within the life branch. For it is the medium that is the most stable. The medium has the characteristics on which the life branch is based. If the lesser or greater were the vast majority, the life branch would weaken and act against that which is best for the life branch. The greater are such, life is sought to a greater extent. But life is not sought to a greater extent in every and in many respects. The greater seek greater life in specific ways and in specific fields, being developed to a great extent in such manner, being greater in specific ways and in specific fields. In ways and fields outside the field of strength for the branch, the greater are lacking in development. In the process, lacking development to a greater extent than the medium, making the greater an unstable base for the life branch. The life branches seek that which is of most benefit and stability. The medium provides that benefit and stability to the greatest extent. The medium is the vast majority. Making the life branch stable and successful. The lesser and greater life qualities are in direct proportion to the vast majority of the medium, to the proportion where the life branch would be benefited to the greatest extent. All contribute to the well-being of the life branch. The life branch contributes to the well-being of all. At the lead of the greater are the fewer. At the lead is the one.

The greater are a stimulus for growth. The greater cannot but be an influence on the life branch. That influence is to whatever extent it happens to be. That influence cannot not exist. No life branch cannot not exist. No life quality cannot not exist. Life's being is one. Life's path is one, the same as life's being. Life's destiny is one, the same as life's path, the same as life's being. Life's being can never be changed. Life's path can never be changed. Life's destiny can never be changed. No event can occur that would change life's being, life's path, life's destiny. Life's being is always fulfilled. The life of any one life quality is always fulfilled. The accomplishment of any one life quality is always fulfilled. Each life quality achieves all. Each life quality has all. Each life quality possesses the self. The objective of any one life quality would not be accomplished only if the self's identity were lacked. The self's identity is never lacked. All that occurs to the self occurs to the complete self. Life's destiny is final. The destiny of any one life quality is final. Having the self, destiny is fulfilled. The self's life is fulfilled. Less than the complete self is never lived. No life quality ever lacks the complete self. For the self to be less than complete, the finality of destiny would have to be altered. The finality of destiny would have to be sought to be altered without making destiny final. No event can ever occur that does not serve the purpose of the one destiny. The one destiny is such as the one destiny is. The one destiny of any one life quality is such as the one destiny is. The one destiny cannot be altered. No life quality is ever less than complete. Being complete, the one destiny is fulfilled. The one destiny is always fulfilled. No life quality achieves less than all. Less than the fulfilled life is never lived.

Seeking life and achieving life, basic life leads into more complex life. The influence of any life quality on life is never not felt. The influence of no life quality cannot not exist. That influence is as the influence should be, never lesser, never greater. Subsequent life leads into life branches. Each branch consisting of the vast majority of medium life qualities, the few lesser, and the few greater life qualities. The same principle of lesser, medium, and greater is the principle with life, life containing lesser, medium, and greater. The same principle is the principle for each life quality. Each life quality containing lesser, medium, and greater, in the proper extent, to the proper extent. Seeking life and achieving life, basic life, primal life, leads into subsequent life. Subsequent life is never the same as primal life. Primal life is never the same as subsequent life. Subsequent life leads into developed life. Developed life is never the same as previous life. Previous life is never the same as developed life. The change is constant. Seeking and achieving life, life undergoes constant change. The change is that which the change happens to be, always occurring. This is due to the individuality of each life quality. This is due to the individuality of each self. Building on the previous, each life quality lives in that life quality's own particular way. Building on the previous proves that subsequent life is different from previous life.

By the fact that subsequent life is subsequent to the previous shows that change is undergone. By the fact of the individuality of each life form, it is shown that change occurs. By the fact of the individuality of each self, it is shown that change occurs. If no change occurred, in seeking and achieving life, it would mean that all life is the same identical life. If no change occurred, it would mean that all primal life is identical. It would mean that all primal life is identical to all subsequent life. It would mean that all subsequent life is identical to all developed life. It would mean that all developed life is identical to all previous life. All developed life being identical to primal life. If no change occurred, in seeking and achieving life, it would mean that each individual self is identical to each other individual self. It would mean that each individual self is identical to all previous life qualities. It would mean that each individual self is identical to all primal life, making all life the same one. The change always leads into what is best for life. The change occurs within life's one best path at living. Life's one best path, life contains all. Life always contained all. Life always contained the one best path.

The search for life by any life member is not lesser or greater to the identity of that life member. The search for life is not different from the identity of the life member. The achievement of life by any life member is not lesser or greater to the identity of that same life member. The achievement of life is not different from the identity of that life member. Each life member achieves what is possible for the life member to achieve. The identity of each life member is the personal identity of the self. There is no alienation from the self. The self lives all. To think that life is lacking, to think that life is impersonal, is to misunderstand life. No identity of any life member is lost or minimized. Living all, each life member makes a decision on all that concerns the self. Living all, each life member establishes the self's personal path at life, making all personal decisions, making all personal judgments. Each life member seeking and achieving life according to personal judgment. The moral obligation is the obligation for all. To decide against morality, to decide against the good is to do so at the self's own expense.

As life is in complete possession of life, as life is complete, so is every life member in complete possession of the self, so is every life member complete. As life achieves all, so does each life member achieve all. As life is fulfilled, so is the life of every life member fulfilled. No life member lives a lesser, greater, or different life from the complete life. Every life member lives, decides, and judges in accordance with the self, in accordance with the best interest of the self. The seeking, the attaining of life necessarily involves the attaining of knowledge. The search for life is also the search for knowledge. Knowledge is central to development. Once any one knowledge is achieved, that knowledge is equal to the status of that knowledge made known. No knowledge was ever discovered that was not made known. By its nature, the achieving of knowledge is the equal revealing of that knowledge. Knowledge is revealed through its achievement. Any discovered truth is known by the person making the discovery. Consequently no discovered truth remains unknown. No discovered truth is ever not revealed. For any truth to have been discovered, that truth must have a range of interest to the person making the discovery. The achieved knowledge has a range of interest. The achievement of knowledge affects its own range of interest. To seek to attain knowledge is to seek to reveal that knowledge, if at least to the person achieving that knowledge. The range of revealed knowledge is exactly such as it is, not lesser, not greater. The range of revealing does not exist beyond itself. No individual is aware of all knowledge. There is existing knowledge that is unknown. There is existing knowledge that is unknown beyond the range of the revealing of that knowledge. There are those who fall outside the range of revealing of any one specific knowledge. That does not mean that the knowledge was not discovered. That does not mean that the knowledge doesn't exist. It is the status of any one knowledge, its range of interest, that determines the extent of that knowledge being known. The range of each knowledge exists. The range of each knowledge is a fact. All attained knowledge is always revealed. All attained knowledge is always revealed to the extent of the range of that revealed knowledge. The path at life by each life branch is guided by the life qualities, which contribute to the identity of the particular life branch. Each life member affecting the path at life by the particular life branch. Seeking life and attaining life, seeking knowledge and attaining knowledge, each life member affects the path at life to the extent of the range of personal influence. Attaining life, attaining knowledge is central to personal development. Attaining life, attaining knowledge, revealing knowledge is central to the development of any life branch. If the revealing of knowledge was not central to the development of any life branch, then no knowledge would have been ever revealed. Instead it is the complete opposite that occurs. All knowledge is to its range of interest made known. Attaining life, attaining knowledge, the path at life by each life branch is established.

Seeking life, attaining life is living life. Life initiates the living path; life is successful at living. The fact that life exists is proof that life is successful. The fact that life exists is proof that life is not denied and cannot be denied success. The question of success as result is a question of degree of success. The success at life is complete. The search for life and the attainment of life is life's basis. It is the reason for life's existence. If the search for life, if the attainment of life, were unsuccessful, then life would be denied life's most beneficial aspect. Life would in fact be a failure. Life would vanish. Life would not exist. The living path at life by the life members is in accordance with life's living path. Life cannot not exist. The same and equal to life, life's living path cannot not exist. Life's success at living cannot be denied. Just as life cannot be denied in existing, so it is that life's living path cannot be denied in existing, so it is that life's success at living cannot be denied. Life's success at living is complete. Just as life is complete, just as life's living path is complete, so is life's success at living complete. The success is life's path. The success is all that life achieves. The success is life's being. Life achieves all. Life has the complete ability to achieve all. Life's ability is complete, as it is that life is complete. The equivalent ability to life's being cannot but be possessed, the complete ability. It is life that initiates life's living path. It is life that searches for greater life. It is life that seeks life's destiny. It is life that is responsible for life's own well-being. Life has a purpose, and that purpose can only be attributed to life. Life seeks that which is best. Life accomplishes that which is best.

The intended is achieved, and the achieved is the intended. Life is in control. Life is in control to the exact extent of life's being, Life is in control to the extent of life's ability. Life is not lesser. Life is not greater. Life's ability is not lesser. Life's ability is not greater. Life's ability is the same as life's being. Life's ability is life's being. Life has the complete ability to achieve life's being. Life has the complete ability to achieve life's destiny. There is a reason for life's particular development, and that is life's complete ability to achieve the most beneficial. Life has no hindrance to the achievement of that which is best. For it is that life's ability is such as life's ability is. Life's ability will result in the corresponding success, in the equivalent to the ability success, in the achievement of life's being and destiny. Any attempt at understanding any aspect of life is therefore an attempt at understanding life's ability and intent. Life's intent is to, under all circumstances, achieve that which is best. Life's intent is to achieve life's one best path at life. Life's intent is to achieve life's being. Life's ability achieves life's being. Life's ability achieves life's one best path at life. Life's Ability is Life's Intent. Life's Intent is Life's Ability.

Central to understanding life is understanding life's successful nature. Central to understanding life is understanding life's victorious nature. Life achieves all. Life is victorious.

Setting upon the living path, life has done so in life's victorious nature. By taking the action that is most favorable, life accomplishes all. Setting upon the living path, life is faced with the task of fulfilling life's destiny. To accomplish this, life creates the most favorable, the most beneficial condition. Life by seeking that which is of most benefit, Life does not engage in seeking that which is less than the most beneficial. Seeking the most beneficial, the most beneficial is created. In the beginning of the present stage, life achieved the most favorable condition. The fulfilling of life's destiny requires that during the present stage, life develops and grows. That development and growth has occurred in the most favorable manner. That development and growth has occurred in the most favorable manner of achieving the desired. Setting upon the path of destiny, life has always achieved the intended. With the end of the previous life stage and the advent of the current life stage, life is guided by life's laws. It is the reality of life that guides life. It is the reality of life that guides life's current stage. Life's existence is a certainty. It is the certainty of life that secures life's existence. The current life stage is a fact. Guided by life's laws, life's existence is never in doubt. The Middle Ground, the Reality of Life is the Sanctuary. Life is the Sanctuary. Life's living path is based on the fact of life's being. No event can occur that is external to life. No event can occur that is external to life's living path. Life's being is fulfilled. Life's destiny is fulfilled. No event can occur that can change life. No event can occur that can change life's destiny. The current stage is secured. Life is secured. As it is, that Life cannot not exist, so it is that life cannot not exist. The current stage leads to life. The current stage results in the fulfilling of the current stage.

The advent of the current stage is marked by the creation of the most favorable conditions. It is not within life to create less than the best. To do so is to harm the one path at life, the one best path at life. Life is one. The living path is one, the best one. Life seeks that which is best. Life's living path is fulfilled only in the one best way. To each life occurrence, there is one best intent. To each life occurrence, there is one best ability. Flourishing under the most favorable condition, the beginning of the current stage leads to basic life. Basic life cannot have always existed. Just as the earth has a beginning, so does basic life have a beginning. Arising from the previous life stage, arising from nonlife, the necessary, the most favorable measures are taken to ensure the success of the present stage. The most favorable measures are taken to ensure the fulfilling of the present stage. It is a transforming state with the intent of fulfilling the living path. Such is the intent, such is the result. Most favorable condition follows most favorable condition. During the beginning of the present stage, the most favorable condition equal to the beginning of the present stage was created. At such most appropriate moment, during such most appropriate condition, basic life comes into existence. The intent is the securing of life's existence. With the creation of the most beneficial condition, this is accomplished. The most beneficial moment can only be one. The most beneficial condition can only be one. It cannot be that the most beneficial, the most beneficial condition, will not lead to life. Life will be the result. Life's existence is not in doubt. Basic life arises from such most beneficial source. Thereby seeking greater life, basic life achieves greater life. No basic life quality remains in the most rudimentary state. Achieving greater life, basic life leads into complex and developed life. Basic life leads to new and distinct existence. All existence that is new and distinct from the previous is established and founded by one source, the one most beneficial source, by the best source to lead into the new. The number one is central to life. The origin of life is the one life, the one life originating from the cross between unlimited nonlife and unlimited life. Life contains all life, making life one. All manifestations of life have one best manifestation, the one most beneficial source leading to basic life and the one most beneficial to complex life source. All complex life is one. All complex life has one source of origin. All basic life that leads to complex life is one. All basic life that leads to complex life has one source of origin, the most beneficial to basic life origin. Life by seeking that which is best, once then achieving that which is best, there is no need for another, which is not equal to the best. All in life originates from the best. All in life originates from the one life. Only one life, only one source, can lead into that which is new and distinct. Any variation from the one such best life, from the one such best source, will not lead into the new and distinct but into something different. As all is different in life, any variation from the new and distinct will not lead into the new and distinct. Basic life originates from one basic life quality. One basic life quality leads to all complex life.

Early life led to complex life. All new attained level of distinct life originates from one source, the founder that is closest to that new life, the founder that is closest to that new life form. All new attained level of life is distinct from all other life. Being distinct, the new life form seeks life and greater life, in the same and distinct to the life form way, life. Being distinct, qualities of the same distinct nature are created. The life form leads into the same life form nature, which is different from all else. The life form achieves and creates of the same life form nature. The life form seeks the similar and same to the life form qualities. Incompatible to the life form qualities are not desired. Incompatible to the life form qualities are not developed. If they were, that would be undertaken by another distinct life form. By seeking the compatible, identity is created, the identity of the distinct life form. It is an irreversible act, in that each life form is separated and distinguished from all others. It is an irreversible act, in that each life form includes only what is of the same life form. Each life form differs from all other life forms, as it is that each life form was founded by the distinct, single. and closest to the origin founder. All differing life forms are excluded from all other life forms. If they are not, that would mean that all life forms are one and the same. The differentiation of each life form is where the differentiation happens to be. The attaining of the life form's identity takes place in its own particular way. All that was previous was previous and was lived in the previous manner. Undergoing the change, life lives in the new manner. Life's existence cannot be prevented. Life's manifestations cannot be prevented. All that life does was always present within life to do. All that life exhibits was always present within life to exhibit. Life's being is the same as life's manifestation. Life's being is the same as life's destiny. Life's being, life's manifestation, life's destiny are one and the same.

The inclusion of all that is of the same nature and the exclusion of all that is not is the life form. The life form is the inclusion of every single life quality, every single life form that is of the same distinct nature and the exclusion of every single life form that is not of the same distinct nature. Whatever the distinguishing point of any life form may be, that is the point of distinction. Only the same quality is included within any life form because any differing life quality would be a different life form. All and only of the same life form is included within any life form. This is due to the distinguishing point, the existing and therefore accurate distinguishing point. The distinguishing point cannot be inaccurate. The distinguishing point cannot not exist unless it were said that all is identical. The distinguishing point also includes life's final and unchangeable being and destiny. As life's being cannot be altered, neither can any one life form be altered. Life's being is final, making all within life final, including all life forms. As result making any one life form include all and only of the same life form. Humanity includes all and only that is human. No nonhuman branch can be a part of humanity. Humanity achieves all that is human. Humanity attains all that is human. Humanity is human, being only of the human nature.

Humanity is one. There is no other humanity. There can be no other humanity. There can never be another humanity. The distinguishing point, being and destiny ensure that humanity is one and can only be one. The distinguishing point, being and destiny ensure that no life form is different from that same life form. The distinguishing point, being and destiny ensure that no life form can become something that life form is not. Only that which is within any one life form manifests itself. Any characteristic that manifests itself from within any one life form belongs to that life form and no other, as it is that all life forms differ. Therefore no life form can take on the status of another life form. No life form can become different from the possibility of that same life form. Any life form, any life quality, any life member leads to that which is possible. The achievement of the possible is never less nor more than the possible. Each life form, each life member differs. The possible in each instance differs, as does achievement in each instance differ. Life cannot fail to occur in life's own way. Doing so, all and only the possible takes place. Life will not develop in a way that is foreign to life and is not present within life. No life member develops in a way that is foreign to that life member. No life member develops in a way that is not present within that life member. Life occurs in one best way. Every life member develops in a single one way. That way is the best way. Life is guided by that which is best. Every life member is guided by that which is best. To any one life occurrence, there is one best solution. Life in all life occurrence does that which is best. Making the way for life to develop one best way. Every life member is guided by that which is best. To any one life occurrence, there is one best solution. Every life member in all life occurrence does that which is best. Making the way for the life member to develop one single best way. The single and best way of development is not difficult to undertake and fulfill; it is the only way. The single and best way is the end result. The end result occurs due to life seeking and doing that which is best. The end result occurs due to life fulfilling life's one identity. Making the end result one, the same as life's being. As it is therefore, the chance for life to occur in the best and one way is not exceedingly negligible. The seemingly infinite different variations that life could have led have no meaning. The seemingly infinite different variations that life could have led to have no status. Life's end result is unbreakable and unchanging. However that life results, that result was always present within life in the exact same way. There is no possibility for life not to occur in one best way. Each life member attains all, and nothing can prevent all from occurring. Making life complete, making all life complete. Life's characteristics of ability and intent are central to life. Life's intent is life's ability. Life's ability is life's intent. Life's intent is to fulfill life's being. Life's ability is the fulfilling of life's being.

Seeking greater life, early life achieves greater life. Life forms taking shape, each arising from the single closest to the life form predecessor. Each life form builds on the life form's own nature, including all life members of the same to the life form nature and excluding all life members which are not of the same to the life form nature. Each life form is closest, in relations, to the founder of the life form. The predecessor is closest to the life form. The objective of each predecessor is the achievement of each such life form. New and more advanced life is then established. The purpose of the predecessor is then fulfilled. Doing so, all predecessors are extinguished; all predecessors become extinct. The predecessor does not have it within to survive for an extended period of time. The purpose of the predecessor having been accomplished, there is no further purpose in life. As result, the predecessor ends; the predecessor is extinguished. In the process, the new takes shape. The human branch is distinctly human and arises from the single predecessor. The single predecessor had a matching counterpart. Just as the existence of the single founder is assured, so it is with the counterpart. No event can occur that would prevent the single founder from existing and accomplishing all. No event can occur that could prevent the counterpart from existing. As it is that the single founder is closest to the new life form, so it is that one counterpart is closest to the one founder. Humanity achieves the distinctly human identity by developing the human character, by seeking the same compatible, human characteristics in others.

The matching pair led to humanity. It is not within a nonhuman branch to be human. Humanity is purely human, accepting within only human characteristics. The predecessor having accomplished the objective of giving life to humanity becomes extinct. Humanity cannot be mixed with the predecessor; that leads to extinction. The matching pair have the characteristics to lead to humanity. The matching pair are the only ones that have the necessary such characteristics. No other member from within the predecessor life form has them. Humanity cannot mix with the predecessor life form, nor can the single founder mix outside the matching counterpart. That would be done outside the human identity. That leads to extinction. Any life form arises from the best source. Humanity arises from the best source. The best source is the single founder. The best source is the single counterpart. The single founder, the single counterpart is the best source. All in life arises from that which is best. The best, and solely the best, gives rise to all within life. Humanity seeks that which is human and rejects that which is not.

All life forms follow the same principle, separating from the past and achieving identity. All predecessor life forms are in the process extinguished. No predecessor life form lives. The reason the past is extinguished is due to the past's nature. The end of the predecessor life form is brought about from within. It is within the nature to end. The struggle for life by the predecessor life form continues after achieving the objective. However, the achievement of the objective is the turning point. It is then that it becomes accentuated of what the purpose of the predecessor was, which was the creation of the new existence. It becomes accentuated that the past is not the new existence of life. The objective of the predecessor is the new existence, which the predecessor is not and cannot be. The predecessor by seeking greater life, by seeking the new existence, shows that the objective, the new existence is lacked. The development and growth of the predecessor can only occur within the limit of the predecessor, which was to give rise to the new. The new existence is the way forward; the predecessor is not. Development and growth by the predecessor is completely fulfilled once the new existence is achieved. Giving rise to the new existence and completely fulfilling life. The predecessor accomplishes all. Not being the way forward, the predecessor becomes extinct.

Humanity has then lived life and sought life. Every individual is distinct. There is one self. Each individual living and seeking life in one's own particular way. The human objective is the achievement of greater life. To seek less than greater life is to be contrary to the motives of original founding humanity. It is to be contrary to greater life, contrary to the Good. Greater life is thereby equated with the Good. Achievement of the good is a fact. Just as life accomplishes being and destiny, so it is with humanity. The human accomplishment is complete. Within being and destiny, within the human, all is present, including all effort at the good. Just as each individual is distinct, so it is that each effort is distinct, some achieving greater good. Within each individual's identity of good is the undertaking at life to that same good level. Whenever the good behave counter, in an opposing way, to someone else's view of the good, to someone else's proper view of the undertaking at life, it is the good that is the rightful side. In concluding which is the more just side, it is the good, the greater level of good, that is the deciding factor. The good is thoroughly such, the good cannot behave in an improper manner. It cannot be that the good can be achieved by all, the differences in achievement often resulting in opposing the good, in not recognizing the good as such. Just because the good is not recognized as such by some does not mean that the good is not the good, nor does it mean that the good does not exist. Being opposed, the good is often mistreated. The good has been imposed upon and harmed. The level of existence by the nongood being lacking, therefore leading to injustice. In the process, the good suffering an injustice. The good then falling victim to the good's nemesis in this world. It has always been that life has attempted to achieve that which is best. That having been the attempt, that has been the achievement. All of life's existence is to the best of life's ability, including this present life stage. Life by being guided by the search for the dominant existence strives toward such attainment. The dominant existence is where the greatest life is attained. The dominant existence is where the good is to the highest extent. It is where the height of good, the height of justice governs life. Striving for the dominant existence, the dominant existence is achieved. Life's boundaries, the reality of life assures the existence of the dominant state. Within the reality of life, the possible is accomplished, the range of which. Within that range, all states of existence are included. One of which accomplishes the most, the most desired, the dominant state doing so. It cannot be that the dominant state achieves less than the height of life. It is the height of life of fact. Life's basis is the good. Life's basis is those qualities which best serve life. Life does not seek, nor is life founded upon qualities which are detrimental to life. Those qualities are included within the good. Life's basis is that which is best, the seeking of the height of good. The seeking of the height of life, truth, and justice. It cannot be that life's basis is neither truth nor justice, neither the good nor the best. If life were based on that which is false, then life would not exist. If life were based on injustice, then life would not be able to accomplish anything of benefit to life. Life being unjust to life ensures life's nonexistence. This present life stage is not the most desired, the dominant state. During the dominant state, the good is at the height of existence, which means that the good's rule is complete, which means that the good could not be harmed. Currently the good's rule is not complete, as it is that the good is harmed. As result, this present stage is not the dominant life stage. Life fully recognizes the good. Life fully understands the good. The good is life's basis. When less than the dominant good is attained, that is fully known by life. If life attained the dominant good, the most desired state, at all times, then life would possess unlimited power. Lacking unlimited power, less than the most desired is experienced. Which is recognized as such, and the effort at the greater and greatest good is undertaken. The issue of concern then is whether this present life stage is considered to be imperfect by life. The issue is whether this present stage is considered as not being the stage of dominant good by life. Life regards the truth as such. In the inescapable fact of creation, life is limited and yet unlimited. The inability to do more than the possible, the inability to possess unlimited power is life's boundary. In the struggle for achievement, life loses the self. No situation can be controlled to an unreal, unlimited extent. In the same process of achievement however, life finds the self. Through that same struggle, through life's boundaries, identity is achieved. Life's laws favor life. Life's laws serve life and life's purpose. Life overcomes all laws. Life makes all laws life's. Life is the master of all. If life did not make all laws life's own, then life would not exist. Life achieves all through the struggle for life. It is based on life's limited, unlimited power that all is achieved. Life makes the effort at life. Life makes the effort at living. Life is real. Life does not disregard the truth. Life seeks the truth. Life's basis is the effort. Life's basis is the truth. A true observation within life is therefore true under all circumstances in life's existence. Life never acts against the truth. Life empowers the truth. In the greatest form of life's laws, in the greatest form of life's being, the greatest good is created. The question then becomes, is it true that life's foundation, the good, currently does not have complete rule? Is it true that the good suffers and is harmed by the good's nemesis and as result is the greatest good created? Under the good's complete rule, there is no injustice. This world is not the most desired state. This world is imperfect. The dominant state, the dominant good is not imperfect. The current imperfection is from within life. The imperfection is undergone by life. The effort is made, leading to perfection during the dominant state. Just as life has the power to achieve this existence, so does life have the power to achieve the dominant good. Life has the power to achieve being. Life has the power to achieve full being. The sanctuary is life. All laws serve life. No truth can be false. From within life's boundaries is the range of life. Lesser states and greater states of existence. Life lives the range of life. Life does not live only the lesser. Life lives the greater and the greatest state. The lesser state is when the good is not in full control. The greater state is when the good is in full control. This is a life truth. Life empowers all truth. No truth is false. Life seeks the best. Life achieves the best. Life achieves the dominant good.

Life makes the effort to achieve all. Within the range of life. Life achieves all. Life achieves full being. Life creates the self. Unlimited life and unlimited nonlife are life's boundaries. Which cannot be considered in life's creation. They can be considered in setting life's guidelines. Life is a fact. Life is living. Life is the source of life's creation. By making the effort, life has created the possible. Life has created the desired. By struggling to create all, life creates all. Life creates the self. Life's existence is a fact. Achieved life cannot be denied. The achievement is life's. The equal to the achievement effort is made by life, creating the self. Life's self-creation is not without limit. The limitation is set by the boundaries. To that extent, life self-creates. To that extent, life is created. If life self-created without limit, then the existence of the opposite would be denied. The middle ground would be denied. If life is created without limit, then the existence of the opposite is also denied. The middle ground would be denied. The medium is found. To think that life does not self-create is to misunderstand life's achieving effort, the achievement of all is the life effort.

The qualities of unlimited life and unlimited nonlife in not existing are recognized and known by life. They are risen above and controlled by life. To that extent, to that real extent, they are within life. Life being limited, all within life is also limited, including the risen above qualities of unlimited life and unlimited nonlife, their remnant states of which. Life being in complete control more than recognizes the opposing qualities. In their remnant state, they are both within life. It is a state above which life rises. As result, attaining identity, attaining the self: life achieves all.

By living life, early humanity has set upon the path of growth and development. It is a development that is solely human. The predecessor being the closest branch, the human line of development revealing itself, occurring in its own particular way. Seeking and achieving answers in that same particular way. No event occurring out of place, all occurrence being bound to its proper historical moment. The taken path being such as it is and not different. Each individual has lived at the appropriate moment, in the appropriate manner, living in one's own way, achieving the self. In the process defining the historical moment. Seeking greater life, humanity seeks knowledge. At the center of which is philosophy. As greater knowledge is attained, so is the good equally attained. To have knowledge is better than not having knowledge. Once having knowledge, the proper course of action is then taken; life is lived accordingly. Greater knowledge being greater good, the greatest knowledge is the greatest good. And so it is that knowledge is not unattainable. The seeking of knowledge has met with results. The good is the basis of greater life. It can only be that achievement of greater life is the achievement of the good. The existence of any life member is due to a level of positive feeling regarding the self. If there were no such feeling, all life members would be at war with the self. Life would be at war with the self. The motives of the self would not be struggled for. They would be nonexistent. Ensuring the nonexistence of all life members, including life. That positive feeling means that the self is struggled for, that the life of the self is possessed, that the self's basis is the personal good. Based on this personal good, the survival of each life member is assured. All that exists does so due a level of good. Life's basis is the good. In understanding any individual, it is the level of good that must be assessed. Life's basis being the good, it is through the good that life rises to the greatest height. In the process, the good and the observance of the good is the criteria in life. The possession of the good is of primary importance. Lacking the good being flaw. Greater life, the good is attainable. The effort in the field must be made. Knowledge of the good must be desired; knowledge of the good must be searched for. Philosophy being central to human development is engaged in seeking answers. The answers philosophy seeks are of life.

Life by struggling to achieve all seeks to achieve all, including self-knowledge. Nothing is given to life. The effort makes life. Life being master of all is the authority. The greatest attributes life has to the greatest extent, to the complete extent. As such, life does not have inadequate self-knowledge. Life has full knowledge of the self. Life's being is such as life's being is. Life achieves full being. Within life are present all the attributes, including full self-knowledge. Life is the justice of fact. There is none greater. Life is the authority of fact. There is none greater. In achieving that which is best, the necessary knowledge is required. In being the authority, the equal knowledge must be possessed, the equal self-knowledge. There is an order to life's being. Life creates all. Life creates the order. Life must know the order. If life did not have full knowledge, life could not be the

Authority. Life could not be Just. It has to be known what to be Just about. It has to be known what to be the Authority about. Behind any life manifestation is the necessary and equal to the manifestation knowledge. Behind the greatest life manifestation is the equal to that manifestation knowledge. In knowing how to self-create, in knowing how to achieve that which is best, in knowing how to be the authority, life has the greatest life manifestation within life. As result, life has full knowledge. Life has complete self-knowledge. The reality of life is unmistaken thought. Accurate correct thought, knowledge of the good is the reality of life. Life is not foreign and unknowable. A true observation is true under all circumstances. It is life that is attempted to be understood, life's ability, life's intent.

Life has the ability to accomplish all within the medium. The accomplishment of the dominant objective must in fact be real. It is the good and the accomplishment of the good that is life's basis. Life seeks that which is best. For life to be less than the best would be an act detrimental to the self. Life is searching for complete justice. Life is searching for the good's complete rule. Life's full being occurs within the medium, including the less desired states and the most desired. This stage of life is not the most desired. There isn't complete justice. The achievement of the most desired state is therefore in fact real, as this stage is not the most desired state. It cannot be that the most desired does not occur. As this existence is not, it therefore will. Life by seeking complete justice during the most desired state achieves complete justice. In life's eternal being, within the reality of life exists the state of greatest good. Life's power being limited, that state is not without end. In then ending, life initiates the most basic state. That state also being limited also ends. Leading to the next, that state then leading to the next. In the occurrence, in life's effort, leading back to the state of greatest good. Life once again achieves the greatest good. At which point life's living occurrence repeats, doing so eternally in the same exact way. Within the boundaries of unlimited life and unlimited nonlife, life's being cannot be changed. Life cannot obtain a characteristic not of life. Life's power cannot be increased or decreased. That would change life being the same. Life will always take the same course of action under the same circumstances. There is one reality of life. The reality of life is always the same. Life's eternal existence means that life will forever occur in the same way. It also means that life has forever occurred in the same way. That which occurs once, the present, will forever occur and has forever occurred. It is only the present that is experienced. Neither the future nor the past can be experienced. It cannot be that the exact past and exact future can occur without them being experienced. The exact future and exact past take place. As it is that they do exist, they must be experienced, but they are not. The present, the past, and the future take place at the same time. Life's eternal future and past existence occur within the present. The past and future cannot pass not felt. Existing within the present, the past and future are experienced. The eternity of life occurs within the present. The eternity of life is experienced through the present. The eternity of past and future exists to the proper extent within the present. Life's laws serve life. Life's power and being is the issue. Life's ability and intent is the issue. Within the one present existence, life forever repeats in the exact same way. The future and past are not inexperienced.

With the past, present, and future simultaneously taking place, life's living occurrence is forever assured. Nothing can interfere with which because nothing has interfered, nor will anything interfere. Life guides the living path to the successful life occurrence. Life's living path successfully occurs because that same living path was always successful and always will be.

Life is successful with all aspects of life's being. Existing within the boundaries, life self-creates. Life struggles to achieve that which is best. Life is not less than the self. Life does not experience less than the self. Life's power is limited, but life achieves all. Life is completely fulfilled. Unlimited power is not needed to live life. Unlimited power is not needed to experience the self. There is no alienation from the self. The self is thoroughly loved. Life is limited and cannot do the impossible, but there is no need to do so. Life flows from life to life. No stage is without end. Being limited in power, each life stage ends. Doing so, initiating the beginning of the next. No life stage is without a beginning. Fulfilling the living occurrence and being eternal does not make life unlimited, as no act of life is unlimited. Proof for life's eternity is found in the reality of life. It is found in the nonexistence of unlimited nonlife. It is found with real nature of nonlife, possessing life within. Life never leads into unlimited nonlife. Unlimited nonlife never leads to life. Life is therefore eternal. It is within the eternity of life that the life stage has beginning and end. Unlimited nonlife does not and cannot exist. Life does. Unlimited power does not and cannot exist. If life leads into unlimited nonlife, then life would vanish. Only to once again reappear. As the creating element had the ability to bring life into existence once, so must the creating element have the ability to bring life into existence once more. If not, the reason for the first and current existence would be denied. If life occurs once, life must occur twice. At which point life would then once again vanish. Only to reappear again, doing so eternally. That would make the creating element unlimited. It would mean that the creating element possesses unlimited power. Life could not forever vanish and forever reappear. The creating element in reality is therefore life and not the unreality of life. Once unlimited power is negated, so are then unlimited life and unlimited nonlife negated. The reality of life takes place. The laws of the medium are observed. The laws of the middle ground are made life's laws. Life does not eternally vanish and eternally reappear. It would require unlimited power to eternally deny life's existence, whereas limited power is needed to fulfill life's being. It would require unlimited power for life to eternally exist without effort changeless and so willed. All that life does is limited in power. The limitation of power is from within life. Unlimited power is not needed in life's occurrence. Unlimited power is needed to stop life from occurring. Life is limited, eternally taking place within the reality of life. Life's eternal existence is wholly limited. That existence is not as the would-be existence of unlimited life, where without effort all is achieved, where existence is without change and limitless, willed however wished. Life's existence is not as the would-be existence of unlimited nonlife, where that existence is without limit, where it is forever without change, forever denying life. Life exists on life's own terms. That is why life is limited and yet eternal. That is the reason why limited power is needed to eternally sustain life, and unlimited power is needed to end life.

Life is eternal in the sense that life's existence cannot be terminated. Life does not originate from an element that is foreign to life. Life does not lead into a state that is foreign, that is not identified with life. Within the eternal setting is life's occurrence. Ranging from seeking greater life to achieving greater life, from imperfection to perfection. Being limited, no stage is endless. Seeking that which is best, the range of life is experienced. Each stage is recognized for what that stage is, the imperfect and the perfect. It can only be that life has a stage that is the most desired, that is the greatest. If not, then life's denial would ensue. As life exists, so does life's greatest stage exist. The stage of imperfection must in fact be overcome. By being forever imperfect, life would not exist. If life were forever imperfect, then life's existence would be denied. Whatever the most desired stage may be, that stage does exist. It is the stage of greatest good. Being the greatest, the stage that achieves the most, that stage is the height of life.

Life originates from life quality. Life leads to life quality. Life lives the life occurrence. Life always existed and always will. The Being of Life has no beginning. The Being of Life has no end. Life's eternity answers the question of when it is that life comes into existence. As for how it is that life comes into existence, unlimited life and unlimited nonlife do not exist. Life cannot not exist. Life's eternity makes the question of which it is that comes into being first, the stage of greatest good or the most basic, meaningless. No accurate assessment of life can be made with the improper understanding of the dominant stage. The focus in considering life has to be the dominant good. It is where life is complete. It is where all life is attained. By the fact that the stage of greatest good is the height of life. It is therefore the stage of primary importance in the consideration of life. The path to which is that, the path, with such of the path importance in the understanding of life. Within the path, life strives to attain the objective of full being. In the process denying the primary importance of the path in the considering of life. The dominant good achieves more than the path, achieving the most, achieving perfection, achieving the height of life. At which point, if life were less than perfect, life would be imperfect at the moment of life's perfection. Life can eternally remain within the boundaries, no greater, unreal existence is needed.

Seeking that which is Best, the Good is Life's Being. As it is that life is the authority, life cannot fail in any objective. Guided by the good, life accomplishes all. The good is of central importance to life. Life achieves the good, the highest justice, the highest truth. The beneficial characteristics being present within the good to that same level of good. It cannot be that truth, justice, and life can be separated from the same level of good. Being limited, life occurs accordingly, within the reality of life. As result, life is mastering every situation. Life must be accepted. Just as life self-creates, so does all within life self-create. The point to consider is the undeniable existence, the effort made for which, the equal to the self-content. Life cannot not exist. Life occurs in life's undeniable way. Life does and create so much, the equal to the life content. The responsibility for which can only be attributed to life. It is life that is the authority. Life is the good. As life cannot not exist, all within life cannot not exist. All within life must take place. Possessing the equal to the self-content and exerting the same equal effort to realize the self, the responsibility for the self's creation can only be attributed to the self. Each one is responsible for the self. For the self's actions, for the self's personality. Consequently, each one is responsible for self-creation. The issue of decisive importance is the choice made for the self. Each individual chooses the self. All choice is made from the self; therefore the original choice is the self. No being is different from the self. The self decides and chooses all. All choice is based on the self. If the self is not chosen, if another self were chosen, or the one self rejected, no such actual choice could be made, including the rejection of the self and the choice for another. If self-improvement is wished for, then self-improvement can be engaged in. All behavior is initiated by the self. The love for the self is complete. The self is chosen for. As life exists within the reality of life, so does all else. The reality of life cannot be changed, but no such change is wished for. Life achieves all. Life is complete. As life is complete and achieve all, so it is with each individual. Living within the boundaries of life, each individual self-creates; each individual chooses the self. Living within the boundaries, no one other self can be chosen; no one other self can be created. However, no one other than the self is wished for. No one other than the self is lived. The self achieves all. The self is complete. As result, each individual self-creates, each individual chooses the self. Each one is responsible for the self. The love for the self is the deciding factor. Each individual seeks that which is best for the self. The love for the self cannot be denied. To the specific extent to the reality of life, all within life is to that specific extent created, and to that specific extent, all within life self-creates. The choice for the self is the same and equal nature as self creation. All the while the search for the good is everyone's objective. To seek less than the most good is to achieve less. It is to be lacking in the possession of the good. All effort must be made in the search for the good. The effort will produce the results, and the results cannot be known until the full effort is made. There can be no limitation on desired self-improvement. There can be no limitation on the desired search for the good.

The human objective has throughout all human history been the greater achievement of personal good. A failure in the matter has at all times been done at the expense of the self, at the expense of the self's higher personal standing. Under any one circumstance in each individual's life, the individual advocates the personal view, to whatever extent that may be. The only way that view can be advocated is if it is considered correct, is considered as good. A claim to a level of good is therefore made by everyone. The deciding issue, as to what is considered correct behavior, is in all instances the personal regard as good. To seek greater good is only natural. The good elevates the human being. The good strengthens the human being. The human objective is the greater achievement of personal good. In seeking greater good, humanity seeks greater morality. Humanity's historical path, the descendant of the predecessor path, does not take away from the human moral obligation. The choice for the self has at all times, all through human history, been completely fulfilling. During any point in human existence, the choice for the self is complete. Everyone is responsible for the self. Everyone is responsible for the personal search for the good. Past humanity is not to be diminished. Past humanity has accomplished all within the human realm. That will always be the case in the human historical path. The made-full effort at achieving the good will meet with the equal results. Possession of the good will lead to a just and moral character, a character founded upon truth and greater life. If truth, justice, greater life are not possessed by the self, then these qualities will be acted out against. Those who possess these qualities will be acted out against. As it is that it is the human desire to lead a peaceful existence, lacking the good leads to human confrontation. The good leads to correct and moral behavior. When relating to others, it is the same correct and moral behavior that will guide the good individual. The good is of the greatest importance. The only way humanity can engage in good behavior is through the good character. The idea that humanity will be judged for the human behavior has never been a positive check to wrongdoing. The idea of judgment is mistaken human thought. Mistaken thinking is not beneficial. The refuting of the idea of judgment is an accurate thought. It is accuracy in thinking that is desired. Accurate thought is of benefit. The truth can only be founded upon the good. Knowledge of the truth can only be attained through possession of the good. The truth is law. The truth is the good. Knowledge of the good can only be a positive. The good will never lead to wrongdoing. To attain the truth is to seek the truth. It is to respect the truth. It is to seek the good. It is to respect the good. The personal conduct that results from attaining the good is the same and equal to the possessed good. It is the possession of the good that is desired. The good leads to good behavior. It is the good that prevents wrongdoing. Consequently lack of knowledge of the truth means that the good is lacked. By lacking the good, the resulting behavior is just as lacking. It is lack of the good that leads to what is incorrect. Any one considered topic has an extent of influence on related issues and personal behavior. All of which will be positive if the good is observed, and all of which will be negative if the good is lacked. To seek less than the greatest good is at all times done at the expense of the self. The only way for humanity to live is by observing the good. The idea of judgment, that attachment to it will lead to good behavior due to the possibility of punishment and reward, makes a complete reversal. Attachment to the idea of judgment does not lead to good behavior. It leads to wrong behavior. Whereas attachment to nonjudgment does not lead to wrong behavior, it leads to good behavior. Any claim that freedom of judgment has led to bad behavior is a false claim. Bad behavior can only result from insufficient level of personal good. Freedom of judgment does not mean that wrongdoing can be then readily engaged in. It means the opposite; the search for the good should be ever greater. Being guided by the idea of reward and punishment, such freedom of behavior is then achieved. Freedom of behavior which is due to the same tool of mistaken thought that then guides it, the same lacking the good tool. Fulfilling the flaw in the process, the lacking of the good behavior.

The choice for the self, self-creation, occurs within the reality of life. The choice is fulfilling. Self-creation cannot be exceeded. During the dominant stage of good, the good has complete rule over all of life. All the possible good is achieved. Prior to the dominant stage, the good was not complete. For life to punish evil during the dominant stage is to punish the not complete level of prior good. Life does not possess unlimited power. states less than the dominant must be experienced. If not, life would have unlimited power. Life cannot eternally exist in the dominant state. During the less-than-dominant states, less than the greatest good is experienced. Life seeks the greatest good. In achieving the greatest good, all wrongdoing is then removed. Life's intent is the attainment of the highest justice. During the dominant state, the highest justice reigns. Life solves the less-than-dominant states by elevating the self. That includes all within life. There is no purpose in life not achieving the highest justice. The constant growth of each individual is key. Humanity's moral obligation is not less. The human desire for the good is critical.

The idea of nonjudgment is central to the human assessment of life. The meaning of nonjudgment is that humanity can act in the way that is self considered as best toward the achievement of the established objective. This has been the case in all of human history. This is the implemented behavior with all from within life. By understanding nonjudgment and enacting the subsequent and related behavior, humanity sets the groundwork for a full and accurate assessment of life. The basis for the complete self is established. In conducting oneself in the considered best way, humanity lives without making any errors. Life is lived to the fullest, humanity fulfilling life. The idea of nonjudgment can be followed without the fear of not understanding life, without the fear of making any mistakes in living life. In so doing, achieving mental freedom, achieving mental growth. The truth, greater life are the characteristics of the good. The truth in life's being is to be searched for. The good is supreme. The more that the good is lacked, the greater the flaw. It is that the personal good, life, cannot be exceeded, and the considered as good has been enacted by the self, but when that good is lacking, an act against the good has been made. The good is to be observed by all. The lacking of the good cannot be equated with the good. To lack the good is to commit a wrong. The more that the good is opposed the greater, the wrong. It is to seek to harm the good. It is to be devoid of the good. It is to be evil.

Life occurs in one single and best way. That way leads to the dominant state. The having occurred is irreversible. The less-than-dominant states can only be imperfect, resulting in such imperfect occurrence. No error can be realized in life's occurrence. Humanity is a part of life. No error can be realized in human existence. The having occurred is irreversible. If self-improvement is wished for, then self-improvement should be engaged in. The only way good behavior can be engaged in is by observing the good, by being a mature and complete human being. By observing the good, it is always greater good that is wished for and struggled for. To seek less is to be detrimental to the self. It is to harm the self. By seeking self-improvement, by seeking the good, humanity achieves mental growth, mental freedom. The question of what is right and just is settled. It is humanity that is the source of the idea of judgment. Many of those calling for humanity to be judged should not be so eager to do so. The results may not be what was envisioned. The results may not be what was desired. Any attempt to deceive the good will end in failure. Certainly philosophy is at the core of human thought. It is only philosophy that deals with the most important issues. As such, only philosophy can solve them. Philosophical truth can be attained.

Through the wish for philosophical knowledge, through the made effort, philosophical truth will be revealed.

The laws governing the world are achievable. Evidence for this can be found in the fact that all the different branches of human knowledge have attained truths in their own field. Truths which are undeniable because human existence is based upon them. Truth is separate from falsehood. False human assessment does not destroy true human assessment. That which is false is false; that which is true is true. As result, humanity is guided by truth. If the false were the guide to true human assessment, that would make all human under-standing false, denying human existence. Humanity could never live if all within the human world were false. Among this then it should come as no surprise when philosophy arrives at its own answers. Philosophy is the supreme human development. It is only natural that philosophy should answer the most pressing questions. Philosophy has as its purpose the understanding of the fundamental reasons for life's existence. Philosophy has as its purpose the understanding of life's ultimate being. These issues are fundamental in the sense that they reveal the most about life: upon understanding these issues, the most is then known of life. Having such focus, philosophy achieves such understanding. Philosophy achieves all within its realm. The questions of proof, refutation, and validity are answered. Philosophy seeks the most, philosophy is the highest good. Philosophy being the greatest good ensures its own true outlook. It cannot be that the greatest good can fail, can misrepresent. If that were the case, then philosophy would not be the greatest good. Philosophy being the greatest good has the greatest reasoning, the greatest love for knowl-edge, the greatest proof. The achievement within philosophy is equal to the effort, and the effort is the most. An incorrect philosophical outlook does not destroy the correct ones. There are a number of varying laws guiding life. Humanity achieves all the possible laws. There cannot be a disproportionate amount of life laws and human-achieved laws. The human limit is equated with life's laws. This is because no law that is humanly unknown can be used to humanly reveal life's being. Making the correct outlook superior and law. That is the case with philosophy. Philosophical truth exists, and since it is that no greater exists to refute and reject the superior, that makes the superior correct and law. All human laws are attained. All philosophical laws are attained. No act can occur as to prevent life from taking place in the one and best way. Therefore humanity achieves all. Philosophy achieves all. In seeking truth, philosophy bases itself upon self-evident conclusions. The alternatives to which are self-denying, are at their root opposed to the truth, and the only possible way of life's being. Within the philosophical world, truth must in fact exist, whatever that truth may be. Nor can it be concluded that philosophy does not lead to truth, to any truth at all. Such an assessment can only be made by a nonphilosopher, by someone who has no love for the greatest knowledge of all. The made such conclusion is based on philosophy. It is in fact saying that there is no philosophical truth while advocating one. The contradiction is obvious. How can a nonphilosopher know this, how can a nonphilosopher know philosophical issues? The validity of philosophy cannot be questioned by a nonphilosopher. The task of philosophy is philosophical truth. Only a philosophical view may bring another philosophical view into question. As it is that the nonphilosopher is wrong to advocate that philosophy does not lead to truth. It may still be that philosophy does not lead to any truth. To wonder if philosophy leads to truth is a fair endeavor. One which is answered in the positive. Philosophy is founded on proof of achieved truth. Philosophy has a historical process, throughout which there have been great philosophers, great philosophical thinkers. These great philosophers must have some achievement, achievement equal to the philosopher. Any study of the history of philosophy must primarily concern itself with Socrates and Plato. Philosophy achieves philosophical truth, which is unequaled in the understanding of life. Philosophy is the greatest humanism. Basing itself on self-denying or self-evident ideas, philosophy makes conclusions, conclusions which if correct cannot be overturned. Philosophy seeks to understand the unseen laws, the world of truth, the world of ideas. The world of truth is the basis of all. The world of truth can only be reached through thought. Any correct philosophical theory is proven through the world of ideas. A correct analysis cannot be false. Philosophy leads to truth. Correct philosophy does not need to be physically tested and affirmed. Nor is philosophy based on the experience. Philosophy makes conclusions based on thought, that is the proof, irrefutable thought. Just because it cannot be brought to physical test does not mean that philosophy is wrong. It isn't that all life is the basis of the world of ideas. It is the reverse. The world of ideas is the basis of all life. The proof to any idea is in the world of truth, not to a physical test. A correct philosophical analysis is as result correct. Philosophy does not make conclusions on the experienced, rather on that which is true. There is philosophical truth within this stage of life. To achieve that truth is possible. That philosophical truth is based on the experience of the present, but the present is not to be diminished or discounted. To engage in philosophy is to seek truth in the present stage, and that is all possible philosophical truth. It is to make observations from within the present stage. It is to be to that extent dependent on and limited by the present stage. That does not mean that the range of philosophical truth within this stage cannot be attained, nor does it mean that the present truth is without value. The philosophical laws guiding this stage are valid. They cannot be wrong. This stage is not separate from all else, any and all future stages. As such, no future stage can overturn and negate the valid present laws. It is that during the dominant stage the most life is achieved, which cannot be achieved during the present, but the laws of the present cannot be denied. Any and all life development can only be based on the present, to whatever extent that may be. This means that the experienced does not limit philosophy, the inexperienced does. Philosophical laws achieve the possible. Philosophy does not need to be tested to be affirmed. Philosophy's proof is the strongest of all irrefutable thought. Philosophy's proof is the world of truth, the world of unseen laws. The world of ideas is perfect. The world of ideas is life's basis. The world of ideas cannot fail. Life cannot fail. Only philosophy deals with life's ultimate being. Philosophy achieves the greatest understanding. Philosophy leads to truth.

Philosophy is the made effort at philosophical issues. It is to systematically search for truth. It is to create an explanatory system regarding life. The search for philosophical truth entails that a system be built and that the system is explained. Any philosophical issue is related to others, hence the explanatory system of all the issues. Explaining must occur in order to show that knowledge of the issue is possessed, and a system must be built in order to explain all the related issues. Making the sufficient effort, philosophy is then engaged in. To engage in philosophy does not necessarily mean that philosophical truth is achieved with every single analysis. Philosophy is defined as the genuine and sufficient effort. Such effort is accessible to all. Philosophy is humanity's primary interest. In creating the explanatory system, the philosopher will give full credibility and analysis to all involved ideas. In arriving at a certain view, and in the process rejecting some ideas, the philosopher will continually return to the beginning and repeatedly question the made conclusions, giving full credibility and analysis to all involved ideas, including the rejected ones. Having arrived at truth can only mean that such effort was made. If it were insufficient, the truth could not have been achieved. All opposing views must have been adequately addressed to have achieved the true analysis. Philosophy is not an answer to desired need for specific view. If it were, then philosophy would not be engaged in. The genuine and sufficient effort would not be made. The arrived-at truth presents all, in the process enlightening the individual. The turning to desired view is not a philosophical act. Basing itself on reason, the achieved philosophical truth is therefore knowledge and not belief. Having made the effort at achieved truth, the philosopher has done and accomplished all. No higher understanding is possible. The achieved truth by the philosopher can only be defined as knowledge. Belief may or may not be correct. If ideas which are incorrect are adhered to, then this is not knowledge but belief. If ideas which are correct are adhered to, without having made the full philosophical effort, then this is belief. It is belief with reasons which lead to truth, the inherent such character is as result possessed. Attaining knowledge of philosophical truth, philosophy is not a personal interpretation. Philosophy stands for something, and that is philosophical truth. The value of which cannot be taken away. Human philosophical achievement cannot be negated.

The task of philosophy is to achieve all, to reveal all. Life's existence is a natural occurrence. Life cannot be prevented from occurring. Life cannot be prevented from being. The key to life, the key to life's being is possessed only by life. The key to life's being is unattainable to anyone other than life. Life's being cannot be created by anyone other than life. If the key to life were attainable to anyone other than life, that would make that creator in fact life.

It may be wondered, it may be thought that after the undeniable existence of life, a life member had gathered great and sufficient knowledge and had possibly recreated life. It may be thought that a life member had attained the key to life's being. Such an event has not occurred, and such an event could never occur. Under this circumstance, what is in question is not life's undeniable existence but the possibility of someone recreating life. The issue is not the creation of life but the exact same life duplication. Any creation of life, and not life's being, occurs within the already existing reality of life. As such, any such creation would be done to the possible within life extent. The laws of existence that would be followed are life's. No act could then occur whose basis is not life. As result, creation of life is not the exact recreation of the already existing life. For life's being to be recreated the exact same to life ability would be required. Life already has the exact ability for life's being. Life has the key to life. The key is unattainable to anyone other than life. Life's being is one. There can only be one key. Anything else is not the key to the recreation of life's being. Life cannot be recreated.

Within the boundaries of unlimited nonlife and unlimited life, the one reality of life is achieved. There can only be one life, capturing all within life. All that exists does so within the one life. Nothing exists outside of life. Life's objective is to fulfill life's own being. Life does this in the best way possible. If life sought that which is less than best for the self, then life would be acting against the self. Life would not be fulfilling life's cyclical and eternal being. By accomplishing that which is best, life proceeds upon life's living path.

Life accomplishes what is best according to life's living existence, according to that which further perpetuates life to the best of life's ability. In doing so, Life never considers time and space.

Neither time nor space is considered in life's living existence. Neither time nor space has a guiding effect on life. Time and space do not exist outside of life. They are both meaningless outside of life. One space would be the same as another. One time would be the same as another. No matter how great they are thought to become, as a way of defining them, they would always come back to the smallest measure. Not existing outside of life, the only way time and space may possibly be thought to take place is therefore from within life. It may be thought that just as life is undeniable, so too are time and space undeniable, being an integral part of life. Within the reality of life, life is in complete control over the self. Life is in complete control of all. No function, no aspect of life which does not serve life can take place in life's being. Only that which is best for life takes part in life. That which is less than best would not serve life. It would be foreign to life, as such, would be excluded from life. In living, life considers only life. If life considered time and space, life would not be considering only life. Life would not be considering only that which is best for life. Life would not be in complete control of all. Life would not be life's own master. Life would be constantly checking with time and space to verify what is appropriate. Life would lose contact with the self. Life would lose contact with life's living existence. Life in the process would be destroyed. And yet life is not destroyed. Therefore life does not consider time and space. Time and space do not serve in life's best ability and effort at living. They are foreign to life; as such, they do not exist. Time and space would have a restrictive, limiting effect on life. Life would be subjugated and defeated. Life would be lifeless. There is no entity that can rule over life. There is no entity that can defeat life.

In understanding life, time and space are not primary. Time and space are not primary in life's being. Life does not take into consideration the period of time nor the space that may be necessary for the fulfilling of life's existence and objective. Life lives according to the effort put forth in the achievement of life's mission. The primary factor in understanding life is life. The primary factor within life is life. Time and space serve no purpose in life's being. Time and space don't exist. What exists is life and all aspects of life. Any seeming measurement of time and space is mistaken human thought. Such assessment is not of time and space. It may appear that it is, but it is not. Such assessment is made regarding life. Time and space have no definition. They have no rule guiding them. The rule is life. The definitions attributed to time and space are human. The definitions are from within life. Those definitions are mistaken. Those definitions don't have the reality of life in mind. Life never behaves as result of time and space having come to point where life's response at living is required. Time and space have no guiding effect on life. It is life that has the guiding effect. Not being real, time and space are not included within life. Life would never include elements which are foreign to life. All human endeavors at knowledge must have the reality of life as its priority. In the process achieving greater and better understanding. By excluding time and space, that greater and better understanding is achieved. It is life that is wished to be understood. The assessments of time and space are not of time and space, they are of life. The made assessments are wrongly attributed to time and space when in reality they are of life. Hence the appearance that time and space do exist.

By excluding time and space, life proceeds upon life's living effort, taking into consideration only the living effort. If time and space were included within life's being, then life would behave according to reasons which would serve time and space and not life. As result life would be negated. Life's being is as life's being is. Life is life's own master. Life's laws serve life. The issue of life's cause, the issue of cause and effect, is likewise guided by life's being. As it is that life exists, life is the effect. As it is that life self-creates, life is also the cause. Life's status in this respect is central to the issue of cause and effect. Life cannot not exist. Life is inevitable. Life is a fact. Life's creator, life's cause, is neither unlimited nonlife nor unlimited life. Life is life's own creator. Life is life's own cause. In that life self-creates, life's ability, life's being is better understood. Life exists. Life is the effect. Life self-creates. Life is the cause. Life being central to the issue, cause and effect are inherently connected. All that occurs within life is life's living existence. All of which is the effect. The effect is life. The cause of the effect is life. The cause and the effect are the same property, they are one and the same. The effect by existing captures its own self completely, its own quality completely. Within which no foreign element is included. The effect could never originate from a source which is not identified with the effect. The cause cannot produce the effect while remaining separate from the effect. The effect makes the qualities of the cause its own, and the cause makes the qualities of the effect its own. No resulting effect is ever dependent for its existence to a source other than that of itself. If the effect is not dependent for its existence to itself, to its own cause, then that would end all association between the cause and the effect. The cause would be of different quality to the effect, and the effect would be of different quality to the cause. No interaction could then possibly result, denying life's fact.

If the effect were not of the same nature as the cause, if the effect did not make the qualities of the cause its own, then the effect could never originate from the cause. The cause is not of different and distinct nature from the effect. The effect has a personality, and that personality captures all that is its own. Excluding all that is foreign and including all the same nature. The effect should not be underestimated. The link between cause and effect should be understood. The cause and the effect are inseparable. The effect cannot not exist, making the effect the cause. The effect could never originate from an element which is not identified with the effect. The cause cannot produce the effect while remaining separate, distinct, from the effect. The cause cannot be of a different nature from the effect. If it were, all association would be ended with the effect. The effect would originate from a source foreign to the effect's own, ending all association with itself. Denying the effect's existence.

Life is life's own cause. Life is the effect. That being so, it follows that all within life is its own cause and effect. All within life is a manifestation of life and observes life's being of self cause and effect. With life's living existence taking place, all of life is made manifest. The cause of which is life. Life is the cause and the effect. All within life is its own cause and effect. Life's such manifestation will behave in the life way, doing and creating. The effect of which cannot be separated from the cause and the cause from the effect, the effect owing its existence to itself. The effect including within the effect's own characteristics, making itself the cause. All life manifestations are related to the cause, life. No manifestation can be unrelated to the cause, life. Every such relationship therefore must be properly understood. Life cannot not exist. The effect cannot not exist. The effect includes all and only its own characteristics. The effect is not foreign to itself. Making the effect the cause.

Life exists. Life is the cause of all. Life is the cause of life. All life is the effect. The effect is its own cause. If the effect owes its existence to a cause not its own, not to itself, then that would make the cause different, distinct, from the effect. The importance of the effect should not be minimized. The importance of the cause should not be exaggerated. If the importance of the cause is exaggerated, the effect would be at the mercy of the cause, behaving however the cause wills. The effect would not make the factors responsible for its action its own, thereby would achieve a separation from itself. Thereby would achieve a separation from the cause. As result, no act could ever take place. There would be no existence. The cause cannot be exaggerated at the expense of the effect. The key is the effect, not the cause. The separate and distinct, the superior cause to the effect. The existence of the effect cannot be denied: with the effect not being minimized, all proper attention is turned to the effect, and as result, all proper attention is turned to the cause. The issue of cause and effect is a solvable philosophical issue. All the greatest and most fundamental issues can only be solved by philosophy. All challenges to philosophy will end in failure. Philosophy will forever crush all pretenders to the greatest human knowledge of all, which solely belongs to philosophy. Causal reasoning needs to be understood for what it really is. All that occurs does so within life, owing its existence to life. Life can only receive life's own life quality from life. Life and all within life arises from one's own life quality. Making life and all within life one's own effect, one's own cause. Making all within life one's own creator.

In the reality of life, the cross between unlimited nonlife and unlimited life, life achieves all. As result, life lacks nothing. This is also the case with all life manifestations. All life members attaining all and lacking nothing. Although the self-creating ability cannot be exceeded beyond life's boundaries, that self-creating ability is in all instances completely fulfilling. A greater self cannot be created. A different self cannot be created. However, the love for the self is decisive. It cannot be thought that life achieves less than the most, less than the best. It is the duty of all to seek the greater good. To fail in the process is to do so at one's own expense. Hence being one's own cause, being one's own creator is in all instances completely fulfilling.

Life would never seek less than the most. Life achieving the most is assured. Life's existence is assured. The occurring of life in the best way possible is assured. Life's existence can never be prevented from occurring. No event can ever take place which would interfere with life's occurring in the best way possible. Nothing in life is by chance. All in life is in the best development. Within life's boundaries life accomplishes all. Life's identity is revealed through ideas, provable ideas, irrefutable ideas. Being provable, these ideas exist in fact. They are life's identity. Life's basis is such as life's basis is. Life's basis can only be truth. That truth must exist in fact. What makes the truth such are irrefutable ideas. The truth, the world of ideas is life's basis. The world of ideas cannot be negated just as life's existence cannot be negated. In the world of ideas, all is correct; all is without error. In the world of ideas, there are no mishaps. Such also is the situation with life. Nothing is by chance. Life is without error. Life is the sanctuary of all. The world of ideas gives life stability. The world of ideas is life's haven. In the world of ideas, the good is in complete control. The highest justice there reigns. Life is in life's fully accurate being. All attains its true status. All is understood. That understanding is struggled for by life. Nothing is given to life. By exerting the most genuine struggle, life achieves all. Life achieves all understanding. Knowledge can only be primary. Through knowledge, life achieves order. Through knowledge, life is the just authority. The effort, the struggle by life to attain all is real. Nothing is given to life. That effort is wholly successful. Life is not denied anything. The justice is life's. There is none greater. It cannot be that life is unjust. It cannot be that life is flawed. It serves life no purpose with life's full and complete knowledge and understanding of all, to be less than just. Life's effort is to be just, not unjust. With life seeking and doing that which is best, with life being the authority, life achieves all of life's being. With life being completely self-aware, life has full knowledge. Life has full understanding. By doing that which is best, by understanding all, life engages in justice. It is made clear that life's objective is justice. There is justice in understanding all. There is justice in seeking that which is best. It is by understanding all that life exerts the complete effort at justice. It is justice to exert the complete effort at living. It is justice for life to be victorious.

If it is thought that unlimited, without change, life may exist, then it would have to be considered that unlimited, without change, nonlife may exist. If only the opposite were to occur, that would be done at the expense of the other. Neither unlimited opposite is real. The reality of life takes place. Where to that certain extent the opposites are included. The inclusion of opposites is an integral part of life's being. As result, life is created, and life self-creates. Likewise the material and the ideal are also included. Neither can the material exclude the ideal, nor can the ideal exclude the material. They both contribute to life's one being. The issue of the material and the ideal is of great importance. It needs to be understood. Life is a fact, and life must have a substance, whatever that substance may be. The material cannot solely exist, nor can the ideal solely exist. They both contribute to the identity of the one life. The material is the physical substance to life. The ideal is the conscious. They are both representations of life. They are life. They owe their existence to the self. They owe their existence to life. Each quality should be understood under the light that it does not solely contribute to life's identity, that the opposite is in all instances included. It isn't that any one of the qualities owes its existence to its opposite as much as to life and to its own quality. In the combining of opposites, the material and ideal take part in life. Life is the creative force of all from within life, including the material and ideal. Both opposites are real. Each opposite is part of life, possessing such life qualities. No opposite can originate from a quality not its own, from a nonlife quality. Any opposite has a lot more in common with its own quality than it does with its opposite. No opposite is denied any aspect of its quality, being in full possession of itself, mastering itself completely. Opposites are a part of life but are to that correct extent separate from each other. Any opposite can only arise from its own quality and not from the quality of the opposite. The ideal arising from its own quality and the material from its. No opposite, no life quality, is denied any aspect of itself because life exists in the one best way.

To ponder the future, what life's entering into nonlife brings, is to consider life's being. Life is eternal. Life is indestructible. The real nonlife has nothing to do with the eternal, without change, nonlife. Life leads to life. Life originates from life. To conclude that the ideal owes its existence to the material is to be mistaken. To conclude that life owes life's existence not to the self but to the material is to be mistaken. The apparent termination of the material does not lead to the termination of the ideal. The ideal owes its existence to itself and to life. The opposite quality of the ideal, the material, does not create the ideal. Therefore upon ending does not terminate the ideal. The material is a foreign quality to the ideal. It cannot have a greater to the limited and not decisive effect upon the ideal. As the ideal is fact, as the ideal has more in common with itself than with the material, as life's complete being of including the ideal and material is assessed, the effect of the material on the ideal can only be limited, and to the extent of the material. If it is said that the ideal owes its existence to the material, then it should also be said that the material owes its existence to the ideal. It is obvious that the ideal exists, in so doing making life complete. Without the ideal, life would not be life. The material does not alone constitute life. The material owes its existence as much to the ideal as does the ideal owes its existence to the material. Thereby negating the seeming overwhelming importance of the material. Thereby making the ideal life eternal. The material, to that correct extent, owes its existence to the ideal. The material, upon ending therefore, does not terminate the ideal. The ideal is necessarily eternal, making the material eternal. No life quality can be terminated as the termination would come from a foreign to the life quality source. The real termination comes from Life. The termination comes from Life. The termination obeys Life's Laws.

It is life's being that is attempted to be understood. Life enters from stage to stage, all of which life controls to life's extent. All stages are from within life. As result, all stages are life. In attempting to understand life, it is complete such effort that is desired. It is the complete understanding of life's being that is desired. Materialism, the view which gives excessive importance to the material, at the expense of the ideal, at the expense of understanding life, is not such complete effort. Materialism is not a real effort at understanding life. Philosophy welcomes all philosophical doctrines. Materialism is a part of philosophy, but it is undeveloped. It is not concerned with knowing life's being. Materialism is the most undeveloped part of philosophy.

The material and the ideal are both from within life. Both contribute to life's one being. Neither one exceeds one's own boundaries. By the same measure, neither element is less than fully complete, fully attaining one's status and not less. Consciousness is possessed only by the conscious bearing part of life, to the exact, required, and personal extent. Not missing what isn't present and being aware of one's own only. Life is at all times one. Within life exist all opposites, all of which are a part of life. The basis of life is the middle ground, the reality of life between all opposites. The basis of life is not the inclusion of one quality and exclusion of its opposite. Any termination of life is a result, not the consideration of the ending of one of the opposites, the material, as the material is not the embodiment of all life but is the representation of one of the opposites. To address the issue of terminating life is to take life's being into consideration. It is to take the reality of life into consideration. An incomplete, half effort at understanding life is insufficient. Any appearance that the ideal, that life, is dependent on the material is a false appearance. Such assessment does not come from an attempt at understanding philosophy. Such assessment does not come from an attempt at understanding life.

Life makes life's own opposite, nonlife, life's own. In the process making life, the self, eternal. Being eternal means that the life quality is always handed down, that the life quality is never terminated. The life quality consists of the ideal as well as the material. Life is necessarily eternal, so is the ideal eternal. Otherwise if life did not preserve the ideal, life would not be preserving anything. Life would not be the reality of life. Life would not be eternal. Life would not be hand-ing down the life element. As life has occurred in the same manner for eternity, and as life will occur in the same manner for eternity, it shows that the ideal was always present. If the ideal were not present, then the ideal could not have been obtained. Life either possesses the ideal or doesn't. The ideal is a part of life. Life is eternal, so is the ideal eternal. The only source that the ideal can originate from is life. If life did not possess the ideal, then the ideal could never be obtained. The ideal is a part of life. Life is eternal, so is the ideal eternal. The sanctuary is life. For the same reasons, the material, too, is eternal. The only source the material can originate from is life. If life did not possess the material, then the material could never be obtained. The material is a part of life. Life is eternal, so is the material eternal.

Flowing from stage to stage, each stage possesses the particular characteristics. There are reasons why no following stage can be expe-rienced by the preceding stage. There are reasons why any one life stage can be experienced only through that same life stage. It is only the particular present stage that has the characteristics to experience that same self life stage. Any one life stage has its own characteristic and not the characteristics of any one other stage. Only that particu-lar, only that present stage can be experienced. Life flows from stage to stage, undergoing change. That change can only be experienced by the stage of change and not the previous. And so it cannot be thought that because the following stage cannot be experienced by the preceding that the following therefore does not exist.

Life cannot do the impossible. Life cannot negate life's opposite. Life's power is limited. Unlimited power does not exist. Unlimited power where all is willed however wished without an effort. Not only is life's power limited, in fact, life's power is great and unlimited. Life achieves all there is to achieve. Above all, life achieves possession of the greatest prize of all, the self. Life's wishes are achieved. The achieved is life's wishes. Life cannot be destroyed, and the greatest power of all is life. Possessing the self, life's power is in fact unlimited. Life desires nothing other than life's being. To that certain extent, life's power is unlimited and yet limited. In the reality of life, the cross between the opposites of unlimited nonlife and unlimited life,

life's power is to that certain extent unlimited. Within the reality of life, life is not denied anything. Life attains all. Life is completely fulfilling. It is the reality of life that matters. Knowledge of life's power serves to better understand life.

Life's ability, life should not be underestimated. Having unlimited ability life achieves all in the same unlimited manner. It is the reality of life that decides all issues. Life's ability is from within the reality of life and is unlimited in the limited way. Life thereby achieving all. There is no greater power to life's. Making life's ability unlimited. Outside the reality of life there is nonentity, which does not serve in understanding life. Life resolves all issues in the same unlimited way. Life's basis are the qualities which secure life's existence. Life is based on truth and justice, knowledge and goodness. If life were not, life could never exist. If life were based on falsehood and injustice, lack of knowledge and lack of goodness, that would bring about life's destruction. Each beneficial quality being such to the height of life's ability, each quality achieves all. As life's ability is increased, to the point where all laws serve life to the level of the unlimited manner, life resolves all questions, all issues, in an easier and easier way. Allowing life to attain all, allowing life to know all. All that is from within life. All that occurs within life falls within the qualities of truth, justice, knowledge, and goodness. These qualities are brought to their height. As result, life has full knowledge of all. Life has the ability to bring these qualities to their height. Based on Life's Spirit, Life achieves all.

Just as life's basis is these beneficial qualities, so should the human being be based on truth, justice, knowledge, and goodness. The human objective must be to be truthful, just, knowing, and good. The human being can only be a developed human being. The primary way of being developed is by strengthening the human character. To seek the truth is better than to seek that which is false. To seek that which is false is to be false, it is to have such character. It is a character which is greatly lacking. It is a character greatly inferior to the developed human being. To seek to be unjust is to see something wrong with justice. It is to minimize the self. Not to seek knowledge is to lack knowledge. It is not to know how to behave. Not to seek the good is to do so at one's own expense. It is to seek evil. It is to be evil. It is to be greatly inferior to the good human being. To lack the beneficial qualities is destructive to the self. It is to present a morally undeveloped individual. It is to be lacking the greatest prize of all, the only criteria, the good. As it can only be that the good is the greatest prize, the qualities of truth, justice, knowledge, and goodness must be better understood.

According to the personality of each individual, life is engaged. Each individual living life in the personal way. Each individual's personality being one's own. All that is lived is lived through the self. In the process fulfilling the personality. Doing and accomplishing all, doing and accomplishing the possible. Grasping all that is possible, all that is one's own. The thinking capability and consciousness of any one individual is never different from what it is. If personal growth is wished for, then it should be engaged in. The bond with the self is complete. Each individual is free to live life in the personal way. The limitations of the self cannot be exceeded, but there is no need to do so. Each individual lives life to the fullest. No aspect of life is missed out upon, just as no aspect of the self is missed out upon. Life is experienced through the self. Being the self is completely fulfilling. The self lacks nothing, lest it be thought that life is lacking. That life is insufficient. That life does not achieve all. The self's bond with life is complete. Everyone is responsible for the self. If the way of the good is rejected, then that is the personal choice. There is significance for having made that choice. The good is then lacked. The self then lacks the good's positive qualities. The good is struggled against. What is possessed is detrimental attributes. No individual is ever different from oneself. No individual is ever less than the self. Humanity is free in its behavior. And as such, the way of the good must be observed. If the good is rejected, it is done freely. Negative judgment cannot but be made of those who follow the way of evil. This human assessment of those who reject the good is to be clarified and defended as correct. The good cannot be equated with nemesis.

Life lives all in the appropriate manner. There is justice to all that life does. If there is justice for a human being to regard another as evil, then so it must be. Living all in the appropriate manner, all that life does is always correct. The consciousness achieved is always correct. Life is never less than complete. The human being is never less than complete. During any of life's stages, all the opposites are in their, at that stage's, particular development. With life's drive toward life's destiny, it is life's inescapable future that is suppressed by anyone prior to the destiny stage. The opposites contribute to the one life. In life's living occurrence, life undergoes change, including the opposites. The question then of which opposites suppresses which is meaningless. All is lived in the appropriate manner. All is always lived. Consciousness is always attained.

The opposites are not to be viewed as foreign to life. All opposites contribute to the one life. All opposites are life. As life flows from stage to stage, life flows from life to life. Life's intent being at all times to rise to the possible height, to achieve life's full being. In the process of flowing from stage to stage, life and life's members behave in the self-observed best manner to realize the fulfillment of the personal self. In so doing, the human being enacts the personal behavior, the personally regarded good behavior. That level of good is often not considered as such by others. Each individual lives life to the best of the self's ability. As it is that considered flaws can be attributed by some to others who regard their own behavior as good, that does not mean that such assessment is correct. It does not mean that good human behavior does not exist. It does not mean that because flaw is found in someone else's good behavior that good behavior is not truly such. As it is, that good human behavior does exist, so does the best human behavior exist.

Along life's cyclical development, life's present stage does not consist of the greatest measure of good. During the point of destiny, the good is in the good's most perfect form. The good is in the full and complete state. As life is then in life's most perfect form, so is all within life then in the perfect form. The achieved good of the present stage is equivalent to its own extent. It is not of the magnitude of life's guiding objective, the greatest good. Life's current stage is lacking in comparison with the point of destiny. The achieved present good cannot exceed its own possible limit. This stage is not the stage of dominant good. Life having to look after life's own best interests, the complete measure of life must be lived, including the full measure of the current stage. The current stage must be fulfilled. The current stage must be lived to the full. At the same time this present stage has to be rejected as being the guiding good. Life cannot seek life's own imperfection. During the states of imperfection, life seeks perfection. When less than perfect, life rejects that imperfection. Just as life recognizes imperfection, life recognizes the desired high point in living. By making the effort, the struggled for is attained.

The similar principle holds true for humanity. Humanity is aware of the desired and undesired. By rejecting the state of imperfection, an effort toward the desired in life is made. The individual, by seeking to overcome the negative state, does so through a genuine struggle. The struggle is to self-improve. In this search, only genuine self-improvement is of value. The most genuine of all struggles is knowledge of the good, knowledge of good and proper behavior. Knowledge of the good, possession of the good cannot be obtained without an effort. The greater the effort, the better. The attained good is equal to the search for the good. To seek to escape the effort is to lack possession of the good. It is to lack creation.

Life consists of less desirable and more desirable stages. Those stages are whatever they may happen to be. They are regarded as such according to life. They are regarded as such by the individual. As some stages are more desirable, those stages are the high point in existence. Those high points in existence cannot but be a fact; they are attainable. It is within their nature to be attainable. The effort to attain the wished-for stage is met with success. The point of imperfection has perfection within. If it didn't, life would forever remain imperfect. Life would forever remain in the less desirable states, denying life's actuality. Life cannot be less perfect than life's level of perfection. That perfection is such as the fact that it is. Imperfection necessarily leads to perfection. All creation occurs during times of regarded inadequacy, during the times of the less-desirable states. The more desirable state having been achieved has imperfection within. Just as the point of imperfection has perfection within, so does the state of perfection have imperfection within. If it didn't, the state of perfection would have no way of attaining its being. Life would be forever perfect. And as life is cyclical, having no further to progress, the point of perfection has the same imperfection that led to perfection. The perfect condition is the end result of the not perfect. Imperfection leads to perfection. Perfection is within life.

Life's being is such as life's being is. Life is not greater. Life is not lesser. Life achieves all within life's being. The range is from the less desirable to the more desirable stages. Throughout it all, it is life that does the living. Life is not different from what life is. Life is real. Life is limited, yet life achieves all. During no instance does life live to a lesser degree than the possible. Life and every life member is one with the self. Life is lived to the fullest. In all of life's manifestations, life exhibits the part that makes life the authority. Life's achieving of all cannot be less than life's being. Life's laws rule. Life's laws serve life. Life is the criteria. All issues are regarding life, life's laws are the answer to all issues. As life cannot be lessened, as life is real, life is completely fulfilling. And if it appears that life does not achieve all and that life is not completely fulfilling, then that is a mistaken assessment. Life must be accepted and the search for unlimited life abandoned. During all stages, life accomplishes the possible. During the less-desired stages, life accomplishes all so that the desirable stage is then attained. The desirable stage would not have been achieved had not the less desirable stage not achieved all. All stages accomplish all. The point of life's highest and dominant stage of good must be sufficiently such so as to fully take up within all past and leading to perfection stages and turn their inadequacy into complete living fulfillment. If that were not done, life would remain imperfect during life's point of perfection.

Life's dominant stage is where the good has compete control and authority. It is where there is complete justice. Unless it were thought that injustice is a good thing. Unless it were thought that humanity can see that injustice is wrong but life cannot. Unless it were thought that humanity can see that the good must rule all to the greatest extent, but life cannot recognize this. Understanding imperfection, life understands perfection. Life understands the dominant good. Doing so, life achieves the dominant good. If life could not achieve the dominant good, life could not understand the dominant good.

Life's understanding, life's search for the best achieves the stage of dominant good. With the good having complete control and authority, the issue of injustice is then solved. It cannot be thought that the good cannot rule all to the greatest extent, unless life's power is not understood, unless life is not understood. It is the dominant good that life seeks. It is the dominant good that life achieves. Seeking the dominant stage, life is not always living the dominant stage. All of life's qualities must in fact exist. The good is not in the greatest status presently. The suffering of the good, the suffering of life, is a part of the present stage. The present stage cannot be denied and must be fully lived. The present stage, all stages, are a part of life, and life is supreme. Life is never less than the most, including this stage and all stages. The present good may be inadequate when compared with the good of life's destiny, but present life must be lived fully. And the greatest good possible must be attempted to be established. As is the case, the human being is involved in the matter. It can only be that the good is observed by all. It can only be that the existence of the human good is a fact. The supremacy of the human good is provable. The human good must therefore be law. The good's message cannot be ignored. To act against the good is to lack the good.

Life is living life's own being. Life lives in one single best way. Doing so, life never makes an error. Life never behaves in what is less than the best one way. There is one path to take. The path can never be mistaken. As life makes no mistakes, no life member makes any mistakes. Life doesn't just exist, having no purpose. Life is guided by an objective, the fulfilling of life's being. Life's objective is one. Life's being is one. To that end, life is guided by one path of development, which is best. All that occurs within life does so within the single best path. All that occurs within life does so with the intent to fulfill that single best path, life's single being, life's single objective. The only possible and best alternative to life's fulfillment is always taken. Life's actual path is the single proper and best course to take. If it weren't, and were any less so, life would be of inferior nature to life's own being. Making the hypothetical, and not real, greater in nature to the real. This means that life never makes a mistake.

To look back upon the path which has led to the present and consider that a wrong line of development had been followed is not to assess the issue. The best choice is always made. That is proven based on the fact that the made choice exists, and life and all life members are the result of the choice made. All is the result of the development pursued. The existent feeling for life was always fulfilled. Life's existence cannot be denied, nor can that of any life member. The actuality of life is dependent on the taken line of development. In which occurrence, if an error were made, that would make life false and false life real. The conclusion that the past has led to errors is reached through the present. The past has led to the present. The present is a product of the past. All present assessment is based on the past, which has led to the present. Making all made conclusions the work of the past. The origin of the present thought is in the past. If that origin is denied, so is the present thought then denied. As it would have to be considered that the present thinking and behavior is correct, and that of the past incorrect, then the past thinking and behavior could not have been incorrect to such an extent as to prevent the present thinking and behavior from being correct. Making the thinking and behavior of the past sufficiently correct, making the past correct. The past is to be built upon, and a genuine effort at the greater good must be made. The error is not made in carrying out life's sole living path. Inadequate and false human evaluation of life's laws remains such, inadequate and false. The idea of errors is such. Life's laws must be understood and the false refuted.

Life's living existence is guided by that which is best. All of life's acts arise from within life. All life members behave according to one's own personality and never in an opposing way. No life member is different from the self. No life member is, or can be, greater than the self. No life member can be more self-aware than the personal extent. Life behaves only according to life's own being. Life and all life members behave on an instinctive basis. Instinct would have to be identified through the idea that it is an impulse of behavior which cannot be denied, cannot be acted against. The resulting behavior being due to the undeniable impulse. The life member being unable to behave differently from the impulse. In such occurrence, the attained consciousness being strictly equivalent to the extent of the arising impulse. Instinct is all undertaken action, all thought and all behavior. Instinct is not solely a basic level of thought. It is all thought and all behavior. Basic level of thought and more complex thought have one thing in common, the undeniable impulse of behavior. Regardless of how complex the thought pattern may be, it originates from the undeniable impulse, even if the impulse is to think more and more. No life member can do that which is not within. No act can be taken independent from the inner need. The need cannot be denied; that is why all action is taken. No life member can change the self. Life cannot change life's being. Even if a change is undergone, that change cannot be different. It cannot be greater. Life forever behaves in accordance with life's being. Life's actions are life's. To behave in a contrary way from the actual is impossible to do. Any undergone change is the result of the need for the change, the possible, the existing need for the change. Which need is not denied. The attained consciousness is therefore always equal to that of the present feeling, the present impulse. Never does the awareness exceed its limit. The limit is set by the present feeling. All is aware of the self and the reasons for the taken action to the possible extent. Life's being and consciousness are exactly what they are. Life cannot become greater or more aware of the self. Life is limited. The limit is life's. Instinct is the behaving in accordance with the self. This can but be done by every life member and life. For life's acts to become noninstinctive, it would require that life become greater than life's being. It would require that life act independent of life's being. Lack of instinct is for life to have no being. It is for life to be unlimited. Lack of instinct is for the self's consciousness to be raised however wished without limit.

Nor does the definition of instinct have a negative meaning. At no time is the self denied. At no time is the self any less. All is experienced by the self. Growth by the self is at all times possible. The greater the growth, the better. The search for the good can at all times be pursued. The results of the growth are not known until the full effort is exerted. The self achieves all. Life achieves all. It cannot be that to achieve all is insufficient. It cannot be that life has no meaning. It cannot be that the struggle for the good is not rewarded with greater good. The struggle for life must readily be fully engaged. Life is to be lived. In life's eternal repetition, life attains knowledge. However great that knowledge may be or however slight. No knowledge is to be taken away from. All knowledge belongs to life. All personal knowledge belongs to each individual life member. No impulse of behavior, no knowledge is to be taken away from. Not even the slightest nor the greatest. All belongs to life. All belongs to the self.

Humanity in behaving in accordance with the human personality has fulfilled humanity's mission in life. Humanity has at all times done and accomplished the possible. All that has taken place in human history must in fact have done so. Humanity has become social in the attempt to create the desired existence. Within society, everyone has completed one's mission, never doing less than the intended. Rising to one's personal level of life and achievement. Society has inevitably faced questions as to its development. The issue of how society is to be lawfully based is and has been answered by humanity. The selected political system has at all times been the only way for humanity to progress. The true political system has always risen and assumed the role of leadership. Human history occurs in only one way. No political system other than the present may exist. No societal development other than the present may exist. As society has taken shape, society has undergone various stages. All stages lasting as long as the possessed power, no stage being without end. Any one desired stage is not without end. Its power is limited; it will end. By the same measure, so will the undesired stage end. The duration of each phase is determined by the particular societal development. The key to the successful society is the proper foundation. The key is the proper understanding of the involved factors. An analysis of which can at all times be carried out. Upon analyzing, it is realized the correct societal structure has its origin in the dominant branch of human thought, philosophy. Being dominant, philosophy is dominant for a reason. The powers of philosophy must be turned toward the creation of the correct society. As philosophy wishes to know the laws guiding life to the greatest extent, so it is that philosophy wishes to know the laws of building the correct society to the greatest extent.

With the individual entering society, the individual exhibits the personal search for greater life. The individual exhibits the personal effort at greater achievement. The characteristic of which, each individual possesses. With the individual initiating the effort at greater life, at greater achievement, the individual enters a state of not having achieved the desired. The individual enters a state of imperfection. Through the sufficient effort, the desired objective is then achieved. Upon doing so, the individual enters into perfection. The individual reveals the self. The process could repeat, the effort at the desired and the achievement of the desired. The individual does not remain without change. Though changing, it is at all times the individual self. The individual's identity is achieved through the sufficient effort to include within the self the personal living quality in its highest and complete form. All evaluation of the individual is to be made according to the completed desired personal state. The effort at which should be recognized as such, the made effort of the less than perfect state to achieve the state of perfection. By leading into change, the individual is defined. The individual is revealed. At all times it is the individual self that undergoes the living effort. At no point is the individual less than the self. And no matter what may occur, the bond with the self is never denied. The self is never lost.

Life originates with life. Life's identity belongs to life. Life is the result of the boundaries as well as the self. Life is limited. Life does not have to be unlimited to be true to the self. In being limited, less than the possible life is never lived. An alienation from the self never occurs. The self is the source of the self. The self is the source of life. All outlook originates with the self. To be displeased or pleased with the self is to be such through the identity of the self. If self-improvement were wished for, the possible will be achieved. Knowledge of the reality of life is of importance. The self makes all the personal acts. Humanity does the possible. Humanity achieves all. The boundaries guide life. Life guides the boundaries. It is the reality of life that matters. It is unreality that diminishes life. It is the unreal human being that diminishes humanity. Within life, within the limitation of the self, all that belongs to the self is granted. No individual is ever denied one's full identity. All personal actions are taken in accordance with the self. Life is limited, but life cannot be lesser to life's being. Humanity cannot be of lesser nature. The achieved consciousness is one's own. The love for the self is eternal. The self is chosen. Therefore the self is not wished to be rejected. Only those qualities are included within the self which belong to the self. The choice made is only for the self. Being limited, life is not lifeless. Instead life is the authority of all. Within the range of life, every life aspect must in fact exist. The variety of life members is observable. There are the adherents of the good and those who oppose the good. The result can only be the inferior experience of life by those who lack the good. The good has by those individuals been rejected, as has the superior experience of life been also rejected. Making the individual satisfied with the self, not desiring not one's own, living life to the fullest. Being the self, life, humanity is incapable of the impossible. The impossible cannot be done, but the impossible consists of qualities not one's own. The impossible is distinct from the self. It is absent from the self. In being distinct from the self, being absent from within the self, the quality to do the impossible plays no role in the self's personality; The lack of the quality capable of the impossible, from within the human being, does not diminish the human being, the self. Only the self takes part in the self. All that is foreign is excluded. Making the self complete, not lacking what is not one's own. Humanity's existence is crucial to life's being. Life lives to the best of life's ability. Life must exist in life's best way. All within life exists in the best way.

Life is to be understood. Life is to be respected. Any attempt to try to take away from life's powers will end in failure. It is the reality of life that is attempted to be understood and not the unreality of life. Life is limited. Life cannot do the impossible. If life were unlimited, life would be able to become something that life is not. All circumstances would be capable being shaped beyond their limit. With lack of effort, all would be accomplished. With lack of effort, the living path would be abandoned and not engaged. The struggle for life's purpose becoming unknown. The undesired becoming foreign. Being at all times not less than perfect. Only the real is of value. The living path cannot be abandoned. Life has to struggle for all achievement. The achievement cannot exceed life's being. Imperfection and states of the undesired are not foreign.

Life's status is also humanity's status. Humanity is an integral part of life. Behaving in accordance with life being limited. It is observable that humanity is not without limit. The human status can never be demeaning Humanity is equal to any one life stage: Never achieving less, or more, to the possibility of that stage. During the stages of imperfection behaving in an imperfect way. Behaving within the limit of that imperfection. During the stage of perfection behaving in the likewise perfect manner. Life creates the self. Humanity creates the self. The individual chooses the self. The choice for the self is complete. At the same time, the choice for the self cannot be exceeded. A greater self cannot be created. The existence of the good's nemesis is a fact. The existence of those lacking the good is a fact. In achieving the state of dominant good, life achieves the greatest justice. During that stage, all injustice is removed. Being guided by justice, life elevates life's own status during the stage of perfection. Achieving the good, life elevates the self. Prior to the height of life, life lacked the dominant good. And only such lacking of the good achievement could have resulted, including life and all within life. Life's intent is to attain justice and remove all injustice. Life's intent is not to judge life, the self, and all within, in a punitive way, for having been imperfect during the stages of imperfection. Any such judgment would serve no purpose. The fact of the self choosing the self within life's boundaries, within life's being, can but be considered by life. The existence of the good's nemesis is a fact. By attaining the highest justice, the highest justice governs. The dominant good resolves all accordingly. There is no purpose for life not to achieve the dominant good. There is no purpose for life not to govern according to the dominant good. With life's understanding, that can be done.

Life's founding element is the Good. Life being the authority only seeks that which is good. To seek less is detrimental and fatal to life. Being based on the good, seeking the good, life is the greatest justice. The good that life attains is the one and true level. Life's path cannot be less than possible, the most good. Life's living path must occur. Humanity is a member of life, the human path must occur.

Acting in accordance with life, humanity also seeks the good. The human search for the good is the fulfillment of the human range, whatever that range may be. All that exists from within life must do so. It is life's living path. For if any part of life did not exist, life's occurrence would not be fulfilled. So it is with humanity, fulfilling the living path, fulfilling the human range. The judge as to the validity and nature of the good is in each instance the individual self. Arising from the self, all taken actions are viewed as necessary and fulfilling. In the process, humanity takes part in the living path. The individual enacts one's own personal behavior. The individual self is the only one that can do so. Although that behavior is fulfilling in life's path and is viewed as good and proper by the individual self, that does not mean that it is so, being good and proper. As does life seek the greatest good, so does humanity seek the greatest good. To seek less is detrimental and fatal to the human character. As humanity fulfills the human range, as humanity seeks to grow, it is the good that leads the way. The judge as to the validity and nature of the good is in each instance the individual self. However, to neglect the good, to seek less than the greatest good is to do so at one's own expense. The human range includes all possible personal improvement. The effort must be made for the good. To lack the good is to be the enemy of the good; it is to deceive oneself. But it is not to deceive the good. All assessment is based on the good. To lack the good is to lack the good. It means that the good exists, but the good is not personally possessed. It is the good, the including of truth and justice, that leads the way; that is the sole criteria. It is the good that creates all law. To lack the good means that the individual has no standing. It means that no value is to be attributed to the personal regard of good. To lack the good is to have no say in the creation of law. It is to be defeated by the good each and every time. Being an enemy of the good is to inevitably wage a struggle against the good. It is a struggle for which the good cannot be blamed. The blame is at all times with the lack of good. And so the human range is completed. In the form of the individual who lacks the good, who does not seek the good, and the individual who possesses the good, the individual who seeks the good. The human task in the matter is clear. The good must always be sided with; the good must always prevail.

Life being real, under all circumstances can only have achieved the most possible good. Life always seeks that which is best. Life always achieves that which is best. Under any one circumstance, there is only one best alternative. Such alternative is always taken by life. Making life's path the one path of most possible good. Just as life's road to the greatest good can only be a single one, so it is with the human-relevant good. Knowledge of the good is required, and the greatest good can only be revealed by philosophy. The greatest good can only come from philosophy. The greatest good can only be revealed to philosophy. The greatest knowledge belongs to philosophy. The greatest humanism belongs to philosophy. The good is the greatest characteristic. Only the greatest human development can reveal the good. Knowledge of the good is attainable by philosophy, and no event can occur to prevent this from happening. Any such event would not be from within life's one best path. Life always being at life's best leads to the enacting and revealing of all the possible good, including all the possible human good, and that is philosophy. At one point or another, human historical development has produced advancements in the fields of human endeavor. Those advancements could not have always existed; rather, those advancements have occurred at their appropriate moments, having been preceded by a line of development. The new knowledge is based on the previous knowledge. It could not be that the line of development leading to the advancement had not occurred. That line of progress is an essential part to human historical growth. It is essential to the achievement of the advancement. The new knowledge is the clarification of the preceding. The new knowledge seeks to work with that which has been previous. The past has in fact taken place. The enlightenment that was created due to the past achievement is equal to itself. The concern of the advancement is to progress and initiate a new beginning. As the new knowledge seeks to work with that which has been before, so must the past work with the new knowledge. With the necessity of the past, there is no fault with the past in having lacked the advancement. The fault begins when the new knowledge upon being stated is rejected by the past. The good must always be sided with. The past can only work with the new. As philosophy reveals the good, the preceding must work with the new. Philosophy must be worked with. To reject philosophy is to distinguish oneself as a nonphilosopher. It is to distinguish oneself as someone who cannot attain the good. The human wish must not be the rejection of the good. To be of good character is to seek the good. It is to be able to recognize and work with the good. With the necessary effort, knowledge of the good is attainable.

The accomplished good is always equal to that of the potential of life's stage. During the present stage of life, the possible good has a limit, and that limit cannot be exceeded. The good must nonetheless be sought. The choice to engage in good has to be made by the self. In the individual's choice for the self, the choice for the level of good wished for is also made. The search for the good begins with the self, as based on the choice for the self. It is the self that decides all issues. It is the self that creates the self and not the setting, not the environment. The setting cannot bring about a characteristic not present within the self. The environment cannot create a characteristic beyond the limit of the self. The effect that any setting produces within any individual is to the extent made possible by the self. The human being is defined. The human being has human limits. The self has the limit of the self. Within that limit, the complete self is attained. The limit of the self cannot be exceeded. Making each individual one's own personal level and measure of life. If the environment created the human being, then the personal level and identity would be exceeded. If the environment created the individual, that would make all of humanity the one and same identical individual.

The evident differences resulting from the variety of settings. Any one human being, at all times, lives under the same real and personal setting, a change making it the one same personal setting. Regardless of how many times, or how much, any setting is changed to any one individual. The setting is the one real personal setting. It is the setting of fact. Throughout it all, throughout any and all changes, it is the individual, oneself, that does the living, that does the assessing. That living and assessing is done by the one single self. The self is at all times the same single self. The self cannot be altered. Any event, any change in anyone's life is lived and considered by the self, to the level of the self. Any and all behavior is within the range of the self. As result, the environment cannot be altered, as neither can the self be altered by the environment. To think that a change in environment can change the individual is to therefore do so hypothetically as no change in environment nor self can occur. The environment does not create the human being. The self creates the self. Each individual chooses the self. This does not mean that the environment is not important, that creating the right environment is not important. It is crucial that the proper existence is established so that the individual and society may prosper. With the proper existence, the best chance for societal and individual success is created. Under all setting, the final decision as to behavior is made by the self. The creative force behind the individual is the self.

The choice for the self has occurred during all points in life's existence to all life members, including humanity. With the rise of early life and humanity, only the possible has taken place. The early stages of life had to exist, as is the case with of all life stages, including the present and all future ones. Early humanity could not have known what was to be subsequently known. Starting on the path of life, humanity has in the beginning dealt with issues present and pressing at the particular time. And the ideas of early humanity could not have surpassed the point in life's development. Humanity cannot achieve beyond the possible. The discovery of any knowledge cannot occur before its rightful time. Life and humanity must fulfill the living purpose. Past knowledge has led to the present, and the present will lead to that of the future. The completing of life's and humanity's purpose is dependent upon each point in development. Life's purpose in living is to attain the most possible knowledge, to know the self, to live as opposed to not live, to establish the link with the self, to create the greatest good. Humanity is an integral part of life. Humanity's purpose is to attain the most possible knowledge concerning life. Human knowledge reveals a fact and truth of life's being. Humanity achieves the knowledge equated with the period of existence. The early stages of human historical development the equal to those stages knowledge was achieved. The equal life was lived. During the later stages, the equal to those stage knowledge was achieved. The equal life was lived. Each period of human development must in fact take place. A greater knowledge, a different life from the actual of the particular stage cannot be achieved. The human historical process is restrictive. At the same time, less than the complete fulfillment never occurs. Within the restrictions, all of life's benefits are found. Truth and life are never denied. The fact of the self is never denied. The truth and life are always in their complete state. The truth at all times remains such, whichever the truth may be. The possibility of the search for the truth is ever present. Human ideas cannot exceed the times. Human ideas, however, do determine the times. An alienation from the self never occurs. Life is fully lived. The choice for the self is made and holds true under all circumstances, under all setting, including the particular time of human historical development. As the self is at all times in one's own possession, less than the self's life, an inferior and undesired life is never lived. There can never be a superior, more desired human being to the self, future or past. The choice for the self is always based on the self. Therefore the preference will forever be for the self. The individual is restricted to the personal particular time of existence. By living, the individual fulfills life's process. By attaining the self, the human limitation of every historical time period is undergone. The limitation is in fact without limit. Less than the self is never lived. Search for truth can always be engaged in. As human knowledge has increased, past humanity remains undiminished. All was at all times done. All was at all times achieved.

In the occurrence of human history, no individual is different from the self. No individual ever achieves more than the self's ability. No individual achieves less. The fully becoming of everyone takes place during the rightful period. Not during a previous or later period. The individual cannot be taken out of one's own actual period of existence. The personally attained views and ideas cannot be altered. The personal conduct cannot be altered. The individual's existence is proof that life is and has been assessed, that life is taken part in. The personal living of life is and has been exactly the same as it is. If the study of people past is engaged in, then it should be with the understanding that the personality of the person studied is complete, that life has been lived, life has been assessed, the views have been formed. If there is truth in those views, then the truth must live on, forever being true. If the individual has engaged in good behavior, then that good behavior must forever remain such. The full life has been lived. The study of people past should be done within the bounds of reason. The person studied has lived according to one's assessment of life. That assessment is exactly the same as it is. It cannot be changed. The one responsible for the adhered to views is the individual of study. That individual is responsible for oneself. What is required is a fair evaluation of human history.

No one is ever untrue to the self. No one is ever a lesser being to the self. Life exists in one way, the best and only way. As result, life lacks nothing. Life is in complete possession of the self. No life member lacks anything. Every life member is in complete possession of the self. Each individual human being is the one and only. The quality of greatest worth is the quality of good. In the consideration of the human being, it is the status of the good that is of primary importance. The good is the only criteria. The good makes all possible. The good creates all. The good leads to proper human behavior. To attain the good is to attain the greatest prize. It is to have the greatest knowledge, the greatest enlightenment. Knowledge of the good is the greatest knowledge. The law of the good is the supreme law. The good is life's foundation. It is based on the good that life achieves the greatest justice. As is the law of the good supreme with life, so is the law of the good supreme with humanity. Only truth takes part in the world of the good. That which is false is excluded from the world of the good. That which is false can only be detrimental. That which is true can only be beneficial. With the good being the supreme development, the human wish can only be to possess the good to the greatest extent. In so doing, presenting the most grown human being, the greatest human being. To lack the good is the greatest flaw. The observation of the good is at all times possible. The search for the good can always be engaged in. The greater the search, the greater the achievement. The way of the good is not hidden. It is only hidden to those who do not seek it, to those who lack the good. As humanity has historically progressed, it has become more and more clear that the way of the good must be searched for by all. It has become more and more clear that the good takes precedence over all other human qualities. The greater the achieved good, the better. It is better for humanity. It is better for the self. In the way of the good is the best way for the human being to develop. Humanity knowing that the cause of the good must be aided however possible, to the best way possible. The cause of the good must be struggled for, in the process achieving greater good. With humanity seeking the good, humanity seeks truth. The truth is an integral part of the good. Only the truth enlightens. Only the truth leads to good human behavior. Only the truth is of value. As such, humanity must base human behavior on truth and the search for truth. It is only the good, only the truth, that can lead to the proper, to understanding, to peaceful human existence. With humanity seeking the good, with humanity seeking the truth, it can only be that humanity rejects the false. As it is that the false is detrimental to the human being, to human growth, to understanding, to peaceful human existence. The study of the good, the stating of the good's content, is the study the stating of life's laws. The good only reveals truth, only leads to truth. That is what makes the good such, that can only be good. The good only revealing truth. It is truth regarding life, whichever the truth may be. In so doing, the truth is such as the truth is. The truth is unchangeable. If there is error in understanding the truth, then it is human error and is not an error by the good. Since the truth is such and is truth, the truth is of value. And lacking value is that which is false. That which is false is often regarded as truth. That does not mean that it is truth. That is a human failing making the analysis. It is possible to make a false analysis. Belief in the false does occur. The false is distinct from the true. The false is an inaccurate estimation of life law. The false is not equal to the true. It is based on truth that life achieves life's being. The false is detrimental and is detrimental to understanding life, detrimental to attaining the good. The search for the good is a particularly human effort, particularly human such characteristic. To evaluate the good's content is to humanly do so. It is to do so within the range of the human being, within the range of the individual. With the effort being genuine, such results will be produced. The results will then also be genuine, revealing some aspect of the good. The arrived at understanding of the good is from within the human range, within the human limit. Whatever that limit is, the made genuine analysis stands for something genuine and good. And if any one such evaluation should only be engaged in and known only by a single individual, that evaluation remains such, genuine and good. It doesn't mean that such analysis doesn't exist, that such behavior doesn't exist. The human being behaves within the range of the human being. The accurate evaluation of the good is open to being questioned and rejected by external to the good sources, by those who lack the good, as being truly good. And according to that reasoning, making the lack of good good. Making the genuine and good lacking the good. However that which is inaccurate in understanding remains inaccurate and false, regardless if it is endorsed by some. And that which is correct and true remains correct and the truth, even if it is regarded as incorrect and false by some. The human range can only be fulfilled. The good human being remains such. Attaining the human good. Which cannot be denied, the human good exists.

To falsely evaluate Life's Laws, to falsely evaluate the Good is possible. Belief in the false does occur. This present life stage is not the dominant and greatest life stage. The present can only be lived. With the possibility of the false existing during the present stage, then so it must be. That does not mean that the false cannot be pointed out. It does not mean that the false cannot be and should not be refuted. This present stage cannot be minimized but must be lived fully. The human need to understand life's laws is real and can only be fulfilled. If in the effort to understand life mistakes are made, then those mistakes should be corrected upon knowing otherwise. In the effort to understand life's laws, it should always be the search for the truth, the search for the good that is the guide. Life's laws are not incomprehensible. Life is not of foreign nature to life's own being. The possibility for humanity to understand is such, possible to understand. In the process, humanity achieves all. It takes truth to understand truth. If this weren't so, the theoretical human truth would in fact be false. Making all human observance false, therefore equating the false with the truth. That which is false is distinct from that which is true. By grasping life's laws, humanity is realized. A separation between humanity and the human understanding of life cannot be made. A separation between the individual and the individual's estimation of life cannot be made. Humanity is the thought. The understanding of life's laws involves the attempt to understand the good. The supreme life law is the good. Within life's being, it is the good that makes all possible. It is the good that ensures life's success. As the human being searches for the good and achieves aspects of the good, the human being achieves the greatest knowledge. No knowledge is equal to knowledge of the good. The regard for the search for the truth, the regard for the revealed truth, the regard for the fellow man, the regard for the personal conduct, the personal regard of the self are all human aspects of possessing the good. As the good is taken part in, all of one's personality rises to the height of humanism. Allowing for the complete experience of life. The greater the possession of good, the greater the human being. The rightful outlook elevates the human being. The self's identity rests upon the self's possession of the good. The good is the criteria in all life. As respect for the good decreases, so does the individual decrease. It is to then lack the superior life. It is to lead a life where comfort is found in lacking the good, in opposing the good. It is to lead a devoid of the good life. It is to distinguish oneself from the good. The inherent difference being the lack of good. The human being is the thought. To possess the good is to do so. To lack the good is to lack the good. Humanity can only wish to be guided by the good. The way of the good is the most desirable quality. By seeking the good, the possible personal level of good will be achieved. That level could not have been achieved prior to the seeking of the good. The effort can only be made.

Self-improvement can only be engaged in. As the individual self improves, led by reason and thought, the physical must not be overlooked. The human being has always had the reasoning ability as well as the physical. Seeking knowledge of the good does not omit the physical, does not omit manual labor. The thought process does not interfere with the physical aspect of the self. The mental evaluation of the good cannot be without end, without stop. The physical can be taken part in when the thought process is not engaged. Whenever the need for manual labor arises, it must not be avoided, thinking that the self is too busy attaining knowledge of the good or that labor is not something that is done by thoughtful people. All responsibility must be met. Manual labor can be taken part in when it is so necessary. The personal responsibility should not be met only when the solution to the problem cannot be personally offered. The reasoning of being above work, for its avoidance, certainly cannot be used by someone who in fact has engaged the intellect. The search for the good was not engaged, at least not sufficiently so. Not to then engage in work is the result of weakness of mind, not strength. It cannot be that work is avoided due to being in pursuit of intellectual wisdom. Only a nonintellectual may enter into the world of the false, into the world of lack of good.

With the individual seeking self-improvement, as the individual achieves and creates, all achievement and creation is due to personal initiative, due to personal effort. The effort is the individual. The greater the effort, the better. The more that is achieved, the better. In the process the individual and humanity are growing, and it is that the greatest effort in the attempt is to attain the good. All personal acts must be guided by the good. With the individual creating, it should be remembered that creation is of value and not boasting about creation. The original purpose was to self-improve, to create, to attain the good. The good is the self's guide. To attain less of the good is to create less. As the good is the self's guide, all acts are equally so guided by the good, including the regard for personal creation. Just as error in the evaluation of the good has not been made, so too one's outlook in the matter of regard for personal achievement is free from error. The self is accountable to the self's possession of good, viewing the self with justice. To seek to glorify the self beyond the limit of the good is to do so at the expense of creation. As the limit of justice is lost, the achievement is less, directly due to the transgressing of the good's limit. To be engaged in the transgression is the end result of lacking the good. To misunderstand the reasonable consideration of the self is equal to misunderstanding the good. The objective in living is to attain the greatest life possible, the greatest good possible. The going beyond reason of personal estimation of the self is the consequence of the lack of search for life, the lack of search for the good. To be boasting about the self, about personal achievement, is not to be achieving but boasting. As the good is lacked in the self's own estimation, it is ensured that the boasted-about achievement was in fact less than the claim. It is ensured that the self is less than the claim. The greatest achievement is to achieve the good. The good can only lead to good. As the good is minimized, so is all creation minimized. The greater the good, the greater the achievement. The proper consideration of the self, of personal creation, is with those who have attained the good. The greater the flaw, the lesser the individual. What is therefore required is a personal consideration of fact.

Human historical development by occurring has an objective which will be achieved. That objective is whatever it happens to be. Human history will occur in the manner of the objective, fulfilling the objective. In the process of the historical development, humanity has become aware of the need for the good. As the need for the good becomes clear, human history will develop in the like manner. Human history will in that specific way be influenced by the need for the good. The human historical objective will inevitably include the need for the good. The human need for the good is the individual's need for the good. The individual seeks to behave in a good manner. The individual seeks an ever greater good. In living, the individual grows. Greater levels of good are sought. Greater levels of good are attained. If it is felt that the bounds of the good had been infringed upon during some point in the self's life, then the only alternative to improvement in behavior is the good's stricter observance. If it is personally considered that an act of wrong had been committed, then the best remedy is the greater attainment of the good, not the asking for forgiveness. To pray for forgiveness shows that the state of improvement has not been entered, the way of the good has not been searched for. The good can only be wished for at the highest extent. The good can only be attained through the most genuine effort, through the most supreme, most sincere effort. Likewise that is the effort that is needed, that is the effort that should be engaged in to attain the good. Prayer plays no role in seeking the good. Prayer plays no part in increasing the value given to the good. Prayer takes away from the search for the good. To pray is to shift the focus of required improvement to that of an act which is not a part of seeking the good. It is as result an act of not wishing self-improvement, as compared to the needed, genuine act of seeking the good. To pray for forgiveness is to seek a favor without ever taking the necessary measures to self-improve. The remedy for inadequate and wrong behavior is better and good behavior. Praying for forgiveness is an attempted deception directed toward the power that is prayed to. In that the insincere gesture, lack of substance gesture of seeking to self-improve through prayer, of seeking the good through prayer, is presented to the power prayed to as an earnest effort at the good. The claim is made that thence forward the good will be observed, when no such measure has been taken. The seeking of the good is a deliberate, purposeful effort. To recognize that a wrong had been done is to do so, recognize that a wrong had been done. It is to be improved. That is the only way the recognition could be made. The issue is the search for the good. The answer is the ever greater effort at the good. For which purpose prayer plays no part. If it is thought that the search for the good is taken part in, despite praying, that praying does not take away from the effort at the good, then it should be known that praying is not a real effort. It should be known that prayer does not reveal the good. Thus ensuring that the thinking is flawed. The thinking, the effort, cannot lead to understanding the good, to attaining the good, based on the fact that it was not known that prayer plays no part in the effort at the good. To pray is to seek freedom in the good's abuse, as prayer does not have the good. Prayer's deception is not only directed toward the power prayed to; the deception also includes the fellow man. In that the good is not wished for. The good is disrespected, yet the claim to the opposite is made. It is claimed that the good is worshiped, that the good is revered. The fact of the prayerful tendency cannot but become apparent to the possible people of interaction. Prayer, it would be proposed, is done out of respect for the good. Having done wrong, the highest state of repentance is claimed to be entered. The individual has such esteem for the good that upon acting against the good, the power is prayed to for forgiveness, the primary method of improvement, the primary method for atonement. It would be thought that the individual's respect for the good is proven based on the fact of praying. As this individual is respectful of the good, so this individual needs to be respected. If the fellow human's positive opinion is gained, or the accuracy of discernment confused, then the deception would have served its purpose. The good's abuse will then be further perpetuated. To abuse the good morally, to abuse the good in theory, is to abuse the good in fact. To pray for forgiveness is not to seek the good. The praying individual disrespects the good. The praying individual disrespects the power that is prayed to. The deception also includes the self. To pray, it is imagined that all within one's power has been done in the effort to improve the self. The wish to possess the good can only be complete. An inadequate effort is not aimed at knowing and attaining the good. As the wish can only be complete, so must the effort be complete. Not to grasp the good is not an impossibility. The lack of good is then viewed as good. Whether the power that is prayed to exists or not has no bearing on the topic. The issue of concern is the personal search for the good. Prayer is defined as the asking for forgiveness, or the asking for a desired favor to be answered. In both instances, the principle is similar. The asking for a favor is to misunderstand the course to be taken in attaining the good, in doing all to the utmost, to have events turn out in the desired way. Life is to be lived. The best way to achieve a wished state is through the not lessened effort. The most effectual life is that which is not decreased in effort. Prayer plays no part in living life to the utmost. To pray is to decrease the effort at living. It is to decrease the effort at attaining the good. For the prayer to be answered, it would mean that the power prayed to rewards the deception. That there is greater benefit in the inadequate attempt than the genuine. By lacking the effort to live life to the fullest, benefits which are otherwise absent in the most sincere attempt at life are capable of being obtained through that same lack of effort. The power prayed to would have to be supremely just. To grant the wish is to reward the inadequate attempt to a greater extent than the greater, sincere effort at life. The effort to create the most fruitful life, the effort of having taken all the necessary measures to live the full life would meet with less benefit than the lax, not-genuine effort. The issue of concern is justice. Who from the two lives examined has done more to succeed? How can it be that the lesser attempt is granted favors which haven't been sufficiently struggled for, favors, rewards which had the life of superior effort been led would not have been experienced? Praying for favors will not be answered. Nor can it be thought that the superior effort is failing in the way of not recognizing the power that would be prayed to and is not being respectful of the power. That the power is neglected and that therefore is a failing, a failing worthy of lack of success. As result is a benefit to the lax, insincere effort, for having turned to the power for help. Doing so, not neglecting the power, respecting the power. That therefore is a benefit, a benefit worthy of success, a benefit worthy of help. The greatest human attribute is the possession of the good. The good is only attained through the most sincere, most genuine effort. The effort that guides the individual under all circumstances, guides the individual through life. As the good is attained, the good is the guide in all respects, in all fields. Including the issue of respect for the power. It is the good that has the respect. It is the genuine, sincere effort that has the respect for the power that would be prayed to. It is the lax, insincere effort that lacks the good, that lacks respect for the power prayed to. That is so, unless it is thought that lacking the good is better than possessing the good. The power prayed to can only recognize the sincere effort, the sincere good. The results of the effort by the good at life will be equal to the made effort and not more. There will be no interference in which by an external source. Life lives in the single and best way. In that single and best way, Life achieves the most possible. Life achieves all possible. The good individual also achieves all possible. As result, there will be no interference with the made effort, with the equal and deserved results by an external to life source. To pray for life to occur in the single and best way is not needed. It is how life is going to occur anyway. The question of prayer is in fact the question of how humanity is to live. If the self's situation in life is considered unfavorable, the solution is to work hard to change that situation to the liking. The answer to living is to seek the good. Once achieving the good, all within the self's power will have been done to lead the most productive life. Life's path does not need to be altered or feared. The fact that prayer is not engaged in does not mean that the way of the good necessarily follows. All attempts to deceive the good will end in failure. Not to seek the good is not to have the good. It is to lack the greatest prize. Prayer does not seek the good. Prayer does not reveal the good. Prayer is foreign to the good. Only the clear mental evaluation can lead to the good. If the good is wished for, then the required understanding of the good's content must be philosophically attained. For which cause, prayer serves no purpose. To seek to gain knowledge of the good through prayer is to engage in the insincere effort. To pray, in an attempt to gain knowledge of the good, is not a real attempt. It is not an effort at knowing the good. To engage in prayer is to do so due to reasons other than the wish to know the good. Just as prayer is not useful in providing knowledge of the good, prayer is not useful in living the life of the good. Only that individual may do good who is aware of the good. Prayer can be engaged in if it is so desired. But a claim to being good due to praying cannot be made. It is the reverse. It is due to lacking the good that prayer is engaged in. The life of the praying individual is distinct from the life of the individual who seeks the good. One attains the good, and the other doesn't. As the effort at the good is lessened, the equal proportion of lessened good is achieved. Prayer will not be answered. The greatest favor that the good grants is the sincere life, the sincere effort. The greatest favor is knowledge and possession of the good. The greatest prize, the greatest reward in life is the good. There can be no other greater favor, no greater achievement. Prayer does not reach the good, prayer is not answered. Only the greatest effort can reveal, can attain the greatest good. The greatest effort is with philosophy. Only philosophy can lead to the greatest good. Prayer is not a part of philosophy. Any claim that prayer is part of philosophy can only be made by a non-philosopher. The good is there for humanity to seek.

Life is not to be altered. Life is not to be feared. Life achieves all. Life is not to be indifferent about. What should be hated is the lack of personal good, the lack of personal effort. What should be hated is making the self a lesser individual. Being there to be crushed by the good every single time. Not to seek the good is not to have the good. It is to be defeated by the good every time the good is rejected. By turning away from the good, the personal failure is then inherent. The making of the self into a lesser individual cannot be avoided. The personal defeat by the good is automatic. The fact that prayer is not engaged in does not mean that the way of the good necessarily follows. Conversely the fact that prayer is engaged in does not mean that the good can never be observed. The question of seeking the good involves a comprehensive approach to knowing the good. As the approach is thorough, such level of good will be achieved. It does not mean that the good will be immediately with the least amount of effort achieved. It means that the good will be in due time achieved. Prior to which only lower levels of good were the self's guide. As the levels of good were lower, such behavior was engaged in. A lacking of the desired good behavior. Once that desired good is achieved, the individual reaches personal growth. The individual reaches personal maturity. At this point, the individual may very well consider the behavior of the past as insufficient. Meaning that what was once considered as good is no longer viewed as such. What is important is that the good is personally attained. What is important is that the good is accepted when revealed. As the individual seeks to morally mature, so does humanity seek to morally mature. Humanity can only seek to be guided by the good. To do otherwise is to do so at the self's expense. The individual is best when guided by the good. Humanity is best when guided by the good. Humanity's most beneficial growth can only occur when humanity is guided by the good. For that purpose, humanity must seek the good. Humanity must attain the good. Humanity must accept the good. The identity of the human good is based on irrefutable truth. To oppose the good is to therefore lack the good. It is to isolate oneself from the good. Upon the good's rise, the good is recognized as such by those who have the good character and not recognized by those who lack the good. For the good not to be regarded as such by those who lack the good is not the fault or the doing of the good. To side against the good, for whatever reason, ranging from lack of knowledge to personal misery, is to take upon oneself the identity of opposing the good, of achieving lesser development, lesser understanding of life. To oppose that which is good for humanity is to seek human suffering. It is to seek the suffering of the good, the suffering of the greatest creative element. The way of the good is thoroughly such, taking up within all issues to the same level of good. The good would never endorse a view or solution that is less than the good. The good individual can never mistreat another but, due to being good, always treats all others in the same proper, good manner. In the all-inclusive question of right and wrong, there is always a good and proper assessment to all issues. That assessment is always superior to all others. To think that there is no such good and superior view, better than all others, is to reveal that the good is lacked. If the good were possessed, the good would never be not considered as superior. And though a claim by the lesser to being the superior is continually made, that doesn't make it so. That claim does nothing to take away from the superior nature of the good. With philosophy capturing the supreme essence, order to the question of human good is given. As result, all greater good is distinct from the lesser. To oppose the good is to disrespect the good. Being unable to properly associate with the good, the result is human conflict. All human conflict is caused by the lesser, by those who lack the good. For the human good to err in behavior is to do so to the equivalent level of good. The level of personal good is constant. The human good's error, or imperfection, can only occur and be at the same level of unchangeable good. That is what makes the good such, possession of the good. The lesser at no time becomes the greater. For the imperfection of the lesser is always equal to that same lesser level, lacking of good level. The rightful answers to all issues facing humanity must be implemented, with the good having deciding power. Only then will the possible human justice be served. If the good is not in control, then justice is oppressed, and injustice is the rule. The good being such and good can only seek leadership of humanity, leadership in all issues. The good can only seek the destruction of nemesis. Led by philosophy, led by the good, no error can be ever made. The way of the good is thoroughly such. The good individual can never mistreat another. The good can never be not good. Philosophy's search for the good, philosophy's search for knowledge, is all inclusive. That search includes all issues that are considered of importance. And all those issues are assessed in the same philosophical, supreme manner. Whenever there is a number of points of view regarding the possible answer to any one question of human societal development, it is the point of view of greater good that should be sided with. Philosophy is the supreme branch of human knowledge. Philosophy is the supreme branch of humanism. Therefore it should be philosophy that should be sided with. There are other branches of knowledge, but no other branch has knowledge of life's reality as their purpose. The answers given to life's reality are none. The answers that are come up with are limited in scope. Those answers don't deal with life's reality only because knowledge of life's reality was not their purpose. Instead the answers given only apply to their limited fields of inquiry, limited fields of knowledge. Science, also, will be put in its place. It is best for the good to be sided with. It is best for philosophy to be sided with. The human being's roots are with philosophy. Philosophy is central to the human consciousness. And as such, philosophy will forever remain the most integral part to the human historical awakening. To think that philosophy is no more, that philosophy was something of the past, is to be mistaken. It is not to understand the powers of philosophy. If it is accepted that philosophy is supreme, then the question of the proper consideration of the differing philosophies arises. The history of philosophy is there to be analyzed. The central philosophies are generally, within the world of philosophy, considered as such. Any one philosophical doctrine has respect for any one other. That will forever remain so.

With philosophy achieving the most, life is better understood. Life's reality is revealed. Life renders the greatest justice. Life is real. Only that which is real takes part in life's being. Less than life's living occurrence is never lived. No life member lives less than the most. Life's basis cannot be anything other than the truth. Life's existence is due to life's laws. Life's existence is due to life's own powers. All that exists within life does so due to its undeniable identity. All that exists does so due to its powers being able to achieve undeniable identity.

Any one life member's status is defined through the personal evaluation of life's being. A false such evaluation is capable of being made. The correct understanding of life reveals a truth, reveals an independent truth. One which exists in fact, is dependent on the truth's own powers of existence and is not dependent on the truth's existence on mental discovery. Life's truth can only be reached through an intellectual analysis. It is thought that reveals all truth. Appearance does not lead to the understanding of life. Life's truth is accessible only to the intellectual effort. It is that effort that defines any life member. The intellectual achieves a consciousness. That consciousness cannot be derived without the mental ability. Life's self-awareness is neither greater nor lesser to life's being. Life consists of the mental ability. Life is fully aware of the self. The intellectual, the mind is life's basis. Life empowers life's laws. Life's laws sustain life. Life's laws serve life's purpose. Life's purpose is to attain all, to know all. As life attempts to know all, life understands all. Life creates all. With life's laws sustaining life, those laws exist in fact and are not dependent on human discovery for their existence. If life's laws did not exist in fact and independently, then life would also not exist. The question then is, what is the real nature of life's laws? The laws cannot be acted against. They are life's foundation. And yet they can only be discovered through thought. Therefore the basis of life's laws is thought. Life's laws are knowledge, knowledge which life is responsible for as it is that life has created all. It is life that is attempted to be understood, life's ability, life's intent. When humanity achieves a truth, it is life's reasoning that is discovered. All that occurs within life does within life law. Life and all within life is thought. No act is ever taken without thought. Since all acts do occur, then they do so as result of mind. Without mind, life could never be alive. Mind is life's basis. Mind is life's substance. All true reality is to be found in the realm of mind. All true reality is accessible only to mind, not to any one sense. Life's reality is such as life's reality is. Life's reality is neither greater nor lesser. To be correct in one's reasoning is to reveal an existing life truth. The only verification of necessity is the accurate evaluation. Philosophical truth cannot be overturned. Philosophy has a range. The present life stage has a range of knowledge and achievement.

Philosophy can only fulfill its own range. Doing so, achieving philosophical truth. And no future life stage can overturn present philosophical truth. Unless it is that the present stage stands for nothing. Unless it is that all human knowledge stands for nothing. If present philosophical truth is subject to revision by any one future life stage, then all human knowledge would be subject to revision in the future.

Life will only seek the good, in the process empowering the good. Life would never engage in wrongdoing. All acts are taken in the effort to attain the good. Life's decision is thoroughly just. And if imperfection and unjust suffering are encountered, then it is due to being inevitable and not due to life effort for the undesired. The imperfection and injustice are within life. It is life that undergoes less than perfection, less than justice. It is life that suffers the imperfection, the injustice. It is life that suffers during the states of less than the most wished for, during the states of less than the dominant good. That is why life makes the greatest effort at the good. That is why life will in the end prove to be successful. The dominant good will be attained during the dominant stage. The greatest justice will be served. Imperfection and injustice are then removed. Life's basis is none other than the good, the good for the self. If the good were not life's basis, life would not be able to exist. Just as the good is life's basis, just as life seeks the greater and greatest good, so it must be with humanity. To seek the good is the greatest possible deed. Not to seek the good is to be imperfect. Not to seek the good is to be morally deficient. To oppose the good is to commit the greatest crime. The individual must seek the good. Human society must seek the good. The best political system is that which creates the highest level of good. The individual and society must work toward the same common goal, the greater achievement of good. That then is the check to human behavior, the good. It is the human obligation to grow, to achieve greater and greater levels of good. That is the most complete individual, one guided by the good. As society must be guided by the good, society will establish an existence where there is the most chance for the good to flourish, where each individual will have the best chance to seek the good, the best chance to observe the good. The self is chosen. The personal level of good is also chosen.

However, it is the duty of society to establish the best existence. And if there is no check to human behavior other than the human personality, other than the human possession of good, none other is needed. Each individual is responsible for the self. To choose nemesis is to do so according to one's own will. It is done at the self's expense, at the good's expense. Led by philosophy, the content of the good must be so stated. The understanding, the revealing of the good's content can only come from philosophy. Levels of good are no doubt achieved by other branches of thought, but the supreme good is revealed to only philosophy. It is inherent that nemesis seeks to harm the good, seeks to destroy the good. As the good was personally destroyed within the individual, so is the good sought to be destroyed within others who do possess the good. No amount of pretense can conceal the nature of nemesis. What is wished for is the suffering of the good. What is wished for is to struggle against the good. The good therefore calls on all to join the good. The good calls on all to work with the good. The good's response can only be good in nature.

Life's unlimited power is within the reality of life. To that certain extent, life's power is limited. Life is not greater to the reality of life. Hence the existence of imperfection, the existence of imperfect stages within life is understood. All stages of less than the highest good are viewed as such. Life views all stages of less than the highest good as stages of less than highest good. By always seeking the good, life achieves the good. Life rewards the self. Life does not punish the self. For life to judge humanity, for life to punish humanity, is for life to judge the self, is for life to punish the self. During the stages of imperfection, only imperfect behavior can be engaged in. To judge humanity for being imperfect during the stages of imperfection would be an injustice. To judge humanity when humanity is less than the most complete would be an injustice. It is during the stage of dominant good that life and all within life, including humanity, is at the most complete being. During which stage, the dominant good governs all, making imperfect behavior impossible to engage in, making imperfect behavior something of the past. As the good then governs all, the good is at the highest level, making judgment unnecessary. As it is that at that point there is only good within life.

It is the idea of lack of judgment that leads to better and good human behavior, and not the reverse, being fearful of the possibility of negative judgment and therefore engaging in good behavior so as to avoid punishment. What is of concern is the truth. The truth can only lead to good. What is desired for the human is to be grown and mature. Only such individual can engage in good. To be less than mature is not desired. To think that responsibility to good behavior ends upon the refutation of judgment is to be mistaken. It is when responsibility begins. To observe any truth is to have the necessary level of good. The good can never lead to wrong and bad behavior. Wrong and bad behavior is the result of being less than mature, less than grown. It is lack of truth, lack of good, that leads to wrong being committed.

Seeking the good, humanity achieves the good. The guide to human behavior is the good. With the personal level of good being chosen, so is the personal level of lack of good chosen. To reject the good shows that the superior character is lacked. It shows that the characteristic of ever-enlightening wisdom is lacked. No individual can choose the good, no individual can engage in good behavior if that individual is less than intelligent. The good can never be adhered to if the false were the self's guide. Intellect is a prerequisite for knowledge of the truth, knowledge of the good. To observe the good, to observe the truth, it is required that such equal intellect be possessed. To achieve the good is to achieve such truth. It is to have such intellect. It is to have such superior personality. It is to be closer aligned with life's being. The good individual is of the most genuinely alive nature. The good individual has greater life. The individual lacking the good is inferior to the good individual. The good lead a life of the highest order and are guided by the most sincere purpose. Behaving in accordance with the source of life. Not abandoning the good, never engaging in less than the superior life. The results of lacking the good are the opposite. The superior life is absent. The motive before the self is less than the most sincere. The wish is not for the good's success. What is sought is the good's failure. What is sought is the good's destruction. As result, life is inexorably abandoned. The achieved good creates the individual. The achieved life creates the individual. Lack of good, lack of life, destroys the individual. Lack of good destroys the morality of the individual. By lacking the good, the inferior and defective life is more and more readily engaged in. Leading further and further away from life. Leading to an individual who receives strength not from life but from the absence of life. Such strength no doubt exists. Individuals who lack the good do in fact exist. If the nongood did not achieve life, then they wouldn't exist. The quality of nongood would be forever rejected by everyone. The strength of the lacking-the-good individual is equal to that same lack of good, same lack of life. Strength, true strength, can only be attained and possessed by the good. Only life, only the good, can create the most sound human being, the most powerful human being. The strength held by the nongood is a deception, for only the good may be powerful. If nemesis had power, then that power would be used to abandon the way of lack of good. The power would be used to become good. Instead the possessed is used to reject the good, to abuse the good. Proving that that is not real power, proving that true power is not possessed. Instead of being in accord with life and the good, life and the good are constantly then opposed. Creating a lesser individual, creating a life of perpetual injustice. The good creates the individual. The lack of good destroys the individual. Accurate thought creates; false thought destroys. The idea before the self must be true and good. Only then will the most upright human being be realized.

All strength is with the good. This is proven based on the fact that the sufficient strength was possessed to had attained the good, the greatest prize. The equal to the good strength was in fact possessed. Having such strength does not make the good individual more than human, more than the possible human. It is the fulfilling of the good personality. All in the self's ability would have been done to create the most grown, the most mature, human being, living life to the fullest. The supremacy of the good is established and substantiated on the only possible ground, and that is mental evaluation. The good leads the superior life. In any intellectual analysis, the good is dominant. Therefore evil can never be victorious over the good. Any encounter ending in the apparent victory of evil over the good is that, apparent and not real. The good can never be defeated. The good empowers the greatest justice. What is needed is the honest mental evaluation. The lack of good is due to weakness. To harm the good is the greatest injustice.

If the good is not wished for, then the good will not be attained. The good is not known by all. Those who have no need for the good do not know the good. The different levels of search for the good, for the truth, produce different levels of attained good. The objective of the good society is for the good to work together toward the same good objective. The objective is not to compete as to who has achieved a greater level of good. The search for the truth will reveal the truth at the appropriate moment. The truth cannot be realized before then. This is the fact with the individual. This is the fact with society. Upon achieving the good, the good is then observed. Prior to which occurrence the good was not observed. The life that was led up to that point was an inadequate life. A life that was guided by the lack of good. The good is lacked by those who haven't engaged in the sufficient effort to attain the good. In due time, the good will be achieved by those who have made the effort. The good will not be achieved by those who haven't made the effort. In either case, when the good, when the truth is lacked, the individual is guided by the false, by that same lack of good. Attachment to the false is possible. It is a false estimation of life. Any one life truth is not false. What is false is the understanding of a life truth. The world of the false is guided by its own set of rules. Which are thoroughly false. The world of the false exists due to the false understanding of a life truth. The life truth is fact. What is not fact, what is not real, is the false understanding. The false only exists to the level of the false based on the reality of life. Yet the false gives a false understanding of the true reality of life. The false therefore wages a struggle against life. The very source that made all possible, including the ability to proclaim the false as true, the ability to proclaim life as false. The shallowness of the false, the parasitic nature of the false is obvious. Being guided by the false, all answers given have as their identity the rejection of truth, the rejection of the good. The struggle against the good is then inevitably waged. The length to which the false resorts to so as to further the parasitic cause. The allure of the false is no doubt tempting for those who lack the good.

The individual, and society, by having the good as the objective will overcome stages of inadequacy, stages of false existence. As the good will not be achieved before the rightful time. Upon doing so, the individual, society, will then be based on the good. And all acts will originate from the good, prior to which the individual, society, were lacking the good. And all behavior was so lacking. The achievement of the good was needed and was the proper change. The previous to the good development was previous to the good. That development was of such nature. The nature was such that the result was the good. The path to the good can only be taken. Any assessment of that path must also take into consideration the final result, the achievement of the good. If the path were so lacking, then the desired good would never have been achieved. It is the totality that must be assessed, including the grown and mature development. In the instance of the individual, in the instance of society. The desired in life is at all times lived, the desired being the living path. As the living path takes place, that living path is at all times based on the result of the desired. To behave counter to the desired is not possible. Within the living path, there are less desirable stages and more desirable stages. Each stage cannot but be recognized as such. Each is a stage of fact. Each is a stage of life's reality. Just as life achieves all, so does humanity, and all within life achieve all, including the most desired states. Life cannot be greater from life. No life achievement, no achievement by any one life member can be increased from the actual level. Making the achieved desired and the most desired inescapable. The good in life must not be underestimated.

With the living path being the result of the desired, to commit an error in life is therefore not possible. For an error to occur is for an act to be taken not based on the desired. It is for an act to be taken not based on the life felt. Error is as result not possible. When the mature grown state is achieved, it may then be considered that prior to which lacking behavior was engaged in. That behavior may have been lacking; that behavior, however, was not an error. If it were, the good would not have been attained. If it were, life would not have been lived. To ponder the question of error is to direct the analysis to the issue of truth. All behavior originates from the established personality. To behave contrary to the self's personality is not possible. Whether the behavior is lacking or not, it is the self's own living path. There is none other. The existence of the individual is due to the self's personality. It is due to the individual's single path at life. As error is not a factor, so is the idea of sin not a factor. The idea of sin would have to be defined as a severe error, a severe error which was done against the good. Such error would involve misbehavior against the good. The error would be as great that the individual would be worthy of punishment. The individual would feel that the self is worthy of being punished, that the error was most grievous. To think that error is committed in life is to be mistaken, to think that the self has committed a most grievous error is also to be mistaken. Any one individual's behavior is from within the reality of life. To misbehave against the good is not to know any better. It is to lack the good. The misbehavior is not done at the expense of the good. The misbehavior would not harm the good. The misbehavior would not insult the good. No misbehavior harms the good. All misbehavior harms the self. The objective in life is to attain the good. Not to attain the good makes the individual a lacking, lesser individual. The harm is the lack of good. Life's good is thoroughly good. The good has attained all good. The good is completely good. As result, the good can never be harmed by any lacking the good act. As result, the good would never consider any one act as a grievous error, as sin. The sin would be to harm the good, and the good can never be harmed. The idea of sin therefore does not originate with life. The source of the idea of sin is humanity. With the good, with life not considering sin, so it can only be with humanity. The good cannot be sinned against. Humanity can never sin against the good. What remains then is the issue of grievous personal behavior which may be sinful. Under all circumstances, sin would include the personal self or others. A sinful action would be regarded as having been taken either by the self or someone else. If a completely devoid of the good individual were to at all times behave in the same devoid of the good manner, then that individual considered those completely devoid of the good actions as necessary and needed. If they were not regarded as such, then they would not have been taken. The lacking-the-good individual did not and does not consider the taken acts as sinful. Life does not consider those acts as sinful. No misbehavior harms the good. All personal misbehavior harms the self. If an outsider to the nongood individual were to conclude that the nongood individual is engaged in sinful behavior, that does not mean that such conclusion, such observation, is correct. In fact, it is not correct. Such observation can only arise from not understanding the issue of sin. If an individual who was not at all times guided by the good but after sufficient effort achieved the good is assessed, then the individual considered the taken actions as necessary and needed. The good is attained at the appropriate moment and not before. Prior to which occurrence, the good was lacked, and the behavior was so lacking. But it was not lacking to the extent where the good was not attained. The lacking the good behavior may have been lacking, but it wasn't lacking enough for that lacking behavior not to had occurred. It was not regarded as sinful. The point of it being considered as sinful is when the good is attained. At which point the individual would have to consider the fact that the good cannot be sinned against. With sin not involving the good, that lessens the extent of the so considered sin. The grievous error may well have involved another human being, but it always involves the self. It is the self that considers that a grievous error was committed. Such conclusion can only be made if the individual had to some extent personally improved, that is the only way that lacking past behavior can be recognized as such. The personal improvement can only have been undergone if the good is personally searched for. At which point the individual can seek further and greater self-improvement, greater attaining of the good. By attaining the good, the individual resolves all. The personal path in life is then completed. Having achieved the good shows that the path was very much needed. It shows that no error was committed. The understanding of the issue of sin is what is desired. It is the growth of the human being that is desired. By understanding truth, the human being grows. The intent of life's good is the ever greater attainment of good. As the good cannot be sinned against, the good would not consider any one individual as being worthy of punishment. The good's intent is not punishment. If it were, the good would not be involved in the ever greater attainment of good. The good individual can resolve the self's dilemma by realizing that the good cannot be sinned against, that the good is not there to punish. The dilemma can be further resolved by knowing that the good is the self's objective; otherwise improvement would not have been undergone. It can be known that the greater search for the good, the greater attainment of good, will completely resolve the issue of sin. The completely devoid of the good individual would not be punished, lest the good lose sight of the objective of greater and greater good, lest the good lower the self to the monster's devoid level of good. The greatest prize is the good. The greatest punishment is the lack of good.

With the proper understanding, any one individual can resolve the issue of sin, the issue of grievous error. What remains of the idea is that an individual may conclude that someone else is committing a sin. That then is an inaccurate assessment, resulting from not understanding the idea of sin. If the idea of sin were understood, then the term *sin* would not be used. What would be used is a term of mistake, severe error, or misbehavior. The concluding individual that someone else is committing a sin cannot tell any one individual that sin is being committed as the outsider has no understanding of the idea of sin. Having no such understanding, the outsider's level of good would then be brought into question. By using the term misbehavior, what would then be engaged is the issue of the reality of life. What would then be engaged is the issue of the single and best path of life. Life lives in the single and best way. Any one individual lives in the single and best way. The objective is the good. Humanity must make the effort to attain the good. Doing so, the equal to the effort good will be attained. Life can only be accepted. Life can only be wished to be understood. The human being can only be accepted. Life is to be lived. To conclude that sin is being committed is to not understand life. It is to not understand humanity. It is to make such conclusion based on one's own mistaken thinking. It is to be mistaken in the made false such conclusion. It is to speak for oneself. It is not to express the reality of life. It is not to state a life law, a life truth, as there is no occurrence of sin in life. What there is is the reality of humanity and the human search for the good. What there is is inadequate behavior.

Life is at all times guided by righteous justice. With life attaining the dominant good, life will consider the path which has led to the dominant good. The path which was not equal in level of attained good as compared to the level of good of the most desired state. The lacking of the dominant good path will be elevated to the dominant good in the same righteous just way. Well knowing that what was lackling is no longer so lacking. Life's objective is the good. Based on the made effort, the dominant good will be achieved. Life will then live in the dominant good and just way. Philosophy makes philosophical conclusions which are based in the reality of life. To the philosophical truth, such life law exists. By engaging in philosophy, life laws can be revealed. Philosophical truth is not meant to be hidden. By making the effort, philosophical truth can be achieved.

The reality of life is the middle ground between the opposites. If only one opposite existed, that would be done at the expense of the other. If only one opposite existed, that would make that opposite unlimited. That opposite would be unlimited in power, and unlimited power does not exist. What exists is unlimited power, unlimited power within the reality of life. What exists is life's limited unlimited power, that power is the power of fact. Within the medium of life, unlimited power to that limited extent is attained. If only limited power existed, that would be done at expense of the opposite, unlimited power. The reality of life takes place. Unlimited power to the limited extent is achieved. Limited power to the unlimited extent is achieved. The reality of life includes all. Life is both infinite and finite, finite and infinite. Life is complete and lacks nothing. Life achieves all. As life is complete, life has the equal power to achieve all and have all. And that is unlimited power. If life's power were any less, life would not achieve all and have all. As life is complete, as life achieves all and life has all, life is unlimited. As life is unlimited, so is life's power unlimited. Life's unlimited power is the unlimited power of fact. Life's unlimited power is associated and equated with life's being. With life being unlimited, life is infinite. Infinity is associated and equated with life's being. Life is unlimited. Life has unlimited power. Life is infinite. Infinity is not to be equated with any one number but is to be equated with life. Life is not unlimited in false to life manner. Being so unlimited, life is to that certain extent limited. Life is to that certain extent finite. As life is limited, life is also finite. Infinity cannot be equated with any one number. Infinity cannot be equated with anyone not real life factor. Infinity can only be equated with the real life being. That which is not real does not serve in understanding life. All that is of life is within the infinity of life. With life being finite, all infinity is reduced to one. Life's being is one. Life's infinity is one. Life, infinity, is contained within the one. The one contains infinity. The one contains all life. The one of life, the one of infinity, is such specific numeral one, containing life, containing infinity. That specific one is not any one numeral one. The one represents life. The one stands for the infinity of life. Any other numeral one would be representing some life factor but is not the same nature as the one. Any one number must represent a life factor if that number is to have any meaning. Any one individual, any one self, can only be one and can only be represented by the corresponding and equal number one. Each self is finite, yet from that finitude infinity is the result. No individual lacks anything. Each individual possesses the self completely. Each individual achieves all. Each individual achieves infinity. With each individual being finite, each individual is limited. Each individual is limited to the extent of the self. Beyond which limit, the self cannot occur. Within each one's limitation, there is lack of limit. The limit is the self's own. Making all that is done, done to the limited extent, to the personal capability. No separation from the self ever occurs. All that is done is done with the self's need for the taken action. No action is ever taken without the agreement of the self. No personal alienation is possible. The self is as result unlimited. The complete choice for the self, the love for the self, is ever the decisive issue. Breaking the boundaries of limitation. Forever ruling out impersonal behavior. Giving rise to the complete and unlimited self. It is life that is attempted to be understood, and these are life's laws. All life has to be understood in the real life way. Life possesses all. The individual possesses all. As life is unlimited, in the limited way, so is the individual limited and unlimited in the similar manner.

The lack of limit is equated with infinity, limitation with finitude. Each individual can only be equated to the finite numeral one. And the completeness in living by each individual, completeness due to the containment of all the self's own, equated with infinity. The relationship between numbers and life is valid. The world of numbers is authentic. There is only one self. There can only be one self. No other individual is the self. No other individual is the same as the self. Each individual is different. Each individual is different, so is the numeral one representing each self different. Though the number one in each instance of the self is one, it is a different number one. The number one which captures the identity of each self always varies, just as each self varies. No one else is the same as the self. No one else can be equated with the self. No individual can be equated to another. The only way any individual can be equated to another is if the difference is overlooked. And an equating, not indicative of much, is carried out. Just as no individuals can be equated, so too is the numeral one representing each self not capable of being equated to another. This is due to the spirit of the number. This is due to the life contained by the number. Such numeral one therefore is not a lifeless number but is very much a number containing life. Such is the instance with all real life numbers representing a life factor, containing the life factor. Any number which does not represent a life factor is a meaningless, lifeless number and cannot be used in understanding life.

Life self-creates. Life's boundaries are unlimited life and unlimited nonlife. Life's middle ground can only be one. Life contains all life. Life achieves infinity, the one infinity. All within life is due to the middle ground. Any one achieved single identity is the result of the middle ground. Any one achieved single life member achieves all and is infinite. As does life have one infinity, so does any one single life member have one infinity. The living earth captures the one infinity of life. All life, in any one life stage, is directly related to the living earth. The living earth is the sole representation of life. If life existed elsewhere, that life would be different from earth life. However slight the difference may be, that difference would be an irreversible fact. Making the other life different from the living earth. If life existed elsewhere, life's one infinity would not be able to be reduced to one. If the other life is thought to be a representation of the one infinity of life, that would negate the living earth as capturing the one infinity of life, which cannot occur. The living earth is a fact. With Earth being a fact, it is the possibility of the existence of the other life that is negated. The living earth cannot be duplicated. There is only one self. With the earth being fact, the other life could not also exist. There is only one infinity of life. Infinity is reduced to one, the one earth. To that certain extent, life is infinite. To that certain extent, life is finite. There is one infinity. The opposite to infinity is one. Life contains the opposites, material, ideal, nonlife, life, infinity, and one. Only what exists is real, and no duplication of reality is possible. If any duplication were possible, that would change from one the number. Infinity would no longer be reducible to one. The opposite to infinity would no longer be one.

The thinking process, the reasoning pattern, is central to the human being. The thinking process is the identity of each life member. Distinction in life is drawn along the line of thought process. All life varies, so does the thinking pattern in each instance vary. The truth by existing is attached to by those who have the sufficient reasoning potential. The truth is attached to by those who have made the sufficient effort. Any achievement is the result of effort. The engaging in the effort to achieve truth is central to human development. If the effort is lacking, so will the reasoning process be equally lacking. Making the attachment to the false possible. To advocate the false is to oppose the truth and those who side with the truth. It is to attain one's identity at the expense of reality. The truth governs all issues. By making the effort at thought, at life, the human being is thus serious and sincere. In such serious and sincere manner, the individual then achieves the self. The effort must be genuine. The human being can only be a good human being. It is the effort that creates, the lack of effort that destroys. The good can only be searched for by all. And if the good is opposed by mindless enemies, then so it must be. It is mindless hysteria that satisfies those lacking the good. The present stage has been produced by life's effort at the good.

Life's state of dominant good will be realized. And no act can ever occur to prevent this from happening. No act can ever occur that would lessen the level of attained good during which. All that occurs in life serves to fulfill the state of dominant good. No act can ever occur that would diminish, take away from the state of dominant good. No act can ever occur that could diminish, take away from life. All that occurs to life occurs within life. All occurrence is a life occurrence. Occurring within life, by life. Life cannot be altered. Different stages are entered; however, all occurs within life, by life. Life therefore never lives less than fully. Life has life's range. Life has life's path. Within which all stages are included; none of which are diminished. Just as life's dominant good cannot be diminished. Life's dominant good is from within life's occurrence, from within life's range. Life's stage of dominant good is life's stage of dominant good. The stage of dominant good cannot not be within life. It is the dominant good that life searches for. It is the dominant good that guides life.

Life lives life's occurrence during the appropriate stages. And no stage is out of sequence. No stage is experienced by another during another stage. As life lacks nothing, so does the individual lack nothing, always living life to the full, experiencing the less desired and more desired stages and aspects of life. Throughout it all, the self remains complete. Experiencing and living all during the appropriate stages, in the appropriate manner. With no stage being out of sequence, the self lives life accordingly. Achieving consciousness and full consciousness, living the full life. The encountered negative aspect of the self's life is lived by the complete self. Just as the desired is lived by the complete self. Life must be understood. The truth of life must be accepted. By encountering the less desired, the effort is then made. By engaging the effort fully, the equal level of desired existence is then achieved. The effort is the integral part of life. With the individual struggling to achieve the possible, all is then achieved. Any assessment of any one individual must include the complete such individual. It is the mature and grown human being that must be assessed. With life achieving all, so the individual achieves all. No stage of the self's life is lacking, just as the self is never lacking. The life that the individual lives is the individual's own. No stage can be lesser; no stage can be greater. The life lived is the complete life, lived by the complete self.

The negative setting can only be experienced by the negative setting. And regardless of how detrimental it may be, the individual never lacks any portion of the self. For that same reason, any beneficial setting is experienced by the same beneficial setting. And regardless of how beneficial it may be, the individual never has an excess portion of the self. By flowing from stage to stage, by living life, the individual lives the full life, the individual achieves the full self. At all times the individual behaves in accordance with the self. All taken action is due to a reason. As the individual grows and matures, those reasons are in such manner mature. As the individual grows and matures, greater thought is engaged. That thought produces such understanding, such behavior. By living life to the full, the individual understands the self completely. With each action being due to a reason, the individual is completely self-aware. It may well be that greater good can be attained at a later point, presently at any one point, no greater good can be achieved. Making the individual always completely self-aware. Engaging the effort at life, engaging the effort at thought, the individual sets upon one's own personal path at life. The individual reveals the complete self. The individual understands the complete self. As life is lived to the full, so is the self fully understood. Living life is a fact, living the different stages of life is also a fact. Each stage in the self's life reveals itself completely. It is the self that lives each stage. It is the self that grows to each stage, doing so fully, doing so to the extent of the self. As the complete life is lived, the individual attains all. The individual attains all self-awareness. The individual, the human being lacks nothing.

Without the needed effort in life, nothing would get accomplished. Life must struggle for all. Nothing is given to life. Life is the result of effort, effort to attain all, effort to attain the good. Though the necessary effort is needed, life achieves all. Life reveals all. Life has complete knowledge. Life has complete knowledge of the self. By living, life takes the necessary measures to live. Life takes the path best for life's fulfillment and being. It is the path which life alone decides upon. The path is based on thought. Life only seeks that which is best. Doing so, the required and equal knowledge is possessed. Life makes an effort at living. It is based on the made effort. It is based on the taken best path, that life achieves all, that life has complete knowledge. Life cannot know less than the extent to life's existence. Since all laws are fact, then all laws are understood to the level of the law. The confirmation of life's laws as fact is to be found in life's knowledge of all. No other and external to life source is needed to confirm and substantiate life's laws. No other and external to life source is needed to confirm and substantiate life's being, life's ability. Unlimited power is not needed in life's success. Any one law is fact. Any one life law serves the law's purpose. Any one life law achieves that law's purpose. All life laws are life's. All life laws constitute life. Life achieves that which is best. Life achieves all. Life therefore has complete knowledge. Life cannot lack knowledge, for it is that life creates all. Life creates all laws.

It is life that sets upon the living path. It is life that encounters each stage. It is life that lives each stage. Doing so fully, doing so to the extent of life. The attained knowledge is the lived path. As the path is lived, the equal knowledge is attained. As the path is complete, so is life's knowledge complete. Life's knowledge is the taken measures at living. Life's knowledge is the living path. Life experiences the living path. As result, life understands the living path. Life understands all. Life understands the self. Life only occurs within life's path. Life only occurs within life. Life will not lead into not of life. Life will not lead into falsehood. Life's path, life's living effort cannot be false. Life cannot have false knowledge. Based on the effort, it is the reality of life that is engaged. The reality of life is fact. There is truth to the reality of life. If there weren't, the reality of life would never occur. The truth of the reality of life is equal to the reality of life. Life lives accordingly. Life is the reality of life. There is reason for any life act. There is reason for any life stage. That reason cannot be false but only true. It is the truth of all that sustains life. Life has always had the equal knowledge to the truth of the reality of life. Life lives the living path.

Life understands the living path. As the living path is true, so is life's knowledge true. Achieving all, life never leads to falsehood. Life cannot lack knowledge. Life cannot have mistaken and false knowledge.

It is the state of dominant good that is life's objective. Life always seeks that which is best. The living path is life's best undertaking. Within the living path is the state of dominant good. As the living path is achieved, so is the state of dominant good achieved. The dominant good is the state where life achieves the most. It is the stage where life achieves more than during any other. The stage of dominant good is a fact as life is fact. During the living path, life achieves all knowledge. During the stage of dominant good, life achieves the most knowledge, the most good. No life stage can be negated. No life stage cannot not occur. The living path leading to the dominant good cannot not occur. The present stage is proof of this. Life cannot attain all in one single stage. The present stage is proof of this. Not having unlimited power, life lives the entirety of the living path. Life does not eternally, without change, live in one stage. The living path leading to the dominant good cannot be of the same nature as the attained desired objective. Instead the path achieves the possible throughout it all. It is life that takes all course of action. It is life that life's laws serve. It is life that governs all.

In living, life encounters the possibility of the living path. In living, life comes up with solutions. Consequently the result is the living path. The living path is life's solution to living. All throughout of which, life's intent is to accomplish the best. Life's intent is to achieve the greatest good, the greatest knowledge, the greatest life. Life is equal to life's objective. The living path is the equal result to life's ability to accomplishing that which is best. Life will not seek less than that which is best. Life will not seek less than the greatest good, less than the greatest knowledge, less than the greatest life. Life is not lacking in any way. Life does not lack knowledge. Life does not lack the good. Life's ability is equal to life's intent. Achieving the most during the dominant good stage, life achieves less than the most during the rest of life's path. Life achieves lesser and greater levels of good during the different life stages. The living path must be accepted for that which the living path is. A different way of attaining the guiding good does not exist. Proof for this is found in the fact that the path does exist. Making the path the best possible way to achieve life's mission. Accepting life's effort does not mean a human effort at improving the level of good cannot be made. Such an effort is a must. Such human effort is to the extent of the human ability. The achieved improvement is to the extent of the human ability. Which cannot be exceeded. In seeking to improve the human condition, it is always the good that must be the human guide. Humanity can only be guided by knowledge. It is the good and knowing human being that is the objective. Such human being cannot engage in wrong behavior. The good is the greatest prize. The objective of the human being must be the good. To attain the human good is not an impossibility. Certainly a genuine and sincere effort must be made. The human good must in fact exist. An effort will produce greater results than lack of effort. Proving that the human good is a fact. All human conduct should be based on the good. The human being should be assessed according to the possessed level of good. To be guided by the good is to conduct the self in a responsible manner. The good presents the desired human being. Having done all in the self's power to be a good human being. The good human being can only be good and cannot engage in wrong. All law is to side with the good individual. In seeking the good, all human law can only be guided by the good. All human law can only be created by the good. To do otherwise is to have a law which cannot serve the purpose of the good. It is to have an illegitimate law. It is to have a law which empowers the lack of good and restricts the good. It is to have an unjust law. The good individual, by existing, naturally sides with the good and opposes the lack of good. The good individual defines the nongood as such. It is a definition which must be correct. If that definition were incorrect, then it would not be made by the good. Being good, the human good can only be correct in defining the nongood as nongood. Human opinion, the opinion of the good stands for something, stands for the status of the human being. The human being cannot be negated. Though human justice is limited, that does not mean that the search for human justice should be abandoned. This is not the stage of dominant good. The achieved good presently can only of such lesser nature. If this were the stage of dominant good, it would be known and recognized as such. If this were the stage of dominant good, all would be known about life. Life would be completely understood. The dominant good cannot but be known and recognized when it is experienced. As it is that questions remain as to the nature of life's being, then this stage is not the dominant good.

There is one stage of dominant good and one stage only. By setting upon the living path, life seeks to fulfill the living path. Life seeks to complete the living path. The reality is the medium between the opposites. Life has a beginning. Life has an end. That is the living path. At all times accomplishing that which is best, there can be only state which accomplishes the most. Living the path, life recognizes the path. That is the path that life has taken for eternity. That is the path that life will take for eternity. There cannot be more than one state of dominant good. One state accomplishes all. If there were another state that accomplished all, then that state would be the same as the dominant good. Making all other states not the dominant good. Completing the living path is life's objective, the attaining of the dominant good is life's objective. It is where all is attained, all is understood. If life constantly progressed, life would never achieve all. Life would never understand all. Having to always achieve more, life would achieve nothing. If life constantly progressed, life would not be from within the reality of life. Life would have no beginning. Life would have no end. Life would be unlimited. The reality of life is that past the state of dominant good, life would have nothing greater to achieve. At which point life would return to the original and most basic stage of existence. Eventually the return to the most desired state is made. During which life accomplishes all. Beyond which there would be nothing more to accomplish. Returning to the starting point, life would have the guiding purpose to once again accomplish.

To undergo life is to know life. When one life stage leads to another, life achieves knowledge of the self. To experience the living path is to achieve the equal knowledge. It is to understand all. It is know the self completely. Life rises to the extent of the living

NO HARM TO GOOD

path. All is contained within the living path, all life, all knowledge. Life masters the living path. The living path is life. Each and every time life comes up with solutions. The solution is the living path. By understanding the living path, life understands all. Life's objective is to know all. Life's objective is to understand all. Knowledge is central to life's being. It is based on knowledge that life attains all. It is based on knowledge that life resolves all. It is based on knowledge that life establishes the good. It is based on knowledge that life establishes order.

Setting upon the living path, life's mission is the guiding purpose. And so life enters into stages. Each stage has a beginning and an end. The factor which brings about change is the need for greater life, the need for greater knowledge. The idea of limited power bringing about the end of each stage serves its purpose to its own extent and not further. The rest of the idea of limited power is life and life's ability, life's search for greater life, life's attempted achievement of the guiding purpose. Change occurs, each stage ends, due to life's effort at greater life. All that occurs within life serves the purpose of attaining greater life. No event can occur which does not serve the purpose of greater life, greater knowledge. Such is the instance with all suffering, such is the instance with nonlife. Life is master of all. It is the truth of life that is desired. What is not desired is a false and mistaken understanding of life. The truth of life is that life is master of all. Life achieves that which is best. Life achieves greater life, greater knowledge. What appears to harm life doesn't do so. As it is that the good cannot be harmed, so it is that life cannot be harmed. It is the truth of life that is desired, not appearance.

Knowledge is central to life. Knowledge is central to humanity. It is human knowledge that is required. It is the truth of any issue that is desired. To be guided by the truth is better than to be guided by that which is false. It is the grown and mature human being that is desired. It is only by being grown and mature that knowledge can be attained, that the truth can be reached. Certainly the truth to any view can only be good. The effort at attaining knowledge, at attaining the good, can only be serious and sincere, humble, understanding, and mature. It is the sincere, genuine effort that leads to the good. If the effort is any less than genuine, that would show that knowledge of the good is not wished for. What is wished for is the same lacking as the effort. The effort must be humble. For to engage in bragging is to show that the effort was not genuine. If it were, then it would be known that the achievement is what is important, and not the bragging. The effort must be understanding. Understanding of the fellow man. If the effort is not, then the effort is disrespectful of the fellow man. A disrespectful attitude is not an attempt at the good. The effort must be mature. The good is the greatest prize. Only the equal and mature effort can lead to the good. By seeking the good in the genuine manner, such good is attained. The good attained is not in any one single issue, but all issues, all encounters in life. It is based on the good that the individual lives life. And as it is that no individual can discover all truth, then all ideas, all possible truth in one's life, is faced and analyzed with the same level of good. In the process producing the good human being. The good human being is knowing. The good human being is knowing of the good. The good human being is knowing of truth. The good human being is accepting of truth. And so, in such manner, the good human being would have done all. The good human being would have achieved all, living life then to the full. Such is then the life lived.

Possession of the good can only lead to good existence. The seeking of the good is the greatest attribute. The lacking the good is the greatest detriment. The lack of good is due to a disregard of the good. The lack of good is due to a disrespectful attitude of the good. The good is then not wished for. Knowledge is not wished for. The truth is not wished for. Instead of being guided by the good, it is the lack of good that is the guide. By rejecting the good, by rejecting the truth, a world of falsehood is created where the taken personal actions are with the aim to sustain that false world. To lack the good is to be separated from the good. To lack the good is to oppose the good. To be guided by the false is to struggle for the cause of the false. It is to struggle against the truth. It is to struggle against the good. Life always does all in life's power to create the greatest good. For the current stage, that means that the good is not in complete control. It means the opposition of the good by the nongood. It means the actuality of the good and the nongood. Such failing, such lacking the good failing, is detrimental to the human being. It is detrimental to humanity. Negative assessment, negative judgment cannot but be made of those who lack the good. That assessment is human. It is made by the good human being. The good human being stands for something. Such judgment is valid. It cannot be that the nongood be viewed positively by the good. If the nongood were to be viewed in a positive manner, that would show that the good is not possessed. It would show that the good is not understood. The nongood individual is not the result of life unjustly supplying an insufficient level of good to that nongood individual, with that individual wanting and wishing for a greater level of personal good; thus the individual being nongood without the personal choice to be nongood. Rather, the self is chosen. The good is chosen, as is the lack of good chosen. The level of nongood is chosen. And so the nongood individual is responsible for the self. The nongood individual is responsible for all personal acts. The fact that life occurs from within life's reality and is in such manner prohibited from judging humanity due to all choice being from within the limit of life and therefore all choice made is to that extent limited, is the concern of life. Nonjudgment of humanity by life is the concern of life. That is not the concern of the good human being. And if the good human being did something wrong in negatively judging the nongood, then the good human being would not be a good human being, which cannot be. The good human being cannot be mistaken in the negative judgment of the nongood. It is the idea that the good human can be mistaken that is mistaken, and not the good human being. The issue of importance therefore is whether good human beings exist. The issue is not whether the good human being can be less than good and, as result, nongood. The good individual cannot be less than good. The error in behavior is due to the nongood. It is the disrespecting of the good that is the flaw. The disrespecting of the good way for the human being to behave is the flaw.

The intent is to establish what is true. The intent is to establish what is good. The human wish can only be for the good to govern, for the good to establish law. In all circumstances, the good individual is to be given priority. The good has priority over the nongood, just as the truth has priority over the false.

The good human being has such complete outlook of life. The nongood individual has the opposing, complete outlook. The good is not searched for; the attainment of the good is not desired. What is wished for is not the good, but the nongood. Such being the wish, such being the search, such is the find. The effort is not at the good, the effort is not at the truth. The effort is therefore neither genuine nor mature. It is not a genuine effort at the good. The good is not the objective. The nongood is the objective. The nongood is then the prize. The nongood is then the reward. As the search for the nongood becomes greater and greater, so does the furthering from the good become greater. To despise the good is to love the nongood. To despise the truth is to love the false. The personality of the nongood can never be in accordance with life. The struggle is against life. As the struggle is against the good, against the truth, the struggle is against life. In that struggle, all is resorted to. The false and the nongood become the greater and greater prize. The alienation from the good is complete. The proof for this is found in the fact that the good is foreign. Hatred for the good, hatred for life never goes unchecked. Based on that hatred, the personality of the nongood individual is attained. As the good is strayed away from, the good, the only prize of worth, is lost contact with and missed out upon. The nongood individual can feel good about oneself in lacking the good, in feeling victorious over the good, and the requirements of the good, in having the freedom to behave in the desired nongood manner, but such action is deceptive and false, equally as much as the end result, the lacking the good result. By not meeting the standards of the good and in thinking that the good has been defeated in secret, with no one's knowledge and without nongood acts having to be answered for, the deceiving of the self is then complete. Nongood behavior can only be engaged in at the same lacking the good level. It is the good that is lacked. Every time the good is strayed from, the good is then equally lacked. To lack the good is to enjoy the equally lacking the good benefits. It is to enjoy benefits of nongood value. The nongood prize gained is equal to the turning away from the good. To lack the good is to have such nongood personality. To secretly act against the good is to attempt to deceive the good. It is the good that must be fooled. The lack of detection has to be carried out against the good. This task cannot be accomplished. The good is ever present. It is the good that is denied. The rejection of the good cannot go undetected. The nongood personality is evidence of this. For it is that the nongood personality is such, nongood. The good is the source of life. The good is the only prize of value. It is the good that the nongood lacks. The deception is not of the good, the deception is of the self. And the great riches gained by the nongood are riches of great poverty. The only criteria is the good. The good personality is the only criteria. Good character is the only judging point and no other.

The acts of the nongood are answered for. Every act that is harmful to the good is harmful to the self. As result, it is the nongood that suffers and not the good. The good cannot be harmed. By siding against the good the most grave crime is committed. The crime committed is the lack of good. The punishment is the lack of good. The greatest reward is the possession of the good. The greatest punishment is the lack of the good. By behaving against the good, the harm then done to the self is inherent. The punishment of the nongood individual, by the self, is inherent. In all the different ways that the good is harmed, it is the nongood individual that harms the self, in those exact same ways. Every act of harm taken against the good is answered for in that same taken acts. In contrast, the seeking of the good is the achieving of the good. It is to live in peace and harmony with the good. It is to live in peace and harmony with life. There is no greater achievement. There is no greater benefit, no greater reward. The good individual has such complete personality. Living life in the same good manner. The good is beyond harm. The good individual is beyond harm. No harm can ever occur to the good individual. The only way possible to harm the good individual is through the loss of the good identity. That can never happen. The identity of the good individual is constant. It remains constant. The good identity cannot be lost. Proof for this is found in the fact that the individual is in fact good and not nongood. All other harm is therefore meaningless. As the greatest prize of good is achieved, so is the greatest reward of good achieved. The negative reward to the nongood individual is natural. The nongood cannot be rewarded positively. If it were, the same benefit would be gained from being nongood as from being good. The good individual possessing the reward of the good. And therefore to think that the possession of the good is not the greatest reward, the lack of good the greatest punishment, is not to understand the good, not to understand life. It is not to understand philosophy. The good is truth, The good is life's basis. The good is life's positive regard and relation with life's own best interests. The good is life's most superior alignment with the self, with life's own best interests. To stray from the good is to be in absence of life. It is to lack the positive relation and regard for life. It is to misbehave toward the good. It is to misbehave toward life. Misbehavior of such a nature is not a nonoccurrence. Evidence for this is found in human struggles. By lacking the good, the good is then opposed. Once the good is lacked, the nongood individual has the freedom to misbehave against the good. As result, the lack of good is not just living the nongood life; it is also the misbehaving against the good, against the good's cause. The lack of the good becomes more and more involved. It is the waging of a struggle against the good individual. It is a struggle for which it is the nongood individual that is responsible. As the struggle against the good increases, so does the level of nongood increase. As the distance from the good increases, as the level of nongood increases, so does the abuse of the good increase. By wishing for the nongood, the nongood individual must ask if it is truly the wrath of the good that is wished for. The way of the good is far superior. The human being can only wish for the good. By being mature, humanity must realize that there is only one way for the human being to be. Humanity must realize that the nongood character is the greatest human flaw. The good must be wished for. The good must be searched for. The good must be respected.

By achieving the good, all that there is to be humanly done has been accomplished. There is no greater accomplishment than the possession of the good. All of the self's acts will then arise from a source that is stable and at peace. Stability and peace can only arise from the good, from the possession of the good. From the observance of the good. Only the most positive qualities will originate. The individual will in fact lead the good life. All the personal characteristics being from the most superior quality. Once the good is attained, it is the complete personality that does so. All the differing ways in expressing the self's personality are in equal measure as the possessed personal level of good. The differing personal qualities will all be equally good. Having achieved all, the individual is at peace with the good. Being at the height of development, the greatest possible life is then achieved. To be brave, to be intelligent is to be truly so. As is the case with all the positive human attributes. The issue of decisive importance is the good and the possession of the good. The good individual is at peace and is peaceful because all with regard to the good has been done. The individual is peaceful toward the good. The good individual can only be peaceful toward the good. That is the only way that the good may be attained. It is the good that is desired to be attained. It is the good that is attained. It is to have the necessary and required good character to do so, attain the good. It is therefore to be at peace with the good. It is therefore to have peaceful relations with the good. It is only the genuine and sincere effort that can reach the good. Achieving the good, all is then achieved. It is to be at peace with the good. It is to be at peace with the self. The issue of decisive importance is the good. It is the good that is the criteria. All is to be assessed. All is to be judged, from the standpoint of the good. The good can only be not reached based on an insincere and less than genuine effort. To lack the good is to lack the peaceful attitude toward the good. To lack the good is to have the complete such lacking, less than superior personality. It is to be lacking in all respects. To sustain the nonpeaceful existence, all groundless reasons must be turned to. Leading to an empty and pointless life. Such a baseless mentality cannot bring with it peace and comfort. The miserable individual is equally so miserable in the complete sense of life. Therefore being unable to achieve happiness within. The good is the criteria. Such an empty and miserable life is of no value. As the nongood individual is constantly opposing life, the life then led is unprotected. As the individual is constantly opposing life, life is constantly opposing the individual. The individual is subject to life's ever more destructive response. To engage in nongood behavior is to have an ill personality. Of which ill personality, the nongood individual cannot be the judge. For it can only be that the nongood behavior is engaged in because it is viewed as good, which it is not. A taken action can only be considered as good. If it weren't, it would not have been taken. An action taken by the nongood individual can only have been considered as good. A nongood individual is therefore defined as someone who is not an authority of the issue of the good. A non-good individual is someone who cannot be the judge of oneself, for all such personal judgment would be distorted and positive in nature of the nongood. A nongood individual cannot be the judge of the content of the good, for it is that the good is lacked. It is the good that is not understood.

It certainly is the fact that no one good individual can be the judge of all the nongood individuals. In the process verifying the nongood acts by the nongood individual as such. That does not mean that those nongood acts suddenly become good. In assessing the content of the good, it is only philosophy that has the final say on the issue. As result the human good can only arise from within philosophy, arising from the understanding of philosophy, from the engaging in philosophy. Being guided by philosophy, humanity thus will create the greatest human level of good. And in such manner bring all the nongood individuals to judgment. The good human can only evaluate the nongood acts by the nongood to the extent, to the level of the good human being and not beyond. The ultimate judge in the matter is life, life's inevitable progress toward the dominant stage. Life's achieving of the dominant stage is based on the achieving of the dominant good. Prior to which, the dominant good was not in possession. Which means that there is an improvement; there is an increase of the level of good. And the previous to the dominant good is so judged by life as needing improvement so that the previous good to the dominant stage of good may be elevated, may be brought to a higher level of good. That means that all from within life is improved upon. That means that all from within life is judged by life. Life judges all in the life understanding of all manner. Life's existence is life's constant best judgment.

The validity of human judgment extends to its own domain and not beyond. The human observance of nongood acts by the nongood individual is the observance made by the human good and is meaningful and properly so, to the level of the human good. Which cannot be equated with life's judgment. As it is that all from within life is improved upon, that means that all is in a similar such way insufficient. The present stage of life is lacking the supreme good but is founded on a level of good. The only way that the present stage may reach the supreme good is through elevating the present insufficient level of good. All human behavior is therefore lacking the supreme good to either greater or lesser extent. Any one human is in such way inadequately good since it is that the supreme good isn't being taken part in. Varying levels of human good are a fact, however. And those levels cannot be equated. There is human good and nongood. This is evidenced by the fact that the false, and provably so, is often adhered to as truth. This is evidenced by the fact the good is not the objective of many. It is evidenced by the fact that the good is often not genuinely wished for. To define someone as a good individual, or another as a nongood individual, is to humanly do so. Such terminology is not completely without merit. The existence of human good is provable. The objective of the human good is the attainment of the good. The objective is knowledge of the good, the revealing of the good, the clarifying of the good. The human good can only wish to create greater good. That is why the good is engaged, to struggle for the cause of the good. The good is engaged so that the cause of the nongood is exposed and destroyed. The good does not wish to live in peace with the nongood. Any destruction of the nongood must start with the exposing of the real and failing ideology of the nongood. The destruction keeps in mind that prior to the human good, such good ideology was not present, and so it could not have been observed by anyone. The destruction is therefore with the intent that the human good is fairly assessed by all. The destruction is with the intent that all join the human good. The human good is accepting of all who themselves are accepting of the human good. The ideal of any and all nongood causes is subject to being exposed and intellectually destroyed by the human good, by philosophy. Such is the deserving fate of all nongood ideology. It is the nongood that is responsible for any human struggle. And the struggle is automatically initiated when the nongood is endorsed. The exposing of the nongood is an attempt by philosophy to achieve understanding. It is an attempt to achieve truth. Philosophy is concerned with the clarification of philosophical issues. Central to which is knowledge of the good, the engaging in good behavior as opposed to nongood behavior. Knowledge is therefore central to philosophy. And as knowledge is central to philosophy, so is knowledge central to humanity. By attaining knowledge, the human being becomes grown and mature. It is only the grown and mature human that can attain the good. It is only the grown and mature human that can engage in good behavior. The theory of judgment likewise is critical to human understanding, to human growth.

The theory of judgment, that humanity will be either rewarded or punished, is to a great extent the issue of life's being. Life is the middle ground between unlimited nonlife and unlimited life. Within the reality of life, all is achieved by life. Life is not denied anything. No life member lacks anything. The choice for the self is complete. The love for the self is complete. Any attempted improvement of the self is based on the love for the self. It is based on the choice for the self. As the choice is complete, as the love for the self is complete, the self's free will is complete. The free will of any life member is complete. The free will can neither be raised nor lowered, the free will is as result complete. The deciding issue is the love and choice for the self. The free will is complete because the choice, the love for the self is complete. The reality of life cannot be exceeded. To do so is for life to become unlimited, in the process giving rise to the counter, unlimited nonlife. Life makes an effort at the achievement of all. Life succeeds in the effort. For life to judge the human being is for life to exceed the reality of life. Life will not exceed the reality of life. The human being will not exceed the reality of life. As result, there is no such reward and punishment, judgment of humanity. What exists is life's constant effort at achieving that which is best. What exists is life's constant judgment at achieving that which is best. In such manner, in such good manner, the supreme stage of good is attained. All life acts, all life understanding is based on the reality of life. All life judgment of good and best is from within the reality of life.

For the human being to understand any truth can only be a good thing. For humanity to understand the reality of life, for humanity to understand the nonreward and punishment, judgment by life can only be good. The truth can only be good. That is what humanity strives for, the achievement of truth, the achievement of the human good. Being guided by the good, the human being is grown and mature, leading to good behavior. Not to understand the theory of judgment is not to be guided by truth. It is to lack the good. As such, the resulting behavior to the specific extent is to be just as lacking. It is the possession of the good that leads to good human behavior. It is the lack of good that leads to lack of good behavior. The good individual possesses the good. The good individual seeks the good. The good individual cannot engage in nongood behavior. Knowledge of the truth is wished for. Knowledge of the good is wished for. To possess the good is to make the equal to the wish effort. The search for the good is sincere. The motive of the search for the good is the attainment of the good. The idea of the potential of reward and punishment acting as a guide and leading to good human behavior is mistaken. No such good behavior will be the result. To begin with the individual would be based on the falsehood of judgment of humanity. And as such would be lacking the good. The individual is therefore unaware of the content of the good. The individual by responding to the threat of punishment, or the possibility of reward, would be guessing as to what is good. In the end, all actions would revert back to the personal lack of good. The search for the good is not prompted by threats or promises. The search for the good is initiated with the intent of attaining the good. To respond to threats and promises is not a sincere effort at the good and does not attain the good. To respond to threats or promises is to attempt to deceive. It is to attempt to deceive the good. The world of philosophy belongs to philosophy. The world of philosophy belongs to lovers of knowledge, lovers of the good. All pretenders, all frauds will be exposed. The idea of judgment does not help humanity in the search for the good. It has always been that humanity has had freedom of behavior, freedom of will. Even the individual who is guided by the idea of judgment creates freedom of behavior. Believing to be acting in accord with life's laws, freedom of behavior is then achieved. Freedom of will which originates from a mistaken source. All the while believing that the source is correct, thereby creating freedom of will. As the source is mistaken, so is the reasoning mistaken, so is the resulting behavior mistaken. Nonetheless, the resulting behavior was due to free will. The belief then that the idea of judgment has been a check to human behavior, that the idea of judgment has guided human behavior into doing that which is good is mistaken and false. Freedom of behavior is attained, and that freedom of behavior is the same as lacking the good personality.

With the human freedom of behavior comes the human responsibility for the self. The refutation of judgment creates the more aware human being, the human being who is in accord with life. Being in agreement with life, the human being enacts life. Doing so to the full potential of the human being, not achieving more, not achieving less. It is the more conscious, the more aware human being that is desired. Only such human being can create the most, can create the greatest good. The responsibility for the self can only be successfully met. Being guided by the good, the human being seeks the good at all times, seeks the good in all issues. Thereby attaining good at all times. As it is, the refutation of judgment requires clearer understanding of the issue. What is required is clearer understanding of life. All the issues of importance must be so understood. Change can occur. It is the truth that humanity seeks. Doing so, making the individual fair and just. Human history is there to be examined. All the while, freedom of will was always the taken course of action. The idea of judgment is a human idea; it is not a fact. Judgment has never occurred. If there is mistaken human thinking, then the one responsible for that is mankind. The flaw is with humanity. With the idea of judgment having been so prevalent in history, the idea of judgment must be so historically accepted. The idea of judgment has been central to human thinking. In the process, human history has unfolded in such human way. What has occurred has done so. And human creation has been such as human creation has been. The fact of the idea of judgment being mistaken hasn't prevented and stopped human progress. Human history is there to be examined. As result, in many cases, attachment to such idea has not prevented humanity from producing, has not prevented humanity from having a level of good. The idea of judgment therefore is not completely devoid of good. This is evidenced by the fact that many creative people were attached to the idea. The presence of good, in many of the instances of such people, has been undeniable. And it is not for anyone to assess the level of good in each such instance. The question then becomes to what extent is the idea attached to, and for what reasons? As the reasons become less and less sound, the thinking becomes less sound, the possession of the good becomes equally so less. The good created by any truth therefore begins with the good created to human understanding. The good created begins with the good accomplished for the human mentality. It is the truth that is of value. It is the truth that is searched for. And as attachment to the idea of judgment has nonetheless resulted in human achievement, attachment to the reality of life will lead to greater human achievement. The greater achievement has already begun with the understanding of the reality of life. A new beginning awaits humanity. Nowhere does philosophy call for nongood human behavior. Nowhere does the good call for non-good human behavior. It is the lack of good that does so. The human wish can only be for the good. The human wish can only be for the truth. Change is a part of life. Change is a part of history. Change from the past can occur. The human mentality can only be elevated. Humanity can only be in accord with life. The reality of life can only be accepted. The most conscious, the most aware humanity must be realized. In the process, the most good would have been engaged in. The most good would have been humanly accomplished. Whatever the exact content of the most human good may be, it would have been accomplished. Being guided by truth, humanity is then guided by the human level, the human extent of good. All possible, in the creation of the greatest human good, would have been done.

All life issues are related since it is that all life issues deal with life. The refutation of the idea of judgment is founded upon the reality of life. The refutation of the idea of judgment, hence the idea of freedom of behavior, is central to human thought. And the many issues directly related to the idea of freedom of behavior will likewise be positively and accurately affected and assessed. Humanity is not perfect. What is desired is to achieve the least amount of imperfection. Freedom of behavior accomplishes just that. It is the idea of judgment that is mistaken. It is the idea of judgment that leads to flawed human behavior. In many of the human instances of attachment to the idea of judgment, the origin of this thought is due to acceptable reasoning. In many instances, it originates from a need for justice. Observing the evidence of nongood human behavior, the idea of judgment is then seen as a remedy to that injustice. As result, there is reason to such thought. The idea of judgment therefore originated long ago in human history. The originator of the idea has been humanity. The idea of judgment has never been confirmed by an external to humanity source. It could not have been confirmed due to the fact that it is incorrect. The idea of judgment is a philosophical issue. The origin of the idea being humanity, the intellectual considering of the idea is a human effort at achieving truth. It is a human effort at philosophy. Philosophy is accessible to all. It is the engaging in philosophy that is desired, as it is that philosophy has all the supreme answers. It is the philosophical assessment of the issue that is desired. Such assessment will reveal a definite level of good by many who have in such manner reasoned that there is justice to judgment. The level of good is due to an authentic and genuine effort at philosophy and reason. The made conclusions are equally as authentic and genuine. In such manner, there is a level of good. The idea of judgment is a part of human history. The level of possessed good by many who sided with the idea is undeniable, and it isn't the place for any one human being to attempt to judge the level of good possessed by others, others who have achieved an undeniable level of good. It is philosophy that was turned to in order to clarify the issue. Philosophy has accomplished the task. The philosophical assessment of the issue of judgment reveals that there is definite level of good by many who have sided with the idea. At the same time, the philosophical assessment of the idea reveals that there is a definite, undeniable lack of good by many who attach themselves to the idea of judgment.

In those instances, belief in judgment is due to sinister motives. In those instances, belief in judgment is due to sinister reasons.

If there is mistaken human thinking, then the one responsible for that is humanity. The flaw is with humanity. And regardless of however long a falsehood has existed, that doesn't make the falsehood correct. It is up to humanity to develop and grow. It is the clear understanding of the issue that is desired. As the effort at philosophy is less than authentic, less than genuine, the reasoning is less than genuine, the reasoning is less than authentic. As the reasoning is less and less sound, the lack of good is then equally so increased. The lack of good is defined as the lack of achievement of truth, the lack of love of knowledge. If philosophy were loved, then philosophy would be engaged in, which it is not. If philosophy were engaged in, then sound philosophical reasons would be presented. Sound philosophical reasons which would be presented in systematic form, going to great detail to prove or disprove an issue. If philosophy is not engaged in, then knowledge is not loved. The truth is not loved. The good is therefore lacked. The made conclusions are equal to the good lacked. In the process, the individual believes oneself to be representing a level of good, when in fact it is the lack of good that is represented. With the individual lacking the good, the individual does not know the content of the good. As result, regarding oneself as good. In the process revealing the real and true nature, the lacking the good nature. Not only is the individual lacking an authentic attempt at knowledge, the individual is lacking in the attainment of knowledge, namely the refutation of the idea of judgment. With the idea of judgment being central to the reality of life, the individual then by failing to understand the idea then fails to understand the reality of life, fails to understand many critical to human knowledge issues. The made conclusions regarding those critical issues are just as lacking in knowledge, are just as lacking in good. With the individual lacking knowledge, lacking the good, the individual lacks justice. The idea of judgment is considered by that individual as a form of justice. The question therefore is, why would an unjust individual seek justice? How can an unjust individual seek justice? The answer is that the unjust individual does not seek justice. The unjust individual seeks injustice. The justice desired is not justice. The justice desired by the unjust is not justice. It is injustice. Failing to understand that the good is personally lacked, unfounded importance to the personal view is then given. As that self-importance is increased, the level of personal good is decreased. Excessive attachment to the idea of judgment is equal to excessive lack of good. The unjust individual seeks the unjust suffering of the just. For it is that the unjust individual is neither good nor just. The enemy of the unjust individual is the just individual. The friend to the unjust individual is another unjust individual. Therefore the unjust would be rewarded and the just punished. The neither good nor just individual is such, neither good nor just for a reason. It is the suffering of the good that is desired. It is the rewarding of the unjust that is desired. Such lack of good is due to the original mistaken act, the lack of desire for knowledge, the lack of desire for the good. By lacking the good, the individual then proceeds to reveal the real personal nature. The lacking the good nature, not recognized as such by the lacking-the-good individual. The individual willingly reveals the personal lack of good. The idea of judgment has never been confirmed by an external to humanity source. It has not been confirmed as correct only because it is incorrect. The idea of judgment is a human idea. It is a human failing. Attachment to it reveals the sinister reasons by many. This is due to the personal nonrecognition by those lacking the good as a lack of personal good. According to the neither good nor just individual, the just are deserving of punishment, the unjust deserving of reward. Accordingly, the neither good nor just individual is undoubtedly most deserving of reward. Justice for the neither good nor just individual is for the just in life to be punished, for the unjust to be rewarded. As excessive attachment to the idea of judgment is an excessive failing by the neither good nor just individual, the rewarding of the unjust is wished for. As excessive attachment to the idea of judgment is an excessive failing by the neither good nor just individual, the punishment of the just is wished for. The days of the beast will soon be over.

The cause of the good must be struggled for. It is the way of life. As it is that life struggles for life's attainment of all, so must the good struggle for the cause of the good. The struggle is a life characteristic. It is based on the struggle that all in life is achieved. Possessing limited power, life must struggle to achieve all. Nothing is attained by life without an effort. It is the effort, it is the struggle that defines life. The equal to the made effort is the achievement. It is the effort that is the achievement. The effort is the creator of life. It is the effort that is the creator of all. It is based on the effort that there is a sense of creation, that there is unison with life. Based on limited power, life is genuine and worth living. If life had unlimited power, all experiences would lose interest. Unlimited power leads to the loss of the living quality. Unlimited power negates the effort. Unlimited power negates creation and achievement. By negating the effort, by negating the sense of achievement, contact with the self would be lost; contact with life would be lost. The life lived would be pointless and uninteresting. Through limited power, life feels and life experiences. Life is completely fulfilling. It is limitation that makes life fulfilling. Setting upon the living path, life encounters all, life lives all. Not all the stages are the same. Some are greater than others. Some stages achieve more. Throughout it all, life is in control. No event occurs of which life is not in control in the life way. The living path, by consisting of all stages, consists of the lesser and all the greater stages. None of which can fail to be undergone by life. Ensuring that the range of life is lived, ensuring that the greatest good cannot but be created, ensuring that the greatest good cannot but be lived. And if the living path allows for negativity to be experienced, then so it must be. It must be endured. Throughout it all, the identity of the self remains uncompromised. No event can occur to the self of which the self is not in control in the self way. By undergoing the negative, the self is assured of living the positive, based on that same negative act. For it is that the self can never be compromised. The self can never be lost. The individual self can never be taken out of any to the self-occurring circumstance. The possible would have been always done. Life is limited in power, but life is ruler of all. Life is always true to life's own being. All acts are initiated by life. All acts are initiated by the self. All acts are life. All acts are the self. Life is never foreign to life's own being. The self is never foreign to the self. The complete reality of life is lived. As the negative is lived, so will the positive be lived.

The fact of the reality of life is proof that life has achieved all. The fact of the self is proof that all favors have been granted. The fact of the self is proof that all others have been rejected, and instead the choice for the self was made. The self is never inadequate. Life is never inadequate. Life does not miss out on any qualities. The truth of life cannot be inadequate. It is only the reality of life that is of value. It is the unreal that is of no value. The limitation of life is not demeaning. Instead, the limitation of life is the one characteristic that makes life live. Based on that limitation, the being of life is attained. All is attained. It is only life's true being that is of concern. No life member can exist if the self is not chosen. Through that choice, all is granted. Through that choice, all is lived. The self is not imposed upon any one life member. The self is loved. When life chooses life's being, the choice is not unlimited in nature. The world of the unreal need not be entered. The choice made for the self originates from the world of limitation. Within that world, the choice has no limit, or it is meaningless to speak of one. No personal quality was forced on anyone. No personal quality was denied to anyone. To wish to reject the self is to once again choose the self. The love for the self is binding. No rejection of the self is wished for. Self-improvement can be engaged in by anyone.

It can only be that it is the truth of life that is wished to be understood. Any attempt at understanding life can only have the truth as its objective. The truth can only be attained by the equal to the truth effort. To desire an understanding different from the truth is to have an immature and incorrect concept of life. Life's being is the result of the limiting opposites of unlimited nonlife and unlimited life. Life is therefore limited. Within that limitation is the total and complete life being. Within that limitation is unlimited life. Life is so unlimited due to the fact that life attains all. All that life has belongs to life. The opposite is what limits life. Life by living within the limitation does so to the full life potential. All life acts belong to life. All life acts exist due to their need. All acts are to the extent of the full life potential. All life acts are to the extent of life's being. Life's being cannot be increased. Life's being cannot be decreased. All that is done is initiated by life. By doing so, life is equally aware of each act and that act's defining quality. Each act being, to that extent, an identity of life. Life cannot be unconscious of the self. Life cannot be unconscious of the motivating factor for each life act, for each life feeling. If such were the case, life would be unaware of life to the slightest and all degree. If that were the case, then no life act would ever occur. If that were the case, then life would not be a fact. It is that life is a fact. It is that life's being cannot be raised. Life's being cannot be lowered. Life is conscious to the life extent, not more, not less. Such also is the personally moving factor of all deed with all life members, including humanity. Nor is humanity any different, in this sense, from any other life member. Nor is humanity any different, in this sense, from the supreme life laws. And that is the enacting of the human character. Not more, not less than which. Enacting all that is human. Enacting all that is human from within the limiting opposites of unlimited life and unlimited nonlife. All that is of humanity is due to the reality of life. All that is of humanity belongs to humanity. All that is done by humanity is due to the human character. All that is done by humanity is initiated by humanity. Human behavior is to the extent of the full human potential. All human behavior is human. All human behavior originates from the human need for that behavior. By being so, the human being is equally aware of each act and its defining content. Each act being to that extent the identity of the human being. The human consciousness cannot be lowered. The human consciousness cannot be raised. That would make humanity not human. Humanity cannot be not human. The human character does not restrict the human being, making humanity oblivious and unconscious, lacking all knowledge of the reason for the human behavior. The human personality does not lack thought and reason. Humanity is not the servant of a foreign will, being unable to question or oppose that will. Humanity does not lack choice. The human character is not lacking. The will belongs to the self. The choice belongs to the self. All acts are taken due to reason and thought. Humanity possesses the complete human character. For humanity to be unconscious is for humanity not to exist. No life member is any different in this sense from any other. And that is the fulfilling of the particular personality. Not achieving more, not achieving less. The human specialty is not found in the idea that all other life members are instinctive, whereas humanity is not. All life, all life members are equally to their character aware. The term *instinct* is a human term. It is a human definition. There can be no negative meaning to it. Unless there would be a negative meaning to all, unless there would be a negative meaning to life. The special human status is founded upon humanity's own unique and solely human personality.

Humanity has complete reasoning ability, up to the point of questioning any and all personal thought. Only afterward does the thought become final. An act contrary to which is not wished to be taken. All life members are completely fulfilled. Humanity is completely fulfilled, the self is completely fulfilling. As the struggle, as the effort is the way of life, the human being must make the effort to achieve all. Humanity must make the effort to attain the good. It can only be that humanity seeks constant greater and greater growth. All growth begins with knowledge, and the primary human knowledge is philosophy. By engaging in philosophy, by studying philosophy, by observing philosophical answers, the greatest step would have been taken in the attaining of the good. It is only philosophy that can lead to the good. And so it is the good human that each human being must be. For it is that any philosophy will reveal that possession of the good is the greatest prize. Led by philosophy, led by the good, the human being then can only engage in good behavior. The deterrent to improper human behavior is the possession of the good. The good individual always seeks the good. For not to seek the good is fatal to the good character. Nongood behavior is fatal to the good individual. If improper human behavior is engaged in, that improper behavior cannot be engaged in by a good individual. It can only be engaged in by a nongood individual. Circumstances, the environment does not result in improper behavior by the good individual. The primary effort by the good individual is the attainment of the good. The good individual would know that engaging in improper behavior is detrimental to the primary effort of attaining the good, it would be known that improper behavior is detrimental to the self. The individual is responsible for all personal acts. It is the individual that is responsible for the status of the self. If the good was insufficiently possessed, and a greater effort at the good is wished to be undertaken, then such should be the personal action. The individual and society can only work toward the same good cause. To work toward the good cause is to struggle for the good cause. It is to struggle against the nongood. By engaging in good, a step is already taken against the nongood. The struggle against the nongood is inherent. If not, the good was not attained. It is the duty of the good to wage the struggle against the nongood. It is the nongood that is responsible for all human wrong, for all human suffering. Waging the struggle, the defeat of the nongood is imminent. The nongood is lacking, lacking in all respects. It is in the world of ideas that the original struggle will be waged. It is there that the nongood must be thoroughly destroyed.

The good seeks to create the greatest possible good. The good seeks to create that which is of most benefit to life. All life members seek to create that which is of most benefit to the self. As life seeks the greatest good, it is the range of life that is lived. All life stages are lived with the living path. No stage is excluded. No stage is different from what that stage in fact is. Life's living is such as life's living path is. Within which, the dominant stage is found. To think that any less than desired stage can exist without end is to equally think that the most beneficial stage can exist without end. The less than desired stage must be endured. Upon doing so, a more positive stage will be entered. This is due to the fact that all the less desired stages would have been endured. Once the less desired ends, a different stage begins. Once the less desired is endured, there is no more to endure. The effect of the less than desired is as result strictly limited. The less than desired leads to a better existence. Thus the less desired state is not distinct from the positive meaning. The less desired state has a positive meaning. When understanding the negative state, the positive to which it leads must be included. The desired state, the state of dominant good is the guiding objective and can only be taken part in after the experience of the negative state and states. For by being positive, the positive must have overcome the negative to have attained the positive state. Regarding the dominant good, all the negatives are then overcome. They must have been overcome. If they weren't, the dominant good would not have been achieved. There would have been more negativity to overcome, which means that the dominant good could not have been achieved. Life becomes complete based on the desired. Only then can the negative stage and stages be fully understood. On its own, the negative state has no meaning.

Life's wish and purpose is to be alive. Life wishes to live. If life's wish and purpose weren't to be alive, then life would not be living. When the life of any one life member ends, that then occurs contrary to the needs and wishes of that life member. The ending of that life member can only be therefore a negative occurrence. Life can only be identified based upon a positive state. It is through the positive existence that all is understood. If the ending of any life member, which is a negative occurrence, is a permanent ending, then the same, conversely, can be considered of any one positive life state, that that positive state is also permanent. The reality of life takes place. If life led into a permanent negative state, which is life's ending, then life would be identified with this final stage, which is negative. The positive state, based upon which life attains life's identity, would be negated. There would not be any such state. Life by wanting to live regards living as the positive. If life led into a permanent nonexistence, life would then attain a negative status and condition, which would not be balanced out by a positive condition. The positive, based on which life is identified, becomes fully negated. By permanently ending, the negative would become of greater magnitude to the positive, based on the fact that the negative is not followed by a positive. The negative must precede the positive. Life cannot be defined based on a negative.

Each negative will lead into a positive. Each end leads into life. To suffer, to undergo the negative, is to experience characteristics which are not defining of life. It is to experience characteristics which lead into the desired objective and are in themselves meaningless. Life has prevailed. Life is the ruler of all. Throughout life's existence, life is at all times of positive nature. Permanent negative life cannot occur. Life consists of the complete life range. Within which are included all the varying aspects of living, the desired and the less so. When the less desired conditions take place, they do so within life's range. Which can only be founded upon, and be, positive. Making the less desired also positive. It is that positive that will lead into a greater. As result, revealing the negative nature of the previous. By becoming greater, life achieves the more positive nature and, in due course, the most positive. It is always life that undergoes all stages of life's existence. The range of life is lived by life. It is life that lives the range of life. No event can ever occur which would prohibit the transpiring of the complete living path. No event can ever occur which would change the living path. Life's Living Path is unstoppable. Life initiates all. Just as the negative is experienced, so is the positive experienced. No aspect of life is inexperienced. At no time is life in danger of not existing. At no time is life in danger of not occurring.

During no point in life's existence can life be restricted from achieving all, from achieving the dominant good. All events in life serve the purpose to create and establish the greatest good. As such, there is only one best path to be taken. That path therefore cannot be altered as there is always only one best path during any one circumstance. Therefore whatever occurs within life is to the one best ability of life, and life's path cannot be altered. The less desired stages are not the result of life seeking less than the greatest good. But are the result of life's potential, which is limited and not unlimited. Life's living path has a single occurrence. Every living moment can only have a single expression to it. That is the one best expression. Any one life stage begins when the previous ends. Each stage has a beginning and an end. This is correct up to a point. All that is of life has to be understood in accordance with the reality of life. All that is of life has to be understood in accordance with life's ultimate being. Life is not dependent on any one factor but life only. Life occurs independent of time and space. As each life stage has a beginning and end, that beginning and end is independent of time and space. Each life stage has to be in such manner understood. Each life event has to be in such manner understood. Life's past, present, and future, has to be understood as being central to life's being. The beginning and end of each life phase has to be in such manner understood. As life's past, present, and future simultaneously occurring, being central to all life occurrence, being central to the beginning and end to each phase. In such way is life independent of all that is foreign to life. In such manner is life independent of time and space. In such manner does life live in life's own way. In the equal such way does the beginning and end to each stage have to be understood. As life is eternal, so is each life phase eternal. As life's beginning and end has to be understood in the context of eternity, so does the beginning and end to each life phase have to be understood in the context of eternity. Life lives in the manner that life considers as best. Life's laws serve life.

Life does not need any help in living. In attempting to understand life, all attention should be turned to life. Life should not be minimized but must be only understood. Life is the source of life's being. Life is the source of all. Life is the answer. Life is the origin. Life cannot not be a fact. Life cannot not exist. Life is not based on any other quality other than the good. The good is life's foundation. The good is life's objective. Life will never seek less than the good, but only that which is best. Life is binding and just. Justice must not be looked for anywhere else other than life. All that occurs does so within life. There is no extraneous force involved in life's existence. Any force that is involved in life's existence is a life force. That force belongs to life. Life is not inadequate. Life is thoroughly just. Life would never seek injustice. There is no greater justice to life's justice. Life understands all. Life is the creator of all. The fact of life belongs to life. The honor of life belongs to life.

The good is life's greatest characteristic. The good is responsible for all life creation. The good is dominant. The good can only be dominant. Such must also be the process to human society. The good should govern human society. The law of the good is the only legitimate law. All law which originates from a nongood source is not a legitimate law but is a tyranny in disguise as a law. The good can only be empowered. It is only based on the greatest human good that the greatest good in human society, in human affairs, will be realized. Philosophy is the greatest human good. By revealing the most about life, philosophy is a complete development. By philosophy's nature, philosophy attains the supreme answers. Philosophy attains the supreme understanding. Understanding of life can only be founded on the possession of good. In seeking and attaining the greatest knowledge, philosophy does so due to the possession of the most good. The good is then present in all issues of human concern. The human being is complete, addressing all issues. The most important issue is philosophy. Just as the supreme good is achieved based on philosophy, so is the supreme good achieved in all human issues. It cannot be that a varying level of good from the supreme good is possessed by philosophy. The same level of supreme good is the rule for philosophy's complete outlook. It is the greatest good that is humanity's objective. Philosophy achieves that good. Philosophy will address all issues in the same good manner. Philosophy exhibits that same level of supreme good in all issues of human concern. The greatest good in human society will only be established when philosophy is placed in deciding and political power. Philosophy must be king. Only then can the most human good be created. Philosophy proves its supremacy based on the fact that philosophy alone seeks to and understands life's ultimate being. Philosophy alone seeks to and understands the most pressing issues in life. Philosophy by achieving the greatest knowledge, philosophy by achieving the greatest good proves that the greatest good is possessed. That same level of good will manifest itself in all issues of involvement. As philosophy is the supreme human development, it isn't every single philosophy that is the dominant philosophy. It isn't just that philosophy is supreme, but that the dominant philosophies are in fact supreme. The history of philosophy, the greatness of philosophy is there to be examined. Humanity has from the earliest days engaged in philosophical thought in philosophical understanding.

The good can only be recognized as such by those of the similar nature by those of the similar good nature. The good will not be recognized as such by those lacking the good. The good will not be observed by all. Those who are opposed to the dominance of philosophy cannot be convinced otherwise. Philosophy may be challenged, but philosophy cannot be defeated. Philosophy's supremacy will be challenged by philosophical frauds who have done nothing in the world of philosophy, who don't know what philosophy is—the love of knowledge—but nonetheless regard themselves as genuine thinkers. No doubt the out-of-control ego is responsible for such a mentality. Being an intellectual fraud, the egomaniac resorts to deception in order to seek attention, in order to be glorified. Ignorance is central to such a mentality. The days of the fraud, the days of the beast will soon be over. It is best not to challenge the good. It is best not to challenge philosophy. Lest it be a personal wish to be exposed, lest it be a personal wish to be put in one's miserable place.

The great frauds of religion and science must come to the good. The frauds of religion and science can only observe the good. The supremacy of philosophy must be recognized. The good can only be sided with. The detractors of the good are those who claim the false as true. The human wish is to achieve the good. The human wish is to be guided by the good. As such, the cause of the good must be defended. The cause of the good must be struggled for. Such effort must be made. That effort must be made by the observers of the good. No one else is going to struggle for the cause of the good other than the good in society. The responsibility for the full representation of the good rests with the good in society. The defense of the good is inherent in the possession of the good. If the good is not struggled for, then the good is not possessed. The good has it within to defend the good's cause. It is only natural for the good to seek the destruction of all that is false. It is only natural for the good to seek the destruction of all that is evil. It is nemesis that must be destroyed. The undeveloped and evil nemesis has no place in world affairs. The undeveloped and evil nemesis has no place in the world of the good. It is the good that has all the right to seek power. It is in the world of ideas that nemesis has been defeated. That defeat will remain eternal.

The good in society possess the good. The good in society are motivated by the good. To possess the good is to seek to always engage the good. Being good is a complete personal quality. Being good is to engage in an attitude and behavior that is true and rightful in all respects of human involvement. It is to relate properly toward other people. Good relations between people is of primary concern. Such quality in the human being is of primary importance. The good involvement in human affairs can only be attained through knowledge and understanding. Knowledge and understanding of the considered issues. The good could never be sided with if the understanding of the subject matter were not possessed. Humanity is faced with developmental issues and the differing solutions to which. To endorse a view that is inequitable is to lack understanding, it is to lack the truth and the good in the matter. The good human relations is the objective. Understanding is the objective. The truth is the objective. To seek to pursue good interaction with others is knowledge of a truth. This truth can only be carried out in deed if knowledge of the best possible solutions to the developmental issues facing humanity is possessed. Good human interaction cannot occur if good human interaction is not the personal objective. Good human interaction cannot be the objective if the solutions presented are not the best possible. If good human relations were the objective, then the best possible effort at achieving the best possible solutions and answers to human issues would have been made. Such best effort would have achieved such best solutions. Since it is that the solutions presented are not the best, then the effort was lacking, the effort was not sincere. Therefore good human interaction was not the personal objective. If good human relations were the objective, then results would have been produced. If it is claimed that good relations is the personal objective, when the results produced do not serve that purpose, then the made claim is false claim. The objective of good relations requires that the good in others be recognized as such. The objective requires that the lack of good in others be recognized as such. By making the effort at good relations, such then is the result. The individual behaves in the good manner. Always siding with the good, never mistreating the good, never mistreating anyone. The best possible course of actions in the good human relations is the personal achievement of the good individual. For once being good, it is known that good human interaction is of the utmost concern. Error in the field would be strictly avoided, and only the good course of action would be always taken.

The human wish to understand life's laws, to live in the perfect society, and to live a peaceful life can only be carried out. The equal effort in each field must be made. Good human relations is the peaceful life lived. Knowledge of good human relations is central to the human. As such, the equal to the importance of the issue effort would be made. The knowledge attained here by any one individual is equal and the same as the knowledge attained by that same individual in all the varying branches of personal thought. To lack knowledge here is to lack knowledge to the same degree everywhere else in the personal thinking. For it is that knowledge of good relations is central. As result, an effort at knowledge would reveal this fact. If the effort is lacked here, it is lacked everywhere else. If the effort is genuine here, so then is the effort genuine in all aspects of personal knowledge. If an individual were knowledgeable, then knowledge in this most important field is an obvious requirement. No human knowledge is greater to that of knowledge of good human relations. All personal knowledge is equal to the personal knowledge of good relations. All personal knowledge is equal to the personal knowledge of the good.

The greater the level of personal good, the greater the level of personal development is. The good is in fact life. The greater the life within the self, the greater the knowledge of life is. To possess life is to know life. Knowledge of the good reveals life. The only criteria aimed at establishing human intellect is knowledge of the good. The intellect is the same as the understanding of the good. No test can be created to assess human intellect. Other than the test of knowledge of the good. Nor can possession, nor wealth, be used as indicators of intellect. The sole judging ground of intellect is the good. Such a task is not a human concern. The intelligence level of others is not one's own concern. It is the attainment of the good that is the objective, the personal objective. To speak of intellect other than in the possession of the good is to lack intellect. It is the good that is the test. It is life that is the test. The resulting creations, the resulting deeds through life will be the testament to the intelligence, to the possession of the good. The purpose of the human being is to attain the good, the purpose is to be productive in society. In such manner then all individuals contributing to society. The purpose is not the consideration of the intellect of others, the good of others. The individual is to be concerned with cultivating and increasing the personal level of good. The greater the good, the greater the intelligence. To have the good is to have superior knowledge.

Good human relations are critical to the creation of the good society. Arriving at the best solutions to the developmental issues facing humanity is likewise critical. The proposed solutions at achieving the good society, by the good, are equally so good. Their intent is to improve the living condition and must be considered as proper. Opposition to the good is inevitable. The greater the opposition, the greater the lack of good. Those lacking the good do not see themselves as lacking the good. Such is life. Life must be accepted. Life by having always accomplished the most good justifies the existence of all individuals. All are part of life, including the nongood. That fact does not hinder the search of the good by the good. The good is sought for the good's own sake. The good is sought for the self's own personal improvement. Whether the nongood exist has no bearing on the personal search for the good. The good is lived, not thought about being lived. As the good struggle for the cause of the good, all such and deserving credit is to be given to the good in society. The made effort will always be so remembered. The made genuine effort at the good will forever remain such, genuine and good. And if someone falls, that persona does not die. That good individual lives forever. All in life must be faced in the same good manner. In the same good manner bringing nemesis to justice. The foundation of the good society will be truth and justice. The foundation of the good society will be the ever greater search of the good. The complete empowering of the good and the complete suppression of the nongood. With the good society being guided by truth and justice, no error can be ever made. The motive being the ever greater good, no error can be made. The foundation of the good society will be empowered philosophy. It is only philosophy that can offer the best solutions to the developmental issues facing humanity. It is only under the guide of philosophy that peaceful human relations can be achieved. It is only philosophy that understands what good human relations are. Good human relations cannot be achieved within society not founded on the good, within a tyrannical society. The solutions offered at solving the issues facing society are important. If these solutions are not founded in good, then they will not serve in creating the good society. Under such a lacking the good state, such a tyrannical state, there cannot be peaceful human relations. The flaw is with the lack of good. By lacking the good, by not coming up with the best solutions, it is shown that the best solutions was not the intent. Philosophy is the greatest good. Philosophy will be central to the good society. Only then will the best solutions be come up with. And if there is discord, that does not take away from peaceful human relations. It is all the good could have done. The flaw is with the nongood. Peaceful human relations is the empowering of the good. Peaceful human relations is the peaceful existence of the good. The fact of discord does not take away from peaceful relations. Only philosophy can create the good society. All lacking efforts are such, lacking effort failures. By not engaging philosophy, by not engaging the good, it is proven that all nonphilosophical solutions are failures. It is only philosophy that understands what peaceful human relations are. It is only philosophy that can teach what peaceful, good human relations are. Within philosophy there is order and might. Within philosophy there is truth and justice. The question then becomes, what does society wish for philosophy? Whatever the answer may be, philosophy is here to stay. Once again proving the superiority. And if there is only one person aware of philosophy, that is an achievement for humanity, an achievement for the truth. Philosophy can but reveal philosophical content. The influence on society, on human thought, will be whatever it may happen to be. The influence will not be greater. The influence will not be lesser. The influence will not be nonexistent. By the fact that any one truth exists, by the fact that philosophical truth exists, it is proven that influence on society, on human thought, occurs. Not everyone in society can know every truth, not everyone in society will accept every truth. That does not mean that the truth does not exist. It does not mean that the truth is not the truth. It does not mean that the revealing of the truth occurs at the wrong moment in human history. The achievement of the truth is an act by humanity. By the fact that the truth is achieved, it is shown that the moment in human history was the right and appropriate moment. As result, any one truth has a range of influence which cannot but be real. From the moment of the achievement of the truth, society undergoes change. Upon the revealing of the truth, society undergoes further change, and from then on, society will no longer be the same. Society will never be the same to the range of the truth's influence. Philosophical truth being central to human thinking, such range of influence will be realized. Philosophy is a human interest. No one philosophical truth may be revealed by all humanity. For a few to arrive at philosophical truth is for all of humanity to arrive at that truth. It is for all of humanity to achieve that truth. The human wish is for philosophical truth. Humanity is one. To arrive at philosophical truth is not beyond humanity. As philosophical truth is achieved by few, philosophical truth can be achieved by many, the vast majority. There can be no great distinction between the few and the vast majority. Philosophical truth is always accepted. Philosophical truth is always accepted by the vast majority. If the truth is rejected by some, it is then not within philosophy's capabilities to make the truth acceptable to all. The rejection by the minority does not disprove philosophy. Rejection by the minority does not prove that the vast majority is not in agreement with the truth. And so, in such manner, can the good society be built. It is the human task to study philosophy, to engage in philosophy, to empower philosophy. It is the greatest good that is desired. It is the truth that is desired. It cannot be that the human wish is for the false. The false belittles humanity. The false has no part in the human reasoning ability. The false must be recognized as such and discarded. The false is of no value. It cannot serve the purpose of enlightening humanity. The false carries with it its own refutation. The refutation is inherent in the false. That is why it is the false. The false then must be struggled against. Doing so, exposing the inherent refutation, the false will in due time collapse in the eyes of many. The reason for that is the improper foundation in thought. Unlike the false, the truth brings eternal proof. The false can never stand against the truth. The human wish is for the truth. If the false could legitimately attract humanity, it would attain the identity of the truth since it is that only the truth is of value to humanity. To seek to attract humanity to a proposed theory is to state the truth in the matter. The proof that rests with the establishing of the truth of all issues based on reason is sufficient and is the foundation of life. Any appeal to proof, of any theory, can only be based on reason. To seek to disprove a truth is to turn to flawed reason. To seek to prove a truth is to turn to reason. Reason arrives at truth. Reason is sufficient to do so. No further proof is needed. Those who are guided by the truth, those who possess the good need no further confirmation of this fact. The foundation of the good society will be truth, reason, and knowledge. All human ideas will be revealed. The source of all human ideas is and has been humanity. It is humanity that states all human ideas. Their worth is decided by the level of good. No human idea has originated from a nonhuman source. No human idea can claim truth due to it originating from a nonhuman source. Philosophy is the supreme knowledge. Philosophy is based on human reasoning. Philosophy does not originate from any source but the human source. Therefore no truth can claim to be nonhuman or superior to human. And if a claim is made that any one human idea has originated from a nonhuman and superior to human source, and as result finding proof due to its superior nature, proof of the held view as correct due to that view having originated from a superior to human source, is a false claim. Any such claim is not a philosophical claim; it is not based on reason. To claim truth due to an idea's superior to human origin is to reveal that the effort at reaching the truth of the considered idea has been abandoned. It is to reveal that no effort at the truth of the matter has been made. As such, further analysis of the false claim will reveal the true and sinister reasons for the made false claim. Such a false idea has no appeal. The good society will not be attracted to such false idea but only repulsed. The false is of no value. The false does not serve the purpose of enlightening humanity.

That which is good for the self, that which is good for life cannot be unrecognizable. No error as to the content of the good can be made. Life is the sole judge of that content. Since it is that life's governing laws are most just, life's judgment into the content of the good is equally as just. It is life that decides upon the content of the good. Life could never mistake the good. Life will never develop in a manner that strays from the good. The lesser good type of existence of life is known to be such. Life strives toward the greater good. Living the range of life, the lesser good is also experienced. The lesser

THE GOOD, LIFE BEING

gives the equal to itself level of satisfaction. When living through the lesser good, life strives for the greater. The good belongs to life. Life struggles for the good and is successful in the effort. Making life aware of the good. By struggling for the good, it is life that creates the good. Every life act is with the intent of establishing and living the good existence. Based upon this characteristic, life creates and decides upon the content of the good. All levels of created good are recognized for exactly what they are. The less than desired will inevitably be experienced. That is a phase of life. That phase cannot be taken out of life's being. Nor is there such a necessity. In attaining the greatest good, the less desired is very much needed. During that phase is when the greater good is formed. It is upon the work of the less than desired, by seeking to improve, that the greater good is created. The justice to the less desired state of good is that life continuously seeks the good. The good cannot be achieved without an effort. The effort is made during the lesser good state. It is the lesser that makes the greater possible. If the lesser part of life were to be inexperienced, then the search for the greater would be pointless and without aim. Life's purpose in living, of searching for the greater good, would be lost. Life must be understood. Life must be accepted. The struggle in life must not be sought to avoided. But must be looked forward to. It is the struggle that creates the good. It is the struggle that creates all. It is not the struggle that is destructive to life but lack of struggle. The greatest creation of all is the creation of the good. As the struggle is needed to achieve the good, that also is the case everywhere else. To avoid the struggle, to lack struggle is to be noncreative. By living, life accomplishes all. Overcoming all situations and creating the good and the greatest good. Life is limited, and only the possible control over the self can be exhibited. Seeming to indicate to some that life therefore has no control over the self. Life in fact becoming unconscious to all life acts, life being unconscious of the self. That life's limited power presents life that is without any say in the living occurrence. Making life a prisoner of the self, life being alienated from the self. Life in fact not being the initiator of all life acts, life in fact being lifeless. The reverse is the truth. Life may not be able to control all situations to the unrealistic and unlimited extent, but all that is involved in life's being is life. Through living any situation, through living any condition, life is such situation; life is such condition. Life contains all. Life experiences all. Life experiences the self. As result, life is not minimized. Life lives fully. Life is not unaware of any single life act. All life acts belong to life. All life acts originate from a life need. Life initiates all acts. Life seeks that which is best. Life is not foreign to the self. The truth of life cannot minimize the reality of life. It is unreality that minimizes life. It is life that lives the self. No greater control of the self is necessary. Life is real. Life achieves full being. Life has a mission to live and achieve life's objectives. Life does not wish not to live. The wish to live is the most fundamental life characteristic. Life would never have a need not to live but only a need to achieve greater and the greatest life. Life self-creates, the choice for the self is complete. It is through life that the unreal and the false are brought to an end. With life's existence, all attention is turned to life. Every issue of truth is concerned with the reality of life. Every issue of truth is concerned with life's being. Life brings order and reality. Life brings understanding of all. Understanding of all that is life. Life's objective is to achieve full being. Life's objective is the dominant good. By achieving full being, by achieving the dominant good, life lives the dominant good. Life is the dominant good. Life is the full being. For life to achieve full being is for life to achieve full understanding. For life to know all is for life to know the self completely. Life achieves eternity. The idea that life is lacking is then incorrect. It is ill-thought-out.

Life triumphs by living. Life is in possession of the self. Life is without flaw. This is proven based on the fact that life lacks nothing. This is proven based on the fact that life achieves all. Life's justice is life's. Life's justice is that life continuously seeks the good. As result, achieving the greatest good. Life is a fact. Life is complete. The reality of life is lived. The complete range of life is lived. Less than life's being is never lived. By flowing from stage to stage, greater development ensues. That development is naturally occurring. The past phase successfully leads into the next. Thereby successfully undergoing the change. The past stage leads into the without error following stage, with no discord remaining between the two. The character of the past is agreeably resolved into that of the future, without the change being unfulfilling in any manner as result of the insufficient state of the previous. During the lesser state, during the state which seeks the greater, life is supposed to be of that same lesser nature. The lesser nature takes nothing away from the greater. The lesser nature takes nothing away from life. The greater will in due course be fully lived. Life agreeably flows from stage to stage. By living, life exhibits life's being. Within which life consists of numerous life members. Each is a member of life, and all contribute to make the one life. Each experiencing life through the self, in turn, life experiencing each through the self. No life member wishes to be different from the self. No life member wishes to reject the self, but only improve the self. In life's self-creation, each life member has a say as to the personal as well to the creation of the greater and greatest good. Life strives to do that which is proper and just. Where all the various life members are granted the highest level of personal growth, the highest level of living condition. To that cause, every member contributes, as it is that every member is involved in the decision of what the highest personal living condition is. Life's reasoning and laws do not exclude the contribution of any one single life member.

As each life member chooses and creates the self, the identity of life is fully shaped. Which is to an extent founded upon the creation of the single life member. Life is not restrictive or unjust, disallowing personal freedom. It is not a fact that life creates all within the self without the single member having a say in the matter, without having a say in the living condition. Life serves life. Life serves all within life. Each life member, by choosing the self, by creating the self, it is shown that life is not unjust. The greatest wish in life is granted by the possession of the self. It only follows that each life member has a say in the personal development. Humanity is the product of life. Humanity is the product of self-creation. The middle ground is necessarily found. Where life is served, where the individual self is served. The middle ground is that where during any one life stage, the wishes and needs of the individual self are satisfied to the highest extent possible. Life's laws cannot be broken. Life's laws cannot be exceeded. Life is the result of creation, yet life is the result of self-creation. By seeking the middle ground, the middle ground is found. The reality of life is found. By seeking that which is best, life seeks that which is best for life. Life seeks that which is best for each life member. Each life member is as life is, created yet self-created. As life's laws cannot be exceeded, self-creation cannot be exceeded. Yet self-creation is complete. Self-creation is completely fulfilling. No life member wishes to be another. Each life member is represented by the single self. No life member can be duplicated. There is only one self. Therefore the single self cannot be duplicated. By choosing the self, it is ensured that each self cannot be chosen on more than one occasion. Every life member differs. It is according to the differing personality that each individual behaves. Every individual follows through with behavior, which is considered as justified. As such, each individual bears responsibility for all personal behavior. Each individual is responsible for the self. The differing personalities have different objectives. To seek the lesser objective is not to wish to take part in the higher. It is not to seek the good in any one matter. It is to seek to undermine and as best possible suppress the view of the higher. There is inevitable opposition between the two sides. The greater development searches for the truth, for the greater personal and human existence. The greater, the good has the good as the objective in life. The good can only be sought to be revealed. The objective of the good can only be stated. The leadership of the stated good must be realized. The greater power that the good accumulates, the better. The good can only triumph over the lesser. The good can never be defeated. The good is the sole representation of the truth. The truth always prevails over that which is false. The good always triumphs over nemesis. It is always proven that the false is the weaker. It is proven that the false is always defeated, for the only source of strength is the truth. The only source of strength is the good. Making the good invincible, it is the good that rules life. The false can never legitimately challenge the truth. The good prevails each and every time the good's authority is questioned. The good among humanity cannot be denied in existing. Upon being stated, the human good, upon being revealed, becomes the standard. The human good becomes law. The good will leave the good's own inextinguishable mark upon human society, upon human history. All ideas are of mental substance. All ideas are thought. The validity of which can only be determined on the same mental basis. The strength of a theory is judged upon its own merits. Such is the only assessment possible. That assessment is in fact binding. Life is founded upon the good. Life is governed by the good. The good has precedence. It would be senseless to consider the lesser as superior to the greater, as superior to the good. That is in fact what would be done if it were thought that the good suffers defeat from the lesser. There is the truth and the false in life. There is the good and the non-good. There is no lawful source that would consider the false as the truth. The only such lawful source is life and life's supreme justice. Life would never err in judgment. The truth is considered as truth by life. Life considers the truth as superior to the false. If not, life would be based on the false. The truth is as result life's basis. The truth is as result invincible. The human good, the human truth, is invincible.

And so it is that the truth is always the truth. The human truth cannot be overturned. Upon the revealing, upon the stating of the truth, the fall of the false is as result imminent. The starting point in the destruction of the false is the world of ideas. That cannot but be done. If the false has followers, if the nongood is endorsed by some, then those individuals will be viewed as being responsible for the self. Those individuals, by endorsing the false, by siding with the nongood, oppose the good. All opposition to the good can only arise from feelings of animosity toward the good. As those feelings increase, so does the opposition increase. Though such feelings are a fact, they are misguided and do not serve the purpose of the good. The good must be sided with. The ever-present human wish has been the understanding of the good. The ever-present human wish has been the possession of the good. It is the human wish and desire to engage in good behavior. With the revealing of the good, this is possible for all to do. Attachment to the false is detrimental to the human being. The false is such due to detrimental reasons. The false takes away from human growth, human maturity, human under-standing of life. The false can only be wished to be rejected by all. All answers are with the good. It is the knowing, it is the understanding human being that is desired. It is only the grown and mature human being that can lead to the creation of the good society. It is only the grown and mature human being that can lead a peaceful existence. Attachment to the false leads to opposition of the good, to whatever extent that may be. The human good cannot be overturned. The lack of good is the result of animosity toward the good. To possess the good is to seek the good. To possess the good is to love the good. To love the good is to be repelled by the nongood. If there were no such repulsion, then it is the false, the nongood, that would be sided with. By attaining the good, it is the equally such good behavior that will be engaged in. The justice of the good is equally so just, and as the good individual makes an assessment of another, it is the same level of justice that will make that assessment. It is the justice of the good that must be humanity's guide. In the same good and just manner evaluating all issues, all events, all circumstances.

The life led by the good individual is one of justice. The good individual is guided by knowledge and understanding. The engaged in life good individual is the attempt at creation of the greatest good by that good individual. The objective of the good individual is the establishment of the greatest good. The life led by the nongood, the objective of the nongood, is counter to that of the good. The life led is in direct opposition to the good. The objective of the nongood is to thwart the good, to suppress the good, to empower the nongood and lack of justice. The objective is tyranny, the objective is the desired suffering of the good. For that cause, the claim to goodness is made. The guiding purpose of the tyrant is not the good. The good is not understood. The good is not possessed. The claim to the good is an empty claim. It has no substance. The lack of good is due to deficiency in character. As the character is deficient in the possession of the good, so is the character deficient in the claim of representing the good. As the tyrant sees nothing wrong with the lack of good, so does the tyrant see nothing wrong in claiming to represent the good. The tyrant is involved in the deception of oneself as well as others. The purpose of the nongood is to promote the cause of the nongood. The purpose is to harm the good. This is never so stated by the nongood. It can't be so stated, for the nongood sees nothing wrong with being nongood. With the greater effort at attaining the nongood within one's personality comes the automatic destruction of the good, within one's personality. The greater the personal destruction of the good, the greater the desire for the destruction of the good. Just as the good is destroyed within, so is the good sought to be destroyed throughout. This is the objective of the nongood. If the claim to the contrary is made, that the peaceful coexistence with the good is desired, that claim then can only be made as an intended deception with the purpose of weakening the defense of the good. If an attack upon the good, at any one time, is not carried out, it is due to the fact that the power is not seen as sufficient to challenge the good. At the opportune moment, when its strength is at the optimum level, the total destruction of its mortal enemy, the good, will be engaged in. Just as this is so, it is also true for the good. The purpose of the good is to create the good and just society. The purpose of the good is to bring all those who lack the good, all those who engage in the harming of the good, to justice. Only those of the equal to the good character may take part in the good and defend the cause of the good. Opposition to the good is inevitable. Only those who oppose the good themselves lack the good.

If the good is opposed, then so it must be. The opposition does not refute the good. With the creation of the good society, the intent of the good is for all to work together. The purpose of the good society is to create the greatest social good, the purpose is to create the greatest social justice. To that end, each individual must contribute in one's own particular way. The search of the good can only be the objective of every single one. Being guided by the good, each individual will then behave according to that same level of good. In the process, contributing in one's own particular way toward the creation of the good society. The good individual has the mission to seek the good, to observe the good, to understand the good, to love the good. For it is known that the greatest prize in life is the good. All other objectives in life are secondary to the possession of the good. Humanity has existed long enough to know that the good rules all. And so it will be within the good society. Each individual will work toward one's own improvement, toward society's improvement. The good individual will always take that course of interaction with others which will be the most well-thought-out and the best possible under all circumstances. Always taking into account the good, the issue in consideration, and the person that is interacted with. The good individual will not search for disagreement but for common ground. If disagreement should ever arise, the good individual will have the ability to see past the encountered disagreement and will work toward the need for human cooperation in the cause of creating the good society. The individual can only behave and achieve that of the personal self. One human being does not include the capabilities of all others but only the personal capabilities. It takes the combined effort by all good individuals to create the good society. Each contributing in one's own particular way. The personal knowledge, the personal ability, belongs solely to that particular individual. As such, the good individual will have freedom to pursue the personal ability, to pursue the personal initiative and drive. As result, exhibiting the good personality, growing and enriching the good society. Being guided by the good, the good individual will always behave in the same level of possessed good. The core of the good society will be the good. All within the good society will be judged according to the good. The criteria will be the good. The core of the good society will be the good individual. Those who lack the good, those who are opposed to the good will take no part in the good society. In order to create the good society, only those of the equal good character will be allowed to take part. Those who are contrary to the good can never help in the building of the positive state but can only work toward the destruction of the good society. Such people don't have the good at heart. They are not guided by the purpose of the good. The good can only be respected. To oppose the good, to lack the good, is to be flawed in the greatest manner possible. To lack the good is to choose nemesis. It is to seek the suffering of the good. And if the good is not clearly known, then the good should be sided with once the good is made known. It is not required that everyone in possession of the good be identical to all other good individuals. The good society will include all the various levels of human good. By differing, the pursuits in life will likewise differ, being similar to the sufficient extent in the pursuit of the good. The good allows for diversity. Based upon that diversity, the positive state can be successfully built. Each good individual contributing to which in one's own particular way, in one's own particular field of skill. The common bond being the good. It is not required for all members of the good society to be primarily, and restrictively so, engaged in the field of philosophy. Philosophy is there for everyone to engage in. Philosophy is central to human thought. Philosophy is central to human development. The good society can only be built by enlightened people. Not all people can be involved in the highest aspects of philosophy. What is going to be required of the good individual is to pursue life, pursue the good, in the serious and sincere manner, humble, understanding, and mature manner. Such effort will only have beneficial results. Results which will lead to the observance of the good. Results which will lead to the rejection of the nongood and the siding with the good. The good being of central importance is of central importance to humanity. To think differently from this manner is to reveal that the good is lacked. The judge as to the possession of the good will be the good society. The creation of the good society rests upon philosophy's assumption of political power. The good has no need to misjudge anyone. The need of the good is to create justice. The good individual will have complete freedom.

As philosophy is the supreme human knowledge, science is not. As philosophy engages in the effort to understand the reality of life, science does not. It is only philosophy that engages in the effort to understand life's most fundamental being. Science does not have the objective to understand the reality of life. Science does not have the objective of the supreme human knowledge. As result, science cannot claim to have the supreme human knowledge as its objective. Science cannot claim to have the reality of life as its objective. The great intellect the scientist is not. For if that were the case, philosophy would have been engaged in. Not being able to claim that the reality of life is its objective, science does just that, however. According to science, science is the one with the answers. This claim is made due to the limited and blind scope of science. Science was never in search for the reality of life. If science were, science would have come up with the answer to the reality of life. The reality of life is beyond science.

The reality of life is not beyond philosophy. The scientist should not brag so much. Science will always be far inferior to philosophy. So as it is, science is a fraud. The answers that science comes up with are either simple or misleading, seeming to make sense in the world of science but not making sense in the reality of life. The bragging nonintellectual has to be exposed. The one to expose science is philosophy. It is in comparison with philosophy that the inherent flaws of the scientist become noticeable. In the good society, the scientist will always have a place. The contribution of the scientist will always be very much needed. What is in question is the ability of science, what is in question is the content of science. It is not possible for science to understand the reality of life. Any such scientific theory would have to include the life members, including humanity. If any one such theory does not include life members, then that theory is not a theory of the reality of life. No theory of the reality of life can exclude the understanding of life. Having to include the life members, the understanding of the entity of the life members would have to be scientifically carried out. It is a task which science cannot accomplish. Any one life member can only be represented by the number one. There can only be one self. That number one is not just any number one. That number one captures the complete essence of that life member. That number one captures the complete being of the life member. That number one has the spirit of that life member. No other such number one can be equated with the personal number one. The only way that number can be equated to another is if the spirit of the number is removed and is then proceeded to be thought that such number is without spirit. The equating therefore would be made of a without spirit life member. The understanding of a life number being without spirit is not an understanding. It is not an understanding of life. As the personal number one cannot be equated with any other, so it is that the personal number one cannot be quantified. Even if all were identical to another, the personal number one remains distinct. There is one self, making all others different. The one self captures the complete essence of the one self. As that is done, it is made sure that there is no other self. All from then on is different, even from a seemingly identical life member. No life member can be equated to another. No life member can be quantified. Any scientific theory of the reality of life would be making an analysis of without spirit life. The analysis would be of lifeless life.

The inclusion of the complete self makes all the difference. As no life members can be equated, it also is that no life unit can be equated to another. Any scientific theory would deal with life, with life units. No life unit can be equated to another, even if the life units were of the same quality and of the same quantity. The key to life is difference, not equality. As each life unit is distinct from another, each life unit is distinct from all others. As science equates, science runs into mistakes. All scientific theories are incorrect. The formula of the same quality and quantity, two plus two equaling four, is incorrect. The only way that conclusion can be made is if the reality of life is abandoned and a false reality is created. The only way that conclusion can be made is if the inherent difference to all from within life is not understood, and the difference is overlooked. It is life that is attempted to be understood. The connection should as result be with life, not lifeless life. The reason scientific theories seem to be correct is because they are scientifically tested, and science is not the answer. Science does not have it within to test itself. The test should be carried out with the reality of life. In which case, all scientific theories would be exposed as being mistaken. Science approximates. Science creates lifeless life. Science creates life without spirit. Science does not relate to life. Science relates to itself. The reason two plus two does not equal four is due to the content of each life unit. The content which science cannot measure, the content which science does not wish to measure. Energy is not equal to mass. It is that energy is equal to content. A life without spirit is just fine with science.

Each individual is one's own content. Each individual is one's own spirit. Each individual produces one's own content, differing from all others. It is the content that produces the search of the good. It is the self that produces the energy to pursue the good. The good is the greatest prize. The good requires the greatest energy. As result, energy is equal to content. Energy is not equal to mass. With science being deeply flawed, the scientist also is so flawed. The scientist is guilty of excessive self-praise. The scientist does not understand the limitations of science. The scientist does not understand that the reality of life is not the objective of science. The scientist is trapped within a world of inferiority to philosophy. The scientist does not know one's own place. Failing in all respects of being serious, sincere, humble, understanding, and mature. If the scientist wishes to be a braggart, then the scientist must be prepared to be crushed each and every time. The reality of life was never the objective of science. It can only be that science accepts the power of philosophy, power which science never had and never will have.

The question of whether numbers are real therefore arises. Numbers are real as long as the content of the number is included. The content which is equal to the self, content which is equal to the self's own content and such number and not any one lifeless number. There is one self. Within that number one, the content of the self is included. The spirit of each number can only be included. The one life contains all of life. The one life contains infinity. Such numbers help in the understanding of life. The real numbers help in life's living occurrence. For it is that life is one and not any more. The one life containing all and not any less and not any more. To remove the spirit of the number is fatal to understanding the reality of life. It is to then deal with aspects of life but not the reality of life. As the reality of life is wished to be understood, real numbers help in the effort. The key is the content of the number. The key is the soul of the number. The key is the soul of the self.

The human objective is to seek the good. The human objective is to engage in good behavior. The equivalent to the desired good is at all times achieved. The truth of any one topic is central to the achieving of the good. It is the truth that humanity seeks. The truth elevates the human being. To grasp the truth is to base the self upon the truth of life. The truth is the foundation of life. The only way to progress in life is by understanding life and basing the self upon the truth of life. If life were understood, then the greatest possible good will have been accomplished. Life's truth is not searched for by everyone. Not searching for the truth, less than the truth is found. The failure in the proper search for the good is the result of lacking the necessary character. The whole personality then suffers. To question the truth, to oppose the truth is not to make any change in the truth. To oppose the truth is to do so at self's own expense. It is to irreversibly reveal the lacking character. The truth cannot fail. The truth may be challenged but cannot be defeated. The defeat is of the self. As the lesser human good exists, so does the greater human good exist. Life's living path cannot be avoided. Within the path of life, all that is of life has been included. The existence of the lesser and greater good cannot be avoided but must in fact exist. If it is thought that life by mere chance could possibly lose and not have the input of the greater good, then the same thought pattern could be used in respect with the lesser good. That possibly by chance life could lack the input, could lack the existence of the lesser good. Life's path is that which life's path is. Life's path cannot be questioned. Life's path cannot be altered. In the struggle by life to attain all, life has done all possible to attain all. Life is successful in the struggle. Life's objective being the good. Life achieves the good to the life extent. Life's path cannot be devoid of good. Life's path cannot be devoid of the good human being. It cannot be thought that if the good in life were nonexistent, life would not have had the input, the achievement, by the good. The good human being cannot be denied in existing. Life's existence cannot be denied. Human history will unfold in the human way, achieving all in the process, achieving all human creation. Life's path is not insufficient. Life is not insufficient.

With life struggling and achieving all, life attains full being. Life's power and ability are equal to the task of full being. Life's power and ability are equal to being victorious over nonlife. Life achieves supreme justice. Life is the authority. There is no power greater to life. All attention should be turned to life. Life is to be respected. Life is to be understood. Life springs from the truth of life's being. The truth of life's being can have no reservation. Life's being does not limit life. Life's being frees life to achieve all. The good being life's basis, all that life does is guided by the greater attainment of good. Life's need for the good leads to the empowering of the good. To speak of God's attributes, to speak of God, is to speak of life's attributes. It is to speak of life. God is not lost in life's existence. If it is thought that God, in order to be God, must be unlimited, then the answer to that is that God does not have to be unlimited to be God. The issue of central importance is the essence of God. The essence of God is goodness. The essence of God is being victorious in the achievement of all. The essence of God is understanding all. The essence of God is being self-creating. The essence of God is being the Just Authority. These attributes are life's. Life does not have unlimited power, but life has limited yet unlimited power. If it is thought that life is of inferior nature to the unlimited God, then a great mistake would be made. It is the truth that is of concern. The truth of life's being can have no reservations. The truth can only be superior, not inferior. Life, God, that is unlimited is not real. The unlimited life is not worth living. Achieving all without an effort. The life of unlimited God would not be worth living, achieving all without an effort. It is the struggle that creates all. It is the struggle that makes life worth living. If the struggle is taken out, life becomes lifeless. The inferior life is the false life. If it is thought that life does not have such of God attributes, then another great mistake would be made. Life in that case would not be understood. Life would not have been sufficiently understood. If it is wondered where life's attributes, where God can be found, the answer is in the world of ideas. As God cannot be refuted, God is a fact. As life cannot be denied, God is a fact.

Life's attributes can be questioned, but life's attributes cannot be overturned. To conclude that God does not exist is to conclude that life does not exist. It is to conclude that life's attributes do not exist. The highest representation of life's being cannot be denied. Therefore God cannot be denied. To conclude that God is a fact is as result an act of good. It is the truth of any one topic that is of concern, to achieve the truth can only be good. To achieve the truth is to then act in accordance with the truth. It is to produce behavior that is better than not having achieved the truth. The individual who does not understand the truth is flawed, that individual is lacking. That individual does not have the character to arrive at the truth. In the process, claiming truth where there is none, endorsing that which false as true. That which is false is wished to be true. Life's being is rejected. The human objective in life is to be enlightened. The objective is to be the most developed. The objective is to be the most full-grown human being possible. To attach oneself to the false is to fail in the human objective. The truth of any one issue can only be beneficial. The topic of God is not so complicated to understand. To understand to an extent where the meaning of God remains foreign to those who seek the truth of the issue. The meaning of God is not foreign to those who seek the truth. The meaning of God is not foreign to those who seek the good. The meaning of God is only foreign to those who make no effort at understanding the issue. The original understanding of the topic can only be revealed to philosophy. However, understanding of life, understanding of God, rests with the understanding of the good. As the effort is genuine and sincere at life, at the good, such genuine and sincere answer will follow. The human being can only be a good human being. This is the first and only step in understanding God. The issue of importance is the possession of the good. The issue of importance is the need for the good. Without the personal possession of the good, God, life could never be understood. Nor is all professed attachment to the idea of God genuine and sincere. Not all professed attachment to the idea of God is an attachment to God. It is not an understanding of God.

The reality of life, the truth of life can only be revealed to philosophy. It is philosophy that makes the effort at ultimate reality. It is only philosophy that understands life's being. It is only philosophy that can reveal life's being. It is only philosophy that can reveal God. Science can't do it. Religion can't do it. The definition of religion being lack of philosophical thought. As philosophy is engaged, with the sufficient effort, life's eternal laws can be understood. Those laws are then stated. If philosophy cannot state life's laws, then no human-discovered law can be stated. No such human law can be revealed by any branch of human thought. Philosophy has made the effort. Philosophy is supreme. No human idea has originated from a nonhuman source. Every human idea is human. This is evidenced by the fact that philosophy is supreme, and every philosophical idea is such, philosophical and human. Relying on human reasoning, wanting to understand life's being, philosophy respects life. Philosophy respects the reality of life. Philosophy is engaged in because knowledge is loved. Religion makes no philosophical effort. Religion has no philosophical ability. Religion has no love for knowledge. Religion cannot understand life. Religion cannot respect life. Religion cannot understand God. Religion cannot love God. Religion's professed God of worship is not God. The God that is referred to in religion is God in name only, lacking all the attributes of God. It is not religion's effort to achieve any life law, but that is exactly what religion claims to reveal, life laws, life's being, God. The claim to revealing God is made. Religion has nothing to do with life's being. Religion cannot reveal life's being. Religion has nothing to do with God. Religion cannot reveal God. Not only does religion claim to reveal God, religion is constantly speaking for God. Religion is often quoting God. Religion's empty rhetoric of God worship does not mean that God is in fact worshiped. God is not worshiped. The one that is being worshiped is the individual self. The one that is being worshiped is religion. The religious follower is guilty of exaggerated self-praise. It is only based on exaggerated self-praise, only based on personal failings that the claim to speak for God, the claim to reveal God, can be made. It is the personal failings of the religious follower that make it possible to speak of issues for which the religious follower has no respect. Based on those failings, the vision of life is then completed, attributing life, attributing God, with those same personal failings. Consequently, the exaggerated self-praise. Consequently, the worshiping of the self. Religion's object of worship is not God, though religion makes the opposite claim.

Not loving knowledge, not loving God, the religious follower is not prevented from speaking of central life issues. Being conceited and arrogant makes that possible. By speaking for God, by quoting God, the religious follower resorts to conceit and arrogance. Ignorance is key to religion's disrespectful claims. The claims that religion makes originate from conceit, arrogance, and ignorance. The made claims are then associated with God, thereby presenting God with those same attributes, of conceit, arrogance, and ignorance. The professed respect and love for God is not respect and love; it is the reverse. God is disrespected and hated. If God were respected and loved, then God would not be spoken for by those who have done nothing in the world of knowledge. If God were respected and loved,

God would not be attributed with the qualities of conceit, arrogance, and ignorance. The only way God could be worshipped by religion is if God were conceited, arrogant, and ignorant. It is religion that asked for the analysis. These are the results. These are the facts.

Not recognizing the personal failings as such is the religious follower's problem. Not recognizing conceit, not recognizing arrogance as such is religion's problem. The not understanding of either love or hate is religion's problem. And love and hate are not understood, for it is that the central religious claim is that God is loved, loved above all, when it is that God is hated. What religion worships is a cheap imitation of God. What religion worships is a caricature of God. Proving that God is hated. Certainly lack of shame is pivotal to religion's disrespectful attitude. Religion has made no attempt at knowledge. Religion cannot reveal knowledge. Religion cannot reveal life. Religion cannot reveal God. Claiming to do just that, religion exposes religion's personal failings. Religion's professed great love is a false claim. If religion were so loving, then religion would love knowledge first and foremost. If religion were so loving, then religion would love the effort. Religion would love philosophy. Religion would love God. But it is that religion has no love for philosophy. Religion has no love for God. The days of the Beast will soon be over. Humanity has been deceived long enough.

Religion is always talking about right and wrong, how the human being should be righteous and good. But the most detrimental human characteristics are not regarded as such. Having no love for knowledge, religion turns to shameless, disrespectful, fairy tales, and fantasies. Fairy tales and fantasies which are passed off as fact. If life were wished to be understood, such effort would have been made. No effort at understanding life was made. Being figurative has no place in understanding life. To disguise the personal failings, religion turns to deceit. Whenever the failings of religion are about to become clear, religion turns to deceit. Religion is made bigger than reality. Religion attempts to overwhelm and disarm. Telling tales of how peaceful and loving religion is. As religion is not loving, religion is not peaceful. If religion were peaceful, then the first thing that religion would do is love knowledge. The first thing that religion would do is love God. The personal failings would be recognized as such and abandoned. As the good is not loved, as the good is not wished for, religion lacks the peaceful character toward the good. Religion lacks the peaceful character toward knowledge. Religion has the peaceful attitude toward the personal failings. Religion does not have the peaceful attitude toward the lack of personal good. The lie is the constant in religion. The claim to religious miracles is made. No miracle in the name of religion has ever occurred. If religion could perform miracles, then the first miracle that religion would perform is to abandon religion's way of being shameless. The first miracle that religion would perform is to abandon the lack of effort, becoming grown and mature in the process. No such miracle has taken place. Religion is not capable of performing miracles. Religion is more blasphemous than the miserable atheist. The good accepts all those who accept the good. The way of the good is the way forward for humanity.

The recognizing of religion's own flaws is the task of religion to accomplish. The greater effort must be made by all. That greater effort leads to philosophy. With philosophy showing the existence of God, the human status is increased. Humanity is in such way enlightened. The limit to being human is at all times maintained. The human effect on life is human, not affecting life to more than the human extent. Throughout it all, the human objective is the good. The fact of God's existence does not change the human objective. The good has always been the human objective and always will be. To have sought less than the good, to have been less than good was always done at the expense of the self. To seek to be less than good is done at the expense of the self. It is the human wish to be the greatest possible human being, and the way to the greatest human being is the way of the good. At no time in history any one individual denied the wish for the good. That will always continue to be so. The fact of the human knowledge of God's existence only increases the human wish for the good, to whatever extent that may be. It is better to be enlightened than not. It is better to know truth than to not know truth. The truth brings with the truth enlightenment. It is better to conclude that God is a fact than not to do so. It is better to understand the reality of life than not do so. To understand God's fact, to understand the reality of life is to understand God's, life's, justice. It is to know rather than not know. And so as knowledge is the human task, it is better to have achieved knowledge. As result, the grown and mature human being is realized. If the proof of God's existence is beyond any one individual that doesn't prevent that individual from observing the good. What has to be done by the human being is to analyze the issue in a fair way. The good must be searched for. Knowledge must be searched for, philosophy respected. The insidious way of the false must be recognized. The false must be rejected. Fairy tales and fantasies are then recognized as such. The human being must be serious, sincere, understanding, humble, and mature. As the human being is such, the way of the good will be observed. God's existence has always been a fact. God's existence completes life. The height of life's laws are exemplified by the fact of God. As life is fact, as life's supreme authority and justice is fact, so is God fact. As God's supreme justice and authority is fact, so is God fact.

The human presence in life is an integral part of life. Life is completely fulfilling. All that is of life completes life. All that is of life has a reason for existing. Humanity has a reason for existing. Humanity completes life. Engaging in the search of the good, the human being must engage in the search of the good and not engage in telling tales of how intelligent humanity is, in view of the fact that it is philosophy that completes the human being, in view of the fact that philosophy is the supreme human intellect. Completing life, humanity has developed in the human way. At all times achieving the possible. At all times living to the full. Each moment in human history has been completely fulfilling. The human being has always attempted to create the most favorable living condition, even if that condition were the rejection of the present. The rejection of the present can only be carried out based on the need for the achievement of the favorable condition, regarded as such and guiding one's vision of life. That present need for the rejection of the present is the need for the creation of the favorable, regarded as favorable and guiding one's vision of life, including the rejection of the present. The present is always lived to the full potential. It is based on the realization of the full present potential that any decision is made, including the decision that there is better life awaiting any one individual in the future. If humanity is guided by the idea that better life awaits humanity during the stage of dominant good, humanity still lives the present to the full. Each phase of life is equally to that phase important and is equally so lived. The present stage can only be fully engaged. in. Observing the good, stating the good, and struggling for the good. It is the human duty to establish the good. It is the human duty to understand life's laws. It is the human duty to create the most just and peaceful society. It can only be that the good society is attempted to be created. It is only philosophy that can create the good society. Anyone who opposes the good society is an enemy of the good. As the human presence in life is and has been unavoidable, so has the human historical development been unavoidable. Human history is there to be observed. The human potential has been equally so expressed. The human potential can only include the work of philosophy. As humanity matures, the way forward is the way of the good. The way of the good as so stated by philosophy. The good has as the good's mission to struggle against and defeat any one view opposed to the good. It is only the good that is the good's safeguard. The good has rivals, but the defeat of each one is imminent. Life is governed by the supreme good. Any one other level of good is viewed and recognized as such. It is the supreme good that life governs by. The lesser therefore maintains the rank of the lesser, never surpassing the greater in value and importance. The greater good can never be surpassed by the lesser. It is the greater that rules. It is the greater that prevails. Human ideas are based on the same principle. The lesser can never surpass the greater; the lesser can never prevail over the greater. The defeat of all enemies of the good is imminent. Human factors are involved in shaping the human condition, the human society. Each factor is a fact, as is the existence of the good fact. There should be no question as to the superior nature of the good. And if there is any one indicator seeming to result to the contrary, that the good can be defeated and surpassed, then that indicator is incorrect. The deciding principles in the matter have not been properly understood. The victorious good can only seek to create the greatest good. The victorious good can only seek to establish the good society. With the advent of the good, as so stated by philosophy, humanity enters the state of maturity. Only being able to establish the good from that point forward, the good could not have been established prior to the existence of the good. The philosophical good exists with the purpose to state the good, with the purpose to observe the good way of behaving. The philosophical good exists with the purpose to crush all opponents of the good. And so to wonder why it is that the good exists now is to ask an unnecessary question. The safeguard of the good is the good. The way to observe the good human behavior is through the possession of the good. The barrier to human wrong is the good. To grasp the good is to do so through the self's equal to the good character. To grasp the truth is to do so through the self's equal to the truth character. It is of vital importance to possess the good. It is of vital importance to recognize the good in others. The only way to personally achieve the good is to seek the good. The only way to personally achieve the good is through thought and reason.

With human history taking place, the human reasoning has been made evident. To reason is to do so accurately and fairly. It is to be guided by justice. Not all human reasoning has been accurate and fair. Not all human reasoning has been just. Based on the lack of justice, the unjust character is revealed. The lack of personal justice is not personally regarded as such. That is why injustice is so readily stated by the unjust. Injustice is considered to be justice. As result, the unjust individual is neither accurate nor fair. Based on the unjust reasoning by the individual, the character of the unjust individual can be properly assessed as being unjust. The reasoning is the way to assess the personality. And if the individual is just in reason, the individual will be just in personality. If the individual is unjust in reason, the individual will be unjust in personality. With humanity revealing the human historical reasoning, it has been humanity that has been completely responsible for all human reasoning. Not having received advice or confirmation to any one human thought by an external to humanity source, namely God. Nor has any one future to the present life stage been responsible for aiding humanity in thought and reason. All that is, and has been, created and achieved by humanity has as its origin the human being. If humanity were to be advised by God, or by any one future stage to the present, that would take away from the human living effort. That would take away from life's living effort. In the process, humanity would not be made greater. Humanity would instead be diminished. Life would be diminished. Humanity would not achieve what is human. Life would not achieve to the measure of life's ability. Any one life stage is concerned with that same particular life stage and not any other. If not, life would be disregarding the present. Life would be disregarding the living effort. By disregarding the living effort, life could not occur. Hence, no life stage will interfere with or aid another. Life's effort is to achieve the most. The human effort is to achieve the most. To aid humanity is to minimize humanity. It is for humanity to achieve less than the most. It is for humanity to be less than the greatest human. As humanity does not need help in reasoning, humanity does not need help in living. In achieving the mature human being, prayer is not needed. For the human being to seek God's help in living is for the human being to seek to cheat in living. It is for the human being to seek to cheat in living with God's help. Humanity does not need help in living. Humanity does not need help in achieving all that is human. The help has already been given: by life seeking to accomplish, and accomplishing, that which is best; by life accomplishing that which is best for life, for all from within life, including humanity, all the help has already been given. In such manner then does life live, occurring in the best way possible for life and all within life to succeed. Every life member has all the power to live. Within that power, all that is of benefit to the life member has been granted. Every life member is guarded by the self's own power. Within whose full benefit, no harm to the self can occur. With the self's power including all benefit to the self, the self's power is miraculous. In such manner, the miracle of life then occurs, with all the help having been already given.

It is the human reasoning ability that makes all conclusions. The proof that can be presented as to the validity of any one conclusion is the reasoning itself. The life of humanity can only be lived by humanity. As such, it is the human mentality that is involved in human thought. Any human conclusion is humanly provable or disprovable. The human being consists of the human being. It is the human being that makes all human conclusions, not God. Incorrect human reasoning is the fault of the human being. The answer to incorrect reasoning is to try again. With correct reasoning, the human being reveals an aspect of life. It is the human being that reveals life, not the reverse. God has not revealed any truth to humanity. With philosophy being the supreme knowledge, not one philosophical truth has been revealed by God. As result, no truth has been revealed by God. If any truth is going to be revealed by God, then the supreme philosophical truth would have been revealed. That hasn't happened, therefore no truth has been revealed by God. The human task has at all times been to be grown and mature. The task has been the search of the good. To speak falsely is not an act of good; it is an act of nongood. To lack the good is to not have wished for the good. It is to not have engaged in philosophy. To claim that God has revealed any one truth is to speak falsely. It is to lack the good. It is to have failed in the human task to seek the good. Instead a false understanding of good is come up with. A false understanding of good where conceit, ignorance, disrespect, and being shameless are the guiding personal characteristics. A false understanding of good where the most detrimental human characteristics are not recognized as such. It is by being based on these characteristics that the religious claims to reveal God, to speak for God, and quote God can be made. Certainly religion's first victim is the truth. Religion's first victim is the good. To know of religion's abuse of the good is to know all there is to be known of religion. Religion's hideous abuse of the good reveals all about religion. A fraud to the core, which does not recognize its own evil as such.

It is the grown and mature human being humanity must be. It is only the grown and mature human being that can be a good individual, leading then a good life, living life to the full. The good human being cannot be such without the substantial understanding of life. To understand any aspect of life is to have sought to understand life. It is to in such and equal way be seeking the good. It is to in such and equal way possess the good. The level of personal knowledge cannot exceed the level of personal good. It is the good that accomplishes all. It is the good that makes all possible. All understanding of life is made possible by the good. The greater the personal good, the greater the understanding of life. The greater the personal understanding of life, the greater the good. For the human being to be fair and just is for the human being to have a substantial understanding of life. It is for the human being to have a substantial level of good. Being fair and just is to have an understanding of life. The human being is grown and mature by seeking to understand life. The human being is grown and mature by being fair and just.

The good human being seeks to build the good society. The good human being seeks to peacefully coexist. The good human being can never engage in any act of wrongdoing. The objective of the good human being is to seek the good. That means that only good behavior is engaged in. The good human being does not engage in wrong behavior. To do so is contrary to the self. To do so is to no longer be a good individual. The good individual seeks justice. The good individual is peaceful. To not engage in wrongdoing, to be a just individual, makes the good individual peaceful. No one other than the good individual can be peaceful. If the good individual is not considered as peaceful, then no one can be considered as peaceful. The need for peaceful existence is strongest in the good, as proven by the peaceful attitude toward the good. The good, the cause of the good, has its enemies. There are those who are not equal to being good, who despise the way of the good, whose purpose is to harm the good. The first step in harming the good is taken within the nongood individual by being opposed to the good. Contrary and opposed to the good reasoning is come up with, reasoning which harms the cause of the good. The cause of the good is destroyed within the nongood individual. The cause of peace is destroyed within the nongood individual. As the good seeks peace, the nongood does not. And so, the good's wish to peacefully coexist has a limit of possible achievement. Within the good society, the cause of the good takes precedence. The basis of the good society is the good. The basis is the good individual. The cause of the good, the good individual, will be promoted. The cause of the nongood, the nongood individual, will be suppressed. It is only the creation of the good that is desired, any creation of nemesis has no place within the good society. The good society being good, no error in estimating the level of good can occur. No error in deciding what is good and in deciding what is nongood can occur. The good society will always side with the good individual. The good individual being good, no error in behavior can be made; all behavior is equally good. If there is error made, that error will be admitted to and improved upon, making the individual equally good. If the good individual is involved in a dispute, then the good individual will behave in the same good manner. There must be an equally good reason for the good individual's behavior. Making the guilty in the matter the nongood individual, The deciding body, as to the possessed level of good by any one individual, will be the good government. The deciding qualities will be fairness and justice, being sincere and understanding. The greater these qualities, the greater the good.

The nongood will be suppressed for good reason. The nongood harms good people. The greater need that the nongood has for harming the good, the greater the suppression. Such nongood individual will be taken out of society. All such monsters will be taken out of society. Civilization was created with the intent for humanity to live in peace and justice. Only the good society can be peaceful and just. The good's purpose is to create the greatest human good. The greatest human good for everyone. The good therefore recognizes no boundaries, no borders. What the good recognizes is good people. Good people suffering under the effect of nemesis. As such, every nation must side with the good. Every nation must work with the good. Every nation must turn power over to the good. All nongood governments are illegitimate and tyrannical. The good society will teach the good to all people, to all governments. It is the wish of the good for all and everyone to side with the good. The good society has the right to overthrow any government which does not observe the good. The good society has the right to overthrow any government, any nation, which has not turned power over to the good.

It cannot be that any one society is all and equally inclusive and accepting of all views. All societies suppress certain views. Certain views are not politically empowered. As result, they are suppressed.

If the good is not in power, then it is the good that is suppressed. Making that society unjust. All justice originates from the good. The priority within the good society will be the good. Within the good society, the criteria will be the good. The good as possessed by each individual. The good society will always side with the cause of the good. The good society will always side with the good individual. The good society is guided by the level of good as possessed by each individual. In any one dispute, the deciding body will take into consideration the evidence of the case, as well as the level of good of each individual. And if the made decision is not agreed with by any one individual, then the answer will be for that individual to get involved in the search of the good to a greater extent. All parties, all people within the good society, work together toward the cause of the good. Only the good society is guided by the best interest of each individual. The good society has the most genuine reason for existence. Each individual will in the personal way aid the cause of the good. The full freedom to pursue each individual's dreams and aspiration will be the way of the good society. Within all circumstances, it is the cause of the good that will decide all issues. No achieved rank within the good society can ever elevate the personal level of good. No authority will have the right to behave contrary to the cause of the good, contrary to any one good individual.

The purpose of the good society is to create the greatest justice. The purpose of the good society is to judge all on the basis of possessed good. The purpose of the good society is to bring all enemies of the good to justice. The good government of the good society will have complete control. The good government will set up guidelines within which the good society will function. Making the good government have complete control. The good society will be allowed to function. Whenever any one deciding body fails in its task, the good government will have the right to override such body. The good government will have the right to override such failure. Ownership will be private. In the process, each individual's dreams and aspirations will be followed. By observing the good, the private owner behaves in the same good manner. The guide to behavior is the good. The vast majority of citizens are good in character. The good society will function according to the talent of the good society. To seek to control the private ownership of good people by government is to in turn reveal that the good is lacked by government. It is to reveal that the good was never the personal objective. It is to in turn reveal a personally conceited, arrogant, and ignorant attitude. Such an attitude will have no place in the good government. No price or wage guidelines will be mandated by government. Private ownership will decide both price and wage. Any one private ownership that should lack the good will be taken over by the good government and sold off to private ownership. The good is to be worked with by all. The good is not to be opposed. Opposition to the good reveals that the good is lacked. The greater the opposition, the greater the absence of good. The greater the absence of good, the lesser the observance of the good. Such lacking the good individuals cannot help in the creation of the good society. All law will originate from the good government. All bodies of government will enforce such law. All innocent life will be regarded as sacred. All marriage will be between man and woman only. Every guilty individual will be punished. The good is to be worked with. Any opposition of the good exposes that individual as lacking the good. The lack of good is the greatest flaw. The objective of the guilty, the objective of nemesis is the destruction of the good. The good will therefore be protected. The good will be protected by the guardians. The overwhelming might of the good will be felt by all enemies of the good. All politicians, all November impostors, are to work with the good. All November impostors are to submit to the good. Any ally of nemesis best be aware of the wrath of the good.

All power belongs to the good. Being good proves this. Any one individual not representing the good is a tyrant. Any one government not representing the good is tyrannical. What the good individual wants to do is behave in the same good manner. What the good individual wants is the freedom to behave in the same good manner. The good government can only recognize this. The good individual does not have to be told how to behave. Being a private owner, the good individual will behave in the same good manner. To seek to mandate such good individual as to how to carry on with the self's private business is to in turn expose the personal lack of good. It is to expose the fact that the objective of good was never the personal objective. If the objective were the good, then it would have been known that the only criteria is the possession of the good. It would have been further known that the good is to be given full freedom. It would have been known that only a tyrant would interfere in the good's life. Not knowing that the good is the only criteria means that the good was lacked. To lack the good and claim to possess the good is to be then doubly at fault. It is to expose an exaggerated self-praise

Knowledge of the good, possession of the good being central, the good society will accomplish the possible. The creative force being the good individual, the good society will create and accomplish in accordance with the good individual. All the talent and all the ability is with the good individual. All the talent, all the ability is with the good society. As the good individual does not need to be told how to behave in a good manner, the good individual is responsible. The good individual is intellectually developed. The proof for that intellect is the observance of the good. There is no greater knowledge than knowledge of the good. All else follows, the extent of the good individual's talent is fully possessed by that same good individual. It takes intellect to know the good. The good individual is the most intellectual. The good individual does not need help in being responsible. The good individual does not need help in being intellectual. Being responsible and intellectual, the good individual is full grown and mature. It is the full grown and mature human being that is wished for. It is the full grown and mature human being that leads the full life. It is the full grown and mature human being that leads to understanding life. The good individual does not need help in living. The vast majority do not need help in living. To offer help where help is not needed is to reveal the conceited, arrogant, and ignorant personality. Such a personality is not seeking the good. Such a personality is not seeking the creation of the good society. To claim to wish to help someone not in need of help is to do so due to ulterior motives. The unwanted good doer, the tyrannical good doer. All freedom comes from the good. Any view which is not good, which is not accurate, is a tyrannical view. The view is tyrannical and will only lead to tyranny. To help the grown and mature human being is to take away from the grown and mature human being. It is to belittle the grown and mature human being. It is to take away the personal expression of life. By making an effort, the good individual achieves. It is the effort, it is the achievement that is the good individual. It is the responsible, intellectual individual that makes the effort that achieves. To help the good individual is to take away from the good individual's expression of life. It is to take away the effort. It is to take away the achievement. Unneeded help does not help the good individual. Unneeded help harms the individual. Unneeded help does not make the good individual better. Unneeded help makes the good individual worse. Unneeded help is detrimental to the human being. Unneeded help is detrimental to the good society. The good individual's life is not to be interfered with. To interfere is to reveal the personal tyrannical nature. Tyrannical nature which is disguised with unneeded offerings. Hence the pretending good doer. Lacking the good, the pretending good doer's mission is the subjugation and the destruction of the good. The lack of good is the result of not having made the effort to achieve the good. The views that are then come up with are just as lacking. Seeking political power, the tyrant seeks to empower the personal deficiency of good. In the process creating laws which are harmful, laws which are not truly laws. Just as the tyrant is illegitimate, so are the laws illegitimate. Those laws are not beneficial. They oppress society. They oppress the human being.

The tyrant cannot come up with answers. Those answers are flawed; the answers come up with are not answers. Proving that the good was never the objective. Someone so lacking cannot come up with answers. The personality of any one individual is one. It is the same one personality that considers all issues. Lacking the good, it is the same lacking the good personality that considers all. Conversely, having the good, it is the same good personality that considers all. The creation of the perfect society, the cause of peace and the cause of the good are related issues. It is only the good that can lead to the peaceful existence. It is only the good that can lead to the creation of the perfect society. It can only be that the good is such due to the fact that good seeks the peaceful existence. The good individual is fair and just, fair and just in all matters, including human relations.

The result then is peaceful human existence. The good individual is therefore peaceful. The good individual has a peaceful attitude toward all the issues of central importance, namely the good. With the good individual being fair and just, the good individual can only endorse the equally such perfect society. In turn leading to peaceful human relations. To endorse anything less than the perfect society is to lack the good. Any lack of peaceful existence is the result of lack of good. Any lack of perfect society is the result of lack of good. The nongood individual is neither fair nor just, leading to the equally such behavior. Leading to the disregard of the fellow man, leading to less-than-peaceful relations. The equally such neither fair nor just society is endorsed, leading to less-than-peaceful relations. The effort at the good is the same effort at peace, is the same effort at creating the perfect society.

The human effort to understand life's being, the human effort to create the good society, and the human effort to achieve peace, is the same effort. As philosophy is the answer to understanding life's ultimate being, philosophy is the answer to the creation of the good society, and philosophy is the answer to achieving the peaceful human existence. Philosophy's need to understand life is greatest. Philosophy's need to create the good society is greatest, and philosophy's need to achieve peace is greatest. The answers to the central human questions can only come from philosophy. The supreme answers to life's being could not have been come up with prior to the appropriate existence of fact. Philosophy has achieved an immense amount prior to which. With the advent of the good, change is necessarily brought about. Regardless of what society had achieved prior to which, it could not have been the same as the good. Change in that case is only natural. The good is there to be revealed. The good is there to be stated. The good is there to improve the human condition. The human objective is the attainment of the ever greater good. The human objective cannot be the search for the false. The human objective cannot be the rejection of the good. All views in history have been so stated. The impact of any one view upon society, upon humanity, is such as it is. The impact of any one truth is irrefutable. To achieve any one truth is to do so irrefutably. By the fact that the truth is considered, it is assured that the truth does in fact exist. Doing so, the truth cannot but claim the truth's status as such. The truth cannot be denied from existing. No one human view can be denied from existing. No one human being can be denied from existing, from contributing to society, from influencing society. Upon being stated, the truth will oppose that which is false. To prove a theory in thought is to do so in fact. The truth of the idea, the truth of the theory is the fact. The truth of the idea has precedence over that which is false. The truth is always accepted as such. Whatever the impact may be, the truth is always accepted. The truth is always accepted within the world of ideas. With the good impacting society, with the good impacting humanity, the good states the good's ideas. The good teaches the good's ideas. The acceptance of which will depend on each individual. As the self is chosen, so is the personal level of good also chosen. The good, as stated by philosophy, will only be accepted up to a certain point, depending on the personal choice for the good. If the good is not wished for, then the good cannot be taught. The good will not be accepted. That is due to the complete lack of personal good. The duty of the good is to make the good known. Doing so, those individuals in greater possession of personal good will be more accepting of the good. Prior to the good's existence, the good's ideas were nonexistent. The good upon being revealed therefore brings about change. With the vast majority of society being of sound character, the ideas of the good are more readily accepted. The human wish is the ever greater human being. The human wish is knowledge of the good. The good as stated by philosophy then is the way forward. As the human being wishes to be knowledgeable, it is philosophy that presents the supreme knowledge, the supreme good. And so each individual must confirm that it is the good that is personally wished for. Doing so, it will become obvious that philosophy is supreme. Philosophy is central to human thought. Being central, philosophy can only be supreme. Philosophy is equal to the philosophical task. To reveal philosophical truth is to be equal to that truth. To understand philosophical truth is to be equal to that truth. And certainly humanity can only be equal to the possible, not achieving more, not achieving less. Philosophical truth has a limit of appeal. Philosophy is not more appealing than possible. As humanity estimates philosophy, that assessment will be to the human extent. The human desire for philosophy will be to the human extent. The answers that philosophy offers are the supreme answers. Flaw with those answers will always be found by those who lack the good. Philosophy's effort is unwavering. Stating truth, philosophy automatically exposes the false. Philosophy automatically wages a struggle against the false. There is no falsehood that can succeed in disguising itself as truth. The false has it within its own refutation. The false was never correct, regardless of it having been considered as correct. The false has its counterpart. The false has its nemesis. The one that seeks to destroy the false at all times, the good. Philosophy is equal to philosophical truth. Achieving truth, philosophy completes the human effort at truth, the human effort as one humanity truth.

With the philosophical good impacting society, those of the equal good character will side with the philosophical good. In the process aiding the good. The engaging in good behavior is equal to the personal level of good. The good is never missed out upon by anyone. The level of possessed good being the level of desired good. The lived life cannot interfere with the personal search of the good. It cannot be thought that the life lived interferes with the personal attainment of the desired in life. There are stages in anyone's life that are more desired than others. Those stages are a part of anyone's life. As such, the desired is a part of any individual's life and is completely fulfilling. As the self is chosen, so too is the life lived chosen. All related to the self is so wished to be such since it is that the self, the primary wish, is such as desired. Since it is that the self, the primary wish, is granted and attained. The undertaken living path by each individual involves the self. It is the self that does the living. All that the self does and undergoes is in accordance with the self. Each individual always does the possible for the self to do. Making the life lived complete and fulfilling. There are the less desired and the more desired stages in life. Life is beyond the human nonacceptance. Life is to be lived. The choice for the self, the love for the self is the solution. The love for the self resolves all. The self's living path is the personal living path. All that occurs involves the self, the loved self. As the self is chosen, so is the living path chosen. As the self is fulfilling, so is the living path fulfilling. The good in life is never missed out upon. It is always the self that lives. It is always the personal good that experiences all. Making the good, knowledge of the good, in the self's life inescapable. If the good is wished to be improved upon, then such effort should be made. The extent of the effort is decided upon by the self, by the good of the self. The extent is not known until the effort is made. The self's destiny is the personal one. The self is not denied from existing. All is therefore granted.

Life is completely fulfilling. Life does and accomplishes all. During the more desired stages, life accomplishes most, leading to the stage of supreme good. To wish to understand life is to do so. It is to wish to understand life ultimate reality, not just aspects of life. The struggling aspect of life should be properly understood. Victorious life should be accurately understood. Life's struggle is not without victory. Life is in full possession of the self. Life's being is such as life's being is. To wonder why it is that life has attained life's own particular being is to look to the actual. It is to look to the fact of life. Life achieves life's being. Life's being is evident. It is the achieved that is the desired. There is no need to achieve any other, any different form of life's being. Life achieves all. Life's form of being achieves all. Life's form of being can only be the correct one. Life being in the correct life form, life lives the reality of life, the range of life. Life lives the possible. Life being limited, life lives the possible. Within the possible, within the reality of life, life lives all. By always seeking that which is best, life achieves the range of life. Life achieves the state of supreme good. The supreme good is from within the reality of life. The supreme good is the stage where the most good, the most of benefit to life is achieved. The dominant good is where the greatest justice is achieved, where the greatest knowledge is achieved. It is where the good never suffers. It is where no act of evil can occur. It is where all knowledge is attained. The stage of dominant good is the range of life. No greater good can be accomplished. No greater knowledge can be accomplished. The good then is complete. Knowledge then is complete. It is not possible for life to wish to accomplish less than the best, less than the most good, less than the most knowledge. Such being the wish, such is the result. It is a contradictory idea to think that life can wish for less than the best; namely, that life would have a varying and lesser development from the existing life being. It is not possible for life to accomplish less than the best, less than the most good, less than the most knowledge. It is not possible for life to attain less than all, less than all knowledge, less than all good. Life understands all. Life is the supreme justice. Life is the authority. There can be nothing unknown. There can be no injustice. Life sustains all. Life has the equal knowledge. Life is the supreme good. Life has the equal knowledge. Life's complete effort at knowledge is met with complete success. Life's form of being achieves all. There is no need for a different form of being.

Life's complete effort at living is met with complete success. It is only the truth of life that reveals life's being. Life lives based on the truth of life's being. Life lives based on the truth of each stage. No stage of life can be founded upon falsehood. Though any one period of existence is based on truth, no period of existence is without change. Change occurs due to life's search for greater truth. It is always life that undergoes the living occurrence. From stage to stage, it is life that does the living. No one of which is realized before the proper moment. Seeking the greater, life realizes the greater. Life attains the supreme good. During which period, it is the supreme truth of life that guides life. Making the previous stage or stages inadequate, making the previous stage or stages being founded on less than the supreme truth. If the basis of the previous to the dominant good stages were the truth of life, then any one such stage would have achieved what the supreme good achieves. It is the fact that no one other than the stage of supreme good achieves the truth of life. No one other stage achieves the supreme good. As result, all stages strive for the stage of supreme good. Meaning that the truth of any one stage, upon attaining the greater, becomes inadequate and in that certain way false. If such preceding stage were adequate, then that stage would not have led to change. It is life's search for greater good that exposes the inadequate, in the process exposing what in that certain way is false. The previous stage, by attaining the greater in that certain way, becomes false. The false brings about all change.

The truth of the previous stage becomes in that certain way false, without overturning the truth of the previous. Bringing about the end of the previous.

Life includes the range of life. Life includes all life stages. Life is always founded upon laws of truth. During any one life stage, other than the dominant good, life is always striving to attain the dominant good. Life's less than supreme stages achieve the equal to the stages level of good and understanding. It is always life that undergoes the living occurrence. Life always leads to life. Life never becomes different from life. The link with the self is ever present. Seeking and attaining the supreme good, life does not reject the supreme good. No rejection of that which is best for life takes place.

Any one individual seeks that which is best for the self. Any one individual seeks that state of existence of most good. By making such effort, such will be the results. The greater the effort, the greater the results. Humanity is free to seek personal growth, personal development. All effort at personal growth occurs during the present life stage. And so the results will be equivalent to the extent of the present stage. Greater to the possible present growth cannot be achieved. That doesn't mean that upon making an effort, no growth is achieved. To seek knowledge is to attain knowledge. To seek the good is to attain the good. Personal growth is not restricted from occurring. All life occurs within the self. To wonder if humanity is satisfied in the process of living is to look to the human personality. It is to look to life's being. During any one life stage, humanity achieves the possible. Humanity achieves all possible. It is not possible for humanity to wish for less than the best, less than the most knowledge, less than the most good. It is not possible for humanity to achieve less than the best, less than the most knowledge, less than the most good. During any one stage, humanity never achieves less than all. For humanity to wish for more than the most knowledge, for more than the most good, is for the human being to be dissatisfied, dissatisfied with life, dissatisfied with the self. All personal life occurs within the self. The extent of the self includes the range of life. Humanity will achieve the possible human level of achievement from within the reality of life. The reality of life includes the supreme stage. That is where the greatest good is achieved; that is where the greatest knowledge is achieved. To consider human dissatisfaction is to consider the reality of life. It is to consider the supreme good. Humanity achieves all. Humanity achieves all wished for. It is not possible for humanity to accomplish less than all. It is not possible for humanity to know less than all. That is the fact during any one life stage, including the supreme stage. The stage of dominant good cannot be taken out of the reality of life. The question then becomes, how much is it that humanity wishes to live, how much is it that humanity wishes to know? The equal effort can only be made. The answers are found with the effort.

No life member has lesser, varying development from the existing. Making every life member complete. Every life member achieves all. As the human being strives for growth, the human being strives for the greater good. And the greater good will be realized. Seeking the good, the human being proceeds from the basis of good. The individual is based on a level of personal good; that is the only way any existence is possible. Attaining the greater good, the previous to which level of good is overridden. The previous good was nonetheless sufficient to lead to greater good. Making human life without error. Making life without error. If there were error, then the greater good would not have been attained. The previous to which level of good is overridden is considered as inadequate. Through it all, the link with self is ever present. It is the self that does the living. As life seeks the greater good, life accomplishes all. There isn't any negative that life does not convert into positive, that does not lead into greater good. There isn't any negative that does not lead to the stage of supreme good. Life is immune to any negative. Life can never be destroyed. Life seeks growth. Life accomplishes growth. Bringing to an end all previous stages to the dominant good. To wish to know life is to do so. It is to wish to know life. Within the reality of life, life has unlimited power. Life is eternal. Life is victorious. Life is the authority. Life is truth and justice. The guidelines of unlimited nonlife and unlimited life do not force life into any behavior, any contrary to life's being behavior. Life is not lifeless. To think that life is forced into behavior is to think incorrectly. It is to overlook many issues. It is to overlook life's being. It is to not understand life. It is to not understand life's power. It is not to wish to know and understand life. Such an analysis cannot understand life. Such an analysis is not an attempt at philosophy. It is to be overwhelmed by one's own personal ignorance. The key to life is life, living life. Life cannot be taken out of any understanding of life. The central issue of importance to understanding life is the love for life. The central issue is the love for the self, making the idea that life is forced into behavior meaningless. Life has the power of will. Life's effort is deliberate and conscious. If it is that, greater consciousness cannot be attained. Greater consciousness is not needed. Greater consciousness is not wanted. With life having the power of will, with life having the power of consciousness, so does each life member have the equal to the life member power of will, power of consciousness, including humanity.

As humanity cannot attain greater consciousness, greater consciousness is not needed, greater consciousness is not wanted. Not being able to attain greater consciousness, the human being is not unconscious. Rather, the human being does and achieves all. The human power of will, the human power of consciousness, is the self's power of will. It is the self's power of consciousness. The self can never be different from the self. The self can never be alienated from the self. The life lived by the self is the self's life. The self achieves and does all. The power of will, the power of consciousness, can neither be raised nor lowered. Making the human being complete. Making the human being completely conscious. For humanity to be unconscious is for humanity to be lifeless. It is for humanity to be without life. Which obviously is not the case. The human being is responsible for the self. Will and consciousness is what guides the human being. Will and consciousness is what guides human behavior. Will and consciousness is what guides every life member. In process achieving all. In the process achieving complete consciousness. The power of life is to be properly understood.

With each individual developing, the individual naturally develops in that manner that is considered as most appealing. In so doing, the individual's wish is fulfilled. It cannot be that the individual develops in an unappealing to the self manner. The individual always develops toward that which is appealing. Not to do so is for the self to be detrimental to the self. The self cannot be a detriment to the self but only a benefit. By seeking that which is most appealing, the individual engages in thought. The individual engages in creation. The individual engages in personal thought, personal creation. Making the life lived sufficient and fulfilling. It is the personal life. It cannot be that that which is personally considered as unappealing is sought and developed toward. The individual can never take the wrong path of personal progress. As such, the human being never leads an inadequate life, a life which is improper and unfulfilling. The human being never leads the not personal life. By developing, the individual seeks life. To seek life is to, through that same effort, live the same life. The individual behaves according to the life sought and found. The personal line of development and accomplishment is under no instance denied but is always granted. Seeking greater life, the individual sets objectives for the self. Completing one, another objective is then undertaken. All the while the individual has a purpose to pursue and accomplish. The same individual, the same individual living the personal life. The same individual proceeds from objective to objective. Causing to question which one of the personal stages of development is the one to be understood as the most indicative of the personality of that individual. It is so that there is the continuing and connecting link with the self. The self only leads to the self. Any one path at life can only be undertaken by the sole life member to whom it is personally bound. No period of the self's life can have anyone other than the self living that period. Each objective is the personally such. The self is irreversibly present and found during any stage of the self's life. Each stage consists of the self. All stages of the life lived reveal the self. In assessing any one individual, the task is to accurately do so. In understanding the individual, the search of the good by that individual is central. The good cannot have been always possessed. There are periods in the self's life where the good was lacked, and there are periods where the good was attained. It is the content of the good. it is the sincere effort that is of concern. The effort at the good is a conscious, deliberate effort. The effort at any one personal objective is a conscious, deliberate effort. It is an effort involving thought. The core of the human being is thought. Thought is central to life. Thought is central to any one life member. By engaging in thought, the human being lives. By engaging in thought, the human being creates. The human being achieves truth. The human truth has value. The human truth has irreversible human value. There is no human truth that does not enlighten. There is no human truth that does not develop the human being. As the individual chooses the self's line of development, the equal objectives are set before the self. It is through the effort at the objectives. It is through the effort at and the achievement of the objectives that the human being grows. In the process, the individual becoming what the individual truly is. The accomplishment of the identity of the self producing a rewarding feeling, a feeling of good, as regarded as good by the self toward the self. It is thought that achieves truth. It is the idea that enlightens. It is the idea that awakens humanity. It is the idea that is sought. It is the idea that is found. Achieving the desired growth. The human being is equal to the human being, having the same life value. If life is not understood, then the effort at understanding must most eagerly be engaged in. If any one human issue is not understood, then the effort at understanding must most eagerly be engaged in. In the process, awakening humanity.

In living, humanity lives according to life's laws. No event occurs that is not based in life's being. Life's Being is Goodness, Truth, Justice, and Understanding. As the good is life's basis, the good is the motive. Life will never occur in any manner that is any less than good. Human fear only arises from one source, lack of understanding of life. Life is not to be looked upon as presenting a lawless living condition. Lawless living condition which can only be feared. Life is to be lived. Life is not to be feared. Life is to be taken part in. Nor are fairy tales and fantasies needed. By understanding life, the human being grows, the human being lives the full life. Including within the self's thought and deeds only the most genuine reasons. By grasping life's laws, inevitably it is life's goodness that is understood. To know any one life law is to know the justice involved in that same life law. As any one life law is a life law, there is no life law that is unjust. Life's being is founded upon life's laws. Life's laws secure life's being. Life is supreme, achieving all, achieving all the goodness possible. Therefore there is not unjust life law. To think of any one life law as unjust is to not understand the law. It is to not understand life. Mistaken or unjust assessment cannot be made by life. It is not possible for life not to seek the good. It is not possible for life not to attain the good. Life's judgment is the sole criteria. Life is the sole order achieving being. Life is life's own check and affirmation of the just and real. Life can successfully carry out this task due to the fact that life is the height of existence, and there is no higher judgment to life's. Life will never occur in any manner that is less than best. It is life's good that is in control of all events. All that occurs within life serves the purpose of the good as there is no harmful deed that does not result in the achievement of the good. Consequently, there is no unjust life law. Life is to be lived, not feared.

Life by being supreme, life by achieving that which is best, life achieves order. Everything in life is most accurately such. If there were no order to life, then life would never have achieved that which is best. If there were no order to life, then the false would be mistaken as truth. Life would never occur if there were no order to life. That same lack of order destroying life. The identity of every life member would be lost if there were no order within life. Each self would become different from who the self truly is. The claim to being somewhat different from the self's true identity would be successfully made. No aspect of life is different from the truth of that aspect. All within life is most accurately such. As there is order, there is the highest aspect of that order, there is the highest good, there is the greatest good. Life is supreme justice.

The human objective is to seek the truth. The human objective is to understand life. Doing so, the human being is enriched. All that is good originates from the truth. All that is good originates from understanding the truth of life. Understanding any one life truth can only be good thing. The human being by grasping the truth attains the goodness of that truth. As the truth is good, the same level of good to the truth is required to attain the truth. Being guided by the truth, the human being is guided by the good. Humanity does all possible to be guided by the good. As the importance of any one truth is increased, so is the possessed personal level of good increased. As the individual is grounded in truth, as the individual is grounded in good, the individual is grounded in a peaceful attitude. As the truth can only be good, the truth can only be peaceful. And as the understanding of the truth individual is good. The understanding of the truth individual is peaceful. The check to human behavior is the good. Led by the good, the human being has the same good reasons for all that is done. It is the lack of good that leads to improper behavior. With the good being the check to human behavior, it is the lack of the good that is not a check to human behavior. In the process, to lack the good is to do so at the self's personal expense. If the truth is not understood and is rejected, the understanding of the truth was not the personal objective. The achievement of the good was not the personal objective. The peaceful human attitude was not the objective. To lack the truth, to lack the good is to lack the peaceful and loving character. If peace and love were the motive, then the truth, the good would have been achieved. If the personal character were peaceful and loving, then the peace and love would have been made evident by the search for the truth, by seeking the good, by attaining the truth, by attaining the good. There would be peace and love for the good, thereby attaining the good. Not to attain the good is not to love the good. It is not to love the truth. It is not to love peace. Only the good individual loves the good. Only the good individual loves peace, unless it were thought that everyone loves the good, unless it were thought that everyone is peaceful and loving. The peaceful and loving beast will be destroyed. It is the duty of the good, it is the duty of philosophy to destroy all monsters.

By lacking the good, the nongood individual embarks upon the equally such nongood behavior. Not having the good as the self's guide, the nongood individual is unrestrained in the need for evil. The nongood individual is unrestrained in the abuse of the good. The nongood individual seeks to strengthen the personal lack of good. The way of evil is strengthened so that the good may be better abused. Lacking all restraint, the way of evil is pursued in all the different ways. The strength gained in the search for evil is weakness in the search of the good. The gained strength is with the intent to better defend and struggle for the cause of the nongood. The strength gained is not strength but weakness. It is rooted in deception. The strength gained is in the lack of good. Turning to hatred and deception, the nongood individual lacks development. The nongood individual lacks the higher levels of being human. The nongood individual lacks conscience. Lacking conscience, the nongood individual lacks higher human consciousness. Lacking the good, the nongood individual is lacking in conscience. The nongood individual is lacking in consciousness. The height of human consciousness is a must. And the highest consciousness is not acquired through any method that does not seek the good, and the good's constituting characteristic of truth, justice, and understanding. It is only the good that results in good behavior. It is only the good that results in the highest consciousness. Lacking higher consciousness, the struggle that nemesis wages against the good is done to the highest personal cost to nemesis. The lack of restraint in pursuing evil comes at the highest personal price. These are the results of being evil, lack of character, lack of good, lack of soul. There is a difference between good and evil. The inferior status of evil is forever so marked.

Seeking growth and development, the human being achieves growth and development. Not to seek growth and development is contrary to human nature. It is contrary to the nature of life. The human being grows in understanding. The human being grows in attaining the good. Not all of any one individual's life stages consist of the height of personal development. To seek the good is to have lacked the good. That is why the effort at the good was originally initiated. The search for the good signifies that the good was lacked. Upon growing and developing, upon attaining understanding, the individual reaches maturing stages in the self's life. They are maturing stages which combine to at a certain point present the mature individual. That point is where the sufficient level of personal growth and understanding has been attained so as to mark the height of that individual's life. The maturing point being regarded as such by the individual self. From that point, issues and ideas are considered in the same mature way. The effort at growth having achieved maturity, all that has led to which, then being properly understood. Attaining maturity, attaining the good, the past has therefore accomplished its task. Maturity, the attaining of the good, the content of the good must be properly understood and estimated. The past, which has led to the good, by its nature lacked the good, lacked maturity, but the absence of the good was not to the extent where the desire for the good was negated. The then absence of good was not to the extent where the good, the state of maturity, would not be achieved. The past must be viewed in the context of having lacked the good, then having attained the good. The issue for the human being is the desire for growth, the desire for the good. That desire being genuine, the good will be attained. The self will be enriched. Seeking growth and development, growth and development will be achieved. With this process occurring to the individual, it also occurs to the human historical context. As the individual matures, so does humanity mature. Humanity's maturing phase necessarily takes place, as it is that the human search for the truth is real. Achieving that truth which is maturing, matures humanity. The human path at life is one. Within whose boundaries, all that occurs does so to the one humanity. The maturing development in all life is a must, and historical humanity is no exception. The maturing point cannot take place at any one inappropriate phase. The point of maturity distinguishes its own rightful moment of occurrence. And maturity can only be that of understanding life. Maturity can only be that of understanding the good. Philosophy represents the greatest understanding of life. Philosophy represents the understanding of the good. For philosophy to achieve that understanding is for all humanity to achieve the same understanding, as the human path at life is one. As philosophy achieves and matures, so does humanity achieve and mature. Philosophy is and has been central to human development. To think that philosophy is not central is to make a great mistake. To think that it is possible for philosophy not to have occurred, therefore negating the idea that philosophy brings about human maturity, is to be greatly mistaken. It is not possible for philosophy not to exist, just as it is not possible for humanity not to exist, just as it is not possible for life not to exist in the single and one way only. The miracle of life cannot be overturned. Historical philosophy has always taken place, presenting the equal development. Even though philosophical, human maturity is marked by the phase of maturity, that does not negate previous human or philosophical development. If that were the case, maturity would never have been achieved. The necessary was at all times accomplished. Humanity has never been prevented from fulfilling humanity's own character. Humanity has not lived less. Humanity cannot live less than the human potential. There are no hindrances to human growth. All that is involved in the human realm serves the human purpose. There are no diminishing factors. Humanity is free to live the full range of humanity's character, including the state of maturity.

The way for humanity to develop is philosophically. Humanity is to seek the philosophical solutions to all issues. Philosophy has all the answers. No other human thought can compare to philosophical thought. Philosophy is supreme. As such, philosophy is and has been dominant over all other human development. From Plato, to Aristotle, to Hegel, and many others, philosophical achievement is the pride of humanity. And if that achievement is not known, then it will be taught. The philosophical effort is at understanding life. The philosophical effort is at understanding the good. The good is life's supreme laws. The good is life's supreme being. The supreme laws of life can only be beneficial and good, always acting in the best and most just manner. Life's being of truth, justice, and understanding includes the good. Life's being is present with the quality of good. It is the quality of good that brings life to the height of being. Life is thoroughly good. There is no aspect of life that does not serve the purpose of the good. The good makes all the contradictions within life disappear. Life is the medium between the opposites. Life is all contradictions, and yet life does not have a single contradiction. By negating the absoluteness of any one opposite, life creates the reality of life. All within the reality of life serves the purpose of life. Life cannot not exist. Therefore all serves life. Life lives in the life way. Life is victorious over absolute nonlife. Life is victorious over unlimited nonlife. The seeming contradictions are not contradictions. Life does that which is best for life. Life's victorious achievement cannot be wrong. Life's victorious achievement cannot be mistaken. Life's victorious achievement cannot be questioned. As result, there are no contradictions to life. Life contains no contradictions. Understanding life can contain no contradiction.

The human phase of maturity marks a certain change in human thinking. The phase of maturity marks a departure from certain immature human ideas. Maturity is better reasoning. Maturity is better behavior. By maturing, by growing, all issues are then considered in the same grown manner. With philosophy leading the way, solutions to questions of human development are presented. The development of society is central to humanity. Philosophy has more authority on such issue than any one other branch of thought. The solutions to life's being can only come from philosophy. The solutions to human societal development can only come from philosophy. The objective of philosophy is to solve the issues of central importance to humanity. The objective of philosophy is the creation of the good society. The cause of the good can only be promoted. The cause of the good can only be defended. The good, the cause of the good is the basis of the good society. The good individual is the basis of the good society. The objective of the good society is to defend the good individual. The objective of the good society is to promote the cause of the good individual. All within the good society will be judged according to the good, according to the level of possessed good. The vast majority possess the good. Possessing that level of good, the vast majority can only seek the good. The vast majority can only seek to work together toward the common objective of good. The good individual is understanding and respectful. The good individual is understanding and respectful of the good. The good individual is understanding and respectful of others. The good individual is peaceful. The good individual is peaceful toward the good. The good individual is peaceful toward others. The vast majority, by working together, seek to peacefully coexist. The vast majority seek the good. In the event of any one dispute, the good individuals will work together in the common effort to resolve that dispute. If it should occur that such resolution is not found, the good government is to resolve the dispute. The good government is to settle the dispute according to the issues involved, the good government is to settle the dispute according to the individuals involved, always siding with the greater good. The individual representing the greater good is to be sided with. And the good is to be judged according to the honest and sincere search of the good. The good is to be judged according to the honest and sincere understanding and respect. As the personal level of good is increased, the good individual will have greater say in the arrived-at solution to any one dispute. The dispute is to be settled then according to the wishes, as so stated, of the good individual. The dispute is not to be settled according to the wishes of anyone other than the good individual. The dispute is with the good. The harm done is to the good individual. Only the good individual is aware of the extent of that harm. The good individual being good, the good individual cannot misrepresent the good. As result, the good individual is to be sided with. The good individual is to have the say to the solution of any one dispute. The good government will work with both sides. The good government will always encourage for the way of the good to be observed. The found solution will be fair and just. The party that is not sided with will learn the one lesson of importance, to seek the good to a greater extent, thereby improving the self. With the good government siding with the greater good in all disputes, no good individual will ever be imprisoned or punished. Based on the goodness of the individual, no taken act is less so. Therefore there is all the right for behaving in such manner. If the good individual should wrongly encroach upon the rights of another, that can only occur in the form of accident. The good cannot be deliberately less than good. The good's deliberate behavior cannot be misbehavior since it is that all disputes arise with the lesser. No such deliberate and improper deed is the fault of the good individual. Committing the wrong in the form of accident, the good individual will behave in the same good manner and compensate the wronged individual. By working together, the level of compensation will be agreed to by both parties. If no agreement is reached, government will side with the account, the presentation of the greatest good. In the process siding with the good, no party will be offended by the decision of the good government. It is that the good is the objective of all. Only such individuals will be placed in position to judge human right and wrong who themselves know and understand the good. The good government will give complete support to the judging individuals. If the good government is attacked, government will have the right to defend itself and the cause of the good. Anyone who struggles against any part of the good society makes it clear that the good is lacked. To struggle against any part of the good society is a criminal act. Once any aspect of the good society is confirmed as being good by the good government, no effort to harm that part of society will be acceptable or legal. Humanity by achieving historical maturity will progress upon certain previous ideas. The previous has brought about the present. The previous has served its purpose. The good society is such for a reason. The good society serves the good. The good society serves all. The good can only be worked with. The good society can only be improved upon, not struggled against.

The objective of philosophy is the creation of the good society. The good society is a just society. It is justice that governs the good society. Being just and serving the good, the good society serves the cause of the good. As result the good society will do that which is necessary to defend and protect the good. The question of human rights is the question of justice. With the good society being based in justice, it is the cause of justice that will be served. The question of human rights is answered with the justice of the good society. Led by the supremacy of philosophy, the good society cannot be less than good and just. Solutions to human societal development can only come from philosophy. All other solutions will reveal themselves as flawed. Not having the philosophical and supreme nature, they can only be flawed failures.

The objective of philosophy is the good and all that the good represents. The objective of humanity is the good. With the good being the objective, the good can only be treated respectfully and peacefully. There is no reason to treat the good in a disrespectful and harmful to the good way when it is that the good is wished for, when it is that the cause of the good is struggled for. The human being can only be respectful and peaceful. To wish to harm the good, to be disrespectful of the good is to show that the attaining of the good is not the personal objective. Being respectful and peaceful is a personal choice, it is personally regarded as good and proper behavior. It is a behavior of which the individual is fully conscious, as it is a behavior of personal choice and wish. The individual becoming greater, the individual becoming full-grown in the process of being respectful and peaceful. It is the height of personal development that is desired. Being respectful and peaceful is the height of personal development. All that occurs to the respectful and peaceful individual is viewed and considered in the same developed manner, in the most stable and accurate manner. In seeking the good, the good individual does not consider if everyone else has done the same, thinking that if others do not seek the good and are not respectful and peaceful, to then personally seek the good and peaceful human existence is in fact useless, the effort being doomed to failure right from the start. Others not seeking the good doesn't negate the fact the self has taken that all differentiating step. In this respect, all in the self's power has been done to seek the good. All in the self's power has been done to promote and defend the good. The self has control over the self only. Not to wish for the good is to be in the equal way poorer. To personally take up the peaceful and good existence is anything but a waste. There is all the reason to do so. The peaceful attitude is the answer. The good is dominant.

The good government, likewise, by seeking the good is respectful and peaceful. The good is respected. That is why the good is sought. There is an attitude of peace toward the good. That is why the good is attained. The laws of the good government are respectful and peaceful. The good government does not desire to be less than good. The good government does not desire to be nongood. The good government struggles against that which is nongood, against that which is neither respectful nor peaceful. The good government struggles against injustice. The good government can only be said to be neither respectful nor peaceful by those who themselves lack the good and do not understand the good. Those who lack the good are contrary to the good. Those who lack the good will be treated in the equal and such lacking the good, to the nongood, manner. The peaceful law is an extension of the people. Just as the good individual seeks peace, so does human law seek peace. The good individual is given precedence. The existence of the good individual is a fact. If human law does not nor cannot recognize the good individual as such, then human law under the guidance of the good government will learn to do just that. The good individual will be recognized and will be given precedence. The good is of primary importance. The good in people is of primary importance. The criteria in life is the good. By basing itself on the predominance of the good, human law would have excelled. Human law would have been based on the reality of life. Human law would have been based on the supremacy of the good. If imperfection would exist in human law of judging according to the level of good, then that imperfection can be worked upon and improved. The imperfection in other law is greater. By not recognizing the good, it can only be greater. By not fostering the good, by not promoting and defending the good, the imperfection can only be greater. Any one law that does not recognize the predominance of the good is a failure. For it is that such law does not understand the primary need for human law, which is the recognition and empowering of the good. The reorganizing and reestablishing of society will ensue. Society will be restructured according to the leadership of the good. Nor should the leadership of the good be feared. Those who possess the good understand the good and do not fear the good. The fear is with those who lack the good.

The greater the good individual, the greater the magnitude of the importance of that individual. The greater the harm that is inflicted upon the good individual, the greater the say of the good individual as to the punishment of those who are guilty of harming the good. Within the good society, no good individual will be punished or imprisoned. For any one misdeed, the good will be encouraged to seek the good to a greater extent. Observing that the good government is encouraging, instead of being punitive, the good individual will be equally so encouraged to seek the greater good. As it is that the individual possesses the good, the search for greater good will naturally follow as that individual's own wish. Not being punished will only promote the need for greater good. Any such misdeed can only occur in the form of accident or be the result of immaturity. In either case, the good individual will grow more by not being punished. Similarly the good individual will not be imprisoned. Being a member of the good society, the good individual possesses the sufficient and necessary level of good. It serves the good society no benefit to punish the good individual. The good society wishes for the good individual to grow. The wish is for good individuals to inhabit the good society. By not punishing the good individual, greater growth will be promoted.

What sustains the good society is the connective link of seeking the good between its members. What sustains the good society is the common purpose of good by its members and government. The good individual and good government both seeking justice. The good individual and good government both seeking peaceful development. To be governed by the just law is to be governed by a peaceful law. All in this regard of justice and peace is to have been done. Good government is part of the solution. The road to justice and peace also includes the human desire for justice and peace. It is humanity that must seek justice and peace. It is humanity that achieves justice and peace. The good government cannot live the life of the people. The good government cannot live the life of the good citizens. The effort at the good can only be genuine human effort.

Based on the existing fact of philosophical supremacy, it is made evident that humanity has progressed to such philosophical extent. Philosophical truth was wished to be known. Philosophical truth is known. The achievement of philosophy is the achievement of humanity. It is also equally evident that justice and peace are the human objectives. The answers to justice and peace can only come from philosophy. Philosophy then states the answers. Those answers should be understood. Those answers should be attempted to be understood by all. All the while knowing that the philosophical answers are the supreme answers, as no answer to justice and peace can come from outside of philosophy. Any one such answer is a flawed failure. No other comprehensive outlook of life is equal to that of philosophy's. All other answers are based on lack of development. As those answers lack the good, they are pretentious and crude. They exist due to selfish reasons. With the good not being served, they can only be selfish. And as the good is lacked to a greater extent, those views and answers become more selfish. In lacking the good, in being selfish, all the answers and views of justice and peace are tyrannical. All such answers that originate from outside of philosophy are tyrannical. The views offered are not understanding of the issues involved.

Such society, which regards the quality of good of its citizens as primary, has the most firm basis upon which to be built, the good of the human being. All within the good society will be judged according to the good and the level of good. The good individual will behave according to the personal level of good. By seeking the good, by being a member of the good society, the good individual will have done all possible in the achievement of peaceful human existence. In seeking the good, the good individual in interacting with others will take the level of possessed good by the person interacted with into consideration. The good individual and good government are going to work together toward the same common cause of justice and peace. The quality of good is primary in the human being. It is the identity of personal good that defines each individual. Any one other personal attribute can only be understood for what it really is through the identity of good. The good presents a calling to all. The good is the primary attribute. The good is the judging ground. It is the duty of humanity to seek and observe the good. The failure in the matter is the most grievous behavior. To recognize the good, to seek the good, to observe the good is to have the equal to the good personality. It is to have the intelligence of the good. It is to have the equal intelligence to have the good. If there is no intelligence involved in taking part in the good, then the good could not be taken part in. The good cannot be taken part in if the intelligence to do so were lacked. Intelligence equal to the good is of the highest order. It entails the understanding of life. The good individual has the intellect to understand the good. If the good is rejected and lacked, then so is knowledge of the good lacked, so is the intellect equal to the good lacked. Knowledge of the good is of the highest order. If the cause of the good has been sacrificed in favor for that of evil, the attained will be a lack of understanding life, a lack of understanding of the good. The attained will be a lack of intellect. If intelligence were possessed, this would have been shown in the search for the good. The intelligence would have been shown in the understanding of the good, which is not the case. The concepts of intelligence and knowledge can only be properly considered. The concepts of intelligence and knowledge must be properly understood. To lack knowledge of the good, to lack the good, is to be outside the domain of the good. It is to then wage a struggle against the good as a matter of course.

The good is supreme. The good cannot be struggled against. The human objective is the good. Anyone who struggles against the good lacks the good. Anyone who lacks the good is deficient. The objective of nemesis is to harm the good. The objective of nemesis is to destroy the good. For this purpose, nemesis seeks strength. For this purpose, nemesis has attributes of strength. Attributes of strength in the evil purpose of nemesis. Those attributes cannot be used as an indicator as to the nature of the individual. No such attribute, no such ability can be used in assessing intellect and knowledge. For it can only be that any such ability is seeming and apparent. It is not real. Any personal quality can only be as real as the personal good. The nongood individual is defective. It is a defect which is built upon with the intent of becoming more powerful. More powerful in the name of evil, more powerful in the name of nemesis. As the good is so thoroughly struggled against, so will the good so thoroughly defend the cause of the good. It is only by understanding that the good is despised, it is only by understanding that the good is wished to be perpetually harmed, that the good may lead the proper struggle. In such manner will the good society take shape, in the complete defense of the good, in the complete destruction of nemesis. A world shared with evil is not desired.

Human society and culture must be based on the highest of principles, the good. In effect, the highest representation of humanity must govern human society. The highest representation of humanity must govern humanity. The focus of the good society will be the cause of the good. The focus of the good society will be the cause of the good citizen. Those defending the good will be brought closer together. By together struggling for the same common purpose, society will be built, the good's culture expressed. The good society will include all those of the good human character. Not all of whom are the same identical person, all vary. Working together toward the same common cause of good, that variance is meaningless. What is of importance is the cause of the good, the personal self-improvement and growth in attaining the good. All good citizens are from within the domain of the good. For the successful society to be built, the domain of the good must necessarily be sufficient. All the required human skills in creating will be found within. Only the good will take part in the good society. The skills of the good citizens will suffice. The good society will achieve all that is possible. The good can only be the purpose of the vast majority. The accomplishment of the good society will be unmatched. It is that all other societies lack the good. Human history has been to a great extent an attempt to achieve the good. The good, as stated by philosophy, fulfills the human need for the good. By struggling to achieve the good, humanity achieves the good. Humanity understands and accepts the good. The good, the good society, takes all the opposites and brings them to life, all the opposites serving the cause of the good, all the opposites serving the one society. As life includes all the opposites and brings them to life, so does the one society bring all opposites to life. In the process, the one life achieves justice. In the process, the one society achieves justice. The opposites exist to the extent where they do not harm life but build and define life. The opposites exist to the extent where they do not harm the one society but build and define the one society.

The one is of critical importance to life. The one resolves all. The one solves all. Of each life quality, there is one. Within each one life quality, all that is of the same nature is included. The one includes all. All life opposites are included within the one. All life qualities are of life. All life qualities belong to life. All life qualities are included within life. All life qualities are included within the one life. Life is one. Life occurs in life's own way. Life is independent of time and space. The three periods of existence, past, present, and future, occur simultaneously. Life is constant and eternal. The constant and eternal aspect of life guide life. As result, life can never fail. The quality of being constant and being eternal is a life quality. All life qualities, all life laws serve life to the best ability of life. Despite going from change to change, life is constant and eternal. All life laws are included within the one life. All life laws are included within the one. It is the one that gives definition to life. It is the one that gives order to life. In being constant, in being eternal, in achieving the supreme good, life achieves all. The one life achieves all. In considering life's being, it is the qualities of ability and intent that must be understood. Life is victorious. All laws serve life in the victorious form. Life's victorious being, life's supreme being is included within the one. It is the one that makes life's supreme being possible. The One is a Life quality. The One belongs to Life. Life's supreme being belongs to life. The qualities of Truth, Justice, Understanding, the quality of the Good, the quality of the One are all Life qualities. Life's qualities cannot be overturned. Life cannot be overturned. Life's supremacy cannot be denied.

It is life that is attempted to be understood. Life can only be respected. Life can only be worked with. It can only be that humanity wishes to grow. It can only be that humanity wishes for the good. It can only be that humanity wishes to engage in good behavior. No human attribute enriches as the good does. The good presents the most upright, the most righteous human being. Once seeking the good, once attaining the good, the human being has done all possible in living. The human being has done all in growing. All will then be viewed and considered in that same measured and understanding way. By attaining the good, it is the good then that will become the self's guide through life. The good will then become the self's guide through all behavior. Human relations will be elevated to that same and equal level of good. The fellow human being will be understood based upon the quality of good. As result, the most accurate understanding of the human being will be realized. As it is that the good governs life, so it must be that the good must guide the life of the human being. By seeking the good, by attaining the good, it is shown that the character of the good is possessed. It is shown that the necessary and equal to the good character is possessed. Having attained the good means that the previous to the good stages were lacking. And so the good overrides all imperfection. Humanity has never committed sin; therefore it is not possible to live in sin. Not to be in personal possession of a level of good during any one point in the self's life is not possible. To be in possession of a lesser rather than greater good during any one point in the self's life is possible. It is a human need to self-improve. It is human to seek perfection. The only way to do this is by seeking the good. The only way to do this is to continue to seek the good and not abandon the cause of the good. The good resolves all. To misunderstand the lacking of the greater good stages in the self's life is to, an extent, abandon the continuous search for the good. To negatively overestimate the significance of the periods in the self's life during which the greater good was lacked is to fail in the constant search of the good.

As the good leads to good and achieves good, the nongood does not. It is the nongood that is responsible for all negative aspects of human existence, on the social and personal level. The absence of the good creates an individual who lives in misery, for it can only be that only the good can create the good individual, the good individual in every respect. More than the achievement of the good cannot be humanly accomplished. The good individual has accomplished all. The good individual is complete. It is the individual who lacks the good that is lacking. It is the lacking the good individual that is less than complete. It is the lacking the good individual that has not accomplished all and has no desire to accomplish all. To lack the good is to confront the good. To lack the good is to be at war with the good. Lacking the peaceful character, the individual behaves in the same less than peaceful way. By lacking the good, it is the greatest prize that is lacked. The human objective is to attain the good. To lack the good is to have failed in the matter. To lack the good is to be disrespectful of the good. It is to be abusive of the good. The disrespectful and abusive of the good attitude is inherent within the personality which lacks the good. If the good were not abused, then that would mean that the good was in fact possessed, which is not the case. To lack the good is to fail in the attainment of the good. It is to therefore abuse the good. The lacking of the good is fatal to moral character. The lack of the good is at one's own expense. In considering issues, questions of behavior and development, the good is struggled against. The lack of personal good is not escaped. The lack of personal good is fact. The devoid of the good individual is devoid of the good qualities of the human being. The devoid of the good individual is a miserable individual. It is only the good that creates goodness. Lack of goodness creates misery. The devoid of good individual behaves in a miserable way toward oneself and toward others. It is a miserable existence which is not undetected. The individual pays a constant price. The good leads to all that is good, leading to good behavior. The nongood leads to all that is nongood, leading to nongood behavior, leading to nongood attitude. The guide to good behavior, to good attitude, is the good.

In lacking the good, the same lacking the good characteristics are highly regarded. Whereas characteristics of good nature, which should be highly regarded, are not and are detracted from. In lacking the good, nonachieving, nonphilosophical doctrines are endorsed. Atheism and Materialism are nonachieving, nonphilosophical doctrines. Lacking the intellect to engage philosophy, lacking the intelligence to engage the good, atheism and Materialism are turned to. Both doctrines are turned to by pretenders of philosophical endeavor. Both doctrines are turned to by pretenders of intellectual endeavor. Lacking the good, the misery of atheism and Materialism is seen as a solution. Not regarding one's own personal lack of good as such does not mean that the lacking the good individual is not lacking the good. It does not mean that the lacking the good individual is a good individual. The personal lack of good is the personal lack of good. The miserable individual is a miserable individual.

The notion that the good individual is not truly such, that the definition of good is open to interpretation, that such definition of good could very well be mistaken, is false. The human being lives the human life, a greater level to which cannot be lived. That does not mean that human existence is of no value. That does not mean that human opinion, human knowledge, has no value. That does not mean that human knowledge does not exist. It does not mean that human good does not exist. Human truth exists. If human truth did not exist, humanity could not function. The truth can only be good. Human good as result exists. If any one human definition of good is inaccurate, then that is a failure in defining and understanding. That does not mean that human good does not exist. That does not mean that an accurate and understanding definition of the good individual does not exist. The existence of the good individual is a fact. The good individual is immune to any questioning as to the personal possession of good. And if it is thought that there are measures of good in many, then so it must be. That does not mean that the good does not exist, nor that those measures cannot be defined. Order to the good exists, and philosophy is primary in that order. If the good is wished to be better understood, then the ranks of philosophy must be joined.

The supremacy of philosophy can only be accepted. Philosophy is an integral, fundamental part of life. If philosophy ceased, then so would life cease. By achieving truth, philosophy frees the human being. Philosophy makes humanity complete. Life's being is not an unanswerable question. Philosophy, being the top development, is the branch of human thought that fulfills such realm of human capacity. Only philosophy can achieve what philosophy can achieve. Only philosophy can fulfill the top human development. The answers are with philosophy. The answers to human realization are with philosophy. Humanity has a history, philosophy likewise. Throughout which the objective of philosophy has been the achievement of truth. The objective of philosophy has been the enlightenment of humanity. And so philosophy must be seen as one. Each member of philosophy achieving the possible. Each member contributing the possible. No one single philosophy is greater than the one. As human history changes and presents changes, so does historical philosophy present changes. Within any one point in philosophy's existence, the element which will lead to change, the element which will lead to progress is found. The process is continuous. Within any one point in human existence, the element which will lead to change is found. The human path is intertwined with the path of philosophy. When the human historical path undergoes change, the change is to the inherent extent. When historical philosophy undergoes change, that change is to the inherent extent. The change that philosophy brings about in human history is inherent. The change is as philosophy is, integral and fundamental. The human phase of maturity can only be brought about by philosophy. Maturity to humanity is integral, maturity to humanity is fundamental.

Engaging life, humanity, the human being lives life. The human being seeks that which is best for the self. Within any one point in the individual's existence, the element which will lead to change is found. The process is continuous. Hence no phase of the self's life is eternal. By making the effort at life, the equal to the effort is achieved. Entering states of the undesired existence, the effort is made to overcome such states. In the due process of living, this will be done. The undesired will be overcome. The greatest tyranny, the greatest state of personal undesired existence will end, and that which is desired and good will be lived. Within the state of the undesired is found the quality which will bring about change and end the state of the undesired. It is the undesired that is responsible for the creation of the desired. The lacking side of life brings the wealth of life. The quest for the desired is entered solely based on the need to improve the undesired, the state of lacking. Once the lacking state is overcome, the object of the effort will have been attained. The wealth of life is reached upon the previous absence of wealth. Thus life is complete within the self. Greater life is achieved not through mysterious and foreign effort but through life's own effort at greater life. Life's living occurrence serves the purpose of obtaining that which is of most benefit to life, as well as of most benefit to each individual. There is no life stage that does not serve this purpose. It may appear that certain aspects of life are detrimental, but that is an inaccuracy. The greatest state of negative existence only strengthens the state of the positive. When struggling against the undesired, it is only those measures that are of true benefit. It is only those measures which solve the undesired, that are accepted and undertaken. The solutions are those which overcome the negative, the undesired. The negative is always fulfilled within the positive. The question then of what is life's being, how does life live, is thereby answered.

The negative is central to life. Making the effort, life converts the negative. In such unstoppable, relentless life way does life live. In the effort at converting the negative, life seeks greater life. Doing so, change is produced. All change originates from the need to gain greater life. Undergoing the change, the change is complete. The positive is then lived. If it weren't, the negative would still be occurring. The previous by ending, it is the present then that guides behavior. Behavior by originating with the self is the realization of the personal character. It is the self-initiated effort at attaining greater life. In the process, the human consciousness is established. Human consciousness is equal to the undertaken effort at life. The human being is fully conscious. The human being is fully responsible for the self. Humanity is complete within the self. Humanity is complete. Humanity is completely developed. Life is limited. Humanity is limited. Outside of which limitation no behavior can occur. The human attempt at life can only be carried out in that same limited way. Only the limited and possible is capable of being achieved. At the same time, that which is achieved is done so based on the human effort that has been made at life. The human effort at life is set by humanity. Life's living effort is set by life, allowing for full consciousness. With the self having been chosen, so has also all else in life been chosen. No event can negate the love for the self. The consciousness is that which has been wished for. It is the self that produces all in the self's life. The life undertaken and lived is that life based on which the self lives. The originator of all that is within that life is the self. The self achieves all. The self has all. The human being is fully conscious.

It is the effort that creates all. All life achievement is the result of effort. Seeking greater life, achieving greater life is the result of effort. All brought-about change, all brought-about growth is the result of effort. It is effort that creates life. It is effort that creates the human being. Having the objective of greater life, having the objective of greater good, the human being achieves. Not having the objective of greater life, of greater good, the human being does not achieve. Effort creates the individual; lack of effort destroys the individual. Having the good as the objective, the human being seeks the good. The human being achieves the good. The human being lives the full life. Being guided by the good, all issues are solved. All apparent problems are resolved. The human being can only be the full-grown human being. The human being can only be the fully conscious human being. All restrictions to the achievement of the fully developed human being must be overcome.

The good develops the human being. The good matures the human being. The good individual seeks the good. The good creates the good society. In living the full life, the good individual can only seek to create the good society. The answers to what the good society is are found with the good. The good society is founded upon the purpose of improving the life of each of its citizens. The good society is founded upon the purpose of the improvement of its own existence. The purpose of the good society is the achievement of the good. The criteria of the good society is the good. The good society cannot be revealed before its proper time. The good society cannot be built before its proper time. The good society can only be created by the supremacy of philosophy. Any one other claim to the creation of the good society is a false claim. Such claim originates from selfishness and lack of understanding. Being selfish and lacking understanding, any one such claim is tyrannical; any one such claim is a disguised tyranny. Being tyrannical, such claim is punitive. The endorsing individual has a punitive, punishing character. If that weren't fact, then the supremacy of philosophy would have been achieved. Having such need to punish, the target of that punishment is the good individual. The target is the punishing of the good society. The target of punishment is the good. Having such punishing character, reasons are found to justify the punishing attitude. The nongood individual can only behave in the equally nongood manner.

The good society has no equal. The good society will dominate all societies. The good individual is unmatched. The good individual cannot be defeated. The good individual captures the superior human characteristics of intellect, compassion, bravery, and understanding. The superior human character is with the good. As the good is supreme, so is the intellect of the good supreme, so is the compassion of the good supreme, so is the bravery supreme, so is the understanding supreme. It is the call of good that creates the good society. It is the call of the good that brings the good citizens together, working together toward the same common cause of the good. The cause of the good is a conscious, deliberate effort and undertaking. No one single good individual has the capabilities of another. What one lacks, another possesses. Working together, the good society is built. With the good society having undertaken the cause of the good, the good society achieves unity. The good society achieves a single effort toward the cause of the good. Each individual contributing the personal effort toward the objective of the good, contributing the personal way in undertaking the objective of the good. The good society answers the need of humanity. The search of the good, the primary prize in human existence. The good individual is unselfish. The seeking of the good, the attaining of the good, is a thoroughly good act. The good act can only be unselfish. To personally attain the good is for humanity to attain the good. It is to have one good individual. That good individual can only be beneficial to humanity based on the fact that it is beneficial for humanity, to whatever extent that may be, to have one good individual as opposed to not. To whatever extent it may be, the good individual will affect humanity in a positive way. That individual acting in the benefit of others, that good individual is unselfish. Being unselfish, the good individual behaves for the self's own benefit, as well as for the benefit of others. The benefit to others being the individual's good character. Whatever it may be that the good individual achieves, it is for the benefit of humanity, making the good individual unselfish. The good captures all the good and positive characteristics. If the good individual is not unselfish, then no one can be unselfish.

Struggling for the cause of the good, struggling for the cause of the good society, the good individual behaves in such good way. Opposition to the good originates with those who lack the good. Opposition to the good originates with those who lack understanding. Opposition originates with those who are not unselfish but very much selfish, not taking into consideration the cause of the good, not taking into consideration the good and beneficial human character. Instead of the good, it is the nongood that is the objective. In the process, harming the good individual, harming the good society. To be selfish is to put one's own interests ahead of the interests of the greater good. It is to oppose that good which is greater to the personal. In opposing the good, in struggling against the good, the good is then harmed. The harming of the good is the objective of any one view that is contrary to the good. It may not be so stated, but the wish to harm the good is the basis of any one view which opposes the good. If that were not so, then the good would be sided with. The punishment of the good is inherent in any one view which opposes the good. The nongood find reasons for the nongood character. The wishing to harm the good attitude is revealed upon the analysis of the lacking the good reasoning. And so the cause of the nongood can only be exposed and struggled against. The destruction of any one lacking the good reasoning will be carried out in the world of ideas. It is where philosophy is supreme. All monsters are so put on notice.

The human being can only seek to self-improve. Humanity can only seek ever greater growth. By improving and growing, humanity can more readily seek the good. Humanity can more readily attain the good. In requiring the greatest intellect to seek and attain the good, but intellect is not the sole human characteristic responsible for seeking and attaining the good. It is the characteristic of love for the good that makes the achievement of the good possible. The human personality consists of love as well as intellect. If there were no love within the human being, nothing would ever be achieved. Wherever human love is, that is where the human intellect would also be found. Love is the vehicle which brings the intellect into being. The love is the intellect. The two qualities are in fact equated within the self. The balance between intellect and love, mind and heart, is always struck. To achieve any one truth is required that the truth would be needed, that the truth is not hated but loved. Loved to the extent of the truth, loved to the extent of the intellect to achieve the truth. The love for any one truth is identical to the intellect required to achieve that truth. The love for a truth is bound to the intellect of that truth. Intellect and love are connected. They are the same. To lack in one is to lack in the other. To possess love is to possess the same intellect. To lack love is to lack intellect. To lack intellect is to lack love. It is love that initiates all human deed. It is love that achieves all human creation. Humanity, by engaging life, humanity by seeking to understand life, humanity creates, humanity achieves truth. By achieving truth, so also is the love of that truth achieved. The truth becomes a part of the self, as does the love that the truth brings. To attain a truth is to be guided by that truth. It is to be guided by the love of that truth. Without the love for any one objective, that objective would never be realized. No objective would be ever realized. Life would never have taken form if there were no love for life, if there were no love for the self. Love is life's basis. By taking the truth out of life, life ceases, as does love. By taking love out of life, life ceases, as does the truth. The solution to any dilemma will be found in the world of love, the world of intellect, the world of truth, the world of ideas.

In living, the good individual seeks to create. The good individual seeks to achieve. The good individual seeks to live the full life. The search for the highest love, the search for the self's mate, can only meet with success. Life is founded upon life laws. The world of love is a part of life, the world of love is founded upon life laws, the world of love is founded upon the fact of highest love. To be founded upon any less is to deny life's nature, which is in life's highest form. All of life's laws are to the Height of life's existence. The laws of love are in the highest form. Thereby the search for the highest love will meet with success. If the search for the highest love were not successful, that would mean that the human characteristic of love is not real. It would mean that love does not exist altogether, for if love at the primary level is not answered, then love also goes unanswered everywhere else. If the search for highest love were not successful, then that would mean that the life height of existence is less than the possible. It would mean that life's height of existence is founded upon the height of life's laws everywhere else but not in the world of love. The answer to the question of the search for the highest love is found with the miracle of life. The miracle of life contains all. The miracle of life ensures that all is contained. The miracle of life ensures that all will transpire. The miracle of life ensures that the fact of highest love is present. Highest love is that which highest love happens to be. The miracle of life cannot be greater. Each individual by creating the self creates the life lived. They are one and the same. The same will be attained within life as the attained self. Each individual fulfills the miracle of life. The love found is the love searched for. The search for the highest love meets with success. That is attained which has been struggled for. Nonachievement of anything in particular is due to noneffort in the field. To wish to have achieved more from that which has been achieved is to engage in pointless wishful reasoning. The struggled for is at all times attained by the self. The struggled for is always attained by the self in life. To make an effort is to have that effort meet with success. Not to achieve is not to have tried. The content of the effort is the content of the created. It is the self that makes the effort at life. It is the self that makes the effort for the self. It is the self that lives the self's life. The identity of the self is the same as the life lived. That will be done and accomplished in the self's life that has been struggled for. The love found is equal to the love searched for.

All that is of life will necessarily transpire. There is no hindrance to life's occurrence. There is no hindrance to the fact of the highest love. There is no hindrance preventing the good individual from living the full life. Making the effort, the good individual will live the full life. That is created, that is accomplished, that has been struggled for. The self achieves the personal love, the personal intellect that has been struggled for. The self struggles to self-create. The self cannot be denied to the self. The miracle of life is completely fulfilling. Humanity is completely fulfilled. Humanity fulfills life. Humanity is an integral member of life. Without humanity, life would not be the same. The reality of humanity completes life's being. The human being enriches life. Life would lack the human understanding. The human experience would be lacked if there were no humanity. Humanity can only seek to self-improve. Humanity cannot stop seeking the truth. It can only be that humanity would accept the good. It can only be that the good would be empowered. It can only be that the good society will be built. The basis of the good society is the good. The objective of the good society is the achievement of good human existence. The objective of the good society is to assess all within it on the basis of good. The objective of the good society is to judge all within it on the basis of good. The objective is to bring all those who lack the good to justice. The content of the good must be understood by humanity. The content of the good must be known by humanity. By seeking the good, by observing the good, the good individual can never be mistaken as not being good by the good government. The good individual has nothing to fear from the good government. The good citizen seeks the good. The good citizen wishes for the good to govern. The good citizen empowers the good government. The good government is based upon the good of its citizens; the good government wishes for all its citizens to join the good. The good government cannot misbehave against its citizens. All that the good government does is for the benefit of its citizens. And so, all pretenders, all frauds will be destroyed.

The human being can only behave in the good manner. To do otherwise is to be morally diseased. In functioning, the good society will be governed by those who understand the good, by those who love the good. The good society will have those who will protect, those who will guard the good society. The protectors, the guardians will be taught the way of the good. The guardians will know what it is that they are protecting. The guardians will have the good character, the good character of intelligence and bravery, love, and will. As such, the guardians will have no equal. After being in complete possession of the good, the guardians will march against any nation which refuses to voluntarily turn power over to the good. No one has the right to govern other than the good. In refusing to turn power over to the good, the choice of evil is made. The choice to oppose the good is made. The choice to harm the good is made. The good will rule all lands and all people. The good will bring to justice and terminate the life of anyone who should order any opposing enemy to fight and harm the good. The justice is the good's. There is none greater. All justice belongs to the good. The world will function as so stated by the good. As long as the good does not govern all lands, then justice isn't and can't be served.

The claim to the rule of the good cannot be made by anyone other than the good, as so explained and stated by the good. The claim to the good cannot have been made before its time, which is the time of human maturity. Any previous claim, if it had been made, is baseless. As the guardians face an opponent, the guardians will make it clear that this is the army of the good, that it is the voluntary nonresistance that is wished for. If the guardians are challenged, then no unfair advantage is to be sought. If the enemy wishes to gather strength, then the enemy will be allowed to do that. It is the complete destruction of the enemy that is desired. Of that imminent destruction, no excuses would be made. It is the enemy at its most powerful that is wished to be defeated. The army of the good, the guardians, are invincible. No advantage is needed. There can be no fear of a powerless opponent. Being inspired by philosophy and the good, there is no opponent that is a match for the guardians. It is intelligence and bravery, love and will, that is the makeup of the guardians. It is intelligence, bravery, love, and will that will decide all military engagements. It is what the enemy lacks. The enemy of the good is neither intelligent nor brave. The enemy of the good is loveless and without will. If intelligence were possessed, then the good would have been attained. There would have been the required intelligence in order to respect the good, the greatest prize of all. Lacking intelligence, the enemy of the guardians lacks bravery. No bravery can be exhibited in struggling for something that is not in one's possession, the good. Any appearance of bravery is that, an appearance, it is a false appearance. Such act is made out of necessity to that individual's character, the extent of which can only be understood in the possession of the good, and the good is lacked. All is therefore lacked. It is the personality behind the deed that is of value. The deed is defined by personality. Lacking the good, intelligence is lacked. Bravery is lacked. Personality is lacked.

Service in the guardianship will naturally attract a certain type of individual, a type of individual who naturally seeks the good, a type of individual who wishes to know the good. As such, the guardianship will accept all those who wish to protect the good. There will be no test of qualifications other than the assessment of the authentic desire for the good. Being authentic, the guardians will be motivated by the good. The guardians will be inspired by the cause of the good. The waging of battle is carried out through human character. The method is revealing of that character. An army which lacks the good can only wage battle in the same, and equal, to its level of lacking the good manner. The guardians will only wage battle in the same, and equal, to the possessed level of good manner. The guardians will be motivated by the growth of the good. The guardians will be motivated by the cause of bringing all evil individuals to justice. The good does not wish to coexist with those who have chosen the way of evil. That evil is provable based on the ground that the good is opposed, based on the ground that the good is struggled against. The good can only come from philosophy. If humanity wishes to mature, then the way of the good must be observed. The way of philosophy must be observed. That which has transpired in human existence has done so. All that was prior to the existence of the good was lacking the good. All prior human existence was lacking the good. The human wish has all throughout been the good. The human wish for the good can only be fulfilled.

All that has preceded the good will be given the opportunity, the freedom, to study the good, to understand the good. Prior to the good's existence, the good could not have been known. What is then desired of humanity is to judge the good fairly and with justice. Doing so, the good can only be accepted. The good can only be accepted as the proper and future human development. There is no justice greater to the justice of the good. Only the good can govern in the most just way. All is therefore to be governed by the good. As long as there is anywhere in human existence that the good does not govern, then the greatest justice isn't being served. It is the duty of the good to govern all. It is the duty of good to create the greatest justice. Any opposition to the good is a failure by that individual. It is the failure to seek the good. It is the failure to understand the good. The flaw to humanity as not being governed by the good is with those who lack the good. The flaw is with those who do not accept the good. The flaw is with those who wish to harm the good. The side responsible for any battle that the good engages in is the side not accepting of the good. The good can do no wrong, for the good to enter into battle with another is for the good to have been forced to do so. It is the lack of good that leads to all human altercations.

A crime of greater magnitude cannot be perpetrated than not having the good govern. A crime of greater magnitude cannot be perpetrated than having the nongood govern, govern any aspect of human existence. The objective of evil is the defeat and endless suffering of the good. Faced with the situation that the good is thoroughly despised and that the more suffering that is inflicted upon the good, the more joyous the enemies of the good become. The good has one choice in the matter. And that is to defend the good. The good's love for that which is good is equal to the good's hatred for that which is evil. If it is thought that the good is defenseless, then a big mistake is made. All power is with the good. Waging battle, the guardians will behave in the same good manner, in the same intelligent and brave manner. Lacking the good, the enemy of the guardians will behave in the same lacking the good manner, in the same lacking intelligence and bravery manner. The battle waged is decided based on the human character involved. The victor is the superior human. The victor is the good. In the struggle, each guardian will fulfill one's own duty. Each guardian will contribute one's own personal extent of help. The guardian may lose the self's life. That is not to be feared. The life cannot have been pointless. The life cannot have been wasted. The fate in the struggle will have been the self's own and accepted one. What is of concern is the purity of character. For not to have struggled against evil is to have aided evil. To had engaged in the glorious struggle is to have possessed the greatest prize in living, the good. It is better to perish as a good individual than to live as an evil one. The choice for the self has been made. The choice for the good has been made. The life led will at all times be the full life.

In the good's world supremacy, it is the good citizen of each land that will be promoted to political governing of that particular country. The good world society will be bound together by the common search of the good. The bond of the good world society will be the recognition of the good. It is only from within the good society that humanity is full grown. It is only from within the good society that the human being is truly free. Any one other society is not truly free. No other society is full grown. All freedom, all growth, originates with the good. For a society not to be governed by the good is for that society to be neither free nor grown. It is only the good society that can create the greatest good. No other society can achieve the good, as the good is not possessed, as the good is not understood. Creating the greatest good, the good society is the most free. The good society is the most grown. To think that another society achieves more freedom, more growth, to that of the good society, is to neither understand freedom nor growth. The basis of the good society is the good. The good in each individual, the good to any question of societal development. The good individual is the basis of the good society. The good individual will achieve and accomplish all there is to achieve and accomplish. All creation originates with the individual. In creating, the good individual has initiative, drive, and personal responsibility. The good citizen wishes to create. The wish, the desire to create is inherent. The wish, the desire to create is the makeup of the individual. The good individual will possess private property. The good citizen will live in accordance with the personal responsibility The good citizen will live in accordance with personal initiative, the personal drive. By creating, by achieving and accomplishing, the good citizen will acquire wealth, personal wealth. Any one good citizen may acquire greater or lesser wealth than another. The good individual is sincere, humble, understanding, and mature. The good citizen always seeks the truth and justice. The good is always seeking the good. And so wealth cannot be used in assessing human character but rather the personal possession of the good. For a less wealthy individual to be jealous of the wealth of another is for that individual to lack the good. It is for that individual to lack the wish for the good. That jealousy, that lack of personal growth, is not the result of the wealth of another but is the result of lacking the good. If the good were possessed, it would be known that the criteria are the good. If a wealthier than another individual were to feel superiority to the less wealthy on the basis of wealth, then that individual is lacking the good. For if the good were possessed, it would be known that the criteria is the good. Not to assess human character on the basis of the good is to reveal that the good is lacked. Any disrespectful attitude of another individual on the basis of greater or lesser wealth is not due to the issue of wealth but rather due to the issue of lack of good. The creation of a classless society is not the issue, lest it be revealed that by advocating for a classless society, the good is lacked. If the good were possessed, it would be known that the criteria in life is the good and not wealth, and so it would be known that a classless society is not the answer to the creation of the good society. For government to appease the jealous, the lacking wealth individual, by taking the wealth of the wealthy away, is for government to be an accomplice to such envious, lack-of-persona growth, character. It is for government to become envious and less than developed. The issue is not wealth. The issue is the good. In lacking the good, the envious individual will behave in the same lacking the good manner. It will not be in just one instance that lack of development, misbehavior is turned to, but in other and all other instances. Lack of good assures lack of good behavior. The jealousy, the lack of development, will be exhibited elsewhere. As result, government will be the constant appeaser to misbehavior. The hatred of the wealthy by the poor is not the result of being poor; it is the result of lacking the good. By possessing the good, the full and complete life is lived. The wealth of another is not paid attention to. What is paid attention to is the ever greater attaining of the good. Contributing to society, struggling to achieve and create, the full life is lived. With the good government always siding with the good citizen, the full life is lived. If government removes the wealth of the wealthy in an effort to remove the superior, snob attitude by such individuals, then government would not have accomplished anything at all. Removing wealth will not make the arrogant, superior individual good. Nor will it make the arrogant individual seek the good. The good is searched for from within. The good is personally wished for. The arrogant individual will not only misbehave in this one instance but by lacking the good will misbehave anywhere and everywhere else. Government will therefore constantly misbehave along with the arrogant individual in order to appease, in order to appease the nongood individual. The good wealthy or poor individual will not misbehave in any way. The reason for that is the good. The good wealthy or poor individual will assess all in the same good manner. The problem to misbehavior is not wealth, when wealthy, in being wealthy, but lack of good. To remove the wealth, in order to remove the arrogant attitude, is not to produce the good. Lacking the good, misbehavior will follow. What then is the function of government, to remove the endless obstacles to good behavior? That would be an endless and pointless endeavor, an endless and pointless game for government to engage in. Being the constant accomplice to bad behavior. The good is the answer, the promoting of the good in all, including promoting the good for the good society. The good serves the good for all citizens and causes.

The good society will not be a classless society. A society being classless is not the answer. A classless society is not the answer to achieving the good. Society being classless has nothing to do with achieving the good. A classless society would be advocated if the achievement of the good were not the personal objective. To consider that a classless society will achieve the good human existence is to reveal that the good is not understood. It is to reveal that the good is not possessed. What is then possessed is an inadequate, pretentious, and deceptive personality. Pretentious and deceptive in claiming to have an answer, pretentious and deceptive in claiming to aid society, pretentious and deceptive in claiming to aid humanity. It is for someone who has no understanding of the good, to speak of understanding the good. It is to reveal the lack of intelligence, tyrannical character. The fact of someone else's greater wealth to the personal wealth is not the concern of any one single individual. It would be of concern if the good were not of concern. What is of concern is the good, the ever greater attainment of the good. To be observant of someone else's wealth is to exhibit the personal greed, though that greed may be well disguised. If there were no personal greed, then the wealth of another would not be considered. It is the good that fulfills the self's life. Making personal greed a nonissue. The good society will serve all its citizens, all its citizens will serve the good society. Poverty will be eradicated. The core of the good society will be the individual, the responsible, the ever-growing individual. Anyone who is helped by government will in turn help the good society. It is the human being, the individual, that creates. Society is founded upon the creativity of the human being. The good society will achieve all that is within to achieve. For that purpose, the individual will be helped to become more responsible, more ever growing, more creative. It is the human being of initiative and drive that is desired. It is the human being of individualism that is desired. The good society will be governed by the good government. The basis of the good government will be philosophy. It is only philosophy that can achieve the good. It is only philosophy that can reveal the good. The objective of philosophy is the good. The objective of philosophy is the good for the good society. The good for all its citizens. The good government cannot govern in a nongood manner. The good government can only govern in a good manner. It is not within philosophy to seek less than the good. The good government will govern on a permanent basis. Only those will participate in the good government who are of good character. Anyone wishing to engage in governing will do so from within the ranks of the good. The needs of the good society can only be met by the good, the needs of the good society can only be met by philosophy. There is nothing preventing the good citizen from being a good citizen. If it is that governing is not personally wished to be engaged in. There is nothing preventing the good citizen from living the full life. The good government is of the people, by the people in fact, and not in empty theories. The good government will rise from the ranks of philosophy and not just any philosophy. Good government will rise from the philosophy marking humanity's maturity, from the all-inclusive one philosophy. The object of philosophy is to clarify, to achieve truth. The object of philosophy is to grow and develop. The differing philosophies will work together, producing a consensus, producing the good government. It is not confrontation that is sought with the history of philosophy but acceptance.

Philosophy will establish the guidelines of the good society. The founder of the good society will be the one philosophy. All thereafter will be in accordance with the original doctrine. Anyone contrary to the good act, as so determined by the good government, will be a criminal act. The individual committing the criminal act is a criminal. It is time for humanity to grow up. All pretenders will be exposed and crushed. The good will settle accounts with all monsters. The good will uproot and discard all previous to the good society. As has been the human endeavor, it is philosophy that is the core. Philosophy has been central to the human being, and philosophy will forever remain central. It is best not to challenge philosophy.

Philosophy is the answer to the creation of the good society. Philosophy is the answer to human development. Philosophy is the

answer to human knowledge. Philosophy is the answer to understanding life. The human objective is to create the good. The human
objective is to understand life. Life's being is complete. Never is less
than life's complete being lived. Any one life stage is complete. Any
one life stage is fully lived. No life stage can be taken out of life's
being. No life stage can be added to life's being. The addition of any
one, not of life stage, or the removal of any one life stage would be
the destruction of life. The addition of any not-of-life element or
the subtraction of any life element would be the destruction of life.
Life consists solely of life. No alteration can ever occur to life. To add
to life or to subtract from life would be an alteration, an alteration
which would destroy life. Life cannot be destroyed. Life is not missed
out upon. Life is always fully lived. Life's supreme stage will occur.
The supreme stage will be complete. The dominant good cannot be
experienced by another, nor can it be that the dominant good can
experience another. If that were to occur, the experiencing of another
other than the present stage, beyond the inherent extent, then that
would mean that life is not occurring. That would mean that life is
not living. By not living the present life is not living. By not living
the present stage, life is not occurring. Attention is paid to the present. The present is fully lived. That is why it is only the present that
is experienced and not any other stage. If present life lived the stage
of another, that would destroy life. Each stage fulfills life's objective. Each stage is needed in life's being. No stage cannot not occur.
The extent of which is fully lived. No life stage can be replaced with
another life stage. Life's occurrence is such as life's occurrence. Life's
occurrence is the best life occurrence. Life must be accepted. Life
must be respected.

No event can occur that would remove any part of life. No
event can occur that would minimize life. Life is the sovereign ruler
of all. Life is the sovereign ruler of the self. If life's being were minimized, then life would be taken away from. Life would be altered.
Life would be destroyed. As life lives, it is life that is included within
life's being. Life consists of all life. Life consists of all. All consists of
life. To live is to do so within life. To occur is to do so within life.
Life cannot not be taken part in. Each life stage flows into the next,

forever repeating. Life cannot be abandoned. All within life is bound to life. To ponder as to what lies outside of life is to look to life since it is that life consists of all, since it is that life takes place within the realm of life's being. All observation is made by life, regarding life. Life cannot be abandoned. All attention is to be turned toward life. To question what lies outside of life is to look within life. To question where it is that life takes place is to look to life. Life takes place in the sanctuary of life. Life's occurrence is the inclusion of all of life's stages. Each of which is followed by the next. It cannot be that one stage does not flow into the next. Within life occurs all. Life's location is of no concern, what is of concern is life's being. The answer to all questions is found with life. Life's laws serve life. All laws have been molded in life's manner. All laws have been formed in the manner that best serve life. All laws have been formed in the manner where life's richest existence is assured. To wonder how it is that life achieves life's seemingly overwhelming and difficult tasks is to look to life's ability and intent. Life's intent is to achieve that which is best. Life's ability is to achieve that which is best. By seeking that which is best, life cannot but succeed in achieving that which is best. Life cannot but succeed in realizing life's objectives. By living, life has the strength to live. Life is never in danger of occurring in a mistaken way, one which would deny the height of life's being, one which would deny life's one and best path of development. Nothing is by chance. Life's laws ensure life's eternal success. No aspect of life is ever in danger of not occurring. Life has it within to develop in the single and best way.

Life will not develop in a different from the single and best way. All that occurs is from within life's being for it to have occurred. The existence of all was a fact. The existence of all is a fact. The existence of all is assured. Human existence is assured. Human existence was assured. Humanity is of vital importance to life's being. Human consciousness is of vital importance to life's being. The earth's history, human history, could not have developed in a different way. Human creation, the human consciousness enriches life. As it is that life seeks greater life, so does humanity seek greater life. The human search for greater life is within the bounds of life's search. The Human search does not exceed life's but is in accord with life's search. During the less than dominant stage, life lives in less than the dominant way. Life has during the less than dominant stage achieved less than the dominant stage. Life at that point seeks the dominant good. Life then seeks greater life. Resulting in life's ending of the lacking the dominant good stages. Those phases must end for the dominant good to be achieved. Humanity behaves in accord with life's search for greater life, with life's search of the greater good. It is no illness that brings about the end of any one life, rather life's effort for greater life. Never does an event which is not in search for greater life end any one life. Life's laws must be understood. Life's laws serve life.

With life living in life's most victorious form, life lives on life's terms. What concerns life is life. What concerns life is the best way to attain greater life. As result, life's location is of no concern. Space is of no concern. Time is of no concern. Time is certainly meaningless with the past, present, and future occurring simultaneously. Time is certainly meaningless with life achieving that which is best. The past, present, and future occur in their particular way. The present is not taken away from. The present cannot be taken away from. The living in the present cannot be abandoned. For life not to live in the present is for life not to exist. Life's location is of no concern. Life's being cannot be abandoned. Life's being is not wished to be abandoned. The existence of all is dependent on life. It is life that occurs. It is life that lives. All attention must be turned to life. Life is to be understood. Life is to be respected. Life's occurrence can only transpire. Life has done all to the best of life's ability. Life's victory should be kept in mind. Life is the victorious ruler of all.

Life's successful present existence is always assured. Life's present existence is following the same path, that of the past. And the past was successful. Life's present existence is following the path of the future. And the path of the future will be successful. The success of the past and the future is within the success of the present. Life's past existence was successful because that existence was always preceded by the successful past. With the past being successful, that can only mean that the present will be successful. The future will be successful because the past was successful. The future will be successful because the future has it within to be successful. The future is past to the greater future. Life's success is undeniable.

The past and the future occur within the present. They occur to the inherent extent; that extent does not interfere with the present but only aids the present. It is the present that is experienced. It is the present that is lived. The present is the same as the past. To live the present is to live the past. The present is the past, and the past is the present. As life takes place in the past, life takes place in the present. Life always occurs in the present; therefore the past is the present. The past cannot occur separately from the present, for if it could, it would be the past that would be lived and not the present. Consequently life would never transpire, as it is that only the present is lived. The past cannot be separated from the present. Just as the present contains the past and the future, so do the past and future contain the present. Life cannot go unfelt. Past, present, and future are bound together, occurring to the inherent extent. Aiding the present and not interfering with the present. In the process, enriching life.

The endless times that life has occurred and will occur are reducible to the present one, and all life occurrence is included within the present. In life's endless, and same, cyclical repetition, it is the present that is of concern. It is the present that is lived. As such, the present is each cycle. Each cycle is the present. Each cycle is the first and one life occurrence. Regardless of how many times life occurs, all life occurrence is reducible to the one present existence. The deciding point is that life has eternally occurred and will eternally occur in the exact same way as the present. Once life's eternal, and same, repetition is understood, then at that point, precedence to the present will be given. It is the present that lives. It is the present that seeks the good. It is the present that achieves that which is best. Therefore all life occurrence transpires within the present. To understand life is to understand that life's laws favor life. Life's laws serve life.

Philosophy has always been the supreme human development. Philosophy will forever be the supreme human development. The supremacy of philosophy can only be understood and accepted as such by humanity. If it is that humanity wishes greatest growth, then philosophy must be engaged in. Doing so, the greatest development will follow; the greatest answers will follow. Philosophy is the supreme human thought. No other human thought is concerned with knowing life's ultimate being. No other thought is a match for philosophy. No other thought is concerned with knowing the good. No other thought can know the good. No other thought can achieve the good. If it is knowledge that humanity wishes for, then philosophy must be engaged in. The history of philosophy is there to be observed. The history of philosophy is there to be studied. Engaging in philosophy, studying philosophy, the human being grows. Philosophy builds upon the past. Philosophy builds upon philosophy. In the process, including within philosophical thought. In the process, continuing the link with philosophical thought. By turning to philosophy, by growing, the human being achieves truth. That truth is greater than any other. Being greater, it cannot be that philosophy does not bring about change. Change from the nonphilosophical, change from that which has preceded philosophy. Though philosophy brings about change, the nonphilosophical is not devoid of good. That which has preceded philosophy is not devoid of good. The good society will continue the link with the past. The good of the past is not rejected but built upon. All that is of good nature will be accepted within. Change will however occur. Great change can only occur, as it is that philosophy, the good, has been to such a great extent lacked. The good cannot work against the cause of the good. All that is good will be promoted. It serves the good no purpose to minimize the good, to detract from the good in others. It serves the good no purpose not to be founded in the good. It serves the good no purpose not to defend the good. The good citizen is the core of the good society. The cause of the good is the foundations of the good society. Human history reveals that the search for the good has been ever present. Humanity is not unaware of the overriding importance of the good. It is the search for the good that drives humanity. This is the reason that the good has been attained. The good that has been searched for has been the good found. It is philosophy that is the answer to the search of the good. The good society is the answer to the human need for the good. The judging of all within society on the basis of good is the answer to the creation of the good society. Philosophy is the natural progression of human history, as it is that the human search for the good has been ever present. The human search of the good has been found in the supremacy of philosophy. Making an effort at the good allows the human being to attain the good. The good is then understood. The good is then recognized. The good is recognized in others. The good is sided with by those possessing, by those recognizing the good. It cannot be that the good is opposed by those possessing the good, as it is that opposition to the cause of the good would be opposition to the good of the self. Philosophy can only be recognized as supreme by those possessing the good. Philosophy cannot be recognized as supreme by those lacking the good. Siding with philosophy, philosophy is empowered. The good society is built.

The good society can only be built by philosophy. The basis of the good society can only be built by philosophy. The answer to what the good society is can only be found with philosophy. Philosophy achieves the supreme human answers. Philosophy achieves the good. The content of the good constitutes the range of the good, which includes the building of the good society. It is only natural that philosophy would state the basis of the good society. It is only natural that philosophy would build the good society. The answer to the good society cannot come from any source other than philosophy. The good is not the objective of anyone else other than philosophy. The good cannot be claimed to be therefore possessed by anyone other than philosophy. Philosophy cannot allow for anyone else to claim to reveal the good. Philosophy cannot allow anyone to claim to represent the good. Anyone who seeks to create society not in the name of philosophy is seeking to enslave humanity and the good. Anyone who seeks to create society not in the name of philosophy is seeking to harm humanity and the good. Philosophy, by the nature of philosophy, does not allow for anyone other than philosophy to state, to define the content of the good. Philosophy makes the effort. Philosophy makes the achievement. It cannot be that someone other than philosophy can define the good. As it is that philosophy does not allow for foreign definition of the good, philosophy cannot allow for anyone other than philosophy to define the good. No such definition of the good can be made by someone other than philosophy, as it is that no effort at knowing the good has been made by anyone other than philosophy. It is not within philosophy, it is not within the good, to tolerate such false claims. It is not within philosophy to tolerate false representations of the good. The harm caused by nonphilosophical governing is evidenced by all current societies. The results of nonphilosophical governing is evidenced by the Democratic US political history. Countless of know-nothing, wretched fools have sought and gained political power. The objective of democracy is not the good. The objective of democracy is the oppression of the good.

The issue, the objective, is the creation of the good society. The objective cannot be the creation of the less than the good society. To wish to create the less than good society is to admit, it is to indicate, that the good is lacked. It is to therefore wish not to serve the purpose of the good. Not to serve the good is not to serve the good for the people. It is not to serve the good for the citizens of society. Any attempt at building society that does not have the objective of the good is a flawed attempt. It is a flawed, tyrannical attempt, which serves no beneficial purpose in the building of the good society. Such a flawed, not-serving-the-good attempt can only be tyrannical in nature. It is the good that is oppressed. It is the good that is denied freedom. The criteria is the serving of the good. Not to serve the good is to be tyrannical. Any one individual wishing to build a tyrannical society is a tyrant, and anyone wishing to be governed by a tyranny is serving the purpose of being a tyrant. The good citizens of society can only wish to be governed by the good government. The human wish is to reject tyranny, the human wish is to seek the good. It is only philosophy that understands the substance of the good society. There can only be one best understanding of the good society. There can only be one best alternative for the good society. The best alternative cannot be equated to another. That best alternative does not allow to be equated to another. Philosophy does not allow to be equated with any other alternative. To serve a less than best alternative is to equate the less than best with the best. It is not to serve the good. The democratic alternative is not an effort at philosophy. The democratic alternative is not the best understanding of the good. It is not the best understanding of the good society. Democracy equates itself with the best. Democracy equates itself with philosophy. As democracy equates itself with the best, democracy allows for less than the best to be equated with the best. Less than the best alternative is equated to the best alternative. As result, democracy does not serve the needs of the people. Democracy does not serve the good. The claim of democracy is that democracy is desired by the people. The claim is that democracy offers freedom. Such claims are made by those who endorse the democratic understanding. The made claim does not mean that the claim is correct. In fact, the claim is not correct. It is incorrect. The desire of people is not democracy. The desire of people is the good. To desire anything other than the good is to be a tyrant. To desire anything other than the good, by the good of society, is not possible. It is to behave contrary to the self's best interests. Democracy's claim that it is desired by the people only shows that democracy has no understanding of people's needs. Democracy's claim that it is desired by the people only reveals its own tyrannical nature. Democracy doesn't understand the good. The good is not supported. The good is opposed. Democracy is a tyranny. What democracy wishes for is the subjugation of the good. What democracy wishes for is the subjugation of the good society. Driven by its own selfish reasons, democracy puts a mask on its tyrannical nature. Driven by blind ambition, democracy seeks to rule over those who are superior to it, disregarding the harm done to the good society, disregarding the harm done to the good citizen. Claiming to serve the people, democracy tries to disarm. Democracy puts on a false appearance in the effort to disguise its tyrannical nature. Democracy is a tyranny perpetrated by a minority few against humanity. Such is the nature of democracy. Its days have passed. Philosophy has the mission to overthrow all that is false.

The fact of democracy having a history doesn't prove that democracy is an adequate government. The fact that democracy has been apparently successful does not prove that democracy is an adequate government. Nothing proves that democracy is the proper human government, the proper human government for all times. Whatever success any democratic society has had has been due to human ingenuity. Whatever success any democratic government has had has been due to the human spirit. Such success has been the result in spite of democratic rule. Democracy is the unwanted government. In due time its citizens will become aware of its failings. Humanity can only wish to be governed by the good. It is the type of governing that democracy does not provide. Democracy does not meet the needs of the people. Its inherent failings, due to not understanding the good, its inherent corruption, its inherent abuse of the good, in due time become more and more pronounced. As greater and greater, more and more freedom is given to issues which are not understood by democracy, issues which are not supported by the good citizens, those issues only increase in number and severity as the democratic government repeatedly fails in its understanding of the proper and good course for society to take. Democracy leads to the destruction of culture, for what culture democracy endorses is in a constant struggle with the good. The corruption of the democratic government is inherent, just as the abuse of the good is inherent. What greater corruption than the abuse of the good can there be? The problem for democracy is in fact of the good. The problem for democracy is philosophy. As it is that only philosophy can reveal the good. Only philosophy can reveal the flaws within democracy. Only philosophy is superior to democracy. Philosophy is superior to all not philosophical governments. All political power belongs to philosophy. Any one other political development is illegitimate. It is only philosophy that can know the good. The good philosophy can only have complete governing, rejecting democracy. It is the constant struggle with the good that leads to the demise of democracy. No great delight should be taken by any nonphilosophical development in the destruction of democracy by philosophy. The good, philosophy will settle matters with all political deformities.

The good society will reject democracy just as democracy has rejected the good. The good society will accept within all that is of good nature. Democracy was a great human achievement. There is much to be learned from democracy. The great personalities in its creation cannot be denied. The great intelligence behind democracy, the great intelligence behind the US Constitution is not being denied. Democracy has served its purpose. It is time for democracy to grow greater yet. It is within democracy to accept the good. It is within democracy to abandon its own views. Democracy is to a good extent seeking the good. There is good within democracy. It is that need for the good that can lead to the acceptance of the good, to the acceptance of philosophy, by democracy. The good could not have been observed before the good's existence. Democracy could not have observed the good before the content of the good was known. Democracy could not have observed the good due to the fact that the good was not known. Once the good is known, so is the superiority of the good known. To seek the good is to recognize the good. To seek the good is to accept the good. To seek the good is to continuously progress in the search for the good. The search for the good cannot become stagnant. Democracy cannot cease in the search for the good. The need for the good can only be constant. As result, democracy must accept philosophy as the good. If philosophy is not recognized as the good, then the search for the good was never engaged in. What is engaged in is the satisfying of selfish and tyrannical motives. If the peaceful and prosperous human existence is wished for, then the good, philosophy must be accepted.

It cannot be that the good does not wish to create the peaceful and prosperous human state. That is the only way the good can behave. The good includes all good within. To behave in a less than good manner is to have lacked the good. The good cannot seek less than the good. The good cannot seek to harm the good's own cause, and the good is supreme. The good cannot seek to harm a good individual. To harm a good individual is to harm the cause of the good. It is to harm the self. The good can never be contrary to the good. Philosophy can never be contrary to the good. Philosophy can only seek to create the peaceful and prosperous society. It is only philosophy that can create the peaceful and prosperous society. To oppose the good, to oppose philosophy, is to oppose the human peaceful and prosperous existence. To then struggle against the good is to harm the good. The waged such struggle is a part of human existence. The responsible one for the struggle is the lack of good. The good may be struggled against, but that struggle is not in the attempt to achieve the good. That struggle is not an attempt to achieve the peaceful and prosperous society. It may be so stated that to struggle against the good is to seek the peaceful and prosperous human existence, but such a statement can only originate from lack of knowledge, such a statement can only originate from lack of understanding. It is only philosophy that seeks the peaceful and prosperous human existence. With philosophy at the head of society, that peaceful and prosperous existence includes all that is peaceful and prosperous. The waged struggle against peace and prosperity is not the work of the good. The waged struggle against peace and prosperity is not the fault of philosophy. For that reason, the struggle against the good, the effort to harm the good must be completely suppressed. To struggle against the good is to harm the good. It is to lack the good. And so the reasons given for struggling against the good are reasons for lacking the good. They are reasons based on which evil seeks power. And if people side together in the effort against the good and laws are made giving evil political power, those laws are illegitimate, regardless of the manner in which they were established. Regardless if they were democratically established or established by any other political system. Those laws are illegitimate and tyrannical. The given reasons are illegitimate and tyrannical. It is not for anyone other than philosophy to state the understanding of the good. As result, such political power must be turned over to the good. Such political power must be turned over to philosophy. The state of human maturity is marked by philosophy's state of maturity. Humanity well understands that knowledge of life's laws, the peaceful human existence and the creation of the good society, are humanity's primary efforts. All three efforts are in fact a single effort, and philosophy is the supreme human development. Philosophy has the answers to the primary human tasks.

It is not possible for philosophy not to expose that which is phony and pretentious. It is not possible for philosophy not to wage a struggle against nemesis. It is not possible for philosophy not to suppress all evil monsters. It is upon the vanquishing of nemesis that the peaceful human existence can be achieved. It is upon the vanquishing of nemesis that the good society can be built. By possessing the good, by understanding the good, what is also understood is the nature of evil. It is to know that nemesis has one objective, to harm the good, to inflict pain and suffering on the good. Not to expose nemesis, not to suppress nemesis can only be due to lacking the good, can only be due to not understanding nemesis. By possessing the good, the struggle against evil is then inherent. The foul nature of evil can only be exposed. The starting point in waging the struggle against nemesis is the recognition of the good. The starting point is the possession of the good. Once possessing the good, the object of the made effort then can only be the good. It is to then struggle for the good. It is to defend the good. It is to make a distinction between the good and nongood. It is to be accurate in thought. It is to be correct in assessment. Once possessing the good, no mistake can be made. The good is struggled for. Nemesis is struggled against. The good cannot harm the good. The good cannot harm the cause of the good. The good cannot be evil. The good's judgment of evil is justified. The good cannot fear the good. The good citizen cannot fear the good government. The good government works for the benefit of all its good citizens. If the good government is wished to be engaged in, the good government can be engaged in from within the good government. The leaders of the good society will rise from the school of philosophy. The task of philosophy is to be the supreme human development. The task of philosophy is to govern in the supreme and good manner. The task of the good citizen is to be a good citizen. The task is to support the good government. The task is to live the full life. It is not possible for the good government not to know the needs of its citizens. It is not possible for the good government not to meet those needs. Nor is it possible for the good government to be corrupt. The good cannot be less than good. Corruption cannot arise from the good. Corruption can only arise from the lack of good. Which is any one society that does not have philosophy, the good, as its leader.

The human objective is the good. The human objective is the achievement of the good. To struggle against the good is therefore a grave crime. By the fact that the good exists, it is proven that the good is attainable. It is proven that through effort and desire, the good is attainable. Based on the fact of the good's existence, the good, philosophy, can only then state and reveal the good's content. It is only natural for the good to be revealed once possessed. By doing so, differences with inadequate understandings of the good can only be pointed out. The superiority of the good, the superiority of philosophy can only be pointed out. The good can only appear at the appropriate moment in human history. To wonder why the good has come into existence at that appropriate moment is to wonder why any one human event occurs at its appropriate moment. It is to question the workings of life. The human search for the good is a historical fact. Humanity was never denied the search for the good. Humanity was never denied the human spirit. To question the good's moment of existence is to have questioned the good's any one different moment of existence, for whatever reason. If the good's existence were any one different moment, then that moment also can be questioned for whatever reason. As result, attention should be turned toward the stated content of the good. The fact of the good is of critical importance. To reject the good, to struggle against the good is a grave crime. The good does not have to be opposed. Democracy is to peacefully turn political power over to the good. The natural progression of democracy is the acceptance of the good. The natural progression of democracy is its own rejection. The November impostors must peacefully turn political power over to the good. In order to fulfill the legacy of democracy, political power must be peacefully turned over to the good. The day of judgment draws near. All within the good society will be judged according to the level of good. The possessed level of good is of central importance. It has long been the human wish for all to be judged on the basis of the good. The judging of all on the basis of good is central to philosophy. It is only proper for the good society to make such judgment.

Any one human historical occurrence can only take place at its appropriate moment. The good can only appear at the appropriate moment. No human historical event occurs at an inappropriate moment. No one individual misses out on any future human occurrence. No one individual misses out on any future human historical growth. Past humanity, to any human historical growth, has always had the opportunity to seek the good. No one human being is denied the self. Life is completely fulfilling. To think that past humanity misses out on the future is to think that life is not fulfilling. All within the human ability is always accomplished. All within the human ability is always known. With philosophy revealing the good, humanity achieves maturity. Humanity achieves the desired. Prior to the desired, prior to achieved perfection, the undesired, imperfection, was lived. Imperfection leads to perfection. But if imperfection were truly such, it could not have led to perfection. As humanity develops, as humanity seeks truth, humanity achieves truth. It is not the human wish to live in an undeveloped state. It is not the human wish to have the false as the human understanding. Achieving truth necessarily means that the false is recognized as such. Achieving truth means that the false is rejected. Such is the human growing effort. The search for truth leads to truth. The truth is not beyond humanity. The good is not beyond humanity. Philosophical truth is not beyond humanity. Philosophy has long been recognized as the supreme human knowledge. Philosophy is central to the human being. Philosophy is central to human thought. The achievement of the truth is dependent on the search for the truth. Humanity must continue the human legacy of growth. The human legacy of attaining truth. The human nature is not the seeking of the false. Human nature is not the seeking of evil. Lest humanity wish to live in a state of immaturity, lest humanity live the nightmare.

The objective is human growth. The objective is the good. As philosophy is the primary human effort, as philosophy is the primary human development, philosophy welcomes all philosophical efforts. Philosophy welcomes all lovers of knowledge. Philosophy, knowledge, does not welcome any pretense of knowledge. Philosophy does not welcome any not genuine effort at knowledge. Philosophy does not welcome fake lovers of knowledge. No fake lovers of the good will be tolerated. No pretense of intellect will be tolerated. Philosophy will morally settle matters with all such frauds. It is in the world of ideas that all such frauds will be crushed. Philosophy is the love of knowledge. Philosophy is the effort at knowledge. The effort cannot but be made. The effort cannot but be obvious. All philosophical frauds will be crushed. All fake lovers of the good will be crushed. All fake lovers of peace and love will be crushed. The greater the pretense, the greater the deception, the greater the philosophical destruction of such frauds shall be. The good is to be respected. The good is not to be abused. The states of immaturity cannot be the human objective, lest humanity wish to live the nightmare. Philosophy is there to enlighten. The objective of philosophy is the grown and mature human being. The objective of philosophy is the moral and knowing human being.

With the human historical development taking place, the need for the good has been ever present. The need for the good has been the primary human development. The moral and knowing human being has always been the human objective. The moral and knowing human being has always been the dominant human being. The deciding factor to any issue is the good. As the good is life's basis, so is the good the basis of any one issue. The dominance of the good has been a part of human historical development right from the start. To seek less than the good is to be a lesser human. As the lesser struggles against the superior, the lesser fulfills its level of lack of morality, the lesser fulfills its level of being the lesser. The acts of the lesser are from within life's being. The range of which should not be overestimated. It is a fact that the lesser harms the superior to its good. It is a fact that the lesser continually opposes and struggles against the good. It may therefore appear that the lesser, the lacking the good, is victorious in its struggle with the good. At no time does the lesser, the nongood, become other than being the nongood. By opposing and struggling against the good, it is ensured that the lesser, the nongood is such. The nongood fulfills its status as nongood through its struggle against the good. In so doing bringing order to life, in so doing becoming the lesser, becoming the nongood. Life's justice is life's foundation. The nongood, based on its actions, enters the world of the good. The world of the good's law is entered. The judging law is the good. The judging criteria is the good. The good is supreme. Possession of the good is supreme. To lack the good is to lack the good. No attempted deception as to the possession of the good is possible. The fact which ensures that the nongood is such is the struggle against the good. The factor which ensures that the nongood is never victorious in its struggle with the good is the nongood's struggle with the good. The nongood is never victorious over the good. The nongood is never the good. The struggle against the good is lost right from the start. It is the struggle that makes the good the greater. It is the struggle that makes the nongood the lesser. The appearance that the nongood has power over the good is a false appearance. The good cannot be harmed. The good is never harmed. The range of the nongood's acts should not be overestimated. The range of the nongood's acts should be properly understood. The objective is the good. To lack the good is to achieve less. To lack the good is to be less. To seek evil, to engage in evil is to be destroyed by evil. Engaging in good elevates the human status. Engaging in evil lowers the human status. The greater the evil, the greater the lowering of the human status. Then lowering the human status to the point where the term *human* is only figuratively used. Then joining the ranks of the Subhuman Factor. Evil is so eagerly wished to be engaged in. It is the one wish that evil will pay the highest price for. The evil human being, by struggling against the good, leads to evil's destruction each and every time. The good exists for a reason, for the needed observance of the good. To disregard the good is a grave crime. The leadership of the good must be observed. The leadership of philosophy must be observed.

The good is dominant. The cause of the good is dominant. The good human being has been dominant all through human history. No evil act was ever victorious over the good. No evil individual was ever victorious over a good individual. The absence of the good has always been fatal to moral character. And if the immoral individual should defend immorality, then the immoral individual has no comprehension of the good. The immoral individual has no comprehension of philosophy. The immoral individual has no understanding of life. The evil individual lacks the greatest prize in life. The key is the good. The good is the only prize. The good makes attaining the good possible. To attain the good is to have the equal and necessary level of good to attain the good. The good makes the understanding of life possible. It is better to understand life than not to understand life. To understand life is to have the equal to the understanding character. It is to have done all possible to have attained the good. By possessing the good, by understanding life, the individual will behave in the same good way. The individual will behave in the same of life understanding good way. All good stems from life's understanding. Not to understand life is to lack life. It is to lack the good. To understand life is to have the equal intellect to do so. To understand the good is to have the greatest intellect. Only an intelligent individual can achieve the good. Only an intelligent individual can behave in a good manner. To understand the good is to understand life's lawful goodness. To understand life is to understand that life's basis is the good. It is to understand that the good is the law. As the fact of life's goodness cannot be denied, neither can the fact of God be denied. What other definition can there be of God other than life's lawful eternal goodness? To achieve understanding of life can only be good. To achieve understanding of God can only be good. Not to understand life, not to understand God is to lack the character to do so. It is to lack the character to engage in good behavior. It is to lack the effort. It is to lack the intelligence to understand the good. To speak of God's nonexistence is to have such lacking character. It is to have such lacking the good character. It is only philosophy that can attain the good. For anyone outside of philosophy to speak of the good, for anyone outside of philosophy to speak of God is to have such lacking of the good character. Just because God's existence is affirmed by those outside of philosophy doesn't mean that God's existence is in fact affirmed. Only philosophy can affirm God's existence. Lacking the effort, lacking the ability to attain the good, any external to philosophy affirmation of God is an affirmation of the title, God, and not any further. No further connection to God can be made, other than to say the word God. This is due to the fact that no effort at philosophy has been made, and there can be no philosophical knowledge. There can be no philosophical knowledge of the good, there can be no knowledge of God. The nonphilosopher then proceeds to attribute nonphilosophical, nonknowing qualities to God. The nonphilosopher attributes noneffort and nonintelligence to God. The nonphilosopher does not approach God. The nonphilosopher does not define God. The nonphilosopher defines the noneffort, the nonknowing personal noneffort as being God. The nonknowing nonphilosopher by speaking for God, the nonknowing nonphilosopher speaks for the personal self. There is no connection between nonphilosophy, religion, and God. The connection is with the non-effort-making, nonknowing self. Lacking shame, the non-knowing maniac proceeds to speak for God. The claim of knowing, the claim of worshiping God is made. The one being that religion does not know, the one being that religion does not worship is God. The object of worship is the personal conceit and ignorance.

Life's most fundamental questions can only be answered by philosophy. Philosophy is here to change the way of the past. The effort at knowledge is with philosophy. The effort of seeking the good is with philosophy. The effort at truth, the effort at justice is with philosophy. The effort at God is with philosophy. It is only philosophy that can reveal the good. It is only philosophy that can reveal God. Religion makes no effort at the good. Religion makes no effort at knowledge. Religion makes no effort at truth. Religion makes no effort at justice. Religion makes no effort at God. If an effort were made, religion would become philosophy, proving or disproving any one idea would be engaged in. Lacking effort, religion lacks achievement. Religion cannot reveal the good. Religion cannot reveal God. Not seeking the good, religion does not attain the good. Religion does not know the good. Religion does not reveal the good. Religion does not attain truth. Religion does not attain justice. The achievement of religion is the false. The achievement of religion is injustice. Religion's qualities of falsehood and injustice, religion attributes to the God of religion. God is truth. God is justice. The God of religion is neither truth nor justice. Religion does not believe in God. Religion does not worship God. The God of religion is evil. By lacking the character to seek the good, by lacking the good, religion makes the false claim of possessing the good. Lacking the good, being maniacal and ignorant, religion voluntarily reveals its own deficient character. Religion voluntarily reveals its immoral character. Religion does not recognize its own immorality as such, The immorality of pretending to possess the good, the immorality of pretending to worship the good, the immorality of pretending to worship God.

Religion's excessive and hysterical rhetoric is an attack on philosophy. Religion's excessive and hysterical rhetoric is an attack on the good. Religion asks to be analyzed. Religion asks for the analysis. Religion has to be put in its place. If it is that religion wishes for truth and justice, then religion is free to join philosophy. Religion is free to abandon its ways and join the good. The good accepts all those who accept the good. The natural progression of religion is its own abandonment. Once religion's inherent evil is made clear, abandonment will then follow. The progression is the good. The progression is philosophy. Religion is a part of human history. That being so does not mean that religion cannot accept the good. The good could not have been joined before the good's time. There is so much the religious follower does not know. There is so much the religious follower does not know about the religious figure of worship. Once known, abandonment will follow. The natural state of humanity is to know. The natural state of humanity is to be mature.

The natural state of the human being is to seek the good. The natural state of the human being is to engage in good behavior. To do otherwise is to do so at the self expense. To do otherwise is to diminish the self. The human being naturally seeks the full realization of the self. The human being naturally seeks to self-improve. The human being then comes up with solutions, solutions of self-improvement, solutions aimed at the achievement of the full realization of the self. Achieving any kind of self-improving solution always includes others, as well as the self. To improve the self is to also improve others, to whatever extent that may be. To self-improve is at the minimum not to be harmful to others. It is to be beneficial to others. It is to improve the life of others. To offer improvement of others is to self-realize. It is to self-improve. Any kind of self-improvement is an improvement of others. Any kind of improvement of others is a self-improvement. To self-improve is to seek a better living existence. No two individuals have the exact same needs for what is personally regarded as better living existence. The different individuals give different solutions, Society is created. The basis of society is the need for better living. The basis of society is the need for self-improvement. Society takes shape as result of the life that is capable of being lived within it. Society takes shape as result of the potential of the human being to self-improve. Self-realizing, self-improving means that an issue, or problem, to development is observed. Solutions to the resolving of which are then come up with. Society achieves progress. To the achieved progress, further solutions are offered. The process is continuous. Society cannot lose the factors for its existence. The basis of society is the human being. The basis of society is the individual. The human being naturally achieves. The human being naturally creates. Achievement and creation are central to self-realization. The ability to achieve, the ability to create, is with the individual. The ability to achieve and create is with the citizens of society. Society then developing in the manner of its citizens. Offering solutions to the encountered problems to better living.

Any achievement, any creation, is of value. It must be of value for it to have been pursued. Any one single creation is of value to at least the person responsible for the creation. Any one creation must be of value to the creator. Otherwise the creation would not have been engaged in. Any creation that is considered as important not only by its creator but also by others becomes more valuable. It becomes more valuable to others. It becomes more valuable to society. As the creation is considered as important to a greater and greater extent, the creation becomes more and more valuable. Wealth is therefore created. It is creation and achievement that is the moving factor behind all wealth creation. If there is no achievement, no solving of problems, no self-improvement, there is no wealth. There is no economic growth. Creation, achievement, is wealth. With the differing people within society, differing solutions to the problems to better living are offered. There are differing measures of self-improvement, each of which has a differing value to society. The wealth of the individual takes shape. The wealth of society takes shape. The creating and achieving human being is responsible for wealth creation. The basis of wealth is the individual. The basis of society is the individual, the creating and achieving individual. As society cannot lose the factors for its existence, the human being, so it is that wealth of society cannot lose the factors for its existence, the human being. Having wealth, the world of wealth is engaged in. Economy is then created.

Society is the creation of the human being. Wealth is the creation of the human being. The economy is the creation of the human being. As the human being gains wealth, the human being engages in the exchange of wealth with others. The human being either purchases goods or labor. Any one valued achievement or creation that is sought to be obtained by another is obtained by returning the equivalent wealth for which. Wealth is therefore exchanged. Wealth moves through society. The economy is formed. As with society, the economy serves the purpose of achieving better living. By coming up with solutions aimed at self-improvement, the economy is created. The creator of the economy is the human being. The economy is self-sustaining. The economy cannot lose the factors responsible for its existence, the human being.

The good society will be founded on the purpose of attaining the good. The economy of the good society will likewise serve the purpose of the good. The human being will be empowered in the creation of the good society. The good human being is the basis of the good society. The good human being can only live in the same and equal good way. The good human being can only act in a good manner. The good human being can only desire that which is good. The good government can only desire that which is good for society, that which is good for the good human being. The good human being can only wish to be mature. The good human being can only wish to be free. The human being wishes to live the mature and free life. The human being wishes to self-realize. The human being wishes to self-improve. The citizen of the good society will be free to live the desired life. The citizen of the good society will be free to self-realize, free to self-improve. The good individual is at all times guided by the good. The basis of the good society is the freedom of the good individual. For a society not to be founded on the freedom of the good human being is for that society not to be engaged in the search of the good. That society does not seek the good. Such society does not possess the good. Ownership within the good society will be private. The economy of the good society will develop according to the creative ability of its citizens. That development will not be lesser or greater from that which it is. It achieves the possible. The creative ability is with the vast majority of its citizens. The vast majority are of mature and good character. Creation, achievement, is inherent to the vast majority. The vast majority are naturally capable. The vast majority naturally seek the good. The vast majority naturally live the full life. To that extent, the vast majority don't need help in creating. The vast majority don't need help in living.

In creating the good society, a comprehensive approach is needed. The basis of the good society is the good. The basis of the good society is the good individual. All aspects of the good society will be brought under the control of the good government. Whatever the extent that it may be, it will serve the purpose of the good. With the vast majority having the freedom to achieve and create, the economy of the good society will take form. Government will engage itself in setting guidelines to good behavior, beyond which government will not interfere. In so doing, the life within the good society will be expressed. With the citizen of the good society being guided by the good, by maturity and freedom, the result will be good citizen behavior, good citizen behavior which will be beneficial to the individual as well as to society. What is desired of the human being is to be grown and mature. There are times in the existence of the good society when aid would be required to be given to any one citizen. In those circumstances, aid will be given. The good government will help those in need of help, to the extent of the needed help and not beyond. To aid beyond the needed help is not to aid such individual but is to harm that individual. It is to harm society. To seek the good, to seek maturity, freedom, and independence, is to make an effort. It is to make an effort at life. It is to succeed in the effort. It is to lead to benefit in all life circumstances. To aid where aid is not needed is to harm the individual. It is to take away the effort. It is to take away achievement. It is to diminish the individual. The diminished individual cannot lead to benefit in the life circumstances, neither to the self nor to society. It can only be that humanity wishes to achieve the good. It can only be that humanity wishes to make the effort at achieving the good. The human effort at life must be a complete effort. The greater the effort at life, the greater the effort at the good, the greater the achievement. The lesser the effort, the lesser the achievement. To make a diminished effort at life, to make a diminished effort at maturity, independence, and freedom is to achieve less in life. It is to attain less life. It is to be a lesser individual. The lesser human being is not the objective. For a society not to be based on the good of the human being is for that society to oppose the good. It is for that society to struggle against the good. It is for the citizen of that society to achieve less independence, less maturity, less freedom. It is for that society to lack freedom, growth, and independence. It is for that society to harm the good and the good human being.

The good society will be based on the effort at the good. The good society will study the good. The good society will teach the good. The citizen of the good society will be observant of the good. The good will be the primary development of each citizen. Knowledge of the good, understanding the good will be primary with each citizen. Each citizen will be sincere, understanding, and mature. Each citizen will live the full life. The cause of the good will be defended. The cause of the good will be struggled for. It will be known that the achievement of the good is humanity's objective. Possession of the good is the greatest prize, the lack of good the greatest flaw. The good citizen will struggle against all enemies of the good. All enemies of the good will be recognized as such, as so revealed by philosophy.

With the good being the guide, the good citizen, the good society will develop in the possible and good manner. Achieving all in the process. With the good society being founded on the good individual, the free, mature, and independent citizen, economic production will follow. Through the process of which, there are going to be more productive and less productive times. The less productive times will be overcome as long the principles are maintained, the principles of the free and independent citizen. By its definition, the low point of production is not endless. It being a low point, means that there is a high point. With the proper approach, the low point will be improved upon, the low point will lead to better production, to greater creation. A low point in societal production is a low point of production by the individual. When the citizens of society fail to produce, fail to create on a large scale, the economy of society slows down. Failure to create occurs when the solution to creation is insufficient, the solution offered at creation being ineffective. Being insufficient and ineffective, the solution is economically undesired. Personal economic failure is the personal failure to self-improve. Economic failure is the result of inaccurate assessing of the economic situation. Personal economic failure is the result of the inaccurate personal assessment to self-improve. As the individual improves, so does the economy improve. The remedy to economic failure is the accurate assessment of the economic condition. The solution to economic slowdown is the proper self-improvement. The solution to economic slowdown in production is the returning to basics. The solution is to address the issue of creation at its most basic level. Doing so, solutions will be come up with at the most basic level. By solving self-improvement at this most basic level, confidence then builds. Greater self-improvement is then pursued with strength and desire. Further solutions to development then follow until the question of development is fully and satisfactorily solved. The vast majority will produce. The vast majority will create and achieve. The role of the good government in economic development is not to be a burden. The role of the good government is to observe the foundation of the good citizen, the foundation of freedom and independence. By being based on the good, the good government will set the tone for the stable and prosperous society. The citizen will know that the good government, led by philosophy, serves all. The citizen will know that the greatest stability is from within philosophy. Thereby having reason to live and prosper. As the good, as philosophy is government's foundation, it is made clear that this government is the supreme government. It is made clear that this is the height of human development, the height of human good. The height of human good cannot be less than the height of human good. It is not possible for the good government to achieve less than the most good.

With the citizen of the good society creating and producing, the citizen can turn to becoming an employer. Fellow citizens can turn to being employed. The employer then works with the employee, and the employee works with the employer. A team is formed. The employee has skills and abilities which are recognized and desired by the employer. The employee is then compensated for the labor. The formed team serves the purpose of the employer, employee, and society. It is of no benefit to anyone if that team were unsuccessful. For the team to be successful, the fact of the team effort must be recognized by both employer and employee. Employer and employee have the same objective, the success of the team. The only way for that to happen is if the team is guided by the good. The employer must consider the employee, and the employee must consider the employer. Led by the good government, employer and employee working together with the good government in the cause of the good, all members of the team fulfill the personal potential of good. As each member of the team serves the cause of the good, neither employee nor employer will engage in behavior that is less than good. The team is then a successful one. The employee has no reason to fear the owner. There is no need for protection from the owner. The owner has no reason to fear the employee. The owner has no reason to fear the good government. It is in the way of the good that the good society will function. All aspects of the good society will be brought under the control of the good government. Any one representation outside the scope of the good government does not serve the purpose of the good. No such representation serves the good. Only the good government serves the cause of the good. Any grievance by any employee can always be revealed to the good government. Any grievance by any employer can always be revealed to the good government. If any one joined team is not to the liking, that team can always be abandoned. The good government serves the team, employee, and employer. The good government serves the good society.

The function of the good government in the economic field is to set the most fair and stable guidelines. The good society will prosper within which. The good government will serve the single citizen. The good government will serve all of society. All will be seen in one, and one will be seen in all. The good government will not be a burden, functioning to the proper extent, aiding where needed, and not beyond. To aid where aid is not needed is not to aid; it is to harm. It doesn't make the individual richer. It makes the individual poorer. Unneeded aid takes away the human spirit. It takes away the human drive. The vast majority are capable and will achieve. The vast majority are self-sufficient for the vast majority of the time. The aid here is to be to the equal and minimal extent given. In knowing its function, and limit, the good government will not harm but only help. In setting its proper and accurate objective, the good government will raise funds. Beyond the limit of which, no further funds will be obtained. The task of the government will be completed with the obtained funds. No greater funds would be needed in fulfilling the task, and no further funds will be sought.

The good government will be recognized as such by the people. The fair and beneficial guidelines will be acknowledged as such. The good government is not beyond the people. The good government sets the tone for life and fairness. As the good government seeks life and fairness, so do the citizens seek life and fairness. Confidence in government builds. Confidence in the self then also builds. Life is eagerly engaged in. Life is eagerly lived. Self-improvement is eagerly engaged in. creation is the result. The economy benefits. The good government creates the positive living atmosphere. A positive living atmosphere which benefits society in every way. The fair and stable guidelines benefit the economy. The fair and stable guidelines benefit the citizens. The citizens are the economy. Ineptitude by government always results in the oppression of the citizen. Ineptitude by government always results in economic oppression. The good government will know its limit. The good government will know its function. The function being the serving of the citizen, the function being the serving of society. The balance will be struck. The good government will not harm the individual. The good government will not harm society. The contribution by all from within the good society to government will be at the most minimal extent. With the good government being in complete control of society, all aspects of society will serve the cause of the good. The good government will in each instance decide as to what is good for society. Thereby, within the guidelines of freedom and fairness, the good society will achieve the good.

By not harming the individual, the individual is helped. By helping the individual, society is in turn helped. The issue is the accurate assessment of life. The issue is the accurate assessment of the good. Humanity is to seek life. Humanity to seek achievement. It is the good that is of value. It is achievement that is of value. Wealth is the result of achievement. The value of wealth is equal to the achievement. Wealth is always equal to wealth, but achievement is not equal to wealth. Greater wealth is not greater achievement. Achievement is greater than wealth. The achievement of the good is of value. The good is the greatest value. Greater wealth does not lead to greater good. The economy is an integral part of human existence. Economic success is economic wealth. As such, wealth cannot be despised. Wealth is needed in living the successful life. At the same time, wealth cannot be loved. It is achievement that is to be loved. To love wealth is to do so at the expense of the good. If greater importance were attributed to wealth than that which is proper, that can only occur at the expense of personal character. It isn't wealth that makes the human being but rather the possession of the good. The wealth of another is therefore of no concern to the self. To be concerned with the wealth of others is not to be concerned with the good in others. It is to reveal that the good is personally lacked. By properly assessing life, by properly assessing the good, the individual achieves growth. The human being achieves all. By understanding the good, by possessing the good, all in life is then understood. All in life is then accurately assessed. The issue of wealth is accurately grasped. The issue of achievement and effort is accurately grasped. What is then loved is achievement and effort, not wealth. If greater importance were given to wealth than to that of achievement, then that would be done at the expense of achievement and effort. Achievement, effort, is therefore not personally valued. The individual is flawed. The individual does not grasp life. The individual does not grasp the good. The individual lacks the good. Achievement, creation, must be properly understood. Effort must be properly understood. Effort is central to achievement. Effort is central to all. To lack effort is not to understand effort. It is not to understand life. It is not to understand the good. Effort can only be appreciated.

It isn't wealth that is the basis of the good society, but rather the good. As such, the good society has differing levels of wealth. The achieving and creating human being is the economy. With the good society being guided by the good, the good society develops. The good society prospers. The good society will always undergo economic change. With the guidelines being stable and fair, the good society will be economically successful. The good society will master any economic situation. Population growth does not lead to lack of work opportunity. Work opportunity arises with the stable and fair government. Work opportunity arises with the creative self. The self-improving human being is always the self-improving human being. In the process of each individual self-improving, each individual creates and achieves. That creation and achievement is then offered to society. It is offered to the economy. Which creation will at all times be accepted at some level. The acceptance will be at the level of the achievement. No economic achievement can fail to be accepted by the economy. For any one economic effort to fail is for that effort to have been insufficient. It is for that achievement to have been insufficient. With the achievement being insufficient, that achievement fails to serve a purpose in the economy. That achievement fails to present a solution to economic development. Economic solutions are accepted based on the fact that the needs of the economy have been properly understood and addressed. Those solutions are the result of effort, effort at self-improvement. That is the instance with the vast majority. The vast majority are capable and creative. The vast majority do not need help in creating and achieving. What the vast majority need is for the guidelines of the good society to be properly set. To offer aid where aid is not needed is to reveal ulterior motives. The good government cannot be a burden to society. By not understanding, issues which are beyond comprehension are then spoken of.

What is desired in life is for the human being to be grown and mature. What the human being desires is to be grown and mature. What the human being values above all is the personal character. What the human being values above all is the good personal character. The individual self can only seek to improve that character. The personal character cannot be wished to be worsened. It is the good that is wished for. It is the good that is attained. Greed and envy are not a part of the self's character. Being hurtful and pretentious are foreign to the self. The good is the issue, not wealth. Having wealth or lacking wealth has no bearing on the level of possessed good. It is the effort that creates all. It is the effort that achieves the good. All that is achieved is equal to the made effort. The greater the effort, the greater the achievement. Achievement in life can only be equal to the made effort. For an achievement to be disproportionate, not equal, to the made effort, is to have and establish a false existence. That false and artificial existence is created when government gets involved in the economy to the unnecessary and mistaken extent. That occurs when government pays excessive attention to wealth and not enough attention to character. In doing so, government becomes involved by taking wealth from an individual who has earned that wealth and gives it to another who has not. To take wealth from one individual and give that wealth to another is to aid neither and harm both.

The then created false and artificial existence is of no benefit. It is of no benefit to society. It is of no benefit to any one individual. To attain, to receive greater wealth than the made effort is to be rewarded for something that hasn't been done. It is to be rewarded for something that hasn't been struggled for. As the false existence is false, so is the false existence detrimental. Receiving that which has not been struggled for diminishes the human effort at life. As the effort is diminished, so is the human being diminished. The human being is diminished as result of the false and artificial existence. To be rewarded for lack of effort is to be made poorer, not wealthier. It is to be made poorer in the only manner of value, the human personality. The diminished human being is not what is desired. The diminished human being behaves in a diminished way. The receiving of someone else's wealth is not what the human wishes for. Rather, what is wished for is that which belongs to the self and not that which belongs to someone else. Led by the misguided government, the human being becomes the least of the self. Lacking effort, lacking character is the result of receiving the wealth of another. The misguided government harms the receiving of wealth individual. The misguided government harms the individual from whom the wealth is taken. It can only be that the wealth is spent wisely, which it isn't, thereby harming society. The misguided government is pretentious. The misguided government pretends to understand issues of importance. The misguided government is envious and greedy. The same characteristics of greed and envy the misguided government brings into existence within the receiving of wealth individual. Assessing the wealth of another so that it can be taken is greed and envy. Pretending to be helpful, the misguided government destroys, all because the good was not the objective. Wealth instead was.

The creating struggle, the creating effort in life is not to be avoided. It is not to be feared. The needed effort is to be desired. The creating effort is to be eagerly engaged in. It is the effort that creates and achieves all, including the self, including the personality of the self. As the effort is decreased, so is achievement decreased, so is the self decreased. All engaged in effort will end in success. The equal measure of success to the made effort. As effort is crucial, personality is crucial. The character of the human being is crucial. All that is of the human being is of the human character. That character can only be wished to be strengthened and not corrupted. Government can only seek to improve the human character. Government will not engage in corruption of the human being. Government can only seek to increase the human effort. Government can only encourage ambition. Government can only encourage self-improvement.

The good society will not reward lack of effort. The good society will reward the good human being. Every aspect of the good society will serve the cause of the good. Every aspect of the good society will serve the good human being. There is only one best cause of the good society. There is only one best way for the good society to develop. Within that one best cause, all that is of the same beneficial and good nature will be included. Within the good government, all that is of the same good nature will be included. There will be no opposition to the good government. To oppose the good is to lack the good. To lack the good is to be tyrant. It is to be ignorant and selfish.

The funds acquired by the good society will be used for the achievement of the highest level of good. All citizens of the good society will monetarily support the good government. The percentage of monetary support, by each citizen, will be tied to the total of society. Any percentage in monetary rate increase will be to the equal proportion borne by all. Any percentage of monetary rate decrease will be to the equal proportion borne by all. As the good government helps any one citizen when help is needed, so will that individual help the good government. Wealth envy will not be a part of the good society. The deciding factor will always be the good, the possession of the good, the recognition of the good, the empowerment of the good. All the citizens of the good society possess the good. All the citizens of the good society are guided by the good. The good is willfully and willingly personally observed by all. After the certain point, and as so decided upon by the good government, as represented by philosophy, there will be 100 percent monetary support of the good government. The good citizen is an extension of the good government. The good government is an extension of the good citizen. The good government always serves the cause of the good.

Philosophy creates the greatest good. Only philosophy can create the greatest good. All good human beings can only join in the cause of the good. Philosophy has no equal. Philosophy achieves the greatest good. Philosophy achieves the greatest justice. That justice is the basis of the good society. That justice is the greatest human justice. That justice is not the greatest justice in life, however. Humanity is an integral part of life. Humanity represents that which is human. The human scope of existence should be understood for its precise nature. The status of humanity should not be mistaken for that of another. Humanity has the proper human place in life. To be human is to desire to be human. As such, only that which is of the human being can be taken part in. All from within life has achieved the searched for, the desired, the self. All contribute to the identity of the one life. Humanity achieves that which is human. Humanity does not create life's laws but discovers life's laws. Life's laws are truth. Life's laws are justice. Life seeks justice. Life is guided by justice. The justice is life's. Life's justice is unsurpassed. Life is never mistaken. Life will never be unjust. Life can never mistake injustice for justice. For life to consider injustice for justice is for life to seek injustice. Life would never seek injustice for the self. The world of justice can only be governed by the height of justice. Less than the dominant justice cannot govern the world of justice. As is with life, so it must be with human society, so it must be with the good society. It can only be that the highest human justice governs. It can only be that the human being is governed by the height of human justice. It can only be that the human being wishes to be governed by the height of human justice. Though human justice is not life's justice, though human justice is not equal to life's justice, human justice is of value. Human justice has a basis for existing, especially so the justice of the good. Humanity is a part of life. Humanity is a fact. The human being cannot be anything other than human. The human being will behave in the human way. Human behavior, human justice is not without value. To be human is to have chosen to be human. Human behavior will thus occur. Human justice is so revealed. Human good is so revealed.

The good's mission is to reveal the good. The good's mission is to bring about enlightenment. The good's mission is to bring about human maturity. The change from immature must be undergone. The good's mission is to reveal truth. The good's mission is to reveal justice. It is the knowing and just human being that is desired. The not knowing and unjust human being belongs to the state of immaturity. The not knowing and unjust human being is not what is desired. The lacking of life human being is not what is desired. The good's mission is to win over all individuals. The mission is to convince all people of the good's character of truth and justice. In revealing truth, the good reveals the absence of truth. In revealing truth, the good exposes the absence of truth. In revealing justice, the good exposes the absence of justice. The good reveals truth and justice. The good exposes falsehood and injustice. The choice is there for humanity to make. The mature and just human being, or the immature and unjust human being. It can only be that humanity wishes to be mature and just. It can only be that humanity chooses the good.

The good's mission is to show the superiority of the good. The good's mission is the destruction of all that is false. All that is pretentious will be destroyed. There will be no peace with enemies of the good. It is the enemy of the good that calls for its own destruction. The existence of the good is inherent in life's being. The destruction of nemesis is inherent within the content of the good. To attain the good is to destroy the enemy of the good. The choice for the good can only be made. To choose the good, to side with the good, is to deliberately, consciously do so. Personal growth takes place within the self. It is deliberately sought. It is consciously attained. The good is consciously wished for. The good is consciously struggled for. To seek the good is to attain the good. To oppose the good is to lack the good. To lack the good is to have sought to lack the good. It is to deliberately and consciously seek to lack the good. Personal lack of growth takes place within the self. The lack of good is personally wished for. To lack the good is to consciously struggle for the cause of lack of good. All justice, all political power belongs to the good. Anyone who is contrary to the good is committing the greatest injustice. Anyone who is not a member of the good has such lacking of the good character. To struggle against the good is to struggle against the cause of the good. To struggle against the dominance of philosophy is to struggle against the good.

To seek the good is to struggle for the cause of the good. It is to make the effort for the cause of the good. Avoidance of the effort, avoidance of the struggle, is not to achieve. The struggle, the effort, creates all. Based on that effort, philosophy achieves all. Philosophy defines the good society. All consideration by the good society is based on the judgment of good. The good society judges all according to the possessed level of good. The human being will be judged according to the possessed level of good. The human being will be judged according to the acceptance, or rejection, of the supremacy of philosophy. The good, as so stated by philosophy, is central to the human being. The good, as so revealed by philosophy, is central to human development. If humanity is to grow and develop, if humanity is to achieve understanding, the philosophical good must be accepted. The philosophical good must be accepted and understood by humanity only because the good wasn't revealed at a prior moment in human history. To think that the philosophical good is not central to the human being is to reject the supremacy of philosophy. To think, that if the philosophical good were central, that the philosophical good would have been therefore revealed at an earlier time in human history, so that early humanity would have been exposed to the philosophical good, so that early humanity would have had the opportunity to know that which is central is to reject the supremacy of philosophy. To think that the philosophical good is not the philosophical good is to reject the supremacy of philosophy. To reject the good is to reject the good. To accept the good is to accept the good. By the fact that the good exists, the good must be accepted. What is of concern is the fact of the good. What is of concern is the content of the good. The decision to either reject or accept the good is to be based on the fact, and content, of the good. The decision should not be based on what early humanity did, or did not, know. Early humanity was never denied the self. Early humanity was never denied the opportunity to create and achieve. The possibility to seek the good has been ever present in human history. Human history has a line of development. That development is such as it is. It cannot be altered. All is at all times achieved. The issue is the central status of the philosophical good. The issue is the acceptance, or rejection, of the supremacy of the philosophical good. As such, the good society will judge the human being according to the acceptance or rejection of the good. It must be that it is the good that humanity desires. The supreme good is that of philosophy.

All the while, the good society will be in full recognition of its own limitations. The good government will not attach excessive and unfounded importance to itself. The primary way for the human being to develop is in the achievement of the good. As this is so, the good government will be understanding of this fact. The good government will be understanding of the human being. The good government will be encouraging. The good government will be lenient wherever lenience is deserved. The human being will be allowed to live. In the process, the countless ways of good will be expressed. The good individual can only turn to less than the height of good behavior during the less than the height of good stages in the self's life. The central factor to be considered is the genuine desire for the good. This is the central factor for the good government to consider. To be genuinely seeking the good and to then misbehave is to do so within the measure of good. The good government can only be understanding and forgiving of the good individual. The good government will be in full recognition of its own limitations. The good government will be in full recognition of the fact that it is life's justice that is supreme and not the justice of the good government.

With the human being engaging in the attainment of life, with the human being engaging in the struggle to attain the good, differing levels of good are attained during the differing personal life stages. By achieving the height of good, stages of less than the height of good are experienced. Those stages must be properly assessed. The deciding factor is the understanding of the issue. Those stages are very much needed. It is the love for the self that decides the issue. The deciding factor is the attained good. The human being does not live based on one static consciousness, where that consciousness is always the same, but lives based on the whole, varying, and inclusive range of which. Each differing stage of being has a differing objective, a differing awareness, a differing existence. Behavior for one state, the guide of which, does not apply for that of another. All stages are in the measure that is consistent with the identity of the self. The achieved, differing levels of good must not be viewed negatively but positively. The different stages are a necessary part of life.

With the human being engaging in the struggle for life, the human being achieves all. The human being lives all. The life lived ranges from the more desired stages to the less desired stages. Through it all, it is the self, the complete self, that does the living. Never and under no circumstance is the self less than the self. The complete self never is denied to the self. No event can ever occur, no event ever occurs, that diminishes or negates the self. It is the self that experiences all. The experienced is such as it is. It cannot be altered. The self is never diminished or negated. In living the desired, the self is never different from the self. In living the undesired, the self is never different from the self. No event ever differentiates the self from the complete self. As the self is complete and fulfilling, so is the life lived complete and fulfilling. No suffering negates the self. No illness negates the self. The love for the self is unconditional. No illness can deny the existence of the self. No illness can deny the love for the self. No illness can prevent anyone from achieving unity with the self. The less desired side of life should be better understood. The illness, the suffering is the self. To take away the illness, to take away the suffering, is to take away the self. To analyze life is to analyze life's being. Illness and suffering are the self. Illness and suffering enrich human life. The struggle for life is stronger yet. The good is to be loved. Life is to be loved. The pursuit of the good ranks above all, and ill and all can answer the good's calling. The good gives the greatest comfort. The good is the greatest prize.

By seeking the good, an aspect of the good will then be achieved. The human being is then enriched. By not seeking the good, no aspect of the good will be achieved. The human being is then lacking of the good. The human being is then lacking of life. The good is the greatest life quality. All life qualities are present within the good. The good gives definition to all. It is the good that defines all other life qualities. No other life quality can achieve the own status without the quality of the good. Understanding, truth, and justice are life characteristics. If the good were lacked, life would stand for neither understanding nor truth nor justice. The good is central. As it is with life, so it is with the human being. It can only be that the human being strives to be the height of the human being. To strive to be less than the height of the human being is to be less than the height of the human being. It is to have no opinion of value of what the height of the human being is. It can only be that the human being is understanding, truthful, and just. The human being must be guided by the good. To be guided by less than the good is to have the equally such opinion of no value of what the good is. To claim, to think, that the good is possessed, when the good is lacked, does not mean that the good is possessed. The good is in fact lacked. The existence of the good in life is a fact. As life is real, so is the good in life real. As any one human being strives to attain the good, it is a level of human good that is attained. That level resembles to the possible and limited to the human extent, the good of life.

The characteristics of understanding, truth, and justice are to the human extent realized. To make an effort at the good is to achieve the good. Not to make an effort is not to achieve the good. And so the lack of good can never be the possession of the good. The height of the human being is the good human being. The denial of the good

THE GOOD IS CRITERIA

is the denial of life. The denial of the good is the ensuring of the same lacking personal character. The good cannot be deceived.

The good human being can only struggle for the cause of the good. The good human being can only struggle for the benefit of the good. The good human being cannot seek to harm the good. The good human being seeks to create the greatest level of good. The good human being is peaceful. As the good human being with peace approaches the good, so is the good human being in such manner always peaceful. The good human being serves the cause of peace. Being peaceful does not mean that the good individual will not struggle for the cause of the good. It is the struggle for the cause of the good that makes the good individual peaceful. With the good being the height of the human being, to assess the character of any one individual is to primarily do so based on the possession, or lack of possession, of good. To think that there is another, more accurate way of assessing the human personality is to reveal that the good is lacked. It is to reveal that the height of humanism is lacked. It is to have the equally such opinion of no value of what the primary way is for the human being to be assessed. To assess any one idea is to primarily do so based on the level of good. With the mission of the good being the defining of the good, the mission of the good is to establish order to human thought, to human good. The human being must be understanding, truthful, and just, being guided by the good, being guided by the need for peace. Such human being can only be judged positively, as having attained the height of life. The height of humanism, the good can only be revealed by philosophy. No other branch of human development is equal to philosophy. It is truth that philosophy is supreme. It is justice that philosophy is supreme. Philosophy must be recognized as the supreme human development. To recognize philosophy as supreme is to have attained truth. It is to have attained justice. Not to recognize philosophy as supreme is to neither attain truth nor justice. The point of importance is the recognition and acceptance of philosophy as the human good. Not to recognize philosophy as the human good is to lack the good. To oppose and struggle against philosophy is to struggle against the good. It is to lack the good. The greater the struggle, the greater the denial, the greater the lack of good. The bragging and blasphemous frauds, science and religion, must admit to the supremacy of philosophy. If not, neither one would be understanding, truthful, or just. If understanding, truth, and justice were their objective, then the inferiority of their nature would be admitted to. Their futile and pretentious nature would be admitted to.

The more the good is struggled against, the more the good is lacked. The objective of the good is to create the greatest good. The objective of the good is to judge all on the basis of good. The objective of the good, the objective of philosophy is the creation of the good society. Seeking to create the greatest good, the good society judges all on the basis of good. The good society is understanding, truthful, and just and is guided by the good, by the need for peace. The good society can only seek that which is beneficial. The human being, life, can only seek that which is beneficial. Achieving that which is beneficial, life suppresses that which is not beneficial. As the human being achieves that which is of benefit, the human being suppresses that which is not of benefit. The human being cannot strive for that which is detrimental to the self. The human being suppresses that which is detrimental to the self. The good society can only suppress that which is detrimental. Only the good society can know what is detrimental. Only the good society can know what is beneficial.

The more the good is struggled for, the more the good is possessed. To seek the good, to observe the good, is to have the equal such understanding, the equal such truth and justice. To observe the good is to have the equal such knowledge. It is to have equal such intellect. To observe the good is to be the height of the human being. To observe the good is to have the height of human knowledge. It is to have the height of human intellect. As the good is supreme, so is knowledge of the good supreme, so is the intellect supreme. Any individual who lacks the good is lacking of the good. And any achievement by that individual is just as lacking, regardless of the achievement. Lacking the good is lacking knowledge. Lacking the good is lacking intellect. It is the inability to figure out that the good is supreme. It is the inability to figure out that the intellect of the good is supreme. All intellect is personified by the intellect of knowledge of the good. Not to possess the good is not to possess intellect. Not to recognize philosophy as the supreme human development is to lack intellect. To recognize philosophy as supreme is to have the equally such intellect. Philosophy is the supreme knowledge. Only philosophy has the answers to life's ultimate being. No other branch of human thought has the objective of knowing life's ultimate being.

The question of intelligence is the question of the possession of the good. To attempt to define intelligence on anything other than the good, on the lack or possession of the good, is to lack knowledge. It is to lack knowledge of what intelligence is. To attempt to define intelligence on anything other than the good is to lack intelligence. It is to lack understanding of what intelligence is. To therefore define intelligence is to define the content of the good. The more that the good lacked. The more that intelligence is lacked. The more the good is struggled against, the more intelligence is lacked. To whatever extent there is intelligence in recognizing the good, in observing the good, the intelligence is greater than the lack of recognition, the lack of observance of the good.

The function of the school system is to fulfill its purpose in society. The teaching of the youth to contribute toward the creation of the good society, to be involved in the workings of society in a positive way. The function of the school system is to promote the intellectual development and growth of the youth. The function is to help and encourage the youth in intellectual development and growth. The function is not to discourage and not help in the intellectual development of the youth. The function is not to test intelligence but to create intelligence. The school system cannot test, cannot measure for intelligence. For intelligence to be tested, the school system would have to know what intelligence is, which the school system does not know. The test of intelligence is the positive contribution to the good society. The test of intelligence is knowledge of the good. As the school system does not have the answer to intelligence, the school system does not have the answer to being successful in society, to being successful in the field of study and profession. What is important is life accomplishment. What is important is the need for knowledge. What is important is the drive to succeed, what is important is the need to self-improve. The school system must not be considered in excessive and unwarranted importance. To consider school in excessive importance is to misunderstand the function of school. It is to misunderstand life. The human objective is to seek the good. To engage the good, the human objective is to contribute to the good society. To attach excessive importance to school is to do so at the cost of the individual. It is to do so at the cost of individual achievement. The purpose of school is not to assess. The purpose of school is not to assess the human being; the purpose of school is to teach. School cannot interfere with the growth of the student.

All human creation is the result of effort. All human creation is the result of drive. That drive, that effort, is personally initiated. The vast majority have the drive to achieve. The vast majority engage in the personal drive to achieve. That drive is personally sought. That drive is personally increased. The drive to self-improve is the self's being. The drive to self-improve can only be worked with. School can only aid in the effort to self-improve. For that purpose, the student is to be helped in the search for personal growth. For that purpose, the student is not to be intimidated. It is up to the student to learn as much as possible. It is up to the student to achieve as much as possible. The teaching will be done at the appropriate pace. The learning of the taught material, the student will not be tested for which. In such manner, the student will be prepared for life. In such manner, the student will learn responsibility. In such manner, the student will seek to genuinely grow. In such manner, the student will achieve as much as possible. The human being is responsible for the self. The student is responsible for the self. Only what is genuine will best promote that which is genuine. The objective of the student is to learn. The objective of the student is to be responsible. The objective of school is to teach. The objective of school is to promote learning. Testing does not promote learning; only teaching promotes learning. That which is best for the student is to be responsible. That which is best for the human being is to be responsible. By not intimidating the student, the student will achieve more. By working with the student, by being respectful of the student, the student will grow more.

Excessive importance should not be attached to school. School must not be a self-fulfilling prophesy, of regarding itself with excessive importance, and considering itself with excessive importance. School will encourage the student's drive for successful contribution to the good society. The student will be set on the path of constant learning. As the student exhibits the preferred fields of study, those fields will be engaged to a greater extent. In the process, school works with the student. The recommended pace of study will serve the benefit of the student. If the pace is not kept up with, it will be due to at that time lack of personal drive. Learning is a lifelong experience. All will be done to work with the student. All will be done to aid the student. The school system will teach the way of the good. Only the good society can know the way of the good. Only the good society can teach the way of the good. The good society will function in the most beneficial manner. The school system will serve the good society. All aspects of society will be brought under the control of the good government. Any effort at opposing the good will be potentially considered as criminal act. The good can only be worked with. The good can only be wished for. The good society, under the leadership of philosophy, is the highest human good. The good is the good for a reason. The good can do no wrong.

The good is the most understanding; The good works with the individual. The good seeks the improvement of the individual. The good seeks the improvement of society. The need for the good needs to be encouraged. Forgiveness is central to the way of the good. Forgiveness is central to the seeking of the good. If error has been engaged in, the good society cannot promote the need for the good based on constant punishment. The good is not interested in punishment but in creating the greater need for the good. By being lenient and forgiving, the good encourages the greater need for the good. The good encourages personal responsibility. It is shown, it is made clear, that the good wishes to be willingly observed. It is made clear that the good wishes to work with any one individual in order to encourage the desire for the good. The erring individual cannot but notice the lenience and benevolence of the good, thereby creating an attraction to the good, thereby encouraging personal responsibility and growth.

Before the stage of personal maturity, human error is inherent. The path leading to the personal stage of maturity is that, the path, it cannot be perfect. It is less than perfect. The need for the good can only be wished to be strengthened. The good, the way of the good, must be taught. By being lenient, that lenience will be made clear. What will also be made clear is the expectation of the individual, the expectation being the seeking and observing of the good. If the erring individual is punished excessively. That punishment can only be detrimental, detrimental to the cause of the good, detrimental to the growth of the individual. The response to lacking the good behavior must be appropriate. At the same time, the objective of the good is to protect the good. The good's objective is to judge humanity. The good's objective is to create the greatest justice. The good's objective is to bring all evil monsters to justice.

The good must not be taken advantage of. The good must not be abused. The good is the greatest quality. The good is the center of philosophy, the good is the center of the good society. The good society is as no other. The good society cannot be equaled. No other society has the good at its center. No other society can achieve the good. Having no equal, the good society behaves as no other. The good society teaches the good. The good society promotes the good. The good government understands the good, the content of the good. It is only natural for the good government to teach the good. It is only natural for the good to be revealed. It is only natural for the good to be supreme. It can only be that the good would be considered as supreme. Once revealed, the good can only be considered as supreme. To reveal the good is to indicate that prior to which the good was not known. It is to indicate that prior to which the good had not been revealed. With the good being absent, such lacking the good behavior was engaged in. Such lacking the good behavior was considered as acceptable and proper. As the good is revealed, it is also revealed the lack of good. The lack of good prior to which, the lack of good outside the realm of the good. The good can only be achieved based on the genuine and sincere effort. The good can only be attained based on the sufficient effort. The sufficient effort had not been made; that is the reason why the good was not attained.

Not having attained the good, such lacking the good mentality was engaged in. Humanity having lacked the good, phony claims of good arise. It is the duty of the good to reveal the good. It is the duty of the good to expose all that is pretentious and false. Those who don't know the good must not pretend to know the good. Those who have no need for the good must not pretend to worship the good. It is the duty of the good to put all in its proper place.

The good is wished for with the clear understanding. To seek the good is to consciously do so. It is to make the effort to achieve the supreme knowledge. It is to make the effort to be a better human being. Attaining the good, it may then appear that the entrenched bureaucracy, the entrenched customs, are far too powerful for change to take place, but all those who oppose the good will be crushed by the good's overwhelming might. The good wishes for all to seek the good. The good wishes for all to join the good. The good seeks all those of good character. The good offers solutions to the issue of the good society. The good offers solutions to the issue of life's being. All that is life arises from the reality of life. All that is life arises from the middle ground. It is where validity is given to all and all opposites. The reality of life consists of truth and justice. All that is good is founded upon the reality of life. The reality of life is thoroughly good. All that life achieves originates from life's reality. All that is achieved, all that is created, originates from life's reality. To choose the self, to create the self, is to do so from within life's reality. To choose the self is to do so above all others. it is to love the self above all others. That doesn't mean that all others are hated or disrespected. Seeking the good, the human being behaves in such good manner. The fellow human being is thus treated with respect. The common ground in living with the fellow human being is found. As the reality of life is the creator of all, all strives and struggles to achieve and create all. Doing so, the life members take on a different nature. The struggle for life cannot be initiated in the exact same way by all the life members. In the process, giving rise to differences. From the earliest times, differing manners of struggle for life have been initiated. There are those struggles, those efforts, which are more similar. They are more similar to each other and less similar to others. The similar struggles for life have repeatedly chosen such similar struggles in others. That which is of the similar nature has repeatedly been chosen for by the life members. The similar life members have repeatedly chosen for the similar life members. Giving rise to differing life forms, giving rise to differing life groups. The life groups have repeatedly chosen for that which is similar. As the personal feelings of attraction to the similar grow stronger, the feelings of attraction to the less similar grow weaker. As result causing animosity toward that which is dissimilar. As the self is chosen, all that is of the self is also chosen. The particular life group that the self is a member of is also chosen. The particular life group that has been achieved has been chosen. Life members have an attraction to that which is similar. That is how the similarity was achieved. That doesn't mean that all other differing life groups are to be hated and disrespected. Seeking the good, the human being behaves in such good manner. The fellow human being that is from a differing group is treated with respect. The common ground in living is found.

With the reality of life including all opposites, the opposites of attraction to that which is similar and the attraction to that which is not as similar are also included. To that certain extent, both opposites exist. To that certain extent both opposites are correct. Both opposites are founded in the good. Within the reality of life, the attraction to the personal life group and the attraction to a life group different from the personal one are both included. Both exist; both are correct. To the certain and correct extent, both views are correct. The human struggling effort at life has resulted in differing ethnic groups. The personal ethnic group can be liked, and ethnic groups different from the personal one can also be liked. Both attractions are possible. Both attractions are real. As humanity grows and matures, grown and mature answers to questions of being are given. The need for the good is a conscious effort. To attain the good is to consciously do so. To attain truth is to consciously do so. Issues which seemed confusing, with no good answer, are no longer confusing, having arrived at the good answer. The appeal of the personal ethnic group is inherent. The appeal of civility and the good is also inherent. The attraction to differing ethnic groups is also inherent. Both views are founded in good. Both views can lead to good. Excessive attachment to one of the opposite views is to do so at the expense of the other. To deny the validity of one of the opposites is to deny the good of that opposite. It is to then in turn lack the good. It is to lack the measured and accurate understanding of the issue. To deny the fact of the attraction to the personal ethnic group is to have no understanding of the issue. To deny the fact of the attraction to differing to the personal ethnic group is to have no understanding of the issue. The answer to the issue is that answer which is correct and proper, to the correct and proper extent. Not to have the answer to life's being is not to have the answer. It is not to pretend to have the answer. It is not to claim to have the answer. Not to have the answer to any one issue is not to have the answer. Not to have the answer to the issue of ethnicity, to the issue of inclusion of opposites, to the issue of love for the self, the issue of civility and respect, is not to have the answer. It is not to pretend to have the answer. It is not to claim to have the answer. It is only philosophy that can arrive at the supreme answers. To achieve an answer, to achieve truth, is to consciously do so. It is to, in the process, become more conscious. It is to become more aware of the involved issues. Arriving at the consciousness of truth can only be good. Arriving at consciousness of truth can only lead to good, can only lead to good behavior. It is to be guided by truth. It is to be guided by the good. To lack knowledge of the truth is to lack the good. It is to be then guided in the same lacking the good manner. To lack the truth, to lack the good, is to lead to thought just as lacking, to behavior just as lacking. As the good is lacked to a greater and greater extent, equally as lacking good behavior is engaged in. Any one life truth is then abused. The good is then abused. The truth, the good, is then struggled against. All the while claiming to be defending the truth, all the while claiming to be defending the good.

The human ethnic issue is such issue, where the extremes, the opposites deny the legitimacy, the validity, of the opposite. It is where such view of denying the validity of the opposite is turned to, is sided with by some. The human ethnic issue is where the love for the self, the attraction to the personal ethnic group is denied validity by the opposite. The human ethnic issue is where respect and civility, where the attraction to a different ethnic group from the personal one is denied validity. Both extreme views of denying the validity of the opposite are incorrect. Neither view is understanding of the issue; neither view is understanding of the good. The personal view, to disregard the opposite, is then considered as the proper way for humanity to exist. It is thought that for humanity to achieve peaceful existence is for humanity to deny the legitimacy of the opposite. If that were correct, if the peaceful human existence were sought, then the truth of the issue would not be denied. For humanity to exist properly, for humanity to achieve peace, humanity can only be founded upon truth. Human existence can only be founded upon the good. The issue is the good, the achievement of the good. The issue is the defending of the good. It can only be that it is the truth, the good, of the issue that is desired to be achieved. It is the good that has dominance in any one issue. It is the good, it is the truth that defeats the false. To seek the false is to be defeated by the truth every time. In any one issue, it is the higher, the better, argument that is wished to be sided with. To side with the false is to be on the incorrect side of the issue. To deny the fact of the truth of any one issue is to side with the false. It is to be defeated by the truth. It is to be defeated by the good. It is to lack the good. To side with one opposite and deny the validity of the other opposite is to side with the false. It is to reject the truth. It is to reject the good. To reject the good, to reject the truth, is to reject the peaceful human existence. The rejection of the good cannot lead to peaceful human existence. The rejection of the good cannot lead to understanding. Neither one of the opposites is seeking the truth. Neither one of the opposites is seeking the good. Neither one of the opposites is seeking peace. It is only the good that can achieve that which is beneficial. It is only the good that can achieve the peaceful human existence. To lack the good is to have no need for the good. It is to have no need for the peaceful human existence. For one of the opposites to claim to be seeking the good is to make a false claim. For one of the opposites to claim to be seeking the peaceful human existence is to make a false claim.

If any one of the opposites were seeking the peaceful human existence, then the truth, the good, would have been achieved. The good was not achieved. The peaceful human existence is not the motive. Nor is it correct to think that any one of the opposites is better than the other. The issue is the good. The issue is the understanding of the good. The issue is not the lack of good. The issue is not the nonunderstanding of the good. The issue is not the understanding of the false as the truth. The issue is not the claim of the false to be the truth. Just because there is advocacy of one of the opposites that does not mean that the advocacy is founded in the good. It is in fact to lack the good. To lack the good is not to understand the good. It is to understand the lack of good as the good. It is to then claim that the lack of good is the possession of the good. Neither one of the opposites is in possession of the good. Neither one of the opposites seeks the good. Neither one of the opposites seeks peace. If the good is truly wished for, then the good must be attempted to be understood. The good must be accepted. The good must be accepted as so stated by philosophy. Philosophy is central to the issue, philosophy is central only because it is only philosophy that can achieve that which is supreme. And so, prior to the knowledge of the good, the good cannot have been known. The philosophical good cannot have been known by humanity prior to the good. If the good is truly wished for, then the good upon being revealed by philosophy must be accepted. The good accepts all those who accept the good. The good accepts all those who abandon the lack of good.

The good society will be founded upon the reality of life. The ethnic issue will likewise be founded upon the reality of life. All aspects of society will be brought under the control of the good government. Anyone opposing the good government will be considered criminal. Opposition to the good government will be considered a criminal act. All individuals within the good society will be expected to seek the good. all individuals within the good society will be expected to engage in good behavior. The ethnic issue will be expected to be considered by all with truth and justice. No exploitation of the ethnic issue will be permitted. Any opinion of the ethnic issue will be in accordance with the reality of life. Any opinion of the ethnic issue will be in accordance with the good government. Any such opinion of value on the issue can only come from within the reality of life.

Only the reality of life reveals truth. Only the reality of life contains truth. All that is foreign to the reality of life is foreign to truth. All that is outside the reality of life is false. All that is outside the reality of life, all that is false is destructive. All opinion which is not accepting of the validity of the opposite is an opinion not founded in the good. It is an opinion which is not founded in truth and justice. By not seeking the peaceful human existence, such views are harmful and destructive. All expressed views of denying the validity of the opposite will be considered criminal acts. All criminal acts will be thereby punished by the good government. Any expressed view of lack of civility and respect shown toward ethnic groups different from the personal one, the expressed view of denying the validity of differing ethnic groups from the personal one, will be so destroyed by the good. The expressed view of denying the attraction to the personal ethnic group will be so destroyed by the good. The expressed rejection of the validity of the attraction to the personal ethnic group will be destroyed by the good. Any use of the term *racism* will come only from within the reality of life. Any use of the term *racism* will be made only by individuals who seek the good, only by those who possess the good and are part of the good. The expressed use of the term racism by any individual who does not seek the good, by any individual who does not possess the good will be a criminal act. As so stated by the good, as so revealed by philosophy.

Such term of *racism* is a term used as a weapon. It is a term used with the intent to overwhelm and disarm. Such term can only come from within the reality of life for it to have meaning; otherwise it has no meaning. Originating from outside the reality of life, such term is used by charlatans and frauds. Charlatans and frauds who have no understanding of the good. Charlatans and frauds who have no understanding of life. Charlatans and frauds who are phony to the core. Such use of the term has no meaning, no legitimate meaning. Such term distorts and disguises. It distorts real racism. It disguises the personal motives, which are often racist, which are pretended not to be racist. It disguises the personal lack of understanding, the personal lack of good. By trying to overwhelm and disarm, the lacking the good views are presented as being their opposite, views founded in the good. If that were the case, then philosophy would be jointed in understanding the issue. It is only the good that has value. It is only that which is true and just that has value. The human being can only be a truthful and just human being. The human being can only seek to achieve the greatest good, thereby creating the greatest good, thereby engaging in the greatest good. It is the truth, the good, of the issue that is of concern. All that is good flows from truth and justice. That which is false cannot lead to good. Only lack of good can arise from the lack of good. And the lack of good is proven by the fact that the truth of the issue is not understood or is not wanted to be understood. The good achieved by any expressed view is equal to the level of good possessed by that view. The achieved level of lack of good by any expressed view is equal to that same level of lack of good. To not understand the ethnic issue is to lack the truth and justice of that issue. It is to lead to the same level of lack of good. The expressed use of the meaningless term *racism* is not a beneficial term. Such term does not lead to the good. Such term is not founded in truth and justice. Such term does not lead to truth and justice. Such use of the term is a claim to goodness, which it is not. Such term can only be a claim to goodness. It is made with the intent of pointing out the lack of good as represented by some. The problem with the use of such term is that it fails to understand its own lack of good, in the process revealing its own lack of good. The term distorts what true racism is. The term takes away from true racism. The term attempts to disguise the personal lack of good. The term often disguises the personal racism. Such false charge of racism is meant to racially harm the person being accused of racism. It is a racial attack made by someone who lacks the good. Lacking the good, it is only such lacking of the good behavior that can be engaged in. To express the false and meaningless charge of racism is to lack the good, it is to reveal the personal racism. The answer is the good, not the lack of good. To make the false charge of racism is to therefore not know what racism is. It is not to know the good. It is to make the false claim to goodness. The false claim to goodness is a false claim to goodness. The false claim of goodness is the false claim of lack of personal racism. The racism falsely found in others is the personal racism. The false charge of racism is made in order to intimidate. It is made in order to disguise the personal racism, the personal lack of good. Lacking the good, such lacking the good behavior is engaged in, hence the false charge found in others is the real personal racism.

Whatever the level of personal good of an individual founded in the reality of life may be, it is genuine. It is authentic. It is not fake. It is not pretended. Whatever the level of personal good of an individual founded in the reality of life may be, it is greater than the good of an individual who is not founded in the reality of life. The lacking the good individual lacks understanding of life. The lacking the good individual is a phony and a fraud. All the motives of such an individual can be questioned. All the motives exist with the purpose of selfish reasons. The motives don't serve the good. The individual is shallow and empty. Whatever advancement a lacking the good individual may be making in life, it is a meaningless personal advancement. The only prize of value is the good. Lacking the good, all behavior is based in the lack of good. All behavior is based in lack of character. All behavior originates from the lack of good. The very source that gives substance to the lacking the good individual is the same source that destroys the individual. By seeking the lack of good, the individual falsely imagines that it is the good that is sought. The individual falsely imagines that life is being advanced in, whereas it is the personal destruction of the self that is advanced in. Falsely imagining to be guided by good, the hate-filled monster voluntarily reveals the personal lack of good. Such use of the term *racism* is a term of war. It is a weapon meant to harm, in the process revealing the personal harmful lack of character. It is a weapon meant to destroy a good human being. It is a weapon that was turned to too many times by evil monsters. To wage war on the good is a criminal offense. Such term used by a lacking the good individual will be a criminal act. The freedom of speech, within the good society, will extend as far as so decided by the good, as far as so decided by philosophy. There are many issues that the great founders of the US Constitution did not understand. Philosophy is here for a reason. Philosophy is supreme for a reason. The natural progression of all governments is philosophic rule. Whatever the achieved level of good by an individual founded in the reality of life may be, it is greater than the level of good by an individual who is not founded in the reality of life. The expressed use of the term *Uncle Tom* will be a criminal act. Any individual using the term *Uncle Tom* will be a criminal.

It is time for humanity to mature. No effort against the good will be tolerated. It is only the good that is in possession of the good. It is only philosophy that can create the greatest good. The good is not understood by those who lack the good. Those who lack the good neither understand the good, nor can they create the good. The way forward is the good.

By seeking the good, by attaining the good, humanity grows, humanity matures. The previous to the achieved maturity and growth, the achievement of humanity was insufficient and inadequate. If it were sufficient and adequate, the good would have been achieved. Growth and maturity would have been achieved. The objective of the human being is to seek the good. Not to do so, not to seek the good, is to be morally diseased. In achieving growth and maturity, humanity undergoes change. It is change that is desired. It is change that is undergone. It is change that is accepted. Having lacked the good, such lacking the good behavior was engaged in. The results of the lacking the good behavior are evident. The results of the lacking the good behavior are there to be seen. They are there to be experienced. They are there to be learned from. And if the failures of the past are not easy to assess, the answer is the turning to philosophy. It is philosophy that will point out the failures of the past. It is philosophy that results in understanding. If the failures of religion and democracy are not so clear, it is philosophy that will make those failures more clear. Both religion and democracy make false claims. Both make false claims of effort. Both make false claims of achievement. The way forward for humanity is to achieve truth, justice, and understanding. The way forward for humanity is philosophy. Humanity must accurately and fairly assess philosophy. Humanity must assess philosophy in the most just manner. Doing so, humanity will engage in maturity and growth.

Both religion and democracy are failures. For humanity to progress, the insufficient and inadequate past must be abandoned.

The insufficient and inadequate past must be rejected. That which is good and just can only be reached by philosophy. That which is good and just cannot be changed from being good and just. It is only goodness and justice that can create the greatest good and the greatest justice. All that is of life is according to goodness and justice. Living in accordance with goodness and justice achieves the same level of goodness and justice. That which is good and just cannot be altered. That which is good and just must not be lessened. All the power and authority must be given to goodness and justice. For the good to have less power and authority is for the good to achieve less goodness and justice. All power belongs to philosophy, all authority belongs to philosophy. For philosophy to have less power and authority is for less than the greatest good to be achieved. Democracy takes authority away from philosophy. Thereby democracy does not create the greatest good. Democracy is unaware of goodness and justice. If democracy were aware of the good, then the good would have been searched for. If the good were searched for, philosophy would have been engaged in. At which point it would have been known that all power and authority belongs to philosophy. Not having achieved the good, the advocates of democracy behave in such manner of not having achieved the good. The good is then denied full power and authority. Not having achieved the good, the advocates of democracy restrict philosophy. Goodness and justice are equated to lack of goodness and justice. If democracy had achieved, had understood goodness and justice, then democracy would never allow for goodness and justice to be equated with lack of goodness and justice. The first thing that would have been known is that the only prize in life is the good, that the most grievous act would be not to defend the good. The reason the good was not defended was because the good was not possessed. No effort to attain goodness and justice was made. If such an effort had been made, then philosophy would have been engaged in. The good would have been so explained in philosophical terms. It is the contention of democracy that democracy grants freedom, and yet the first act of democracy is to negate the good. The first act of democracy is to deny power and authority to the good. The first act of democracy is to lessen the good. The first act is to oppose the good. The first act is to oppose philosophy and the supremacy of philosophy. Of which democracy has no comprehension, for which democracy has no need. Democracy has no greater development. Democracy has no greater understanding. If goodness and justice are possessed, then no act can be taken that is counter to goodness and justice. Goodness and justice are always goodness and justice. Misbehavior is not due to the possession of the good. Misbehavior is due to the lack of possession of the good. It can only be that the good would be granted full power and authority. Not to do so is to lack the good. The good cannot behave in the less than good way. Full power and authority, as possessed by the good, cannot be feared. It is the lack of good that must be feared. It is always and only the lack of good that leads to the same lacking the good behavior. Lacking the good, it is lacking of the good solutions to human development that are offered. Those lacking the good solutions do not serve the cause of the good. They undermine the good. They oppose the good. As result, leading to a miserable societal existence. As result, leading to a chaotic and ungoverned existence. The caused pain and suffering, according to democracy, is never the fault of democracy. Democracy's limited competence cannot be expected to be exceeded. Consequently, according to democracy, no societal problem is ever the fault of democracy. Being weak in understanding, being weak in character, democracy offers such solutions. Solutions which lead to development problems. Solutions which lead to deep societal problems. The answers to which, democracy does not have. The answers to which, democracy cannot offer. No answers, no solutions, can be offered because those answers and solutions are beyond democracy. The inherent development problems of society are thus caused by democracy. Democracy cannot fix something that democracy ruins. If democracy had the answers, then democracy would never allow for equality of thought. Democracy would never allow for the truth to be equated to that which is false. Democracy is therefore defined as the equating of thought. Democracy is defined as the equating of truth to the false. Democracy is the denial of complete power and authority to the good. All that is good in life originates from the good. The human good originates from philosophy. Philosophy represents the human good. All power and authority belongs to the good. All power and authority belongs to philosophy.

That which lacks the good, that which is false, has no place in societal development. That which is good, that which is true, can only be known by philosophy. That which is good contains all that is good within. If the good did not contain all that is good, that would mean that the good is lacking. It would mean that the good is lacking in good. Which cannot be. The good cannot be lacking. The good cannot be less than good. Philosophy cannot be lacking. Philosophy cannot be less than good. Philosophy includes all that is good within. The one and inclusive good, the one and inclusive philosophy. All those possessing the good, all those wishing to contribute to the cause of the good, will be allowed to do so. The one good, the one philosophy contains all that is good within. The way forward for humanity is philosophy. The way forward for humanity is the rejection of democracy. The way forward is the good society. The way forward is philosophic rule. The way forward is the philosopher-king. The good originates from philosophy. The change that philosophy brings about is much needed change. It is only philosophy that has the answers. Having the answers, presenting the answers, brings about change, much needed change. The human wish is and has been to know the answers. It is the human duty to consider the philosophical answers. It is the human duty to consider the one philosophy. Doing so, it will then be realized that change is very much needed. It will then be realized that only philosophy has the answers. Only philosophy can know the reality of life. Only philosophy can create the good society. Only philosophy can achieve the peaceful human existence. Philosophy achieves the most. The human wish to know life's laws, the human wish to know the reality of life, the human wish to create the good society, the human wish to achieve the peaceful human existence is the same wish. It is the same effort. It is the same philosophical effort. By achieving, by understanding the reality of life, it is shown and proven that the effort is the most. The effort is likewise the most in the attempt to create the good society, in the attempt to achieve the peaceful human existence. No other branch is equal to philosophy. The One Philosophy achieves all. The

One Philosophy will be the basis of the good society. All philosophic leadership will be based on the One Philosophy.

Philosophical leaders will arise according to the understanding of philosophy, according to the verbal expression of philosophy, according to the written expression of philosophy. Philosophical leaders will arise from the school of philosophy. The mission of the philosopher will be to clarify philosophy, The mission of the philosopher will be to clarify the supremacy of philosophy. No significance is to be given to any defense of democracy. Such a defense always originates from those who lack the good. Such a defense always originates from those who have no need for the good. Such a defense always originates from those who have no understanding of the good. It is the wish of philosophy to state facts. It is the wish of philosophy to clarify the issues. As humanity lives, humanity matures, humanity grows, humanity achieves solutions, humanity achieves truth. That growth, that maturity, is not within democracy to achieve. It is only natural that humanity would achieve truth, truth which philosophy achieves and democracy does not. The way forward for democracy is its own abandonment, its own rejection. The way forward for democracy is maturity and growth. The way forward for democracy is the one philosophy. No doubt democracy will be clung on to by some, by those who consider the luxurious existence of glorified incompetence as proper. Of the luxurious existence of glorified incompetence, many consider themselves as most deserving. The incompetent and pretentious living is found most tempting. There is then no need for truth. There is no need for all to be put in its proper place. There is no need for all that is evil to be brought to justice. It is philosophy that states the good. It is philosophy that explains the good. It is the one philosophy that will judge all according to the possessed good. Humanity must join the cause of the good. Humanity must join the one philosophy.

Humanity by not having undergone growth and maturity necessarily will undergo growth and maturity. As humanity grows and matures, change from the past occurs. That change does not have to be struggled against. That change can be joined. The one philosophy can be joined. All legitimate governments can only have the cause of the good as their purpose. All legitimate governments can only have the serving of the people as their purpose. Not to serve the cause of the good, not to serve the citizens of society, is to have an illegitimate government. Philosophy serves the people. Philosophy serves the good. The only legitimate government is the good government. The only legitimate government is the government that is guided by the one philosophy. All other governments are illegitimate. Democracy is an illegitimate government. Any legitimate claim to government can only serve the cause of the good. Not to serve the cause of the good is to have an illegitimate government. As result, there can only be one legitimate government, the government of the one philosophy. To seek to achieve less than the good is to have an illegitimate opinion in the matter. It is to have an opinion of no good value. Such an opinion can have no say in the development of the good society. The good society serves the cause of the good, not less than the cause of the good. All within the good society will serve the cause of the good. All opposition to the good, all opposition to the one philosophy will be criminal act. All vice will be suppressed. All governments have existed prior to the one philosophy. All governments are to abandon their way and accept the good.

Human history is there to be learned from. The results from the solutions that humanity has come up with are there to be learned from. The failures of all government are to be learned from. The failure of democracy is to be learned from. The failure of democracy is that it has no comprehension of the good. The failure of democracy is that it has no comprehension of philosophy. Democracy has no need for the good. Half measures will suffice. Democracy is not of the people, by the people. Only the good is of the people, by the people. No political document, which does not have the one philosophy as its basis, has any standing. All such documents can be overturned with the help of the people. The wrath of the good, the wrath of the people, is not to be wished for. Only the one philosophy serves the people. All other governments are blind tyrannies. The purpose of democracy is not to serve the people. The purpose of democracy is to oppress the people. As the good is not possessed, the good is oppressed. As the good is oppressed, so are the people oppressed. The task of the one philosophy is to create the greatest good. The task of the one philosophy is to create the greatest justice.

The good government can never be misguided. The good government can never not serve the good. The good government always accomplishes most. The good government cannot accomplish less than most. Philosophy represents the greatest good. It is not possible to accomplish more than philosophy. It is not possible for the supreme answers to come from any source other than philosophy. The only human wish that is of value is the wish for the good. The answer is philosophy. The human wish is for philosophy. Philosophy is at the core of the human being. Never being misguided, the good government can never be tyrannical. It is always the cause of the good that is served. A tyrannical government is any government which does not recognize the good. A tyrannical government is any government which is not founded upon the good. Not recognizing the good, not possessing the good, the good then cannot be served. A tyrannical government is any government which does not serve the cause of the good. The good, the cause of the good, is primary with philosophy. All political power will arise from the one philosophy. All political power will arise from the good citizen. Those who lack the good have no place in politics. Those who lack the good do so for a reason. It is the good that is wished to be harmed. It is the suffering of the human being that is wished for. The selfish monster seeks political power through disguise and deception. The selfish monster is motivated by the need for the human being to suffer. Not having known the good prior to the good's existence, all are welcome to join the good. The necessary change must occur. As the day of judgment draws near, all of humanity must observe the good. Nor can any other government be associated with the good other than the good government, other than the one philosophy. The one philosophy stands alone. The one philosophy is authoritarian in serving the good. No similarities can be drawn. Human history has occurred the way that it has. The one philosophy takes place subsequent to which. The one philosophy is responsible for the one philosophy. All political power will arise from the one philosophy. All political power will arise from the philosopher-king.

It is philosophy and philosophy alone that may succeed democracy. By engaging in philosophy, philosophy necessarily engages in solving the most important issues. By achieving, philosophy necessarily achieves the most important answers. Philosophy is the supreme development. Philosophy has the supreme answers. With the same supreme character, the philosopher will engage all issues. It is only natural that philosophy must govern. As humanity matures, it is philosophy that leads the way. Prior to which, maturity, it was immaturity that guided human existence. As it is that immaturity is not desired, maturity is, philosophy is desired. It is the grown and enlightened human being that is desired. It is the grown and enlightened human being that the human being wishes to be. To be not knowing, to be not understanding is not the human wish. With philosophy leading humanity, all that is possible for humanity to achieve will be achieved. All the possible good will be achieved. The justice of philosophy, the justice of the good is the greatest justice. It is only the good that puts all in its proper place. Without the good, there is no order. Without the good, there is no justice. The way of the good will be the way for all societies. The good society will be the development for all societies. The good society will include all lands and all people. The good society will be based on the goodness of the human being. The greater the good, the greater the individual. The language of communication will be the English language. From the mountains of Kashimir, to the beaches of Burgas, to the streets of Trumbull, and beyond, the language of communication will be the English language. The good society will be the guiding political system for the duration of human existence. Maturity is sought. Once achieved, it is built upon. Maturity is never overturned. The One Philosophy, the Good, will never be overturned.

As philosophy is supreme, as philosophy presents the supreme answers, philosophy is fulfilling. Philosophy fulfills the human being. The human wish is knowledge. The human wish is the good. The human wish is truth. The human wish is justice. Such being the human wish, such is philosophy's wish. It cannot be thought that philosophy does not fulfill the human personality. It cannot be thought that truth, justice, knowledge, and the good are not fulfill-

NO GAIN IN EVIL

ing to the human personality. As truth, justice, knowledge, and the good are fulfilling, so is philosophy fulfilling. Achieving truth, spiritualism likewise is answered. Wishing for truth, the human being does not need fairy tales and fantasies. The truth rejects the false. The truth rejects fairy tales and fantasies. Philosophy rejects the false. Philosophy rejects fairy tales and fantasies. Disrespectful fairy tales and fantasies do not fulfill the human being. The pretentious religious fairy tales and fantasies are of the past. They belong to the state of human immaturity. The pretentious, evil character of religion will be exposed. Philosophy is the way forward. The misery of religion is not. Religion has long claimed to be something other than what religion truly is. That includes the beast, the bloodthirsty monster. The Beast will long regret waging war on the Good. The Beast will long regret waging war on philosophy.

The human being by observing the good leads the full life. It is the good that is wished for. It is the good that satisfies. And if the human being were deprived of all else but the good, the human being would have led the full and satisfying life. If a greater prize than the good were wished for, then the wish for the good has not been fully engaged. For by engaging the good, it would be realized that the only prize of value is the good, and regardless of what fate awaits the self, the full and satisfying life would have been lived. The superior life would have been lived. The greatest mistake in life would have been made if the good life hadn't been lived. To think that the good can be deceived as to the nature of the content of the good is to be mistaken. The turning to evil is the immediate turning away from the good. It is to then lack the good. Consequently the good cannot be deceived.

Despite the fact of the good's overwhelming appeal, despite of the good's overwhelming might, many individuals despise the good. Many individuals oppose the good. Many individuals wish to deceive the good. Not understanding that the good is the prize in life. Knowledge of the good, possession of the good is then not sought. Not seeking the good, the just life is not pursued. The life of justice is abandoned. The life of injustice is instead pursued. It is thought that there is benefit in injustice, that there is reward in injustice. It is thought that there is much to be gained in the world of injustice. The benefit of injustice is regarded as most fitting. To regard injustice as beneficial is to regard justice as less than beneficial. Injustice comes at the price of lack of justice. To think that there is gain and profit in injustice is to have the false and mistaken criteria of gain and profit. The unjust life can only achieve gain and profit of the unjust nature. It is to become wealthy in a poor way. It is to become wealthy in the poorest way. The profit is to be a miserable individual, being devoid of true wealth. The gain it to live a miserable life, being devoid of true gain and benefit. To be unjust is to have riches of no value. To be unjust is to have riches of great poverty. The riches of great poverty are not recognized as such but are mistaken for true wealth. As result, living the self-justified unjust life. The rejection of the good is done at the self's own expense. The good is the criteria. The good is supreme.

The good is primary. Knowledge of the good is the highest human knowledge. Philosophy is the way to the good, philosophy is the way to the reality of life. Philosophy is supreme. The task of philosophy is to reveal truth. The task of philosophy is to enlighten. The task of philosophy is to destroy the false. The task of philosophy is to destroy all enemies of the good. Defense of the good is primary. The enemies of the good have no chance in the world of idea. The enemies of the good wish for the good human being to suffer. The enemies of the good are selfish and devoid of feeling. The enemies of the good have no intellectual capacity, for if they did, the first thing that would be known is that the good is the objective. The first thing that would be known is that being a good human is the objective. The good welcomes all those who wish to observe the good. The good welcomes all those who wish to lead the good life. The struggle of the good is for truth and justice. The struggle of the good is with the false. The good's struggle is with evil.

Opposing the good, opposing justice, the enemies of the good oppose truth. The definition of the good is the quality of the good as the truth of the quality of the good. Justice is defined by the quality of justice, as the truth of the quality of justice. The enemy of the good, the enemy of justice, is an enemy of the truth, the truth regarding the quality of justice, the truth regarding the quality of the good.

The good being supreme, the justice of the good is supreme. The truth of the good is supreme. Making the effort at the good, making the effort at truth and justice, the effort at knowledge is made. The effort at understanding is made. Achieving truth, achieving the good, it is knowledge. It is understanding that is achieved. It is the human being that is based in knowledge, knowledge of truth that is desired. The truth is the objective, the truth then producing the grown and mature, the most conscious and enlightened human being. Not making the effort at truth leads to not achieving the truth. A consciousness unaware of truth cannot lead to enlightened and proper behavior. Not to care for the truth is not to care for the good, as it is that the good is founded in truth. The human being can only wish for understanding. The human being can only wish for truth. The human being can only wish for justice. It is knowledge of the good that is desired. Seeking truth, seeking justice, seeking the good, it is philosophy that leads the way. Seeking answers, philosophy reveals answers, answers critical to human consciousness, answers critical to human understanding. Philosophy elevates the human consciousness to the highest extent, leading to the equal and same proper behavior. Lack of knowledge leads to the equal and same misguided behavior.

Philosophy by being central achieves all that there is to achieve in the world of philosophy. Achieving truth, philosophy achieves the reality of life. It's life's overwhelming might that makes all possible. What comforts philosophy, what comforts humanity is truth. Comforting is the reality of life, comforting is life's overwhelming might. All that is life is found within the reality of life. Life achieves all. Life cannot be less than life. Life cannot be less than comforting. The reality of life can only be acceptable and fulfilling. Life's protection, life's care naturally follows. The sanctuary is life. Life is justice. Life is truth. Life is the good. Life is understanding. It is the accurate understanding of life that is desired. Life's ability, life's intent, must be accurately understood. Life's power must not be underestimated. Life's intent is to achieve that which is best. Life's ability is to achieve that which is best. Life's power is to achieve all. The objective is the understanding of life and life's laws. The objective is the understanding of the reality of life. The objective is to live the reality of life.

As philosophy achieves the reality of life, philosophy achieves all. As philosophy achieves all, philosophy produces change. Change from the past, change from widely accepted doctrines. That change is necessary. It is necessary if humanity is going to progress. That change is necessary if humanity is going to mature. The act of change certainly cannot be feared. That change must be looked forward to. The change is for the good of humanity. If it weren't for the change, inadequate doctrines would still persist. Inadequate doctrines would go unchallenged, claiming to be more than the actual, claiming truth where there is none, claiming goodness where there is none. It is only the good, it is only philosophy that creates order. It is only philosophy that can create harmony. The genuine and authentic effort at the good is what is desired. What is not desired is deception in effort at the good. What is not desired is out-of-control egomaniacs. What is not desired is egomaniacal psychopaths, pretenders and frauds who have done nothing in the world of philosophy, pretenders and frauds who have done nothing in the world of the good. For that reason, for putting all in their proper place, change is needed. For the reason of harmony and order, change is needed. For the cause of the good, change is very much needed. It is the duty of philosophy to clarify all. It is the duty of philosophy to destroy all that is false. It is the duty of philosophy to bring to an end to all false doctrines.

That which is righteous, that which is good, can only be approached through effort. That which is righteous, that which is good, can only be attained through effort at knowledge, effort at knowledge of the good. For humanity to engage in good behavior, humanity has to know what good behavior is. Humanity has to have knowledge of the good. If it is considered that any one individual has knowledge of any one other field than the realm of the good, then that individual has such knowledge but lacks knowledge of the good. Having knowledge in any one field other than the good shows that knowledge is needed to know and understand that field, that issue. As it is that knowledge is needed to understand any one issue, it is knowledge and understanding that is needed of that issue in order to lead to proper behavior in association with that issue. The realm of the good is no different. Knowledge and understanding is needed in order to lead to the proper behavior associated with the issue of the good. As it is that knowledge and understanding is needed in all fields of thought, knowledge and understanding is needed in the realm of the good. Knowledge of the good is the greatest knowledge. As the good is the greatest quality, so is knowledge of the good the greatest of all knowledge. Knowledge is needed in any and every field of thought. Such and equal effort is needed. Such and equal effort is made. All knowledge, all acts are achieved based on the same and equal effort. To reach the good, to reach the reality of life, effort is needed. The path to reach the good, the path to reach the reality of life must be taken. That path is philosophy. Nowhere else is the good revealed. Nowhere else is the reality of life revealed. If the good is wished to be known, if the reality of life is wished to be known, then philosophy must be engaged. The effort at philosophy must be made.

Religion is not an effort at philosophy. Religion is not an attempt at knowledge of the good. Religion is not an attempt at the reality of life. Religion does not engage in love of wisdom. Religion does not engage in love of knowledge. Making no effort at philosophy, religion makes no effort at knowledge of the good. Religion does not achieve knowledge of the good. Making no effort at knowledge of the reality of life, religion does not achieve knowledge of the reality of life. Religion is not philosophy, religion does not engage in proving or disproving ideas. Religion does not engage in the effort to prove or disprove ideas. That's because religion has no love of knowledge. If religion had love of knowledge, then religion would engage in rigorous thought. Religion would engage in the love of rigorous thought. Religion is involved in making statements without rigorous thought behind those statements. There may or may not be some value to these such statements. By that same thought, however, there may or may not be some value to any and every doctrine, regardless of how false. Certainly religion is distinguished from philosophy as making no philosophical effort at the good. Religion makes no philosophical effort at the reality of life.

Not achieving knowledge of the good, religion does not achieve the good. Not achieving the good, religion should not claim to having achieved the good. But it is what religion does not do. Religion claims to seek the good. Religion claims to achieve the good. Religion claims to achieve the reality of life. These are false claims. Evidence for this is found in religion's expressed views. Evidence for this is found in religion's doctrines. Lacking the good, lacking knowledge, religion is based in lack of knowledge. Religion is based in lack of the good. The study of religion is carried out in the world of ideas. The study of religion is carried out in moral terms. The study of religion is a moral study. It is morally that religion would reside. It is morally that religion is found to be the opposite. Religion is immoral, the claim to morality is a false claim. Not being based in the good, not being based in morality, religion is not based in peace and love. If religion were based in peace and love, then peace and love would have been shown toward the good. Peace and love would have been shown toward the effort to attain knowledge of the good. To seek the good, to attain the good is to be peaceful and loving toward the good. That is the only reason that the good would have been sought. That is the only reason the good would have been attained. Peace and love for the good makes the need for the good possible. Lacking knowledge, peace, and love for knowledge is also absent. Peace and love for the reality of life is lacked. Peace and love for the good is lacked. Lacking the good, religion has no understanding of the good. Religion is always claiming to be speaking for the reality of life. Religion is always claiming to be speaking for God. That is a disrespectful and blasphemous claim. The blasphemous claim shows religion's immorality, the attempted hiding behind God in order to advance the personal lack of possession of the good. Claiming to speak for God is proclaiming peace and love for God. Religion has no peace and love for God. The proclaimed peace and love is not peace and love for God; it is peace and love for fantasies and fairy tales. The proclaimed peace and love is blasphemous of God. It is disrespectful of God. The proclaimed peace and love is hatred of God. If God were loved, then the good would have been engaged. The good would have been loved. Instead, no such act has taken place. The good, God, can only be approached by the made effort at the good. No such act has taken place. When religion quotes God, when religion speaks for God, religion speaks for itself. Religion quotes itself. Religion actually quotes lack of effort, lack of achievement, lack of good. In the process, God is brought down to the level of religion. God, according to religion, lacks knowledge. God lacks the good. That is disrespect. That is blasphemy. It is not respect. It is not love. It is hatred. It is hatred for the same being for whom such great peace and love is proclaimed. Just because the peace and love for God is so often proclaimed, that doesn't mean that that is peace and love. Religion is not in position to know peace and love. If religion knew and possessed peace and love, then the good would have been loved. Religion does not know peace and love. Religion does not understand peace and love. If God were respected and loved, God would not be brought down to the level of lack of knowledge, to the level of lack of good. God above all is truth and justice. Religion is neither truthful nor just. Religion does not seek the good. Religion does not attain the good. Religion does not attain truth and justice. Religion achieves nothing in the world of the good. Religion reveals nothing in the world of the good. But yet religion is always claiming to achieve all and reveal all. That is neither a just claim nor is it a true claim. Religion is always claiming association with God, making God neither truthful nor just. God would never engage in injustice. God would never be less than truth. If philosophy can't make this statement, if philosophy can't speak to the reality of life, if philosophy cannot speak to the being of God, then no human branch of thought can speak of any truth. If philosophy speaks to the reality of life, it is because philosophy has made the effort to do so, speak to the reality of life.

Disrespecting the good, disrespecting knowledge, disrespecting truth and justice, religion disrespects God. The aim of religion's worship is not God. The object of religion's worship is itself. What religion worships is ignorance and lack of good. What religion worships is lack of truth and lack of justice. What religion worships is blasphemy, the false speaking for God. What religion worships is the attempted hiding behind God. It is lack of character that is the force behind religion. By taking the religious path, as religion does, religion pays a great price. By abandoning truth and justice, by abandoning the reality of life, religion creates a false existence. Religion creates an existence of fantasies and fairy tales. Religion must turn to fantasies and fairy tales as it is that religion cannot approach the reality of life. Fantasies and fairy tales which are considered as the reality of life. Creating a false existence, religion makes many false and blasphemous claims. It is religion's claim that God has chosen a group of people. It is religion's claim that God has said that God has chosen a group of people. It is religion's claim that God has chosen a group of people to reveal God. It is religion's claim that God's chosen group of people are God's favorite people. This is false and blasphemous claim. God has never selected any group of people as God's chosen people. God has never chosen any religious group to reveal God. God has never chosen any group of people as God's favorite people. Religion achieves nothing of value. Religion reveals nothing of value. Knowledge of God, knowledge of the reality of life, is of the greatest value. Religion cannot reveal something that religion makes no effort to reveal. God's revelation would not be from God to religion, as it is that it is philosophy that reveals all. Philosophy reveals all based on philosophical effort, which is not a revelation from God. Knowledge of the reality of life is the greatest value. If that greatest value were possessed by religion, then that would change religion. Religion would then be of the greatest value. Possessing knowledge of the greatest value, knowledge of God's revelation would make religion also of the same and greatest value. Instead, religion remains without value. Religion remains without effort. Religion remains without achievement. The effort is the achievement. The effort is the evidence of the achievement. By making no effort, religion makes no achievement. The claim of religion revealing God is made by religion. It is not an act of God. The claim of God having chosen people is made by religion. It is not an act of God. The claim that religion reveals God is a false claim. Not only is this a false claim, it is a blasphemous claim, blasphemy being the false speaking for God. Religion by falsely speaking for God, religion then involves God in God lacking truth. Religion then involves God in God lacking justice. The claim that God has chosen a favorite people is not only a false claim, it is also a blasphemous claim. The false speaking for God always remains an act of blasphemy. Revelation of God by not occurring from God to religion means that religion makes the revelation. Religion by not seeking knowledge, religion by not attaining knowledge, cannot speak to the content of knowledge. Religion cannot speak to the content of truth. Religion cannot speak to the content of justice. The religious claim of God having chosen a favorite people is not an act of knowledge. It is not an act of truth or justice. Lack of knowledge, truth, and justice cannot lead to knowledge, truth, and justice. God is knowledge, truth, and justice. God cannot be approached through lack of knowledge, through lack of truth and justice. The only way religion can claim to reveal God is by negating and removing God's qualities of truth and justice. The only way the religious claim of God having chosen a favorite people can occur is by negating and removing God's qualities of truth and justice. The only way for the religious claim of God having chosen a favorite people to occur is by lowering God's truth and justice to religion's level of lack of truth and justice. Knowledge, truth, and justice is what is required to approach knowledge, truth, and justice. Religion makes no effort at knowledge, truth, and justice. Religion does not have the answers. The answers are with philosophy.

Religion is of the past. It is a past human development. It perhaps answered needs of past humanity. Religion however no longer answers those needs. What humanity requires is truth. What humanity requires is philosophy. Now that the one philosophy is present, philosophy presents the answers, making it possible for humanity to join the one philosophy. Prior to the existence of the one philosophy, the one philosophy could not have been known. The one philosophy could not have been joined. The flaws of the past are such, flaws of the past. If the one philosophy is presently rejected by religion, religion would make the greatest mistake. Religion would be accentuating the flaws of the past. Religion would be accentuating its flaws. Religion would then be waging a struggle against the one philosophy. Religion would then be waging a struggle against truth and justice. God would never select a religious group of people as God's chosen and most favorite people. God would never be false. God would never be unjust. The claim that God has chosen a favorite people is neither founded in truth nor justice. The claim that God has chosen a favorite people is not an act of God. The false claim is made by religion. The false religious claim of God having chosen a favorite people reveals much about the religion that makes such false claim. Speaking falsely for God, it is to involve God in injustice. It is to involve God in falsehood. It is to be blasphemous of God. It is to be disrespectful of God. It is to be disrespectful of truth and justice. And yet it is to claim to be the opposite, respectful of truth and justice, respectful of God. Respect is substituted for disrespect. Disrespect is not understood as such. Respect is not understood as such. When any one religion reasons falsely, that religion does so, reason falsely. The more the false religion involves God in false reasoning, the more that religion is disrespectful of God, the more that religion is and becomes blasphemous of God. Reasoning to be chosen, religion does not turn to philosophy and knowledge. Religion turns to lack of knowledge, lack of philosophy. Religion turns to ignorance. The basis of religion is not philosophy and knowledge. The basis of religion is ignorance. Being based in ignorance, religion involves itself in topics of which religion has no understanding. Religion involves itself in topics for which religion has no appreciation. Lacking intellect, the false claim of being chosen by God is made. Lacking intellect, being disrespectful of truth, the chosen are disrespectful of the fellow human being. The truth of not having been chosen by God is disrespected, so is the individual who stands by such truth. By falsely claiming to be chosen, by disrespecting the fellow human being, the chosen turns to arrogance and conceit. The chosen are chosen, and the rest are not. The chosen are superior to the rest. The chosen are better than the rest. Regardless of what evidence is presented against the idea of being chosen, excuses by those who so decide to reject the one philosophy are always found to adhere to the false idea of being chosen. Arrogance and conceit are inherent to the idea of being chosen. The morality of the chosen is therefore brought into question. The chosen is careful to disguise the arrogance and conceit. The chosen is careful to conceal the disrespect of the fellow human being. The failing of the chosen is a moral failing. As attachment to the false religion is increased, the moral failing is equally increased. As attachment to the false religion is decreased, the moral failing is equally decreased. The arrogance and conceit is equally decreased. The great moral observer turns out to be the opposite, disrespectful of God, disrespectful of truth and justice, disrespectful of the fellow human being. God has never made any such choice as the made claim of being chosen. That is a flawed human idea. These are the results of being flawed. Substituting respect for disrespect, the chosen doesn't understand what respect is. To conceal the disrespect and hatred of others, the chosen is always speaking of peace. The chosen is peaceful and loving. Proof for this is claimed to be found in the religion of the chosen. God is claimed to be worshiped, truth and justice loved. God was never worshiped. What is worshiped is ignorance, conceit, and arrogance—that is the God of the chosen. The religion of the chosen is shamelessly presented as the Word of God. The shameless book of lies is presented as sacred. This is what happens when there is no shame. This is what happens when there is no intellect. This is what happens when there is no love of knowledge. This is what happens when there is no respect. The failings of the chosen religion are moral. They are failings in character. The moral failings of the chosen are failings of heart. They are failings of mind. It is character that is in question. An immoral character is not desired. The immorality of the chosen religion is certainly extensive. The going to such length to falsely claim of having been chosen by God reveals a lot about the character. The involving of God in falsehood and injustice reveals a lot about the lack of character. An immoral character behaves in an immoral way. What an individual thinks is important, the thinking reveals the individual. The thinking reveals the involved character. To think immorally is to be an immoral individual. Immoral thinking is an act of immorality. To think in an immoral way is to act in an immoral way. The extent of the immorality is dependent on its own level of immorality. The chosen does not understand what blasphemy is. The chosen does not understand what respect is. The chosen does not understand what shame is. Having no respect, having no shame, the chosen so behaves. The chosen is shameless and disrespectful. The outsider, the not chosen, in not being considered and hated, is in such manner treated, is in the shameless and disrespectful manner treated. If the chosen had shame, then the idea of having been chosen by God would not have been turned to. If the chosen had shame, then the idea of speaking for God would not have been considered. If the chosen is respectful, then the first idea that would be respected is the idea of God. The first idea that would be respected is not to be blasphemous of God. The first idea that would be respected is the idea of knowledge. Knowledge would be loved. Philosophy would be engaged in. Instead, philosophy is never engaged in. Philosophy is rejected. The having turned to religion is the having turned away from philosophy. Just because religion keeps praising itself of how good and moral it is, that doesn't mean that is correct. The claim in fact is incorrect. Evidence for this is found in the religion of the chosen, who neither loves God nor morality, all the while claiming to be doing just the opposite. In this manner is religion then destroyed, by revealing the true character of religion.

The pretense of religion can only cease. The pretense of the chosen can only cease. The contemptuous attitude by the chosen, of the not chosen, can only end. Humanity must consider the question, does humanity want answers, or is the pretense of having answers good enough? Humanity can only seek to grow. Humanity can only seek the good. The way forward is the one philosophy. Any claim by the chosen of seeking the good is a false claim. Any claim by the chosen of having ways of seeking and observing the good is a false claim. Philosophy was never engaged. Knowledge of the good was never wished for. Knowledge of the good was never attained. What remains is the claim of seeking the good. What remains is the claim of having attained the good. Both claims are false. The supposed methods that the chosen has for seeking and observing the good are meaningless. The value of those methods is equal to the morality of the chosen. That morality is lacking and deficient. The way out of this inadequacy is the rejection of the false and pretentious religion. The way out of this inadequacy is the one philosophy.

Humanity can only wish for the peaceful human existence. Humanity can only wish to understand the reality of life. Humanity can only engage in such and equal effort. For the human being not to engage in such effort is for the human being to fail. It is for the human being to be a failure. It is not beneficial for humanity not to seek the good. It is not healthy for humanity to believe in fantasies and fairy tales. It is not healthy for humanity to praise evil monsters. It is not healthy for humanity not to recognize evil monsters as such. Not to recognize an evil monster as such doesn't change the evil monster from being an evil monster. Not to recognize the evil monster as such doesn't make the evil monster any different from being the evil monster. That is where the task of the good lies. That is where the task of philosophy is, in the clarification and presentation of truth. All the positive stories that have been told of the peaceful and loving beast are incorrect and false. All the tales told of the peaceful and loving beast are false. Such individual was never peaceful and loving. The followers of the evil monster are not understanding of who it is that they are following. The proclaimed followers of the monster are following a false tale. The person of worship is not the person in reality. Never do the worshipers state that they are worshiping the evil monster. They claim to be worshiping a peaceful and loving individual. The worshipers don't know who it is that they are worshiping. They don't know the character of the beast. They are not following the beast but false tales told about the beast.

No one in history has achieved less and bragged more. No one in history has been as morally evil. No one in history has been a bigger fraud. Humanity by seeking truth, humanity by seeking knowledge, humanity loves knowledge. Humanity loves truth. The reality of life, God, can only be attained through knowledge. Loving knowledge, humanity loves knowledge of the reality of life. Humanity loves knowledge of God. The monster is no lover of knowledge. The monster is no lover of philosophy. If so desired, philosophy can easily be engaged in. No philosophical effort was made. The monster is no lover of truth. The monster is no lover of justice. The monster does not seek the good. The monster is no lover of the reality of life. The monster is no lover of God. The basis of the monster is not knowledge. The basis is the shameless writings of the book of lies. If the monster had any knowledge, the first thing the monster would have made clear is that those writings are blasphemous of God. The first thing the monster would make clear is that those writings are not the way to God. They are not the word of God. The first thing the monster would have made clear is that God's chosen and favorite people are not God's chosen and favorite people. What would be made clear is that God has made no such choice and that it is wrong and false to think that God has chosen a favorite people. What would be made clear is that the claim of being God's chosen people is a false religious claim. The lack of respect, the hatred for the outsider, inherent in the false belief of being chosen would have been exposed. The lack of respect and hatred, to whatever extent it may be, is inherent. If it weren't, no attachment to the false idea would be made. By exposing the disrespect and hatred for the outsider, respect and love for the outsider would then be engaged in. Instead, no such events take place. Proof for this is found in the nonrejection of the blasphemous writings. Proof for this is found in the nonrejection of the false claim of being God's chosen people. The reason the idea of God having chosen people is not rejected is because it is agreed with. The reason the blasphemous writings are not rejected is because they are agreed with.

Lacking love for philosophy, lacking love for knowledge, the monster lacks love for the good. The monster lacks love for truth and justice. The monster is lacking in love. The monster lacks love for the central to the moral human being issues. The monster cannot be moral. For the monster to be moral, the central to the human being issues would have to be engaged and loved. The good would have to be wished for. The good would have to be sought. That is what the monster does not do. Not seeking the good, not attaining the good leads to immorality. The immorality is in not seeking the good. Not loving knowledge, not loving God, not loving God's not chosen people, the monster lacks love. The monster lacks morality. The monster lacks the good. Being immoral, being without love, the monster is without peace. The monster has no peaceful attitude toward issues central to the moral human being. The issue of morality, the good is rejected and struggled against. If the good weren't struggled against, then the good would be studied and sided with. Having no need for the good, having no love for the good, the monster lacks the peaceful attitude for the good. Even though the monster has no peace

VESELIN PENEF

and love, the monster has a very high personal opinion. The monster is thus always speaking for God. The monster thus has God's knowledge. The blasphemous beast is always condemning. The blasphemous beast is not in position to condemn or not condemn. If there is judgment, God will make that judgment. Whether there is judgment by God or there isn't has no bearing on the immorality of the beast. The beast's condemnations are not God's. God has made no such condemnation. Judgment would be a sacred act, only to be understood by God, only to be done by God. Anyone who interferes with that act is insulting God. Anyone who interferes with that sacred act is blasphemous of God. The statement of blessing those who take no offense at the beast is all that is needed to be known of the beast. That is the not of God condemnation of 90 percent of humanity. That is the bloodthirst that the beast has. The beast doesn't seek justice. The beast seeks suffering, suffering which the beast wishes for, suffering which the beast is directly responsible for. The moral sickness, the moral depravity is there to be assessed. The beast is always talking about who is going to heaven and who isn't. That's more peace and love, peace and love for humanity, peace and love for God. Accordingly, incredibly, the beast always winds up in heaven. How convenient, maybe God would have something to say in the matter.

The issue of central importance to understanding the beast is the sick ego. The egomaniacal psychopath is at the core of all this immorality. The mentally sick braggart is at the core of all this bloodthirst. The beast is mentally diseased. Being diseased, the beast has no reasoning ability. The beast has no intellect. Being diseased, the beast has no compassion. The beast has no feelings. Lacking in brain, lacking in heart, the beast behaves accordingly. Being filled with ignorant hate, the beast behaves accordingly. Being a sick braggart, the beast behaves accordingly. Being mentally sick, the beast behaves in accordance. Having no intellect, having no heart, the beast is always making claims of being the opposite. It is not within the beast to be peaceful and loving. It is not within the beast to understand peace and love. The beast has no peace and love. Lacking peace and love for all that is central to the good human being, the beast lacks peace and love. Having a high personal opinion, the beast speaks for God. The beast insults God. The sick egomaniac is responsible for the blasphemous insults. Conceit, arrogance, and ignorance lead to the diseased character. Whatever claim the beast makes, that claim is meaningless. The beast has no forgiveness; that is why humanity is condemned without cause. The beast has no understanding of the good, hence the made claim that the beast will sit in punishing judgment of those who recognize the beast as such. The bloodthirsty wolf in sheep's clothing did not bargain on being exposed. The analysis of the personality of the beast is necessary in human understanding of truth. These are the results. These are the facts. The analysis is the result of the beast's waged struggle against the good. The made analysis will end the nightmare that is the beast. The nightmare that is the beast must end. If pretense and deception, fantasies and fairy tales is the human wish, then the bloodthirsty beast must be praised ever more. It is not healthy for the human being to be immature. It is not healthy for the human being to be less than understanding.

The images that have been handed down to humanity regarding this individual are mythical and false. The reality of the beast is much different. Based on the false tales, the myth, the lie is created. Tales of having been peaceful are told. Tales of having performed miracles are told. Humanity has been attempted to be overwhelmed and disarmed by the magnitude of the false tales. These false tales are told with the intent of creating the unquestionable myth. These tales are told with the intent of creating the greater than human myth. Humanity has been attempted to be intimidated right from the start. The overwhelmed and disarmed human being is what is desired. By creating the greater than human myth, humanity is insulted. The mythical figure is an insult to humanity. By creating the mythical figure, false tales of the beast having been peaceful are told. Being this morally evil, the beast can never be peaceful. The beast never said any peaceful statement. No peaceful statement was said by the beast. What the beast was about was being a mentally sick egomaniac. The beast was about hatred, hatred of knowledge, hatred of God. What the Beast was about was the need for humanity to suffer. The beast wants to punish humanity. The beast wants to punish the innocent.

The beast is the beast for a reason. The beast is the evil character that is the beast. All statements by the beast have to fit the blood-thirsty beast. It is not possible to be peaceful. No call for peace was made. The other mythical and false tale is that the beast performed miracles. No miracle was ever performed by the beast. The range of miracles includes all miracles, important and less important miracles. Anyone who possesses the ability of miracles would engage in the more important miracles first. The beast would perform the most important miracles first. The first miracle the beast would perform is to renounce the bloodthirst. The first miracle would have been to get a brain. The first miracle would have been to get a heart. No such event took place. The beast performed no miracles.

It is only proper that the beast should be exposed. That is what happens when the good is hated. The good exposes that hatred. The good reveals truth. The good most justly destroys the beast. It had to end. The fairy tale of the beast had to end. It is only proper for humanity to recognize truth. It is only proper for humanity to recognize evil. Human growth continues. Human maturity is marked by the fact of the one philosophy.

Certainly the nightmare that is the beast has been a part of human history. Whatever the reasons for humanity not to have recognized the beast as such may have been, they are factual human reasons. Certainly humanity has to a large extent paid only superficial attention. Humanity has to a large extent only analyzed the beast superficially. Due to that superficial and scant analysis, central issues were overlooked. Importance to issues of central nature was not given. The fraudulent personal praise was not recognized as such. The fraudulent personal praise was considered as legitimate. The praising by others of the beast was considered as legitimate. The beast was never analyzed. Endless praising does not mean that that praising is deserved. All it means is that the beast saw nothing wrong with being the beast. Whatever the reasons for misunderstanding the beast were, those reasons are of the past. As humanity matures, humanity becomes enlightened. Issues which seemed to be irreversible are then overturned. Ideas which were considered as fact then become false. Such is the instance with the nightmare that is the beast. As humanity grows, humanity becomes more aware. Humanity then recognizes that which prior to maturity was unrecognizable. The beast, the human nightmare is then brought to an end. The description that has been given of the beast is the result of the beast's fraudulent nature. No one has been a bigger fraud. The description is the result of the beast's bragging nature. No one has achieved less and bragged more. The description is the result of the beast's evil nature. No one has been more morally evil. The beast wanted to wage war against the good. The beast wanted to wage war against philosophy. These are the results of waging war on philosophy. These are the results of waging war on the good. The beast is most justly destroyed. It is the pretense of goodness that is responsible for the made analysis. It is the duty of philosophy to destroy all that is evil. It is the duty of philosophy to destroy all evil monsters.

Despite living through the nightmare, humanity can proceed and progress. Living and learning, humanity grows. What humanity has learned is that philosophy is at the core of the human being. What humanity has learned is to love the supreme knowledge that is philosophy. Loving philosophy, engaging in philosophy, the human being stays in touch with the central development of the human spirit. Living and learning indicates that there is something yet to be learned. Living and seeking the good indicates that the good, the greatest good, has yet to be attained. The states prior to the dominant good can only be imperfect. The key is to engage in genuine growth. The key is the genuine desire for the good. By being guided by philosophy, by genuinely seeking the good, the human being is the strongest yet. Ideas which seemed irreversible are suddenly overturned. Ideas which seemed to be fact suddenly turn out to be false. The greater the human thought, the greater the human being. To lack a desire for the good is to lack the superior thought. It is to lack the superior development. To falsely claim to be seeking the good, to falsely claim of having attained the good is to lack the good. It is to lack the superior development. The book of lies is such false development. It is a false claim of seeking the good. It is a false claim of having attained the good. The false claim to the good is the lack of the good. It is to live in the same lacking the good manner. The book of lies leads to living in the equal lacking the good manner. The book of lies can only be rejected. The good accepts all those who accept the good. All those who accept the one philosophy will be accepted by the one philosophy. The one philosophy is the answer.

The beast voluntarily revealed the beast's own evil, all the while not understanding that the beast's evil is being exposed. Having no need for the good, the beast lacks the good. The beast behaves in such lacking the good manner. The beast has no need for truth. The beast has no need for justice. Being mentally sick, the beast behaves in such mentally sick way. As result, exposing the egomaniac, as result, exposing the bloodthirst. Nothing is as it seemed to be to the beast.

As human history takes place, the one philosophy is realized. The one philosophy is a human historical fact. The one philosophy deals with issues central to philosophy. The one philosophy deals with issues central to the human being, issues central to the development of the human being. The historical human being must not be satisfied with lack of effort. Historical humanity must not be satisfied with inadequacy. Historical humanity must not be satisfied with lack of answers. Humanity must make no pretense of having answers. Humanity must not get deceived by nonanswers. Humanity must not be deceived by false answers. The fair assessment of the one philosophy is desired. Upon doing so, humanity fulfills the highest aspect of the human being, the aspect of fairness and reason. Engaging in fairness, engaging in reason, then reveals the one philosophy. What has occurred in human history has done so and occurred. In many instances of humanity seeking truth, the answers that humanity has come up were inadequate and insufficient. Humanity was satisfied with less than the truth. Appearance was good enough. That is where the task of the one philosophy has been, the understanding of many issues central to the human being, central to human development. Being a human historical fact, the existence of the one philosophy is secured. The triumph of the one philosophy is secured. The triumph of the one philosophy is imminent. The one philosophy has revealed truth. The one philosophy has destroyed evil. The basis of the one philosophy is the world of ideas. The world of ideas contains all. The world of ideas reveals all. The world of ideas is the basis of all. The world of ideas is life's basis.

Philosophy's effort is in the world of ideas. Seeking truth, philosophy achieves truth. No truth is denied from being true in the world of ideas. The world of ideas confirms each truth as such. The world of ideas is perfect. The world of ideas exists in perfect harmony. The world of ideas cannot be imperfect. If the world of ideas were imperfect, life could never occur. There would be no truth. No truth would have any meaning of truth. No truth would be recognized as truth. The world of ideas is fact, just as much as life is fact. The world of ideas contains all truth. The world of ideas contains the human being. The human being is a fact. The range that is the human is included in the world of ideas. No human arrived at truth is denied from being truth. Life's basis being truth, the world of ideas is life's basis. The reality of life is fact. That fact exists as result of life's own laws. Life's laws, life's being is dependent on life's being. Life's being is dependent on life's world of ideas. Life's being, the world of ideas, is discovered by humanity. The world of ideas is independent of humanity. At the same time, the human range is undeniable. No human truth is denied from being truth. No human truth is false. The human being occupies the human range. That range has the worth of the human being. Within that range, that which is false will never be truth, that which is evil will never be good. The human confirmation is found in the world of ideas. Within the world of ideas there is perfect accuracy; there is perfect harmony. That harmony, the good of that harmony, will never exclude the status of the human being. No part of the world of ideas can be in disharmony. That being so, all that belongs to humanity will be attained by humanity.

The issue in question is life's being. The issue in question is the reality of life. It is the understanding of life's ability, the understanding of life's intent that is crucial to understanding the reality of life. Life's intent can only be to seek that which is good. Life's intent is to seek that which is best. Life's ability is to achieve that which is good. Life's ability is to achieve that which is best. All is included within life's intent, within life's ability. All is included within life's being. To conclude that life is inadequate and insufficient is to be mistaken. It is to not understand life. Life is victorious. Life is victorious in all, all that life does. The proof is found in life's existence. There is no obstacle that prevents life from being. There will never be an obstacle which will prevent life from being. Life's single existence is proof that life can never be prevented from being. If there were an obstacle to life's existence, then that obstacle would have prevented life from existing. As there was no such obstacle, no such obstacle exists to prevent life. If that obstacle existed, life would have been prevented. Life would have been negated. The sanctuary is life. Life cannot not exist. Seeking that which is best. Life achieves that which is best. Life is victorious. If life were not victorious, then life would not occur. Life is victorious in achieving that which is best. Life existence is proof that that which is best has been achieved. Life would never seek to achieve less than that which is best. Life being victorious, life is victorious in all that life does. If life were not victorious, then life would not live in the best way. Being victorious in all, life is victorious in life's eternity. It is life's eternity that life seeks most to achieve. Being victorious everywhere else, life could not be less than victorious in life's eternity, life's most desired objective. Life by not not existing, life by having no obstacle, life by being the sanctuary shows that life is victorious in all. Life cannot be victorious in all and then fail in the one way most desired by life. Attempting to achieve eternity, life achieves eternity. Life's laws belong to life. Life's laws serve life's best intent. Life's laws serve life's best ability. Life seeks life. Life attains life. Life is eternal.

Seeking the good, seeking that which is best, life is victorious. Life achieves that which is best. Life achieves the most desired. Life achieves the most desired stage, the stage of supreme good. The supreme good is life's guide. The supreme good is life's objective. Life, by seeking that which is best, seeks the stage of dominant good. By seeking to achieve that which is best, life seeks to achieve the stage of dominant good. In life's eternity, there are differing stages, one of which is the stage of supreme good, one of which achieves the greatest good. The stage of supreme good cannot be denied from existing. It is the stage that achieves the greatest good, whichever stage that may be. Seeking the greatest good, life seeks the greatest justice. Life seeks the greatest truth. Life does not seek injustice. Life does not seek that which is false. During the stage of supreme good, it is the greatest justice that governs. It is the greatest truth that governs. The greatest justice, the greatest truth is that the greatest good must govern. If less than the greatest good governs the stage of supreme good, that would not be the greatest justice. That would not be the greatest truth. The greatest justice, the greatest truth, can only be that the greatest good is achieved during the stage of dominant good. The greatest good then governs. The greatest justice, the greatest truth then governs. The greatest good is that the good achieves all. All serves the good. The good is supreme. The good brings all under the rule of the good. During the stage of supremacy, the good is unharmed. The good cannot be harmed during the stage of supreme good. Life is victorious in all that life does. Being victorious, life achieves all. The good achieves all. Life is fulfilling. Humanity is fulfilled.

Victorious life, fulfilling life, includes the act of self choice, the act of self-creation. As the self is chosen, as the self is loved. Self-creation takes place. The self is not imposed on anyone. The self is granted to everyone. The choice for the self occurs within life's boundaries, and those boundaries cannot be exceeded. However, life achieves all. Life has all. The human being achieves all. The human being has all. The human being having all, the human being has the self. The human being has the choice for the self. The human being has self-creation. No other choice for the self other than the made choice for the self is wished for. Life's laws, life contains all justice. Life contains all goodness. No other choice for the self can be made, but no other choice for the self is wished to be made. Any life lived in seeming misery comes with the choice for the self. The misery in life is not primary. The choice for the self is. Primary in life is the love for the self. The self always has the self. Nor should the meaning of that misery be misunderstood, the seeming misery in life can only be accurately understood. Any such understanding can only include the primary choice for the self. Any such understanding can only include the eternity of life. Any such understanding can only include life's justice, life's goodness, life's supreme good. Such seeming misery is therefore accurately understood. The effort at understanding is then made. The effort at life is then made. The good must be engaged.

The good must be wished for. The creation of the greatest self must be undertaken. Doing so, the human being is then enriched. The real misery in life is not to seek the good. The real misery is to lack the good. The real misery in life is to lack the self. Life is fulfilling. The choice for the self is complete. The choice for the self is fulfilling. No misery ever takes away the self. No misery ever takes away life's goodness. Life's justice is life's own. Life's justice can never be less than just. There is no greater justice. Life's justice is supreme.

Engaging in the effort at life, engaging in the effort at the good, the human being grows and develops. The human being achieves. In the process, the human being overcomes all. In the process, the human being reveals the reality of life. In the process of overcoming all, the human being is revealed. Growing and developing, the human being engages in understanding. The human being engages in philosophy. Central to philosophy is the understanding of the idea of judgment. The accurate understanding of the idea of judgment is to a great extent the understanding of life's reality. The idea of judgment must be understood. The good is the dominant life quality. All takes place under the supremacy of the good. Any one human being who seeks the good will attain a greater level of good from any one individual who does not seek the good. The existence of the good is a fact, as it is that the good is engaged in to the greatest extent by philosophy. As there is human good, there is greater and lesser levels of human good. Not to seek the good is not to attain the good. To engage in less and less good is to engage in evil. Just as the good exists, so does evil exist. Life by seeking the supreme good recognizes that which is good and that which is less good. All about life is the seeking of the good, the greater good. Seeking the greater good, life achieves the supreme good. Life achieves supreme justice. Life achieves supreme understanding. Life will never not seek the good. Life will never not understand the good. That is how life achieves the supreme good. The supreme good involves life's being. The supreme good involves all of life's being, including humanity. Life will never break life's own laws. Life will never contradict the good of life's own laws. The human being cannot exceed being human. The human being cannot be less than human. All that is human is humanly attained. The greatest prize in life is the good. As the human being seeks the good, the human being attains the greatest prize, the good, the human being becomes greater. As there is greater, there is lesser. Each human being attains the true and one self. In life's supreme goodness, in life's supreme understanding, life will never be less than good. Life will never be less than understanding. Life will never engage in wrong. Life will never mistreat the human being. The human being then, under life's guide, attains all. In the process eliminating judgment, the punishing, or rewarding of humanity.

The idea of punishing or rewarding the human being is based on the idea that the human being can be greater than human. The idea of judgment is a human idea. It is not a life idea. All that is human will be attained by humanity. From within the reality of life, the middle ground between the opposites of unlimited nonlife and unlimited life, all of life is attained. All that is human is attained. Life would never break life's own laws of justice and goodness. Life would never contradict life's own understanding. The understanding of humanity being human and not more. The understanding of life's own reality, the middle ground between the opposites of unlimited nonlife and unlimited life, the opposites of being created and self-creating. In the process eliminating judgment, the punishing or rewarding of the human being. Good and evil exists, and all attains the proper and accurate status within Life's Understanding.

The understanding of the middle and accurate ground of self-creation is required, the neither unlimited ground of self-creation nor unlimited ground of being created. The human call for judgment is perhaps the human call for justice. It is perhaps the call for the good to take place. Perhaps it is a genuine human effort at reason. That may or may not be the instance. What is never a human call for justice is when that call for justice is made by those who are themselves unjust. The basis of the idea of judgment is that judgment is an act of justice. The basis is that judgment is an act of good. If an unjust individual calls for judgment to take place, then that individual is calling for one's own condemnation. The unjust individual can only be judged negatively. The unjust individual however does not have one's own condemnation in mind. The unjust individual seeks the personal positive judgment. The unjust individual is therefore seeking injustice. Seeking injustice, the unjust individual seeks the personal positive judgment. The unjust individual seeks the positive judgment of the unjust and the negative judgment of the just. The idea of judgment is of human creation, as such the idea of judgment has the failings of human false thought throughout. Consideration of the idea of judgment requires thought and effort. The greater the effort, the more genuine the effort, the greater the personal reasoning, the greater the personal good, the greater the personal justice is. As the personal effort at the idea of judgment is decreased, so is the personal justice decreased, at least in this one particular field of thought. As the personal good is decreased and the personal call for judgment is maintained, the personal self-estimation is exaggerated. The personal self-estimation is in fact exaggerated; that is the reason for the call for judgment by an individual who lacks effort to a greater and greater extent, who lacks the good to a greater and greater extent. The greater the personal praise by the unjust, the lesser the personal good, the greater the personal injustice. The greater the personal praise, the worse the personal condition. The greater misunderstanding of the good then follows. The good is not recognized as such. The self proclaimed as holy are the unholy. The holy would never tell God what to do. The holy would never be blasphemous of God.

The call for judgment to take place hasn't necessarily been a call for justice to take place. Nor should it have been ever automatically thought that judgment would occur without engaging in reasoning. Nor should it ever be thought that the good can be deceived. Only what is genuine is good. The good must be wished for. Pretense of seeking the good is pretense of seeking the good. The call by the unjust for justice is a deception. It is a personal deception. It is an attempted deception of the good. Any false claim of having attained the good is a false claim of having attained the good. Any attempt to deceive the good ends in failure. The proof is the attempt to deceive. The primary human objective is the engaging in good behavior. By living, the human being grows, the human being changes, the human being better understands the good. By changing, by better understanding the good, by learning, the human being proceeds and progresses. The good could not have been always known. By the fact that the good is attempted to be attained, it is shown that the good was at one time not possessed, then having led to the same lacking the good behavior. That behavior is grown and progressed upon. The issue of importance is the good, the wish for the personal possession of the good. Similarly as the individual, humanity grows and learns. What is important for humanity is the good, the genuine wish for the good. Being guided by the good, humanity will fare well. And the life lived prior to the good was the life lived prior to the good. Being then guided by the good, humanity will abandon all that is evil. Humanity will abandon all false claims of goodness. It is the good, the possession of the good, that makes the transition, the growth possible. What has been has been. The central issue is the good, the possession of the good, the recognition of the good, the recognition of the nongood, the recognition of phony pretenders of being good. And then humanity will grow. Humanity will mature.

Humanity's existence prior to the point of maturity has passed. Matured humanity should not overly and inaccurately consider the idea of what past humanity had known or not known. Matured humanity should not inaccurately consider the life of past humanity. All in life is fulfilled. Humanity is fulfilled. Humanity has grown and developed in the one and best way. All in life assumes its proper place. The present of any one point of human existence is sufficient. To have arrived to the present, past humanity was sufficient. The valid question, of any point in human existence, has been, and is, the genuine and sincere wish for the good. The self is and all through history has been always possessed. The human being is then comforted. Seeking the good, choosing the self, the human being is comforted. Life will then take life's course. Humanity takes the human course. Humanity does not need to be comforted and aided by a foreign to life source. It is the reality of life that comforts. God does not need to comfort and aid humanity in living. What is comforting for humanity is the effort. What is comforting for humanity is the good. If humanity seeks comfort and aid from God, that minimizes the human being, that minimizes the human effort. It is the complete effort at life that is needed. No affirmation by God to any one human issue is needed. None is forthcoming. Humanity is capable of achieving truth. The truth cannot be less than true. That is the affirmation. The truth is the affirmation. Life, God has God's life's place. The human being has the human place. Humanity does the human task. Humanity lives the human life. God lives God's life. God would make no effort outside the original and best effort at living. The human task at living belongs to humanity and the human capability. God would make no interference with which. To step outside the best effort at living is not possible. Any such effort would be the one and best effort. Humanity's ability is founded in life's being. Humanity's status is founded in life's being. Humanity achieves what is human. God is never lost in the process. Truth is never lost in the process. Affirmation, comfort, and aid are never lost in the process. They are present in life's being. They are present in humanity's ability. They are present in the human effort. They are present in the human status. The human status belongs to humanity. The human status captures all that is human. The human status cannot be exceeded. Just as humanity exists, so does human truth exist. Just as humanity exists, so does human effort exist, so does human achievement exist. Human achievement is not lesser. Human achievement is not greater. The confirmation of human truth, the confirmation of the human effort is such as the human confirmation is. The confirmation is the human confirmation. For humanity to want greater than the human confirmation is for humanity to want life to change the taken and best path at living. Life is not concerned with altering life's best path at living. Life's concern is the one and best path at living. Consequently, life will not alter the best path at living. Life's development is dependent on life's being. All that is within life is a representation of life's being. As life develops in life's manner, so does every life representation develop according to life's manner, so does every representation develop according to the manner of the life representation. This is also the instance with humanity. Human existence responds to human effort. As such, human development, human history, will occur according to the human effort, according to the human nature, according to life's being. Human development occurs according to real and natural human forces. Human development occurs according to life's best taken path at living. Humanity does not need any assistance in living, nor is any assistance forthcoming. It is up to humanity to achieve. It is up to humanity to seek the good. All that is of life is found within life's being.

It is humanity that fulfills the human status. No help is required in being human. That help, the human status, the self have already been granted in life's being. All has been granted in life's best path at living. To think that humanity has been left alone, to be fearful, to be resentful of life, to think that life is insufficient is to be mistaken in understanding life's being. Life doesn't have to be attributed with any not of life quality for life to be found to be comforting, sufficient, and fulfilling. Life is life's own ruler. Life does not need the false unlimited power to achieve all. Life's power is unlimited in the real life way. The unlimited power is of fact. If it is that any one human being wishes to know life's being, then philosophy welcomes any such effort. The reality of life, life can only be understood through philosophy. It is only philosophy that seeks the greatest knowledge. It is only philosophy that seeks to know life's ultimate being. By achieving knowledge of life, then all that is of life is humanly known. What is known is that life seeks and attains the good. What is known is that the good is life's guide. By seeking knowledge, the human status is fulfilled. The human purpose is understood. The human purpose is to be a good and enlightened human being. The good human being seeks and attains the human good. Pretense of seeking the good is pretense of seeking the good. Philosophy does not call for excessive and unneeded praise of life. God does not need to be constantly praised. If any one individual wishes to praise God, that individual is free to do so. What that individual has to be certain of however is that the being praised is truly God and not made-up, disrespectful-of-God fairy tales. What the individual has to be certain of is that the praise of God is not an ignorant-of-God praise. An ignorant-of-God praise is not a praise of God but is a praise of the ignorance about God. An ignorant-of-God, God-praising individual is not praising God but is praising the ignorance about God. The praise is of the ignorant of God self. An ignorant of God individual cannot praise and worship

God. The praise and worship is of the ignorant of God self. Pretense of praising and worshiping God is pretense of praising and worshiping God. Being ignorant of God, made up, and shameless fairy tales are then associated with God. The praising and worshiping then is of the made-up and shameless fairy tales. The praise and worship is of the ignorant of God and shameless self. With the human being making certain that the being that is praised and worshiped is God, the human being is free to praise and worship God. The human being is free to praise and worship life. The way to have done this would have been through philosophy. To praise and worship would then be a fine human act. At the same time, the individual must consider the good, the nature of humanity, the achieving and doing that which is human, the living of the full human life. The human nature is to live. Humanity is to achieve. Humanity is to seek and attain the good. The human being is to engage in good human behavior. The groveling and begging for favors human being is not what is desired. If there is any human concern as to whether the good individual is being recognized as having engaged the good human behavior in life, that concern is a meaningless one. Every act of good is always an act of good. No act of good is ever not an act of good. To show respect for God is to seek and attain the good. To show respect for God is to engage in good human behavior. The good is the answer to all. God can never be respected if the good is not respected.

To lack the good, to disrespect the good is to be a human failure. The more the good is lacked, the more the good is disrespected, the greater the human failure, the greater the individual deformity. As the individual wishes to grow and mature, philosophy is the primary way. As humanity wishes to grow and mature, philosophy is the primary way. Philosophy's might has been stated. Philosophy's supremacy has been revealed. The one philosophy is an integral part of human history. The one philosophy is an integral part of human development. From the destruction of democracy, to the destruction of religion, to the revealing of the reality of life, a new beginning awaits humanity. From the destruction of the rotten structures of the past, the new life will arise. From the ruins of the past, the new life will spring. Philosophy belongs to philosophy. Philosophy belongs to philosophers. Philosophy does not belong to empty-headed frauds. It is best not to challenge philosophy. The result will be certain ruin.

Seeking the good, seeking the truth, the human being can only be satisfied by attaining the good. Humanity can only be satisfied by attaining the truth. That which is false, that which is evil has no place in human existence. Humanity cannot be satisfied with the pretending nature of the good's nemesis. The good's nemesis cannot be left unopposed. If humanity is satisfied with the false, if humanity is satisfied with evil, then humanity will pay a price for doing so. Humanity will be lessened. Humanity will live a lesser life. The lessened human being will give rise to know-nothing monsters, whose function in life is to harm the good, whose function in life is to harm humanity. Being satisfied with the false, humanity will never expose, nor understand, the fraud, the beast. Humanity must seek the truth. Humanity must wish for the truth. Humanity must wish for the good. At that point, issues which seemed to be without resolution are suddenly, and easily, resolved. Unclear issues suddenly become clear. If humanity wishes to grow and mature, humanity must make the equal and necessary effort. The struggle to grow, the struggle to attain the good must not be avoided. The struggling, the making the effort human being is the way of humanity. Doing so, humanity will join the one philosophy. The answers are with philosophy. The answers are with the good. Only philosophy can reveal the good. Only philosophy can reveal the injustice of all that is nongood. It can only be that humanity joins philosophy. It can only be that humanity joins the One Philosophy.

The lessened human being is not what is desired. The lessened human achievement is not what is desired. Achieving all, it is the good society that is then built. Philosophy creates the good society. All that is good will be defended. All that is good will be promoted. All that is evil will be destroyed. The good society will take over all societies. The way of the good will govern all of humanity. All those who are evil will be brought to justice. The way to avoid the wrath of the good is to abandon the way of evil. The way to avoid the wrath of the good is to stop harming the good. The communist, the religious monster, all exist with the purpose of harming the good. All must abandon their way of evil or be faced with destruction. If they don't recognize their own evil, that only proves the level of their own evil. The harming of the human being, the harming of the good, the harming of the human soul, all must answer for. The natural progression of democracy is the philosopher-king. As democracy of days past sought the good, democracy must continue the search of the good, which leads to the philosopher-king. Democracy doesn't have the answers. The impostor politician doesn't have the answers. The answers are with philosophy. As democracy seems to be well established, democracy is actually not well established. It is in the world of ideas that democracy fails. It is in the world of ideas that democracy falls. Democracy no longer seeks the good. Democracy seeks to enslave the good. The days of democracy have passed. With the approach of the good society, with the approach of the day of judgment, all humanity must observe the good. The good is the answer to all. All will be judged according to the possessed good. Seemingly well-established doctrines one day suddenly collapse the next. The reason is the failure in the world of ideas.

Philosophy seeks the complete uprooting of all previous political systems. With the acceptance of the one philosophy, philosophy seeks the complete abandonment of all previous human thought. The one philosophy brings great change. The one philosophy must be considered. The one philosophy will be accepted. The one philosophy is the way of the future. The one philosophy reveals the good. For the good to grow and flourish, all that is of the past must be completely torn down. All must be torn down. All is improperly reasoned. The one philosophy, the good society, is founded in the world of ideas. The good society, the one philosophy is indestructible. The human legacy must be the ever greater need for the good. The human legacy must be the complete empowerment of the good. It is within the human character to rise to the new human existence. It is within humanity to fulfill the human mission in life, the achievement of the good. It is within humanity to understand life. It is within humanity to create the good society. It is within humanity to achieve the peaceful existence. By rising to the new height of awareness, humanity will fulfill the human path of development. By rising to the new height of understanding, humanity will fulfill the human level of good. The good will be struggled for. The good will be defended. The good will be sacrificed for. The good will be taught. The greatest prize, the good, will be taught to all. And if someone should fall in the struggle for the good, that would have been for the greatest reason, that would have been done for the greatest purpose, the victory of the good. Struggling for the cause of the good, that individual has such good character. That individual has attained the good. That individual is the greatest prize in life. Living the greatest life, that individual is so remembered, that individual will be forever honored by all powers. This book is dedicated to the good. This book is dedicated to all good people. This book is dedicated to life and the eternal power of life. This book is dedicated to the complete destruction of all that is evil. This book is dedicated to the creation of all that is good. The path for humanity to take is clear. The human will, the human strength, must not be looked for anywhere else other than within humanity. Guided by the good, humanity is invincible. Guided by the good, humanity is ready to face any challenge, knowing that all has been done to understand and attain the good. When the human personality is described, it is best summed up by one characteristic, the need to live in the perfect world, the need to live the perfect life. Through it all, the Good reigns supreme. Through it all, Life Reigns Supreme.

Veselin Penef

ABOUT THE AUTHOR

Philosophers love philosophy. The author is an admirer of historic Greek philosophy. The author is an admirer of the giants in philosophy. By engaging in classical philosophy, by making the effort at classical philosophy, the result is the one philosophy. The one philosophy is the result of such made effort at philosophy. Philosophy will forever be the greatest human knowledge. Philosophical knowledge will always be the greatest human achievement. The author dedicates the book to philosophy. The author dedicates the book to the Good. The book is dedicated to Life's Supreme Being.